Kit Denton's novel was first published in 1973, and it was inspired by a conversation with a Boer War veteran who had actually known Harry "Breaker" Morant—horseman, poet, soldier, and, perhaps, murderer of civilians. The tale the old man told was so extraordinary that Denton followed it up with two and a half years of research, even going to London to try to obtain the documents of Morant's court-martial. The screen version of Breaker Morant's story, presented by the South Australian Film Corporation, centers on the court-martial proceedings which led to Morant's execution in 1902—proceedings which are still shrouded in mystery by the British government despite the eighty years which have since passed.

# Kit Denton

# THE BREAKER

*Breaker Morant*

WASHINGTON SQUARE PRESS
PUBLISHED BY POCKET BOOKS NEW YORK

A Washington Square Press Publication of
POCKET BOOKS, a Simon & Schuster division of
GULF & WESTERN CORPORATION
1230 Avenue of the Americas, New York, N.Y. 10020

ISBN: 0-671-44762-9

First Washington Square Press printing October, 1982

10 9 8 7 6 5 4 3 2 1

WASHINGTON SQUARE PRESS, WSP and colophon are
trademarks of Simon & Schuster.

Printed in the U.S.A.

*It took patience, hard work,*
*understanding, love and much sympathy*
*to write this book.*

*I showed very little of any*
*of them, therefore this is for my wife* LE
*who showed them all.*

# Before you begin . . .

There *was* a Breaker Morant. He lived his life in the times and company of many of the people mentioned in this story, and he went through much of the action in these pages. I had hoped to write a true history of the events and the people concerned, but the obduracy of the British Government in refusing to release a number of essential documents has made this impossible. Nonetheless, this book has in it many of the historical facts and I've departed from history only when the facts weren't discoverable or when I felt it was necessary in the interest of a good story. Morant lived, wrote, fought and died pretty much the way I've pictured it.

For various kinds of assistance with the book I'm indebted to the Australian Council for the Arts; Trevor Beacroft of the Bank of New South Wales; Jim Mac-Dougall of the Sydney *Daily Mirror;* Mrs. Ira Quinlan of South West Rocks; Tony Mays of Canberra; Peter Scasighini; Qantas, and their Public Information Officer, John Ford; Mrs. Cook of the library at Victoria Barracks in Sydney; Lieutenant-Colonel Gentles, Assistant Director, Legal Services in the Australian Army; my sister Stella and her husband Allan and Lieutenant-Colonel Tim Swifte, Assistant Director, Army Public Relations, who's been my friend for sixteen years and never more so than during the writing of this book. My thanks to him and to everyone else who got me to this point.

K. D.

# AUSTRALIA

# November 1901

The corner of the small paddock collected the bars of sunlight sliding through the sapling fence, stretching them in white-gold lines across the green shadows which were almost black. Paddy leaned on the gate, looking into the corner, squinting against the clean hurt of the morning sun, seeing only the light and shadow contrasts. The whistle was sharp and brief, his tongue hard against the back of his teeth, and then more teeth showing as his mouth widened in a grin. There, in there in the barred darkness, Harlequin lifted his head to the sound, his ears pricking forward and his lip lifting in a quiet answering whicker. Then he stepped out, the movement showing him for the first time, a graceful zebra for a moment, for a moment a pale green unicorn, touched with gold, then a golden horse walking dainty-hooved onto the plate of gold that was the short grass between the trees and the gate.

Whenever it happened, as often as it happened, Paddy sucked in a breath, shaking his head a little in admiration, thinking, *No wonder Harry wanted him.*

Harlequin saw the man at the gate and flicked his head to one side, the mane sliding like black silk across the golden arch of his neck, the black tail moving with it, and he came out easily in a trot, half circling, playing his morning game.

"Hey, there, Harlequin." It wasn't a call, just a low-voiced greeting, part of the whole ritual, part of the months behind them both, alone on the property.

"Hey, horse. Come on over here, then."

3

*The man was big across the chest and shoulders, looked big in the way some stocky men do, and the face was a quarry where the years and the weather had dug. The voice was a low rumble and Harlequin heard and felt the affection in the lilt of it, checking on the turn and pausing, his hooves close, his body balanced. Then, head a little lower, he walked with delicacy towards the gate, towards the half-opened hand with the little heap of browny sugar in it. A yard from it the horse spun about and the ritual began again, both of them enjoying it, both knowing exactly how long it should last, both conscious of the admiration and the love that inspired it. When it ended, Harlequin edged his flank against the gatepost, rubbing it gently for the comfort of the rough timber, and his muzzle went down to the sugar, silk lips cool against Paddy's palm. Paddy looped an arm onto the horse's neck, tugging gently at the mane, rubbing knuckles into the crest between the ears and talking.*

*"Ye're a fine feller, so y'are. And ye know it too, don't ye? Ah, ye do so. Ye're a lovely liddle horse an' ye miss yer master, don't ye?" He wiped his damp and empty palm against the side of his trousers and ran it over the soft muzzle, Harlequin leaning his head in, a small grunting noise in his throat.*

*"Ah, well, feller, the both of us misses him, that's the God's truth of it. But he'll be back one of these times, boy, and slap a saddle on that goldy back of yours and ye'll be off like the wind, ye will."*

*Paddy wondered how many times he'd said that, how many times he and Harlequin had stood here like this, or over there in the shed when the weather was bad, half leaning on one another, the man and the horse each remembering—he was sure the horse remembered—each seeing in his mind the pictures of Harry. Outside the Barracks on that going-away night, up at Renmark in the rum-sweat of the breaking-in, on the track down over the hills to Adelaide. All the months since.*

*"That's it, then, me son." He pushed Harlequin gently away, the flat of his hand on the long neck mus-*

4

again, everyone joining in this time, one of them jeering, " 'E got ya there, Sims. Right in the guts."

The giggler, Sims, face flushing, scowling. "I c'd clean *you* up right enough, fancy boy—"

The man turned his back. Near him Magee had the cap, squinting down at it curiously, then handing it back. The man nodded his thanks. Sims' hand on his shoulder was hard and sudden and it spun him fast, so that his back joggled the bar top and his drink slopped.

"How'd ya like it if I was ta knock that bloody great plum outa yer mouth, eh?"

"Stop behaving like a schoolboy."

The hand stabbed out again, the heel jarring against the man's shoulder. Behind the bar, the moist man shifted bottles and glasses and laid a truncheon on the bar top with care. The man reached up and knocked Sims' arm aside. His voice was still low, still tired.

"Look here, you're dirty and you smell and your manners are appalling. But I've no wish to start a brawl with you or anyone else. Go and finish getting drunk, there's a good chap."

Before he could turn his back again, Sims' fist caught him high on the chest, staggering him. The barman took up the truncheon and rapped with it.

" 'Nough, Sims. No fightin' in here, right?"

Around Sims, his friends were pushing at the man, urging.

"Go on, fancy. Take 'im on, why don't ya?"

"Ya not gonna let ol' Simsy knock ya like that, surely!"

"Give 'im a scrap, matey."

The truncheon beat loudly on the bar top, then waved before them. Magee moved closer to the man whose eyes had not left Sims. Magee spoke low, into the man's ear.

"C'mon now, me son. You don't want to be fightin' with annyone—"

The press of men round them pushed him away. Sims was grinning.

"Well, me pretty little porter, ya comin' outside?"

In a swell of sound everyone was shoving towards

7

the door, Sims already rolling his sleeves up, the man caught in the movement, letting himself be taken along. Magee edged close to him as they came out into the lowering sun's blaze, his voice pitched above the excitement.

"Aw, c'mon now boys—it's too hot fer fightin'!"

No one listened, but the man swung a little to look at Magee.

"He's a bad devil, that Sims. Y'll get kilt, y'will."

The man's voice was crisper now. "I think I can take care of myself, thank you."

And then they were all in the street, in a rough ring in the dust, and the silent and sleeping shanties sent out others to make them a crowd. One or two women stood in doorways and the gaps in the crowd's legs filled with boys and yipping dogs. Sims stood, braces hanging over a wide belt, sleeves well up, grinning, waiting.

On the other side of the ring, Paddy Magee spread his elbows to dig himself room at the front and looked across at Sims. The stranger stood just to one side of Paddy, carefully folding the long blue coat. Paddy reached a hand to it. "I'll hold yer clobber for ye, boyo."

"That's kind of you."

"Ah, it would be a damn sight kinder if I was to hit ye over the head with a bit of wood. Quicker, annyway."

"I *have* been taught something about boxing." The man seemed unperturbed as he folded back the cuffs of his shirt to just below the elbow. Paddy thought, Them's good strong wrists he has there, that's true enough. And he stands nice and easy. Maybe . . .

Across the shifting circle of dust Sims stood now with his shirt off, a grey-dirty woollen vest holding in the thick bulges of his shoulders and the swell of his belly.

"That Sims, he's very big, son. But ye'll see he's got a fair piece of a belly there, 'n' if ye was to catch him a knock in it ye'd do him some damage. Not the head, now—it's like a barrel of sand, so it is."

Sims' cronies had been calling across to the man and now Sims raised his voice. "Are ya comin', then? Or do I haveta come an' get ya?"

The man moved forward into the centre, to where Sims was waiting, hands hanging loose at his sides, sweat-stains black on the wool of his vest. There was a second of silence, then the crowd exploded in a crack of laughter, jeers rising out of it. The stranger had placed himself directly in front of the grinning Sims, left toe forward, left arm half extended, right arm cocked high, back straight. Paddy sucked in hard.

"Holy Christ Jesus, he's a Marquess of Queensberry man! He'll be murdered!"

Moving lightly enough, the man stepped a foot closer and jabbed high on Sims' cheek with the left. Sims took the tap, stepped back and kicked the man in the crutch.

The roar of applause drowned the man's gasping grunt of anguish, but Paddy saw the mouth jerk open and the eyes close, saw the sudden tears in the dust on the man's face as he went over, his hands clutching at the tearing pain. Sims walked in flat-footed and clubbed his fist onto the back of the lowered head, and again as the man went crookedly to his knees. The crowd was shouting encouragement and Sims grinned round at them before turning back to the crouched and retching stranger, again going close then jerking a savage knee into the man's cheekbone, watching as he toppled sideways into the dust still doubled round the hands holding his groin.

"The boot, Simsy, give 'im the boot, mate!"

The smile now was a tighter thing, curling the edge of Sims' mouth and slitting his eyes. He measured his distance carefully and swung his foot with deliberation into the bent body in the dirt, the toecap of the heavy boot sinking into the side of the man's gut once and once again. A flood of bile and vomit shot from the man's mouth, opened in speechless pain, and Sims shifted his stance to avoid it, lining himself up for a final kick to the head. As his foot came forward, the man heaved again and the kick took him where his neck and shoulder joined. Sims stirred him with his foot and walked away into the crowd, accepting the backslaps and congratulations and holding his cheek in mock agony for the extra laugh.

Paddy stooped to look down at the unconscious man. "Ye wouldn't be told now, would ye! C'mon—up ye come!"

He dragged the man upright, hitching him like a sick old sheep over his shoulders, and walked heavily to where the tired horse slept standing by the trough.

The man groaned when he was humped across the saddle, groaned and half-opened his eyes. Paddy took the hessian headband off the horse and used it to pass a lashing across the man's back, through his belt and onto the saddle. He tucked the coat and hat into the blanket-roll and went back into the pub, into the smoky dullness and the noise, Sims and his mates still shouting with laughter. Only the barman noticed Paddy and, without speaking, he bent behind his bar, straightened and passed the stranger's bag around the end. Paddy took it out, slung it to his own saddle, took the other horse's reins as he swung up and led off down the dusty afternoon street.

One side of the sleeping man's face was lit by the leaning flames from the fire, yellow-orange and sideways with the early night breeze pushing at them. The thin moonlight on the other side showed a dark patch where his open shirt had pulled away from his neck, a patch darker than the shadows where the skin and the bone beneath were deeply bruised. The billy, propped on a couple of stones, boiled over, hissing into the hot wood-ash and the man stirred, opening unfocused eyes on the fire and the blackness behind it. When he moved his head his face creased in sudden pain and he groaned quietly, not quietly enough for the sound to escape Paddy, dozing with his back against a tree. He rolled upright, moved the billy a little, put another dry branch across the edge of the fire and stooped by the man under the horse-blanket.

The man concentrated on Paddy's face, his forehead

10

skin wrinkling down with the effort. "I've seen you before—"

"Ye have that. It was me tried to stop ye gettin' yerself kilt. D'ye remember that?"

Again the deep frown, then the eyes cleared. "I do indeed." He tried to prop onto an elbow and the pain snatched at him again, stopping him halfway. And he grinned, though it was more of a grimace. "And obviously I *was* killed."

Paddy's laugh crackled into the night. "Ye come close enough to it, and that's the God's truth! Here now —take a sip at this, will ye."

With Paddy's arm behind his shoulders the man managed to get high enough to reach the pannikin of tea that had been stewing by the billy, and he sipped and sank back again. Paddy looked down at the sweat the effort had brought out.

"Ye're not much of a complainin' man, I'll give ye that. I've some food for ye here. Can ye handle yerself up to it?"

Lips tight, the other man edged and worked himself half up in the blankets and Paddy moved a saddle and a bag of feed behind him then spooned some thick stew from the billy onto a tin plate and passed it. The man rested it on his legs, watching as Paddy tipped a rum bottle over the pannikin. Paddy glanced across at him.

"D'ye not want the stew, then? Ye need some food in yer belly, son—it'll put the strength back in ye."

"I don't normally dine with people I haven't met." The man's voice was shaky with pain, but controlled. "My name's Morant. Harry Morant."

Paddy lowered the bottle and beamed. "I *knew* there'd have to be some of the Irish in ye! Morant, eh? No one but an Irishman'd be daft enough to try and fight that devil Sims like a gentleman! I'm a Magee meself. Patrick, naturally, and Paddy just as naturally." He reached a hand.

Morant's hand in his was hot and dry and very firm. "Well, I'm bloody grateful to you, Paddy. Where the hell are we?"

"Oh, just a bit of a camp I've been keepin' for a day or two now. You wouldn't remember ridin' out here, hung across yer own saddle like a dead corpse?" Morant shook his head. "Ah, ye'll be right enough be the time ye've had a sleep."

"I'm glad one of us believes that!"

Paddy watched him as he spooned up the stew, noticing how fast the hot food was reviving him. He swigged from the bottle of rum and spoke with an almost complacent certainty. "Ye're a gentleman of course."

Morant let the spoon drop onto the empty plate and slumped back. "Am I? There are plenty of people who'd argue with you."

"Ah, no—ye've the stink of privilege all over you. Ye've been used to livin' with tablecloths and servants and all the doodads an' there's no way ye can hide it, boyo." He was pushing tobacco into the bowl of a black, short-stemmed pipe. "Did ye run, Harry, or did they chuck ye out to Australia?"

"That's none of your damned business," said Harry Morant.

"Ye're right," said Magee. "It's not."

## November 1901

*Sixteen, seventeen years back. Always on a horse, it seemed, in those times. Young Harry Morant up in the saddle out on Sand Flats the first time they'd worked together with cattle. The fight with Sims was seventy miles and a week behind them, although the word of it had got to the Flats first and the stock-foreman had looked at Harry and said, "It's no job f'r a bloody boxer, Morant, y'know that don't ya?" And Harry had looked straight back at him, the bruises on him going that dull yellow colour by then, and he'd said, "That's quite understood, Mr. Downes—I'm retired from the ring. Temporarily, at any rate." And that flash of a* smile had come out and Downes had grinned back and asked him if he could ride at all? Paddy heard Harry's voice again, a touch of sarcasm in it, just the littlest touch, saying, "Yes, a bit. Haven't had anything to do with cattle, I'm afraid, but I can sit a horse after a fashion." Downes had waved a hand round at the small holding paddock and told Harry to find himself something to hang a saddle on, told him all he had to do was what Downes said and he'd be right enough.

He'd watched then as Harry walked in among the working stock, seen him run a hand down a leg here, across a neck there, talking to the horses as he shoved them aside and looked them over, curling a hand into the mane of a tall five-year-old roan gelding and leading it out to where an old saddle was waiting over the top rail of the fence.

Harry was no stockman then. It was several months before he really began to look as though he knew what to do with a mob of cattle . . . but it was only a couple of days before Downes and the other men were aware that his statement about being able to ride "a bit" was somewhere well below the truth. Downes had put it into words for them all, hunched over his pipe by the fire one evening while the cook's offsider edged in and out collecting tea-mugs and the men turned to warm the side the night-frost was beginning to reach. Old Bull Downes sucked on his pipe and the words came out in blue puffs. "You told me you could sit a horse. Y'never told me you was a professional horse-sitter. If it wasn't f'r yer weight I'd put y'down as a bloody jockey, son. You was brought up with a saddle stitched inside y'trousis 'less I'm mistaken."

Harry, leaning back on an elbow now, face poker-stiff, spoke back across the fire. "Yes, well I have been riding for a year or two, you see. No point in making a great halloo about it though." Downes had looked hard at him. "I s'pose y'drink a little bit too, eh? Just a bit, like?" Harry had agreed, "Just a bit, as you say." He caught the half-bottle Downes threw across to him and held it up to the firelight inquiringly. "Rum?" Downes shook his head. "No—brandy." Harry shrugged

13

*that kind of No Difference shrug, tossed the cork into the darkness behind him and dragged at the neck of the bottle. Then he threw the empty back to Downes while the drovers and drifters and rouseabouts roared their laughter into the night. . . .*

*Paddy pushed himself off the gate and walked back into the big shed, walked back in the years as he did.*

*The saddles were on pegs in the back corner alongside Harlequin's stall . . . the working saddle, high in front, high behind, smooth as beach-stones and dull-glossy under the dubbin, and the racing saddle that Harry had won that time in Orange, the English saddle made of nearly nothing that he'd used so many times in so many races for so many prizes. Including the women.*

*Not that first year, though. That had been a working year, begod! hard yakker right through. That mob of cattle they'd drafted for Bull Downes had taken them as far down as Dubbo where they'd hung about for nearly a fortnight, eating at the Chow's, sleeping late in what seemed like the luxury of the falling-down hotel, drinking, playing cards. That still face of Harry's had helped there, that and the fact that he seemed to know every variety of card game ever invented and every trick ever dreamed up for each of them, and they'd won in ten days more than they'd earned in the previous month. By unspoken agreement, Paddy looked after the money, stitching half of it into an old canvas belly-band against a rough time.*

*Like the sick three weeks on the Victorian side, up in the edge of the high country where Paddy had begun to sneeze and eye-water and Harry had told the boss they were going to stay put till he was well again. The boss had shrugged and given them their pay till then and some supplies and gone on with the sheep they were moving down out of the winter snow, and Harry had made a bough hut and got Paddy into it, weak and sweat-shivering by then. None of it was clear to Paddy for a while, except the chest-pains and the way the coughing seemed to break his bones, but when he came out of it, calf-wobbly and thin, the shelter had been*

14

*flanked by piles of chopped wood and there was a windbreak of wood and saddles and scrub in front of it. Beyond, there was already a couple of inches of sunny snow, crackled with frost. . . . He could smell the rabbit-stew Harry had made for them.*

*The long days of convalescence brought talk with them—Harry's talk mostly. Paddy's quietness in the snug hut had kept Harry's voice low and reminiscent and he'd talked for the first time about his sister Helen and his mother and the admiral, his father. And about himself as he had been, Lieutenant Harry Harbord Morant, begod! of Her Majesty's Royal Navy! Till he gambled and drank his way out of it in disgrace.*

*God, but they'd covered some ground that year— cattle and sheep and fences and even a shearing shed where Harry seemed to draw blood with every blow of the clippers till the ringer had given him an ultimatum and a broom. It looked there for a moment as if Harry was going to put those clippers into the ringer's gut hard enough to show his wrist on the other side. And then he'd grinned and taken the broom and finished that week keeping the floor clean of tailings. Ah, he'd changed that year. Fined down a lot. Hardened up a lot. Picked up his bush-name, too.*

They worked to the front of the crowd as the man hit the ground, hard on his shoulder and upper arm, and even the shouting couldn't hide the dull cracking noise as the collarbone went. Half a dozen men darted in and dragged the yelling man clear and the grubby-looking horse with the Roman nose lashed heels at them, then stood red-eyed watching around him.

Paddy saw Henry, the shopkeeper, and elbowed his way next to him. "Hey, Henry, y're losin' trade, d'ye know that? Harry and me need some tucker and things. And what the hell's goin' on, anyway?"

"G'day, Paddy. It's that brumby. One of Dickson's abos brought him in and Dickson reckons he's no use till he's broke an' there's no one can break 'im, see?"

Harry had heard from behind Paddy. "Who's tried?"

15

"Ah, there, Harry. Well, Dickson's 'ad a go isself, an' the abo 'n' Teddy Roberts there that they just took off."

"Is Dickson paying?"

"Says he'll give a sovereign. Two bob fer anyone who 'as a go an' a sovereign fer the joker that does the job."

Paddy was outraged. "A sovereign, is it? That's bugger-all for a feller to get himself busted up like Teddy Roberts."

"Well, I tell you what, Pad—it don't look like anyone else is game to try it."

Harry broke in. "What sort of odds d'you think people might offer, Henry?"

"Odds? On that little bastard stayin' like 'e is? Christ, Harry, I'd give yer five to one right now."

"I'll take it. Paddy, where's the money?"

"Ah, now, wait on, Harry, wait on! That's a bad little brumby there. You wouldn't want—"

"What I want is whatever we've got—get it out at fives. Or better. I'll go and see Dickson."

A man alongside leaned in. "Oy, you goin' up on that thing?" Harry nodded. "Did ya say ya wanted fives on yaself?" Harry nodded again. "I'll have yer for a quid then. Ya bloody mad, mind, but I'll 'ave yer."

Harry lifted an eyebrow at Paddy while the man dug into his pockets.

Dickson didn't mind who tried and when Harry told him he didn't want two bob or a sovereign but a bet, Dickson put up two guineas at once. By the time Harry had his coat off, Paddy was in the centre of a gambling-mad mob and Henry alongside him was tipping the money into a hat and scribbling down the bets on the back of a scrap of old poster.

The brumby stood, shifting uneasily, puffing little clouds of dust as he stamped a forefoot. The noise went up a little as Harry walked out and studied the horse for a moment. He was talking to it, low so that no one could hear, but Paddy had seen him do it before and watched his lips moving as his hand went out to the trailing headrope, taking it loose and gentle. Paddy had always got pleasure from seeing Harry mount a horse. There seemed to be none of that foot to the stirrup and a pause and a heaving lift. It was a quick and smooth flow from the ground to the horse's back, just like this time, the brumby lifting its head up and to the side in surprise, and a snap of laughter from the crowd.

Henry checked his watch then and said afterwards, "Well, I reckoned he might stay ten or fifteen seconds like Teddy. Damn me, he was there just on two minutes an' 'e 'ad that broken-nose bastard walkin' round like a lady's 'ack!"

The brumby tried. Until that day he'd never had anyone on his back, and on that day he'd quickly got used to the tentative weight bearing down on him and the savaging pulls at his nose and the sting of whips across his eyes and muzzle. He knew he could get rid of those things if he fought, and he'd done it. But not now. Not with this weight, which didn't hit him and didn't kick him. Just stayed there. He tried going down and rolling, but the weight came off while he kicked and squealed in the dust and then came straight back again when he got back to his feet. And suddenly he realized he wasn't *going* to get rid of it and he was tired and the air was cold as it was sucked hard into his chest and the weight wasn't hurting him.

Harry knew it. Up on the horse's back, he could feel the sudden submission and he kneed the sweaty barrel and urged the horse forward into a canter round the dusty yard, hearing for the first time the shouts of applause and the whistles. And a voice rising high and shrill, "Jesus, he's broke 'im. Good on ya, Breaker!"

Paddy, scarlet with joy, gave Henry five guineas for his help and sewed seventy more into his belly-band, keeping fifteen out for supplies and drinks. Not that they had to buy much that night. Everyone wanted to shout a grog for Harry Morant. Breaker Morant, that's what they were calling him.

When they came into the other pub a month or two later, the name was fixed. He was The Breaker. By then Harry had been asked several times to take on

17

tough horses and had done so each time, always for fair pay, always with the odds against him shortening and shortening until they no longer existed. He was The Breaker, and that was that and one of the country newspapers had written a piece about him and now everyone knew him, knew who he was and what he could do.

He was different by then in many ways, aside from the plain physical changes. He still sounded "like a Pommy bastard," still spoke quietly, still offered courtesy where it was never expected. But there were new expressions on his tongue now and new ways of looking at things. Paddy said to him one Sunday morning in a droving camp, breakfast over and a slack day ahead of them, "Harry, ye're a funny feller. Ye're forever washin' yerself an' shavin' whenever ye get half a chance, an' yet ye'll eat terrible tucker when it's given to ye, an' ye'll go filthy dirty when ye're workin' an' ye've a tongue on ye as rough as a blacksmith's file, yet yer a gentleman with it. Ye're a puzzle to me."

"I'm a bit of a puzzle to myself, Paddy." Harry stared at nothing and there was a silence before he went on. "The Navy teaches you not to be too fussy. I'm here because this is where I pretty well have to be. But I've come to like it, I think. Anyway, I accept it. It's not so very different in some ways, I suppose . . . although I do miss some things. . . ." His voice tailed away and Paddy let the silence hang, knowing he should say nothing.

So it was the same Paddy and a different Harry who walked back into that other pub, a full year after Harry had first come there. He showed no feeling about that other time as they loose-tied their horses at the rail and walked up the steps and into the babble of the bar, half-a-dozen men greeting them and the moist-mouthed barman coming to them with a corner-lipped smile and a rum bottle and a "G'day Paddy, Breaker." Harry poured for them both and they drank, silently, companionably, thankfully. Pushing two hundred head of cattle the last ten miles in the dry heat had left them in need of stillness and liquid, and the first two drinks went down before Paddy turned onto one elbow and looked around the dull haze of the bar-room, fuller than usual during the day because theirs was one of three mobs brought in to the holding yards for a little fattening before meeting the rackety train to the abattoirs further south.

Paddy's hand stopped, the glass almost at his lips, as he stared across the room. He nudged at Harry's side, not moving his eyes. Harry swung his head, saw Paddy's fixed stare and swung again to look that way. His face closed for a second or two and the knuckles on his hand tightened the fingers round the glass. Then he relaxed, finished his drink and smiled at Paddy.

"You really ought to say hello to him, you know."

"Aw, now Harry . . ." Paddy caught the meaning in Harry's eyes, and nodded with deep understanding, smiling with the other man. "Ye're quite right, boyo, quite right. Wouldn't do to ignore an old mate now, would it?" He downed his rum, poured another and raised his voice. "Hey—Sims! Is it you, me boy? How are ye then, Sims?" Letting himself sway a little, slurring his voice, he raised his glass above his head in salute, then pounded Harry's shoulder. "Hey, Harry—ye're not drinkin' to me friend Sims there!"

Expressionlessly, Harry lifted his glass a couple of inches, but didn't drink. Across the room, Sims and the same group of cronies laughed and began to shove their way across, crowding close.

"If it ain't the pretty porter-boy! G'day!" Sims' smile was closer to a leer and Harry looked at him dispassionately.

"Hello. How are you, Sims?"

Hearing the voice, Sims pulled a prissy face, one hand flopping onto his hip. "How *am* I? Oh, ai'm very faine, thenk you, my lord. Ai trust you've been keepin' well, Fancy?"

"Well enough. I'd be better if you bought me a drink."

"Me! Me buy *you* a drink! Get out, ya bloody slack-kneed, gutless Pommy dung-fly!"

Paddy watched Harry, motionless, expressionless,

as Sims ranted on. "I c'n see you've been out in the sun too much, it's touched yer 'ead. No, mate, you're gointa buy *me* a drink. An' me friends." He shouted to the barman in the sudden quietness, "Oy—this pretty cove's buyin' drinks all round. Let's 'ave some service."

The barman moved towards them, licking his wet lips, bottle tilting over Sims' glass. Harry's hand stopped the bottle.

"Just a moment, please, there seems to be some mistake. Sims, I'd sooner give a drink to a stinking dingo than to you."

Now the silence was total for a long moment, breaking into splinters of sound, odd shards of edgy laughter. The barman had the truncheon in his hand, waiting. It took Sims several seconds to mouth the words he wanted, his voice thick and a deep flush on his face.

"Outside you! I'm gointa kill ya!"

It was the same scene again, Paddy thought, as they shoved and heaved outside, the same street, the same sun, the same crowd . . . larger now than last time, but otherwise the same. Even the same kids and dogs. Certainly the same Sims. But a different Harry now, tossing his cord coat to Paddy and the wide-brimmed hat, pulling off the grey flannel shirt and shoving back the sleeves of the long undervest. He was leaner than he had been by a little and his face and forearms were deeply burned by the outdoor months, burned and hard. Sims might have been wearing the same foul vest now as then, and Paddy could see the anger in him, spiked and vicious. Folding Harry's coat as he moved closer, Paddy noticed a small bundle of papers slipping from a pocket and pulled them free, shoving them into his own pocket without looking at them.

In the ring the two men faced one another. Again, Harry stepped forward, arms cocked, feet set, adopting the classic pose. One of Sims' mates muttered, "Jees, he's away again," and Sims moved forward.

This time he used the knee, stepping in close enough, fast enough to jerk it suddenly up, both hands out for a headlock, waiting for Harry's head to drop into them as he doubled. It didn't happen. Harry moved aside, no more than a foot, enough to avoid the knee and kick sideways savagely at Sims' other ankle. The boot stopped the anklebone going, but Sims yelped with the pain and toppled, arms flailing. As he began to go over, Harry's forearm slashed sideways and down, rigid as a club, striking across Sims' kidneys, choking the first yell in a deep grunting groan. Harry moved back to his original position while the other man knelt holding his back with one hand, rubbing his ankle with the other. Harry waited till Sims glared up, shaping a curse, then he walked in very deliberately and clubbed a fist to the side of the kneeling man's head, rocking him across to meet the other fist, rocking him back, and again and again, smashing his face into blood and a mash of bone where the nose used to be. He stepped back again, watching as Sims shook his head, blood splashing into the dust and disappearing, spittle and a broken tooth hanging from a pulped mouth. Then he joined his hands into a single fist and swung them together, underhanded to the side of Sims' jaw. The man on his knees went silently down on his side, his jaw loose, and Harry walked away.

Paddy rushed to him, both of them ignoring the pats on Harry's back, ignoring the little group carrying Sims away, and the Irishman shook Harry's hat under his nose, clinking the coins in it.

"Oh, me son, we've made a little goldmine here! There was fools giving me twenty to one about you, d'ye know that!"

Harry took his shirt and coat, shrugging into them. "Stop gibbering, will you, Paddy."

"Gibbering is it? Look, boyo, will ye look at the money in here! There's easy livin' for a month in this old hat of yours!"

Harry turned away.

"Harry! Hey, Harry, where're ye off to?"

He followed, dragging at Harry's sleeve, turning him, face suddenly anxious.

"Harry, are ye all right?"

"No. No, I'm not all right." Now, for the first time,

21

his eyes were fierce and his face showed emotion. "Paddy, would you say I beat him badly—Sims?"

"Beat him? Ye knocked the murderin' tripes out of him, ye know that!"

"I enjoyed it." It was a flat statement.

"Well, of course y'enjoyed it. Why wouldn't ye? Any decent man enjoys a fight, specially if he wins it!"

"Not the fight. Feeling him go down. Feeling the bones go. The blood on him." He looked down at his hands and wiped them on the sides of his trousers. "I enjoyed *that*, Paddy. I *liked* it."

He turned again and walked quickly away, Paddy watching him, the hatful of coins bundled in his hand, his eye puckered with worry.

It was another camp, one of scores they'd set up, lived in, broken and left. Ten feet from their fire, the Bogan River ran low and greening towards the settlement at Nyngan and behind them the track was dry-rutted where it led north to Bourke. There were a couple of tied lines down into the water, the floats carrying them out at sharp angles as the thin current dragged at them. There was the little noise of the river and the wet crunching as the hobbled horses grazed around themselves, and the crackle of the fire and Harry whistling quietly between his teeth as he darned an old pair of trousers. Paddy couldn't see any of it, flat on his back with his hat over his face and his hands under his head, but he could hear the small noises and he knew where they came from. His voice was muffled when he spoke.

"Aaah. There's somethin' about a Sunday mornin', wouldn't ye say?"

Harry looked up, smiling gently round the whistle but said nothing.

"There's a peacefulness about it, y'know. A—a sort of a lovin' feelin'."

The whistle stopped with a short laugh. "You sound like a preacher, Paddy. Why don't you ride in and go to church?"

The hat tumbled to one side as Paddy jerked half up,

then sat up rubbing a hand through the spikes of his hair. "Church, is it? I misremember the last time I went to Mass. Begod! It'd take me a fortnight just to confess me sins!" He poked at the branches under the billy, glancing at Harry. "There's one sin I could confess to you, boyo."

"Whoa, now!" Harry bit off the end of the thread and tossed the trousers aside, tucking the needle into a tin box. "I've enough sins of my own without being worried by yours."

"No, now—I'm serious. I've somethin' of yours. Somethin' belongs to you." He flapped open the saddlebag by his head and pulled out a bundle of papers. "They came from ya pocket last week, the day you took off yer coat to fight Sims."

Harry sat quite still, looking at Paddy. Then he held out his hand, unspeaking.

"Harry, they're damn good stuff, y'know. I didn't know you was any kind of a poet."

"Give them to me."

Paddy handed the little bundle across. "It's the Irish blood in ye for certain, me son. What'll ye do with them, then?"

Harry leafed through the pages, not looking up, voice low. "They're just scribbles." He folded them abruptly. "You think they're good, do you? How the hell would you know?"

"Ah, now, when did ye ever know an Irishman couldn't tell good poetry from bad? I tell ye, they put the whole of the bush in a man's head, they do. And the smell of the cattle and the feel of a horse."

Harry looked up. "You like them! You really do?"

"I do so."

"Then you'd better keep them." He squeezed the pages into a bundle and threw it at Paddy. "Or burn them if you want. Do what you like with them."

"Truly now—ye mean it?" Paddy was carefully unfolding the pages, pressing them down with the flat of his hand on his thigh.

"Why not? They're no use to me."

\* \* \*

The Sunday had gone away from them then, and another, and they'd spent a week in Bourke and teamed up with a mob heading south again, and come back past Nyngan, well down with the cattle to Orange. The boss had been pushing them hard, trying to save a day, and the animals were tired and the men were tired and the dust was sharp and hurtful in the throat and the eyes. Now that the cattle had the smell of the other cattle in the yards and the water there, they began to move along faster and the boss swirled up out of the dust-murk, tugging down the scarf over his face to shout hoarsely at them and at his drovers.

"Come on you bludgers! The sooner you get the bloody beef in there, the sooner the beer's on!" He spat dust and shouted again above the hoof noise. "Hey, Breaker! Harry!"

Harry edged his horse alongside, the snake of the stockwhip looping through his hand. The men looked like twins, coated head to foot in red, gritty dust, sitting horses of dust in a dusty world. The boss pulled up the scarf again and leaned in so that Harry could hear his muffled voice. "Y'stayin' over for Race Week, are ya?"

"Yes, Tom. It'll take that long to get this bloody dust out of my gullet!"

"Yair. Well, we'll be in the pub in an hour with a bit of luck. Are ya ridin' anythin' in the races, then?"

"Might be. That chap Travers, the one from Mudgee —I believe he's got a horse he wants me to push along for him."

One of the other drovers had walked his horse in close enough to catch the last exchange. "Y'not ridin' anythin' in the Cup, Breaker?"

"No, Alec. Not unless Travers' horse is better than I think it is."

The boss had swung towards the second man. "Y've knocked off then, 'ave ya, Alec? No more bloody work to do, is that it? Go on—get yer arse over there with Paddy and let's get this mob locked up. I want a beer."

24

He kicked his horse away and Harry and Alec grinned at one another and followed him.

There was beer, there was rum; there would be the races; and between the rum and the races . . .

Harry heard the banging on his bedroom door in the pub as a distant drum, then as thunder then, with the shouting, realized what it was and half sat up, rubbing a hand across his face. The room was almost dark and cooling and the warm, damp hump alongside him was —was Judy. With the memory of the name he came fully awake, hearing the voice as Paddy's, hearing the renewed thumping.

"Will ye get the bloody door open, Harry? I'm goin' to break it down in a minute, so I am!"

The girl was half awake now, staring around swimmy-eyed. Harry shook her, not too gently. "Come on, Judy, wake up now." He lifted his voice. "Hold on, Paddy. And stop that damn din!"

The knocking stopped and the muffled voice was quieter. "Well, shake yerself then and open up."

The girl was sitting up, Harry's hand still on her shoulder, and she smiled sleepily up at him, sliding closer in the bed, looping a leg across him and flattening her breasts against his chest. "Harry?"

He kissed her lightly on the cheek and pushed her away, his voice as final as his movements. He struck a match and lit the kerosene lamp beside the bed. "Out you get, Judy, and open that door."

"Oh, hell." Sulking, Judy swung to the floor, pulling the blanket with her and around herself, and wrenched back the bolt, jumping back as Paddy barged in, checking himself for a moment to look at her as the blanket slipped down under her breasts. He cupped a hand under the nearer one and planted a kiss on the corner of her mouth. She jerked away.

"Get off, you dirty old bastard, you're drunk!"

"I am, I am indeed, lass!" He turned, beaming at Harry. "Drunk with the drink and drunk with the news." He flourished the papers in his hand. "Look here, will ye, Harry."

25

The pink covers of the *Bulletin* were unmistakable. There were two copies of the Sydney magazine dated three and four weeks earlier and Harry folded them on the bed, not looking at them, looking at Paddy dancing in little jigging steps in front of him.

"It's the poetry, Harry—remember? The poems ye wrote back there?"

"What in hell's name are you gabbling about, you madman?"

"They're in there! They've published them! Here, look!"

He snatched up the magazines, ripping at the pages to find what he wanted, then thrust them back.

"D'ye see? Right there!"

Judy moved forward, careless of the blanket now. "I suppose you've forgot there's a lady present, haven't you?"

Harry didn't look up from the pages, just reached out a hand and scooped some coins off the table, flipping them onto the bed near her. His voice was detached. "You're a working girl, Judy, not a lady. You've done your work and there's your pay and you can go. And thank you."

She grabbed at the coins, scowling, watching Paddy drag an envelope from his pocket and half-crouch over Harry.

"And there's more, me son! Will you look at this— a bank draft. Two guineas it is, made out to Bearer."

Harry's head was still down, his eyes moving from the printed pages to the green cheque.

"Isn't that a great thing now? Your poems printed and money for the writing . . . and d'ye see the name there, eh? 'The Breaker'. See, 'The Brigalow Brigade, a bush-ballad by The Breaker'."

Harry looked up, smiling, not smiling, a little dazed.

"Ye said I could do what I wanted with them, remember? Ye did say that."

Judy had dropped the blanket and stood there naked, looking at them. Now she picked up her dress, stepped into it and did up one of its four buttons, moving towards the door.

26

She pitched her voice coldly at them. "Well, I'll leave you two fancy lads together, then. It don't look as if you need a woman here."

Now Harry looked up at her, the half-smile going chill. "Don't be nasty-minded, Judy. I don't like hitting women. Not even whores." He threw her another coin. "Go on now, there's a good lass."

Close to tears she pulled the door shut behind her, listening to the excitement in their voices through it.

"Ye're not upset, are ye, Harry? That I sent the poems off like that?"

"Not a bit of it, Paddy. I'd never have had the nerve. There's a devil of a lot of people read the *Bulletin*."

"There is, there is. And they'll be reading your poetry! Look at it there. 'The Brigalow Brigade, a bush-ballad by The Breaker'."

With their laughter behind her, Judy wiped her face and walked away, counting the coins in her hand.

It was beginning to drizzle when Judy left, and after that there had been three days of light rain, the first for over a year. It had done almost nothing to relieve the land, sinking into the dust without running off into the creeks, raising the level in the little dams by only a fraction. But it damped the surface enough to stop the dust swirling as much as usual and the lack of even a breeze meant that the hundreds of feet and hooves at the race-track served more to pack down the red dirt than to lift it.

Paddy glanced sideways at Harry as they walked into the crowd, wondering for the hundredth time how the hell he managed to look elegant in the cheap clothes. They were essentially no different from those of most of the men there, but on him the clean moleskins and the stuff jacket looked properly cut, and his dark grey hat had a little tilt that was different somehow. It was maybe the set of the shoulders, Paddy thought, somewhere between the stiffness of a naval officer's and the easy sling of a rider's. It wasn't that Harry was tall or stately—just that he had a movement about him. And a stillness.

Out of the still face, Harry saw the crowds about him with great clarity. It seemed to him that, for the first time since he'd come to Australia, he was a person, something more than just another man. People called to him in the near-crush, most of them simply waving or smiling from a little distance, some of them elbowing closer for a handshake or a pat on the shoulder, all of them using the name he now accepted fully—The Breaker. The outback of the Australia he knew was filled with men who were recognized as "characters," and he supposed himself to be one of them now. He was different, as all such characters were different. For the man they called Guts Robinson, there was the fact that he could eat for hours at a time and then ask when the next meal would be ready; Killer Morrowby once shot his own horse between the ears accidentally while trying to hit a little 'roo from the saddle; there was Col the Galah, a man with a beaked face and a way of ruffling himself in his clothes which gave him the look of the bush bird; Arsehole Thomas, The Sailor, John the Lady . . . there were scores of them. And now there was Harry Morant, The Breaker. His face was quiet and smiling and he made the appropriate answers, occasionally tipping his hat to one of the women, but behind the mask there was an ugly grin, a twist of the inside mouth and a glint of the inside eyes at the thought of his wardroom friends of a few years ago, of his family—Harry Morant, horse-breaker, stockman, boundary-rider, whore-sticker, accepted, liked, looked up to. And now deferred to as a man of letters because a Sydney weekly magazine had printed some of his scribblings. Oh, the admiral would be delighted if he knew! And wouldn't his mother love Paddy Magee, tough old hard-guzzling Irishman out of some Wexford bog? Oddly enough, he thought, she probably would . . . and then he blanked out all the thoughts of the other times, the other places and grabbed Paddy's sleeve.

"Come on, for God's sake, let's get a drink."

Travers stopped them before they got to the pub-stall, a red-faced little man under a fringe of sweaty grey hair, the beer smell leaking out of him in the heat.

"There you are, Morant! I was beginning to think you were off somewhere writing poetry."

His laugh was edged with beer looseness, but Harry saluted him and made no attempt to meet his gaiety. "Mr. Travers, you know my friend Magee, I think."

Travers shook Paddy's hand almost absent-mindedly, his concentration on Harry and his need for him that day. Looping a hand through Harry's arm he led him to the roped-off enclosure where the horses for the races were hobbled, pointing to a leggy black and looking quizzically round at Harry. Paddy ducked under the ropes and ran a hand down the horse's neck, feeling the light dew of excitement on him. The horse tossed his head and stepped mincingly about, watching Harry who'd followed his friend and who gentled the damp muzzle.

"Hallo there, Sunfire." He turned to Travers. "He looks fit, very fit. I hope you've got your money on him."

"He's a good horse, my boy, and he'll have the best rider. You'll win me a tidy bundle between you, even with the odds the way they are." His eyes had gone past Harry and the horse and now he called, "Over here, Lenehan. Spare me a minute."

He moved away from them to meet the man he'd called and Harry looked at him, and at the girl with him, seeing that the man was perhaps forty, neatly and expensively dressed, seeing that the girl was young, maybe twenty at the most, and that the flowered frock was full of her. Travers was leading them together, an arm on Harry's shoulder now. "John, I'd like to introduce Harry Morant to you. Morant—Mr. Lenehan has Eagleton y'know, the big property to the west of here."

Harry's hat was in his hand, his other hand outstretched for Lenehan's cool, dry grip. "I'm honoured to meet you, sir."

"And I you, Mr. Morant. Or am I to call you

29

Breaker?" The smile was deep and friendly, drawing the flash of Harry's in answer.

"Harry will do very well."

"Splendid! And this is my niece. Julia, may I present Mr. Morant? Harry, Miss Davis."

The girl's eyes were the darkest green Harry had seen, almost black, and they locked onto his as her gloved hand went to his fingers. He bowed, breaking the look, but it was still there when he straightened, and her voice was almost as deep in sound as her eyes in colour, deep and low.

"Mr. Morant, if you ride as well as you write poetry, I shall ask Uncle John to place a wager for me."

"If I'm sure you're backing me, Miss Davis, I shall ride all the faster."

Behind him, at Sunfire's head, Paddy tossed a pious glance to Heaven. A steward, one of the local men with a red ribbon tied to his hat and a sheaf of papers in his hand, was moving through the crowd now, calling for starters for the second race. Travers turned from his conversation with Lenehan, tapping Harry's arm.

"This is you, Morant. No instructions—you know better than I do what to do, my boy. Ride to win, that's all."

"I always do, Mr. Travers."

Harry slipped off his coat, handing it with his hat to Paddy who'd been watching the young aboriginal adjusting Sunfire's saddle and bridle. Harry made that fluid move into the saddle, checking the lengths of the leathers, walking Sunfire through a few steps in a tight circle. As the ropes were lowered for the horses to move onto the track, Julia moved in close. Paddy handed up the light crop and stepped back, watching, as Julia slipped off her glove and gave Harry her hand again, smiling at him.

"Good luck, Mr. Morant. And take this as a charm."

She gave him the slim white glove. Smiling down at her he tossed the crop back to Paddy and flicked Sunfire lightly with the glove, moving him onto the track. His face closed in concentration and the people watching disappeared. There were the other horses, there was

Sunfire beneath him, bunching with eagerness to be off. That was the world.

Galloping now down the soft flank of the hill above the property, Harry turned in the saddle to see Julia on the bay only ten feet from him, the horse running freely, her slim body relaxed in the saddle, her head back in a laugh. She reined in alongside him as he stopped, and they walked their horses together.

"Oh, that was wonderful, Harry! I don't believe I've ever ridden like that in my life!"

"You ride very well." The horses still had the friskiness in them, fresh from the gallop, and for a few moments they let them canter, slowing them as they came onto the flat, the house half a mile away beyond the trees. Harry looked at her as she ran a hand down her long hair.

"What else do you do well?"

She hesitated, her eyes darting away from his and her hand fretting at her hair. "I—I think I might do anything well. If you were to ask me." Her look became almost suppliant. "Why don't you ask me?"

She stopped her horse and reached for his rein, pulling his horse close and leaning across to him. Her lips opened on his and he could feel the depth of her breathing, but he made only the slightest response. She pulled away, anger reddening her face, and a touch of shame.

"I see. The great Harry Morant can't be bothered with a simple country girl."

She kicked savagely at her horse, but Harry's hand on the bridle stopped the animal's move, jerking at its head so that the girl had to struggle to hold her seat till the horse quietened again. He kept his hand on her bridle.

"Julia—no, please. You misunderstand."

"Oh? Really?" Voice cold.

"It isn't you, my dear. I—I'm afraid I'm rather out of sorts." Releasing her bridle, he looped an arm around her, taking her to him and kissing her, hot and demanding, his tongue forcing between her lips, his

31

arm feeling the sudden swell of heat in her body. She was pale when he let her go, breathing sharply, her eyes on him as he said, "You see?"

She couldn't answer for a moment, calming herself. Her voice was a little shaky when she did speak. "Yes, I see, Harry. Is it something I can help with?"

He shook his head and moved his horse forward, leading hers with him.

They left the screen of trees and Eagleton was there before them and a little below, a sprawling white house, glaring in the morning sunlight, pepper trees and three huge old gums shading a little of the front and one wing. Off to one side they could see Lenehan leaning on the white-painted rails of the horse-yard, his foreman alongside him, watching as a stockman walked towards the stables. Harry's sweeping arm took in the whole scene. "Look at that. This is the first time I've been in a gentleman's house since—" His voice was calm, but it tailed away with an edge of bitterness, and Julia caught up the unfinished sentence.

"Since you left England?"

"Since I ran away from England."

"Why? Was it something bad you did to make you run away?"

He looked straight at her, his mouth twisting down at one corner. "Bad enough. Running away is always bad."

She looked away, down at the house, and waited before speaking again. "And you miss it? All this sort of thing?"

"Miss it?" He sat very still for so long that she was about to break the silence. But he turned to her again, a hand out to her and she took it, feeling the tightness of his fingers on hers. "Last night, little Julia, last night we dined off good china. There was silver on the table, wasn't there, and we drank a sound wine and we slept between clean sheets." His hand left hers to check her interruption with a finger on her lips, then went back. She listened to the way his voice changed; no louder, but with tiny barbs in it now, little wicked points of irony and brutality. "Last week—for the last hundred weeks and more—I was unshaven and there was dirt and cattle-stink in every crease of my body and lice in my clothes." He was holding her eyes as they widened, and his grip on her was very hard. "I slept under my horse's blanket and took my food from a tin dish. At night when it got cold, I warmed myself a bit at a time by a branchfire and I warmed my guts with grog. I—" He stopped abruptly, collecting himself, realizing he'd started to let too much creep into his voice. "I wasn't born to do those things, Julia. I miss everything I *was* born to do. I thought I'd forgotten . . . but I was wrong."

She took him up at once. "Then go home, Harry. Go back and belong again."

"Belong? I think this is where I belong now, because I have to, you see. I have friends here of a sort, men who don't look the other way when I walk into a room. People like your uncle who take me as I am."

He'd begun to pull his hand away, but now she was gripping him. "I would take you, Harry. As you are, as you were—any way you chose to be. You know that."

"I know. You'd be sorry." He kissed her again, very gently. "Believe me, you'd be sorry. I'm only good enough for the company I keep, the men I work with." Now the bitterness in his voice was open and he made no attempt to hold it back. "I live from one task to the next, from bottle to bottle. Woman to woman, Julia . . . and not your sort of woman."

"Suppose I was prepared to be *your* sort of woman?"

He stared at her, knowing she meant it. "Then I would thank you deeply . . . and tell you to go and find someone better."

He spurred suddenly away from her, tearing his hand away and leaving her with her hand outstretched, the tears blurring her sight of him. By the time she smeared them away, he was halfway to where her uncle was standing, and she urged her horse into a gallop to follow him.

John Lenehan turned from the rail when he heard the hooves coming in behind him, Julia pulling her

33

horse up alongside Harry's, and he waved at them, smiling, thinking how well they looked together. He'd enjoyed having Harry as a guest these past few days, the invitation made at the party Travers threw after Sunfire had romped home, five lengths out and going away. Morant was a different kettle of fish from most of his house-guests and the two men had hit it off well, Harry slipping back into a once-familiar routine and luxuriating in it, Lenehan glad of the chance to talk at a level he wasn't normally able to achieve outside his infrequent visits to Sydney. And Julia . . . Julia was clearly deep in a romantic trance, he thought, seeing her now looking at Morant as though she wanted to eat him. But Morant had eyes only for the horse. Lenehan turned back to the yard, the young stockman now close to the rail, holding the horse's head. From behind him, Morant's voice was quiet, almost reverent.

"My God, Lenehan, that's a splendid looking thing!"

Lenehan waited till the other man had dismounted and joined him at the rail.

"That's Cavalier, Harry. Bred out of the best there is on both sides. And bloody useless."

"I can't believe that." Harry was studying the horse with care: a tall, broad-chested grey, but so deep a grey it was near-black, the sunlight seeming to sink into his hide, the gleams and shadows with a tinge of steel-blueness in them. He stood, stallion-proud, neck arching, bold eyes watching the men watching him.

"He won't take discipline. Oh, he'll let himself be ridden, but only till he's tired of it. Then he seems to explode, that's all. So—no use to hounds, nor on a track, nor across the hurdles. He'd have been better gelded for hacking, I think."

"Oh, Christ, no!" There was something like anguish in Harry's voice, and Lenehan smiled at him.

"He *is* magnificent to look at, isn't he, though?"

"On my oath he is! And fast too, I'll lay odds."

"You won't find a faster one. Jumps like Springheel Jack on top of it. But useless."

Harry looked at him speculatively. "You don't sound

as though he's much use to you." A carefully calculated pause and then, offhand, "Will you sell?"

"Sell? Cavalier?"

The horse pricked his ears and Harry smiled gently at the tone of disbelief in Lenehan's voice.

"Why not? You said he was useless."

Lenehan's look was long and careful, first at the horse, then at Harry, and there was a glitter in his eyes when he answered.

"No, I won't sell. But I'll bargain with you. Not as John Lenehan with Harry Morant, though. As Cavalier's owner with The Breaker."

Harry didn't speak, just looked at Lenehan, level and unsmiling, waiting.

"Look, the big race is on Friday, the District Cup. With you up on him, I don't see how I could lose, and you're the only one I can think of who might stay on him that long."

"So? What's your bargain?" Flat, almost unfriendly.

"If you do it—if you can ride him and win—by the living God, I'll *give* him to you!"

Now Harry smiled, that great flash, and he shook hands hard. "You have a bargain."

"Good!"

"Does he know his name?" He looked round at the horse and Lenehan looked with him.

"I wouldn't be surprised if he knew mine!"

Harry ducked under the rail and Lenehan went on. "Watch him Harry. He's clever."

"Get your chaps out of here, will you?"

Lenehan gestured the stockman and the foreman clear, both of them grinning at the thought that The Breaker had met his match. As Julia came to the rail, dismounted, Harry suddenly remembered she was there, feeling a touch of regret that the beautiful horse had made him forget for a minute the beautiful girl. She stood by her uncle, looking at Harry, and he stepped back to her.

"Will you excuse me, Julia?"

She nodded, her face open, her feelings plain.

"I shouldn't want to see you hurt, Harry."

"You won't."

He walked towards the horse, not hurrying, stopping four or five feet from him. They studied one another, both motionless, contained. Then, slowly, Harry began to rub his hands together, holding them waist-high in front of him, the movement and the dry, rubbing sound pulling the horse's head and eyes to them. He kept up the rubbing, adding a soft chirrup from his lips, and his eyes lightened as the horse began to step in, stretching his neck, lowering his muzzle towards the man's hands. Harry took the rope halter gently, still chirruping and ran an easy hand over the soft muzzle and up between the eyes. His voice when he spoke was confidential and close to the pricked ear.

"Hey then, Cavalier, that's a fine name for a fine horse, isn't it, eh? Now, let's have an understanding, shall we? You're going to be *my* horse, Cavalier. We're going to win that Cup, you and I, and Lenehan can have the purse and the prize. We shall have one another . . . what d'you say to that?"

He had the horse's head half sideways on his chest now, and his voice kept on quietly and hypnotically, just as his hand kept up its soothing massage.

"But the first thing is, I've got to ride you, old son, just so we've both got it clear who's in charge, right? And you're going to behave yourself for me, aren't you? Fine. Now, I'm just going to hop up on that good broad back of yours and you're going to do exactly as you're told, aren't you? Steady now."

The one-piece swinging move took him up and there was a beat of suspense while Cavalier stood stock-still. Harry gathered the slack of the halter in his left hand, the right knuckling the horse's forehead gently. And then at a click of the tongue, the horse was walking easily round the yard, then trotting, responding to the very light pressure on the headrope and the urging of the man's knees. At the rail, the three men watched, shaking their heads in admiration. Julia stood by them, pale, tears on her cheeks, knuckles white. They watched through five minutes as Harry took Cavalier round, checking and wheeling him, once lifting him, forefeet clear, in a curvetting turn, trotting and walking him through figure-eights and finally bringing him to the gate and slipping down, one arm over the horse's neck, fondling him.

"No one understood him till I came along, that's all. We'll win the Cup for you, Lenehan. Make your bets big."

By two o'clock on the Friday afternoon, Harry and Cavalier had spent two full days together, quartering the ground for miles around the homestead, walking diagonally up the long rises, moving along the creeklines at a contained canter, releasing themselves together in a series of bursting gallops across the flat meadows back· to the yard and the house. Harry groomed and fed and watered the horse himself and, as Julia said with a touch of petulance, did everything but sleep in the stall with him. Lenehan, even knowing Harry's reputation as he did, watched in continued amazement as Cavalier responded to every least demand made on him without once showing the desire to rebel. Paddy, putting on weight with the amount of food thrust on him and the comfort of the stockman's cottage, told him it was nothing new.

"Ye see what it is, Mr. Lenehan . . . there's some fellas have a nose for where gold's hid in the ground, and there's some can look at the lie of a bit of desert and find water in it. I knew an old man up on the Tweed River once could drop a net into the water and the fish would swim uphill for a mile to throw themselves in it, that's the God's truth!"

Lenehan, smiling, finished filling his pipe and handed the tobacco to Paddy, who smelled it with enjoyment.

"Ah, that's better than the old horse-turds I've been on this past month or so!" He lit up and puffed deeply, speaking in bursts of smoke. "With Harry, now, it's horses. What was them old creatures one time that was half a horse and half a fella?"

"Centaurs?"

"That's them! Right, well, Harry's a centaur in a

way of speaking, and the horses they know it, d'ye see? He can talk to them and understand them, just like they was people. It's a rare gift."

"Not his only one, either, eh, Magee?"

Paddy's face became cautious. "Ye mean the women, sir? Ah, well now, he's not any kind of a ladies' man, ye'll understand. It's just that they don't seem to be able to let him be, is all."

"I was thinking of his poetry, in fact. But I believe I know what you mean with the other."

Lenehan was seeing in the eye of his mind the look on Julia, wondering whether to speak to her or let her find her own way through her own problems.

By two o'clock on the Friday afternoon, the racetrack was dead dry again, the full week of sun-heat and the beat of men and horses trampling the last of the dampness out of it. The District Cup was the major event and there were people from outlying places who couldn't spare the time to be there for the whole week but who'd ridden in for the Cup race alone.

In the small saddling enclosure, Paddy stood to Cavalier's head. The big steel-grey horse stood quietly, already saddled, listening as Paddy muttered to him. "Ah, ye'll win goin' away, Cavalier, me fine fella. And with old Harry up, you'd win on three legs anyway, ye would." He glanced round. "Where the devil's that useless lump of a blackfeller? Hey, Jackie!"

The young aboriginal, grinning yellowly, came out of a little group of his friends and Paddy handed him the bridle. "Now then, you walk him about just a bit, Jackie. And every now and then you make him jib a little bit, see—get him to kick his heels. I don't want to see him standin' peaceful, otherwise we'll get no kind of odds whatever, d'y'understand?" The lad nodded, his grin widening, and Paddy ducked under the ropes, checking his old turnip watch as he headed for the cluster of people surrounding the riders.

He touched a finger to his hatbrim as he shouldered through them. "Mr. Lenehan, Miss Julia, I beg yer

38

pardon. Harry, it's just about that time, boyo. Ye'll need to be away to mount up."

Harry nodded. "Cavalier all right?"

"He couldn't be better 'less he grew wings."

Harry nodded again, already remote from the chatter and excitement around him, losing himself in the race to come. Without speaking he began to turn away.

Julia pulled off a glove.

"Harry—for good luck."

He looked down, then up at her, not really seeing her.

"No, you keep it, Julia. Pity to break the pair."

Paddy saw, as Harry didn't, the hurt in the girl's eyes. Harry went on. "Cavalier and I will make our own luck. Excuse me—"

This time Lenehan stopped him, holding out a firm hand. "Good luck anyway, Harry."

"Thanks."

His handshake was as curt as the word, and he was gone, Paddy ducking away after him.

Lenehan cupped a hand under Julia's elbow and moved to the roped enclosure, filled now with mounted riders, only Cavalier waiting. Harry swung into the saddle, running a hand down the horse's neck.

"Are ye right, Harry?"

Settling himself, Harry muttered, "This leather doesn't seem to be sitting quite right," and leaned down to adjust the shortened strap to the nearside stirrup. The raking bay on Cavalier's offside shifted step then as it was moving forward, its shoulder brushing Cavalier's flank, and the steel-grey horse's sudden jib and lunge caught Harry head down and off-balance. He fell heavily, no chance to set himself or to roll with the fall, landing on his right arm and shoulder and there was a gasp from the crowd. Julia, white-faced, jerked away from Lenehan and under the rope, but by the time she reached him Harry was up and dusting himself, Paddy patting at him and cursing the other rider. Harry stepped away.

"Don't fuss, for Christ's sake! Give me a boost."

His foot in Paddy's hands, he went back into the

saddle, gentling the horse and gathering the reins and crop. Without a word or a glance back, he followed the field to the start.

Watching, Paddy saw the nine horses line edgily out across the track, Cavalier at number four. With the gun, eight broke clean, and there was a groan when, in the dust, it was seen that Cavalier had swung right-handed and was a length back. Lenehan swore softly, muttering, "Come on Harry, come *on!*"

It was a mile run and at the quarter there was nothing to be seen but an occasional flash through the moving cloud of red dust on the turn. They were squinting as the horses went along the back and Lenehan pounded Paddy's arm.

"Can you see, Paddy? Damn dust—"

Julia, a pair of opera glasses to her eyes, answered him. "Cavalier's lying about halfway back, Uncle John. He's moving up, I think. Harry doesn't seem to be pushing him."

"He's riding funny, sir." Paddy's voice was anxious. "I've never known him not make a run for the front by this time."

In the swirl of the field, Harry sat easily, face still, body moving only as Cavalier's body moved. The crop was unused in his fingers. In the turn to the final quarter-mile, he leaned forward a little more, seeing the three horses ahead of him, the leader a good eight lengths out, and he spoke to Cavalier.

"Sorry boy—a bad start and all my fault. Now, we're going to win this damned race, so let's get after them. Come *on,* Cavalier!"

He loosed the reins and felt the great swell of muscle beneath him respond, tucking himself down behind the horse's head, easing his weight in the saddle and seeing now nothing but the one horse ahead of him, the roll and heave of its rump. Then he was alongside, not looking but seeing from the side of his eye the other rider's arm swinging up and down and back, flailing the crop-driven horse, its head now alongside Harry's knee and then back and out of sight; and there

40

was the red and white post like a barber's pole and they were past and he heard the shout of sound and closed his knees, leaning back a little on the reins and feeling sick and dizzy and clammy with sweat. He pulled Cavalier to a gentle trot, spitting wet dust from his mouth and turned him back to the crowd and the stewards, stopping him and cocking a leg over the saddle to slide down. The noise was swirling round him and the heat was intense and he heard "The Breaker" rising like a chant round his bursting head. Then, there was Paddy, face split in a gaping grin, and Julia, tear-streaked, her hair coming down, and Lenehan, smiling, smiling. Lenehan grabbed at his hand and wrung it and Harry felt the bile in the back of his mouth as Lenehan shouted in his ear.

"Oh, well done, lad! Bloody well ridden!"

Harry's voice seemed metallic in his skull and echoing, as Lenehan pumped his hand up and down.

"Thanks Lenehan . . . I wonder . . . I wonder if you'd mind shaking the other hand? I think that arm's broken."

And the shouting and the pain and the heat went away as he sank to the ground.


The sling was of silk, dark blue silk, elegant and quite in contrast with Harry's clothes. He was back in his old flannel shirt and working trousers, comfortably-worn boots in the stirrups, old jacket thrown across the saddle on Cavalier's back. The horse he'd ridden in was on a lead rein behind him, a pack across its back and Paddy was walking his horse alongside, his voice raised in a croaking bellow of song.

The arm was almost healed now, but Harry had slipped the sling on again knowing it would be a long day's ride, not wanting to jar or tire the arm early in the day. Now, with the sun an hour over the low hills behind them, he reached into the folds of silk and pulled out a flask of brandy, passing it to Paddy.

"Here, you noisy brute—put a stopper in that hole in your face. We'll both feel better for it."

Paddy, still roaring, took the flask, stopping the song

to tug the cap free with his teeth and take a deep swig. His sigh was satisfied. "Ah, now, it's a mornin' for singin' this is! I never was much of a man for sittin' on me arse in a posh house, y'know!" He drank again, deeply, gulping at the brandy, then held it out. "Will ye have some?"

"If you've quite finished, you tosspot!"

"Ah, there's a little left yet." He passed the flask back. "It didn't take ye long to lose yer fancy tongue, did it now? Ye're right back where ye was, rough-tonguin' yer best mate." He sighed and shook his head. "Never mind—'tis good to be away on the track again." They rode silently for a little while, Paddy stewing over something in his mind before he spoke again.

"You now, Harry, that's a different story. Y'know ye could have stayed there, don't ye? I could see the way ye fitted in, in amongst the gentry and that. Ye could have lived like a proper gentleman and written yer poetry and rode for the love of it instead of after a lot of stinkin' cattle." He paused, looking at Harry. "Ye could've married that Miss Julia. She was in a real sweat for ye, Harry."

Harry passed the flask across again. "Not my kind of life. I'm like you, a bushman."

"Ye never are! Oh, ye've the way of it right enough, and ye're a good man on the track and a fine mate. But that's more for you—" he cocked a thumb behind him, the way they'd ridden, "—than this is."

"Might have been once. Not any more. All I'm after, Paddy, is to whack up another cheque in the bush and drink it down at the pub." Even to himself, his voice sounded false, and he didn't meet Paddy's look. He fumbled in a pocket and took out a small gold locket on a thin wisp of chain, clicking the case open with his thumb-nail. Julia's face smiled out at him and he felt a stab of something like pain, remembering the warmth and closeness of her, the tautness of her breasts under his hand, the way she panted and pushed herself at him. Remembering her sudden panic when she lay naked with him and he took her hand and put it on

42

himself, the way she whimpered, "Harry no, no—I can't—I'm afraid. Harry—I'm not your wife!" Remembering the wet face as she dragged her nightgown over herself and ran from his room into the darkness of the sleeping house.

He held the locket out so that Paddy could see the picture. "Not that Julia wasn't a great comfort to me . . . you'd be surprised what a tender little nurse she was. Especially at night when I couldn't sleep for the pain."

"Did she bring yer medicine then, in the night?" Paddy sounded surprised.

"The best medicine for an ailing man."

He heard himself saying it and felt hatred, self-hatred, rise like sickness in his throat. Paddy clicked his tongue against his teeth. "I've said it before—ye're a terrible rogue, Harry Morant. Toyin' with a nice little lady like that. A terrible rogue."

He shook his head again and drained the last of the brandy, letting the flask drop into the dust of the track. Harry's fingers worked at the locket, slipping the portrait free and letting it fall, tucking the gold trinket back into his pocket.

"I wouldn't pretend otherwise, Paddy. I'm not properly cut out for a gentleman, I'm afraid."

Behind them, under the hooves of the led horse, the tiny picture and the empty flask lay side by side in the hoofmarks on the track.

## November 1901

*The afternoon had stretched itself out into a long, red-gold evening and now, with the first of the night's cold creeping in behind the dusk, Paddy was glad of the fire. It wasn't much of a house, but he'd fixed it up well and it let in no draughts and let out no warmth, and with Harlequin stalled and a pile of dry logs by the grate, with a meal in his belly and a glass of grog* in his hand and his old pipe drawing well, he felt mostly content. A bit of company would be nice—he thought that almost every evening, especially in the autumn, when the whole world seemed to be touched with a little loneliness, and the dullness of winter was pulling up close.

He'd not lit the lamp, and he sat there in the flame-flicker, thinking. . . . Harry on Cavalier, his waterproof and the horse's hide both the same gleaming black with the rain teeming down, and the cattle tired and up to the hocks in mud, but Harry always ready with a smile, always with a bottle of something warm tucked away in a pocket to share with Paddy, laughing into the rain, dog-tired though they were. Ah, they'd drunk many a stirring drink that way, the two of them, wet and dirty-dry, working and loafing, card-playing and womanizing and gambling and fighting. Begod, that Breaker could swing a fist like a club, and he never again tried the gentleman's boxing game after that first time with Sims!

Not that he hadn't been knocked about other times, without fighting for it. The polo had done for him more than once, a madman's game for gentlemen only, with the bloody great sticks like hammers flashing about and the little ponies whipping round like watch-wheels, and somebody bound to get hurt. And there'd be the old Breaker—broken in a part of him and tucked away in bed in a hospital somewhere. Roaring at Paddy for a smuggled bottle of liquor and with half the local lassies visiting him, and him lying there in the bed in splints and a spare hand up their skirts or down their fronts and them lining up for more of it!

It seemed to him, staring into the flames, sipping at his grog, that there'd been trouble one way and another ever since they'd ridden away from Eagleton that time, and away from that little Miss Julia. Not that it was all bad—funny some of it. Like that time they went off on that pigsticking jaunt in Victoria somewhere. Harry went anyway, and himself just for the gallop and a friendly bit of a sneer. And there was Harry with this great long lump of bamboo and a pointy *blade on the end of it enough to slice the tripes out of an ox, and half a dozen other men like it and all jinking about in that wicked scrub country with the rocks hidden by the scrub, after a bit of a black bastard of a humpy-backed pig! And himself dismounting for a sip out of the bottle in the saddlebag and seeing Harry alone ride into a clearing after a pig and check and the other man coming out sideways at him, walking his horse and the point of his spear under Harry's chin, very still, just pricking at a tiny spot of blood. He remembered watching frozen, too late to do anything and listening to the two of them, Harry with his head back, and the man saying, "I should hold my horse pretty damn steady if I was you, Morant."*

And Harry lowering the point of his spear and Cavalier standing like a statue while Harry said, "I don't think we've met, have we?"

Cool as ice, and the other man holding down the fire in him, but there was heat in his voice.

"We haven't, but I've been looking forward to it. I want to give you a little advice."

And he'd shifted his point a bit and Harry's head went a bit further up and his back straightened all the way.

"I always take the advice of a man with a blade in my gullet." His voice was tight, but very steady, Paddy remembered, and the other man had said, "Good. Then stay right away from my wife. Right away. Or I'll be hunting you instead of the little pigs."

And he'd given another touch of a jab and ridden away and Harry had sat and watched him go, rubbing his throat and tilting the spear back over his shoulder. Paddy had ridden out to him, his face white, and Harry had smiled ruefully at him and said, "All very well . . . but which one is his wife?"

Paddy kicked the sinking fire into life again and re-filled his glass, thinking, Ah, God, he changed a lot them years did Harry. Kept on with the poetry, though, all that time. And times, behaved like a real gentleman. Like the man he used to be once.

\*   \*   \*

It had taken Harry a week to get used to being back in a city again. It was seven years since he'd landed in Sydney and the place seemed to have grown like a wild pumpkin in damp ground, sprawling tendrils everywhere. He and Paddy had wound up a three-month spell on the one property and had then moved down to the races at Bathurst, and the work and the winnings between them had left them flush, enough money as Paddy had said, "So we can take a bit of a rest, boyo. Eat and drink in style for a month, eh? Why don't we go down to The Smoke?"

New clothes and a decent hotel room and a long lunch with the *Bulletin* people and temporary membership of the Turf Club on Lenehan's letter of introduction. Paddy watched as his friend slid easily away from the roughness of the track and into the smooth patterns of social life, seeing his enjoyment in it, although he worked hard at the pretence that it was all a lot of balderdash. He went to the Turf Club Ball and Paddy looked at him ready to leave the hotel, white tie and tails that he'd bought specially for the occasion, silk hat in a white-gloved hand and the lined cloak swirling round him as he went out to the horse-cab, and he began to wonder if the man would ever come back with him into the outback again. He needn't have worried.

The night after the ball, Harry said, "My God, Paddy, I could do with a decent drink."

"Well, now yer Lordship, ye've nothin' to do but ring the little bell there and one of yer slaves will bring ye some champagne in a golden slipper. Or will I ring it for ye, sir?"

"Paddy, I want a *drink*."

And they went out, plainly dressed, and down to Woolloomooloo, where the pubs were close together and noisy and reeking and full of the oddments of Sydney—journalists and pimps, painters and sailors, whores and thieves.

By the time they'd been at the bar for an hour, Harry was flushed and half-drunk, his eyes fever-lit and no sign of the polished gentleman of the night before. The young man who'd edged in beside him caught his attention and he nudged Paddy and said, "I say, Patrick, look at this young shaver—all fresh and dewy-eyed and drinking small beer."

The youngster half-turned, his face colouring, and managed half a smile. Harry slapped him across the back. "Hey, that stuff'll rot your insides, my lad. I'll buy you a proper drink." Spreading a handful of silver on the bar he shouted for three rums, sliding one of them to Paddy and one to the young man. "What's your name, sonny?"

"Grant, sir. Duncan Grant. And thank you." The voice was quiet, well-enough taught, something of a lilt in it.

"Aha, a polite young Scot! Drink your rum, Duncan Grant, and tell us what a sprat like you comes to Sydney Town for."

"I've . . . I've just landed, sir. Today. I've come to work."

"Hey, Paddy, here's a phenom . . . phenomenal thing. This young man wants to *work!*"

Paddy stared owlishly across at Grant. "Very commendable. Very. The young men of today don't seem to want that any more, so they don't. Just wanta drink. Drink's a curse, that's what it is. I'm very near teetotal meself." He sank his face into his rum again, and Grant smiled a little.

Harry waved a hand for more drinks, his arm still looped across the young man's back. "And what line of business are you in, may I ask, Duncan Grant?"

"None, really, sir. That is—I was working in my uncle's warehouse in London—he's an importer you see, but—"

"But you got tired of it and ran off to the Colonies? Adventure and far places and all that . . . right?"

Grant nodded, smiling, the drink warming him. "I suppose that's what it was. I've read about New South Wales and it seemed to me there were chances for . . . other things out here." Harry looked at him quizzically, and the youngster stumbled on. "I don't mean to stay in Sydney. I . . . I want to be a bushman."

Harry's roar jerked Paddy's head around. "Bushman! You! Hey, Paddy, this little pink thing wants to go bush!"

Paddy leaned in closer. "Don't do it, young fella. 'Tis a terrible life. Stay here where the rum is. Get a job in a pub, why don't ye?"

Harry was running hard fingers up Grant's arm and punching him gently but with firmness on the chest. "You're too soft, sonny. You wouldn't last a week in the brigalow!"

Grant pulled himself away, face clouding. "I may be a little out of condition, sir . . . the sea voyage . . . but I'll harden I don't doubt." Then his curiosity beat him. "What's the brigalow?"

"What is it, sonny? It's all out there—" his sweeping arm made Grant step back again, "—the bush, the backblocks. You need to be a strong man to live out there, Duncan Grant from the warehouse." His voice had gone up and two of the barmen moved along nearer to him, one of them frowning, holding an empty quart bottle by the neck. Paddy tugged at Harry's sleeve.

"Harry, give over will ye! Ye're creatin' a disturbance."

The barman with the bottle leaned across, face close to Harry's. "Oy, you! If you wanta drink, then pay yer money an' drink, right? If yer wanta shout yer 'ead off an' make a bloody shivoo, y'll 'ave to do it somewhere else. Or I'll *knock* ya fuckin' 'ead off with this, see?"

Harry stared at the bottle waving under his nose, then pushed it gently aside with one finger. "My dear man, all I'm doing is telling this young new-chum about the bush, that's all. About living in the brigalow."

"Yair, well keep yer voice down while yer doin' it." He turned to Grant. "You keep yer mate quiet, lad. An' what '*e'd* know about the bush I'd 'ate to think!"

Paddy was suddenly outraged, stretching an arm across and wagging a thick finger in the barman's face.

"Oh, ye're an ignorant man, so y'are! D'ye not know this is Harry Morant? The Breaker?"

48

"Yair, an' I'm the Pope, old feller. Just keep 'im quiet."

Grant looked puzzled. "Who's The Breaker?"

A quietly-dressed, elderly man standing close by chipped in at once. "A balladist, young man. Harry Morant is The Breaker, a man who writes excellent bush verses." He turned to Harry. *"Are* you, sir? Are you Morant?"

Harry sketched a bow. "I am indeed. For what it's worth."

"I consider it to be worth a good deal, sir, and I'm most pleased to make your acquaintance. I've admired your verses since they first appeared."

"Very kind, very kind." Harry was making an attempt to control the slur in his speech as he took the offered hand. Embarrassed, he tried to change the subject. "I was just trying to tell my young friend here, Grant, about life in the brigalow, sir."

The man smiled at Grant. "Then you should ask Mr. Morant to recite you his ballad about 'The Brigalow Brigade'."

Grant's face lit up. "Would you? I'd like fine to hear it if you would."

"Oh, but . . . really, this is hardly the place for recitation—"

Paddy, grinning, broke in. "Ah, go on now, Harry! 'Twouldn't be the first time ye've spouted a piece in a pub!"

The quiet man had had their glasses refilled and slipped one into Harry's hand. Harry took a gulp, looking round at the three of them and shrugged. "Very well, gentlemen, I shall recite!"

With his back to the bar, leaning comfortably on his elbows, he let his eyes lose the sight of the crowded, rackety bar, picturing for them the openness of the country out to the north and west, looking on to the words he'd written five years ago, a notebook balanced on his thigh as he walked his horse:

*"There's a band of decent fellows*
*On a cattle-run outback—*

49

> *You'll hear the timber smashing*
> *If you follow in their track;*
> *Their ways are rough and hearty*
> *And they call a spade a spade;*
> *And a pretty rapid party*
> *Are the Brigalow Brigade!"*

Paddy was beating time with the swing of the lines and Duncan Grant and the quiet man were both smiling, standing close. Several of the people nearby had caught something in what Harry was saying and had edged in a little and there began to be a circle of quietness about the man with his back to the bar and his head back and his voice, low but ringing:

> *"They are mostly short of 'sugar'*
> *And their pockets, if turned out,*
> *Would scarcely yield the needful*
> *For a decent four-man 'shout.'*
> *But they'll scramble through a tight place*
> *Or a big fence unafraid,*
> *And their hearts are in the right place*
> *In the Brigalow Brigade."*

Now the ring around Harry had sucked in most of the people in the bar, and there was a murmur of "The Breaker," and the barmen had shifted along, the scowling one behind Harry at a bit of a loss. Harry's voice hadn't risen, but in the comparative quiet it rang clear in the room:

> *"The Brigalow Brigade are*
> *Fastidious in their taste*
> *In the matter of a maiden*
> *And the inches of her waist;*
> *She must be sweet and tender*
> *And her eyes a decent shade—"*

There were smiles all around the bar now as the words caught them, and they waited for the last line, roaring it with Harry—

The chorus snapped Harry's head down and his
eyes cleared and there were people buying drinks and
calling to him and even the surly barman was smiling
with the new rush of orders.

Harry flushed and frowned, the sudden attention
unwelcome. His head felt clear now, and he muttered
to Paddy, "I'll join you later, back at the hotel," and
pushed his way through the crowd to the door.

A block away from the pub, Harry slowed to a
stroll. He was near the Harbour and the sea-smell came
strongly to him, and the ship-smells—a sweet-sourness
of tarred ropes and salt-steeped timbers and canvas
and a thousand mixed cargoes. The night was clear
and chill and the last of the rum fumes washed out of
him as he walked, remembering other days in other
seaport towns. He didn't hear the running feet, and
the man who cannoned into him at the corner caught
him off balance, sending him lurching to the wall,
clutching at rough cloth. Pulling himself upright by
the man's clothing, he could see in the flicker of a
street-light that he was a sailor, Royal Navy, dishevelled, capless and panting.

"Whoa there, Jack! What's all the hurry?"

The man wrenched at Harry's hand, his voice harsh
with lack of breath. "Lemme go, mate—I gotta find
some help—"

Harry shifted his hand from the tight grip on the
man's shirt and laid it hard on his shoulder, his voice
crisp and cold. "Stand still, man, and talk sense."

The tone of the voice snapped the sailor upright and
still, and he searched Harry's face in the near dark,
listening.

"Now then, what's wrong?"

"We been jumped on, sir. A gang round there, round
the corner a bit. They're knockin' the Jesus outa my
shipmates. I've got to—"

"Show me where."

The sailor swung away at once and Harry followed him back the way he'd come, seeing as they rounded the corner the struggling group at the end of the narrow street under another light. As he ran he summed up the scene: three matelots, one down in the gutter, the other two backed against a wall trying to hold off five—no six—bully-boys. They were so deeply immersed in what they were doing that Harry and the sailor hit them like a swinging club, taking two of them out of the fight at once. From the corner of his eye Harry saw the sailor leap, his bunched knees catching one of the men in the small of the back, his fist swinging sideways at another. Harry used the weight of his running body to drive his arm and fist at an unguarded throat, feeling his knuckles sink in and hearing the choked scream. Then it was a general mêlée, with the two other sailors, heartened by the reinforcements, coming back strongly.

When the police arrived the fight was even and Harry's eyebrow was bleeding where a short cudgel had smacked at him. His knuckles were raw and he was gasping for breath, feeling a dull ache below the breastbone where a knee had dug in.

Paddy walked along the damp stone corridor, the sergeant ahead of him, a bundle of long keys jangling in his hand. The two big cells were off to one side facing the half-dozen single cells across fifteen feet of ill-lit paving slabs. The bully-boys were in the first big cell, lounging back on the floor or on the plank seat along one wall, and they scowled silently as Paddy and the policeman went past them. In the other cell, Harry, a handkerchief still wiping drying blood from his forehead, stood straight, his back to the door, looking at the four sailors sitting in a row, heads down. His voice was crackling.

"You ought to be ashamed of yourselves! Four of Her Majesty's jacks not able to handle a bunch of wharfside ruffians like that!"

One of the sailors, the one Harry had run into,

looked up apologetically. "They caught us on the 'op, sir—"

"Be quiet! And stand up straight!"

The four of them scrambled to their feet, one standing a little crooked, a hand pushed into his side.

"Look at you! Not a hat between you and your uniforms are in a disgusting state." He let a smile creep through. "I'm very glad to have been of service to you."

The sideways sailor grinned at him. "Very pleased to have had you along sir."

One of the others, the side of his face puffed and blackening, said, "Beg pardon, sir, but are you—was you—er, in the Andrew, sir? The Navy?"

Harry was saved from answering by the sergeant, rattling his keys into the lock and swinging the door wide. "Out you come, Morant. Your friend here has paid you out."

Harry spun around. "Paddy! Well done. Have you any money on you?" Without waiting for an answer he turned to the policeman. "Sergeant, what's the damage for these men?"

"Same as yours. Five shillings apiece."

"Good. Paddy, a quid. Quickly now!"

Paddy had been standing through this fast exchange, his mouth open. Now he shut it to swallow before shouting. "Are ye out of yer mind! I'll not spend good silver on a mob of drunken sailors—"

"You'll pay for these men or I'll break your scruffy Irish neck!" The tone of command softened. "Come on now, Paddy. You're still holding a few guineas of mine."

Paddy stared at him, then at the sailors, and the sergeant broke in. "Well, do you or don't you?"

Muttering under his breath and firing salvoes of fury from his eyes, Paddy fumbled coins out of his pockets and his belt. The sailors crowded round Harry, wringing his hand. The one who'd joined him in the attack said, "Yer a toff, sir, a real toff."

"That's all right. But you'd better tidy yourselves before you get back to your ship. Ready, Paddy?"

"Ay, I'm ready. Ready to ding you in the skull, ye madman!"

The four sailors had shuffled themselves into a line under the glance of the one with the bruised face. Now he flicked a look at the four of them and slid words from the corner of his lips.

"Right? Hup!"

As one, the four came rigidly to attention, Bruised Face whipping his hand to his forehead in salute. Very gravely, Harry tipped his battered and dusty hat to them, turned smartly on his heel and walked out. Paddy, skipping to keep up with him, let the irony sting through his voice. "Lovely! Is the captain ready to go ashore now?"

Harry smiled straight ahead, but there was a wistfulness in it.

Sydney? But that was a long time ago. Paddy felt that the cold of this high country had got into his bones. He felt the dullness of the ache across the small of his back as he lifted the axe again, and the deep pull at his shoulders as it came down, clean-splitting the pine log. He stood surrounded knee-deep by split wood and he stopped to wipe the cooling sweat away from his face, looking down the valley to where the snow hadn't settled as it had begun to do up here on the slopes.

He'd knocked together the remains of an old wheelbarrow the week before when they moved into the hut, and he piled it high now with firewood and rolled it, squeaking and leaning, cursing when he saw the door wide open. He stamped in, slamming it behind him, and crossed to the fire, low and half-choked with ash, kneeling and poking it into life again and deliberately rattling the iron bar around to try and stir the sleeping man in the bunk there behind. By the time he'd got the new-cut wood in and stacked and dragged in two or three bigger logs for keeping, the early sun had gone and the feathery clouds had massed and dropped, ready to snow again.

As once before—the time he had got pneumonia,

years ago now—they'd spent a couple of weeks helping bring sheep down out of the upcountry—irritating work because the animals were scattered through several small valleys in the hills. Neither Paddy nor Harry much liked working sheep, but they'd found work increasingly hard to get during the last year or two because of Harry's drinking and his truculence.

Foremen and bosses had found him a problem, drinking not to be friendly or to keep the cold out, only for the sake of it and then spoiling for a fight with someone, anyone. This last job had ended with the boss deducting a good lump of Harry's pay because he'd gone grog-wild one night and just about taken the little tucker-cart to pieces with a cleaver in protest against the cook. Paddy had managed to keep them hanging on till the end and then dickered with the property-owner for the use of the hut up the slopes, planning to settle there for a while and try to dry Harry out a bit. The supplies had taken almost all the money they had, but they were snug enough for the winter if necessary and could make a fresh go of it when the thaw came.

The horses were in a lean-to behind the hut and Paddy raked the straw around, spreading fresh stuff on top of it and dropping some dry feed into the trough, his own horse standing dozing on three legs, Cavalier nosing at his hands as he mixed the feed. Through the wall he could hear Harry moving, stumbling about first, then the creak of the door, then the retching and heaving and, sighing, he went around to the front of the hut, looking at the man standing barefoot in the thin snow.

"Oh, Christ, Harry, if ye don't kill yerself tearing yer guts out like that ye'll do it be freezin' yerself to death!" He got an arm around the crouching figure and half-dragged him back inside, dropping him into the beaten old chair by the fire and throwing a blanket over him. "Sit there a minute and try and get the blood movin' a bit inside ye. I'll clean ye up as soon as I've yer bed fixed."

In the early evening Harry came fully awake for the

first time that day. Paddy was hunched over a piece of harness, a saddler's palm on his hand, the curved needle catching the glint of the fire as he sewed. There was a food smell from the pot to one side of the heat and Harry's stomach contracted with emptiness and need as he pushed back the blankets, noticing that he was in clean underwear and socks. He toppled twice while he was pulling on his trousers and shirt, and he grunted each time. Paddy made no move other than to go on with his repairs and Harry, not speaking, ladled stew into a dish and tore off a piece of damper, slumping onto the stool at the rough table and shovelling food into his mouth, head low. He wiped the plate clean with the last of the damper and fossicked around in a box under the wallshelves, finding the rum and mixing two mugs of it with hot water and a little sugar. Paddy put the harness and sewing-gear away and lit the lamp, looking at Harry, yellow in the yellow light, stubbled and gaunt.

"Ye're a mess, Harry Morant, d'ye know that?"

"I know it." The voice was harsh and blurry. "There's no bastard knows it better."

"Ah, ye're disgustin'!" He started to go on, but stopped himself and swung the chair round to face the other man across the table, sipping at the hot grog while he studied him. When he spoke again his voice was gentle. "We been on the track a long time, Harry. There's no man I'd sooner have rode with, I tell you that straight. Ye're a helluva fella an' I love ye like a brother, but ye've made yerself a stinkin' mess, ye have."

"Oh, for Christ's sake, Magee! I don't need you preaching at me!"

"Magee, is it? Right then—Morant!" Paddy shoved back the chair and stood over him, solid and chunky in the low light, his brows down dark across his face. "Let me tell it to ye straight—ye're a drunk. Ye're a spendthrift, stupid, womanizin' drunk. And what with the one and the other and the lot of them, ye'll put yerself in the grave in jigtime. Ye will!"

Harry looked up at him, a twist of a smile making

him look ugly somehow, and he nodded his head. "Right!"

"Right? It's not right at all! It's a madness!"

Harry drained his mug and reached again for the bottle, but Paddy snatched it from him, holding it away where he couldn't reach, letting the anger seep out of his voice.

"Ah, now, boyo, don't ye see what ye're doin'? Ye're killin' yerself!"

"Exactly! You have the gift of clear sight, Paddy old friend, like all the mystic madmen of Ireland. I'm killing myself. And why not? Why ever the hell not? It's the only privilege I still have." The clear irony changed to a growl. "Give me that bloody bottle."

"Aaah, take it, then, ye drunk fool!"

He watched as Harry poured neat rum this time and gulped at it. "Look, Paddy," he said, "there's nothing I can do will ever put me up on a horse behind a Devonshire fox again, is there? Nothing will take me home again, will it? So it doesn't matter, does it?"

"Harry, the old people at home have a word for fellas like you, and the abos too. Ye're puttin' the death-wish on yerself. Ye're gallopin' to yer own drunk death is what ye're doin'."

"I am, I am indeed."

Harry took another deep drink. "I am indeed." His face was desolate and his voice entirely sober.

Late that night, with Harry snoring and bubbling, Paddy hunted out every bottle of drink he could find, smashed them on a rock and buried the pieces.

They came out of the hills in a softening and a damp warmth, new pale greens all round them and the loud sounds of downhill water proving the end of the winter.

Harry was thin but clear-eyed and Paddy felt good as he rode behind Cavalier, looking at the easy uprightness of Harry's back and hearing his whistling.

The morning after Paddy had got rid of the drink, Harry had had a fit of raging fury which would have ended in Paddy's death or serious injury had the younger man not been weakened by continual drinking and sickness. As it was, he'd done a fair amount of damage to the hut, throwing clothes and food out into the deepening snow and nearly setting fire to the place, and he'd left an aching bruise on Paddy's leg which had taken weeks to fade out. In the end he'd knocked himself out without Paddy having to hit him and for three weeks after that had spent his time either in bed or sulking silently in the chair. He stank and his beard grew in a straggly scrub and he ate only just enough to keep himself alive, glaring at Paddy when the food was put before him.

At the end of a month, still silently, he rose early one morning and by the time Paddy woke, the hut was filled with the smell of food, the fire was high and cheerful and Harry was washed and shaved and in clean clothes. Paddy made no comment till later that day, well into the afternoon, when he heard the sound of the axe and went out to where Harry, sweating and panting, was swinging away at a dead pine. Paddy was alongside him before he noticed, and he lowered the axe and wiped his streaming face with the back of a wet hand. Paddy, face serious, laid a hand on his shoulder and said, "Welcome back, boyo," and they both smiled.

"Ye'd better come inside and wipe that sweat off ye, and get a dry shirt on. Ye wouldn't want another cold now. I'll heat some soup—not as warming as grog, of course."

He lifted an eyebrow at Harry who stared back, poker-faced.

"Grog? You know I don't drink, you mad Irishman."

And that had been that, so that now, with the opening of spring, they rode down into the valleys, pockets empty, tucker-bags almost empty and ready for work.

Harry had held off the drink for a long, hard six months, not refusing two or three beers at the end of a stiff day, but not once taking any of the hard stuff. They settled in on a property outside Yass, a sheep place, where Harry rode the boundary and strung some wire and Paddy, deciding on a bit of a rest, took on as rouseabout, spending much of his time close to the homestead.

It was the most sedate period of their lives in all the years, a settled and near-routine time, without the shifts and starts they'd begun to accept as normal. Harry began to jot down verses again and broke half a dozen new horses and seemed relaxed and comfortable. He began to talk of a trip down to Melbourne or even to Adelaide to see what the racing was like on the city tracks there.

They were back in the high lands that autumn, again to move sheep down out of the cold. It was black rock country, hard and unyielding, the underlying ribs of the slopes covered with a loose skin of sharp stones, almost bare of greenery. Above them the sky was nearly as black, looked almost as hard, and the wind had swung to come out of the north-east, whistling down the gullies and then suddenly carrying swirls of sleet in front of it and chopping across sight-lines in a blur of icy greyness.

Harry and Paddy had been moving well out on a flank, the others across a gully from them and up the slope of the ridge opposite. It had seemed to Harry that Cavalier was making hard going of it and, with the sleet and the wind pushing it directly into their faces, he felt the big horse lose the certainty of his footing, felt a slackness in his movements as they edged upwards almost blindly. He swung down, shaking his head against the tiny ice chips and turned his back to the wind, taking Cavalier's head to his chest, listening with a touch of fear to the stallion's heavy breathing, feeling the tremble in the shoulder muscles under his hand. He realized they weren't any more the great rounded bunches they had been, that Cavalier had lost weight, thinned down. He'd been three, perhaps four, when Lenehan had handed him over that day at Eagleton and that was close to nine years back. It wasn't necessarily much of an age for a horse, but he knew how Cavalier had worked, knew how hard he'd pushed him as a stock-horse, as a saddle-horse, as a race-horse. And now he felt afraid.

The breathing slowed and eased although the trembling was still there. Harry muttered, close to the steel-grey head, "All right, old son. The devil with the sheep. We'll go back." He lifted his head and shouted against the skirl of the sleety wind, hearing Paddy's answering call, thin and tossed about against the rocks, waiting till he loomed out of the murk, covered with the silver crystals of the settling sleet. Mutely Harry swung an arm downhill, back towards the homestead and Paddy nodded, tugging a scarf up over his face and hunching his shoulders. Harry swung into the saddle and they began to move down, letting the horses pick their own paths.

Twice Cavalier stumbled, once where he went through a crisping surface into a wet little bog of a hollow and once when a loose rock skittered away under a forehoof. Then they were almost on the flat, not at the bottom but a place where the slope eased before plunging down again. Cavalier stopped, head down and blowing gouts of steamy breath and as Harry shifted weight into one stirrup to dismount, the big horse went to his knees, a thick sigh shaking him. He tossed his head as though objecting to his own weakness and let himself slide over, lying down, his barrel heaving with the effort of breathing. Harry knelt by him. "My poor old boy. It's too much for you, isn't it? And I'm a bastard!" The wetness in his eyes wasn't all sleet and he blinked, rubbing the horse's head. "You shouldn't be working in this stinking weather, Cav. Let's get you home, eh? Come on now, old son, up you get."

Paddy, riding ahead, realized he was alone and turned his horse into the gusts again, squinting to see. He came on the stooping man and the struggling horse almost before he knew they were there. He was out of the saddle at once, kneeling by Harry, running hard, expert hands over the horse. "Ah, ye good old fella, has the cold got to ye then? All them hard miles, eh?" He looked round at Harry and lowered his voice, close to Harry's ear, as though they were in a sick-room. "He's had enough, Harry. He needs rest—"

He broke off as Harry stood and walked around Cavalier, stooping to the old rifle in the saddle-boot, tugging it clear of the horse's body.

"Ah, ye'll not!"

"I have to, Paddy. He's gone. He's got a few years too many on him for the way I've worked his guts out. He's gone." He checked the breech and looked down.

"If we could get him moving easy . . . get him to shelter—"

"So he can spend a year coughing himself to death? Not my horse, not Cavalier. He wouldn't want that."

Paddy stood, holding out his hand for the rifle, but Harry shook his head. Paddy bent again, patting the horse lightly and coughing, pretending the wind was in his throat, and Harry waited till he'd moved away, kneeling then on the rocks and slipping the bit and bridle from Cavalier's mouth. He slackened the girths and let the saddle slip down, pulling his bags from it and tossing them behind him where Paddy took them up. He shoved his hand deep in the coat pocket where he kept some of the coarse brown sugar Cavalier loved and held it out. The horse had kept his eyes on the man all the time, half-arching his neck and turning his head, and now he dropped his muzzle to the sugar and licked a little of it, not finishing, letting his head drop back, sighing again. Harry lowered his head, dropping his hat alongside him, and rested his forehead against the horse's, still for a long span of seconds. Cavalier whickered softly.

Harry stood abruptly and, in the same movement, cocked the rifle and fired. There was hardly any echo, the wind taking the flat sound and throwing it away in the gullies round them. Paddy mounted, Harry's bags across the saddle in front of him, and waited, saw Harry stand still with the wind whipping at his hair, then eject the shell. Wordlessly he swung up behind Paddy, letting the rifle fall by the dead horse, leaving the saddle where it had slipped. His arms were tight around Paddy's waist and he dug the side of his face hard into the back of Paddy's shoulder as they walked slowly down in the storm.

Horses! There were maybe sixty in the mob . . . not all of them fully wild. A few, perhaps a dozen, were runaways and it was those few who were making it so damned hard to push the brumbies into the rough yard at the bottom of the gully. They knew what the sapling rails were for, they recognized the gate, hanging wide on strap-leather hinges, and every time they were edged down towards it they propped and wheeled, trying to run back through the mob and sending them all scattering up the rough sides of the gully and back towards the half-dozen men behind them. Riding the dapple he had picked up as a replacement for Cavalier—a poor substitute, but he had to have a horse—Harry was half-blinded with dust and sweat. The wild horse whirling up almost directly ahead of him caught him by surprise and he let it by. Over on his right, Spencer, the man for whom they were working now, bellowed. "Don't sit there on y'r arse, Morant, get ahold of him."

By the time Harry had turned the wild horse, the rest of the mob were halfway through the gate, the stockwhips cracking about their heels and the men whistling and shouting. Harry quartered his dapple behind the other horse, trying not to gallop him, not to frighten him more than was necessary. As the bulk of the dust began to settle he could see his quarry more clearly and his eyes widened and he whistled between his teeth. Under the caked mud from a creek somewhere, under the dust, this was something special . . . the coat was rough and thick with burrs, but it looked golden, and the mane and tail, grey-red with dirt, looked to be black below. And the horse, a stallion, moved beautifully, certain-footed and a splendid stride, long and with a raking dash in it. Clever, too, Harry half-smiled to himself, seeing how the horse checked and wheeled, changed gait, spun about, pacing him for a few strides, then stopping suddenly in the hope that Harry would go past him and leave him clear. By the time they'd worked down to the gate, Harry was smiling widely in appreciation and when he cracked his whip six feet behind the horse, it looked at him as though realizing the game was over and trotted sedately in to the yard where the rest of the mob were milling themselves to a standstill. Paddy wheeled alongside.

"Holy Jesus, that was hot work!"

Harry didn't shift his stare. "D'ye see him, Paddy? Don't make it obvious now; just look around casually. I don't want Spencer noticing. There—by the rail—the stallion."

Paddy shifted in the saddle for a clearer look. "I see him. He stands out a bit from that mob of scrubs, don't he? There's breedin' there, boyo."

"D'ye see the colour under all that muck? I believe he's a true Palomino, Paddy!"

"What the hell's that when it's at home?"

"Wait and see!" He wheeled the dapple and walked over to where Spencer was watching the gate being lashed fast. "Mr. Spencer . . . may I talk with you for a moment?"

Spencer, thickset and scowling, looked at him curtly. "Make it smart then, Morant. I want to get home before dark." He half turned to call to the rest of the men. "Come on you lot—y'pay's here!" He turned back to Harry. "What d'you want then?"

"I want you to keep my pay."

Now Spencer gave Harry his full attention, staring at him, suspicious. Then he grunted a laugh. "Do you now? Well, I'll not fight you about that! What's the catch?"

"No catch. I'll take it out in horseflesh."

"What, one of them?" Spencer's thick thumb jerked at the quietening mob and Harry nodded.

"Yes. Will you do it?"

Spencer shrugged. "Why not? The price they're fetching nowadays, I'll be saving money. Go on, help yourself."

Harry raised a hand in thanks, wheeled and stooped from the saddle to undo the gate lashings, Paddy moving along with him. The stallion was watching, a little away from the bunched mob near the centre of the yard and when the gate was swung three or four feet, he moved at once, trotting through the gap. As he came through, Harry dropped a rope halter over his head and took a loop on to his saddle while Paddy shut and lashed the gate again. Spencer watched them, looking at the horse and for a moment it seemed as though he was going to speak. Harry got in first.

"My bargain, I think, Spencer—thanks! Paddy, come and make the acquaintance of—of Harlequin."

Renmark looked inviting when they rode into the town, cool in the first long shadows of the afternoon, fresh from the light shower which had fallen earlier in the day. The dapple on a lead-rope walked behind Harlequin and Paddy's bay, down to the corner hotel in which Harry had got himself arrested a month earlier when he was on the spree after the death of Cavalier.

After the great brumby round-up they'd spent the bulk of the month twenty miles or so up the Murray River towards the Victorian border, putting up with the evening mosquitoes for the chance to camp near big water, the chance for Paddy to pull some fat fish out of the river. The chance for Harry to work with Harlequin. For three days he'd just let the stallion graze on a running-line near the camp, making no attempt to ride him or clean him, simply spending long periods talking to him, knuckling his forehead, getting him used to the cupped handful of brown sugar. He was maybe a hand shorter than Cavalier and not as huge-muscled, but he was, as Paddy said, "A terrible elegant sort of a horse," and there was a quick intelligence in his look. When it came to it, there was really no need for him to be broken. He kicked up his heels a time or two when Harry first settled onto his back, and he spun a little and jinked about, but they both knew at once that this was a game of sorts, token gestures by both the horse and the man. Then Harry began to groom him, walking him into a shallow place where a miniature shingle beach led into the river. Paddy watched from higher up the bank, a line in his hands, his old pipe going like a smokestack, and he let the line hang slack as the horse emerged from its coat of dirt and burrs. Even though Harry had prepared him for it, he hadn't expected quite what he saw, the sleek, deep gold of the hide and the fine black silk of the mane and tail. When Harry led Harlequin back from the water, still shining wet, Paddy stared at the two of them and said quietly, "Ah, now, ye're a pair of champions, so y'are!"

Now, as they tied the horses outside the corner hotel in Renmark, people stopped to admire Harlequin, several boys crowding close, one of them patting the Palomino's muzzle. Harry watched, smiling, till the voice beside him jerked him around.

"Morant, you're not plannin' to start any trouble, I 'ope."

The sergeant towered over him, face grim. Harry, recovering, was all at once glad to be clean and sober. "No, Sergeant, no trouble. Not this time."

"Not *any* time in this town, son, take my word for it."

"Fair enough. May I buy you a drink?"

The sergeant shifted the roll of paper under his arm and looked at his pocket-watch. "Yair, I don't see why not. 'Bout that sorta time anyway. Good on ya."

Paddy watched delighted at the way the pint pewter emptied into the sergeant. "By the livin' God, ye've a hell of a swallow there, Sergeant! I've not seen a better."

"Practice, Magee. I been doin' it a long time." He hunched lower on his forearms, cocking a sideways look at Harry. "Yer still on the hard stuff, I see. I'll remind ya again—no trouble."

"Sergeant, this is a glass of rum. It's the one I bought two or three minutes ago and I shall drink it, *and* the one you buy *and* the one Paddy buys. Then I shall stop for the evening." He downed the drink.

"I believe ya." He waved a large hand and the glasses and his pot were refilled. "I see the *Bulletin* got another of yer pieces in. That one about yer horse, Cavalier. I liked that."

Harry smiled up at the big man. "I wouldn't have suspected you of being a poetry-lover, Sergeant."

The sergeant smiled back. "The way I see it, if a man's got them kinda feelin's about a horse that belongs to him, then he's pretty near orright." He lifted the pot. " 'Ooray, Breaker."

When he'd drunk the beer Paddy bought him he checked his watch again. "Better be gettin' on. Gotta put this up yet." He picked up the long roll of paper which he'd propped against the bar.

"What've you got there, Sergeant—a picture is it?"

"Poster, Paddy. Notice come up from Adelaide—they're goin' up all over. Come an' 'ave a squint."

They followed him out to the low veranda, watching as he dug around for a little box of thumb-tacks and carefully pinned the notice up near the door in the light of a pair of hanging kerosene lamps. Several other men gathered to watch, unable to read the notice till the sergeant's spread shoulders moved and the lettering stood out clear in the lamplight.

As the little crowd built, the words went buzzing back and into the bar, dragging more men out to swell the noise. Paddy listened, his eyes on Harry who was reading the notice with complete attention.

" 'Ey, they're callin' for volunteers, Mick!"

"What for?"

"Join the Yeomanry—go to South Africa."

"Second South Australian Yeomanry . . . see?"

"What the fuck 'appened to the first?" A burst of laughter.

"Maybe they lost 'em!"

"Get out. I 'eard one lot's gorn already. That'd be the first."

"Yair, well whatta they want volunteers *for?*"

"Fight the bloody Bores."

"The who?"

"The Bores. Dutchies. In South Africa."

"Fight 'em for what?"

"I dunno, mate. Don't matter, does it—you're not goin' anyway!"

"I don't see you runnin' off to enlist neither Jacko!"

"Me! No way, digger!" More laughter.

Harry was still reading, close to the poster, leaning forward a little to read the bottom lines. Paddy edged close to him.

"Harry? Ye're—ye're thinkin' of going, are ye?" His voice sounded frightened.

66

Harry straightened, smiling, and Paddy looked at him. It was the full, flashing smile of the young Harry, the Harry of fifteen years ago. He slapped a hand hard onto Paddy's shoulder.

"Going? Of course I'm going!"

They left Renmark just as the sun was lifting, Harry and Paddy and two other men, a little group of people to see them away, the sergeant among them. They rode down south and west to Berri, where another man was already on the road, and then south to Loxton and then edging into the west again through Wanbi to Tailem Bend and Murray Bridge, men in ones and twos turning off tracks and out of gates to ride with them, joining them from places off the Adelaide Road, from Waikerie and Tinkarrie and Mannum, from Pinnaroo on the Victorian border and up from Meningie and Strathalbyn. By the time they topped Mount Pleasant and looked down on Adelaide and the sea, there were more than forty of them, Harry on the golden Harlequin at their head. And they rode into the city like that, along North Terrace to the white block of the Barracks with the guns pointing outwards from the gravel parade-ground corners.

Paddy waited outside the Barracks, Harlequin's rein looped over his wrist as he sat his own horse. He was edgy, nervous. Adelaide was a small and quiet city, but it still made him jumpy. Especially knowing what was coming. He looked across the gravel to the two sentries there, mounted and still, one on either side of the archway. The parade-ground was busy, even now, close to six in the evening, with a file of men in stable-gear moving across it picking up small pieces of litter, and a raucous corporal over on the other side, roaring the step to a fire-picquet marching to their post. And there was Harry, swinging towards him, a gleam of amusement in his eyes. Paddy looked at him, trim in khaki and polished leather, the boots and spurs gleaming, the side of the slouch hat clipped up and letting the last of the light fall on his face. He looked fine.

"Merciful God, 'tis a general at the very least!"

Harry's hands went to Harlequin, and he grinned at Paddy as he mounted.

"Not yet, you mad Irishman, but just you wait!" He slapped the other man on the shoulder. "How are you, Paddy?"

"Oh, well enough, well enough." They turned the horses and walked them along the Terrace. "I've got the place I want, Harry, while you've been playin' soldiers. Thirty miles it is, about, and just a few acres. Enough room for a few vegetables and a run for the horses."

Harry leaned forward. "And how d'you like that, Harlequin, eh?" The horse heard his name and danced a little, pricking his ears. "I wish I could take him with me, Pad—the first lot took their own. He'd enjoy it; and God knows what sort of hacks they'll find us over there!"

"Ah, he'll be right enough with me, y'know that. There's good grass, an' I'll take care of him. Don't worry now." They rode for a while in silence, wheeling through the parkland and heading back towards the Barracks. Harry had an hour's leave. When they saw the guard-post lights, Paddy said, "It's been six weeks now. When are ye off then, d'ye know?"

"Tomorrow." He didn't see Paddy's start, the look of pain. "Big march through the city first. Will you stay over and see us go through?" Paddy coughed and covered the sudden shake in his voice with a laugh. "Not me, boyo, not me! I don't like crowds. An' soldierin's somethin' I can do without." He reached out and grabbed Harry's arm, pulling both horses to a stop. "Are ye sure ye wouldn't want to cut and run now, Harry? We could be away and home tomorrow night, you and me. And Harlequin?"

"You know I couldn't do that, Paddy, even if I wanted to." They moved on. "Look, I've got a fresh hand of cards here, old friend. I haven't had a drink these past six weeks, did you know? I'm as fit as I've ever been. I think I'm cut out for a war. I *want* to go!"

"Ah, ye would, ye would. Well, ye'll do as ye want, Harry Morant. Ye've never done a damn thing else!"

They were back at the corner of the parade-ground. Harry sat quite still for a moment, reins slack, one hand absently sliding down Harlequin's neck. Then he dismounted and passed the rein to Paddy. "Paddy, will you promise me about Harlequin? No one rides him till I get back. Promise?"

"Ye have my word on it. He'll not have a saddle to his back. Not till ye come home."

Harry patted Harlequin again, and the horse nudged at his pocket with a damp muzzle, looking for the sugar which wasn't there this time.

Paddy's hand was square and hard in Harry's, the grip firm and long.

Then Harry spun about and Paddy watched him go, marching easily across the gravel in the shadows, turning for a second to wave in the archway under the light, between the mounted sentries. And then gone.

Paddy looked at the empty space and said it again, quietly. "Not till ye come home, Harry."

# SOUTH AFRICA

Under the loom of Table Mountain, the dock at Cape Town looked like an open-air madhouse. Harry leaned on the rail watching the gangs of Kaffirs walking the mooring ropes to bollards, watching the troops and the naval shore-parties scurrying about, listening to the roar of voices crossing one another in commands and curses, topped by the shrilling of whistles and the gun-thunder made by the wheels of a long string of carts and wagons on the wooden setts of the dock. There was a band playing in the shade of a warehouse and a guard drawn up in review order near them. It was probable, Harry thought, that only the guard could hear the band with all that din. Certainly from the rail of the transport only an occasional treble squeak could be picked out, the bandsmen seeming to be puppets, playing without sound.

Ted Hewett alongside him shook his head admiringly. "You've gotta give the Pommies credit, you blokes. They really know how to make a fella feel welcome. You wouldn't get a shivoo like this anywhere else, now wouldya?"

"Bloody hope not!" Owen Fisher, on the other side of Hewett, spat down over the side of the ship. "If this is how they carry on about unloadin' one lousy ship, what the bloody hell are they gointa be like when it comes to a fight?"

"Harry? Oy, you're one of *them*—are they always like that?" Ted Hewett was grinning, one eye winking at Fisher.

Harry kept his face straight. "I'll tell you, Ted. It's all a very clever ruse. They do it to confuse the enemy into thinking they don't know what's what, you see."

Fisher spat again. "Yair, well I'd say they're doin' a pretty fair job of confusin' *me* for a start." From behind them a bugle sounded and Fisher pushed himself upright. "There ya go, lads. The cruise is over an' the excursion's just about to get under way. Move along."

"Harry an' me'll be along in a minute. You go on, Owen, if ya want."

"Nice of you, Corporal Hewett!" Fisher's voice was quiet, but the snap in it pulled the other two upright. "Now, you and Trooper Morant might just do me a favour. Move!"

Ted, his face assuming a wide-eyed stare of panic, saluted left-handed.

Harry bowed, deeply and gracefully, sweeping his slouch hat along the deck. Fisher's grim face cracked in a grin. "I'll see you jokers later. If you can manage to tear yourselves away."

He wheeled and moved along the deck, chivvying troopers to their disembarkation stations and Harry winked at Ted. "Nice chap, Fisher. For a sergeant."

Ted brushed his two chevrons casually. "Yair; well now he's gone, *I'm* in charge here, Morant. And you heard what the sarge said—move!" He ducked under Harry's flat-handed swipe and they headed forward, into the mass of men forming ranks near the brow of the ship.

On the dock, the Second South Australian Yeomanry stood easy, the men turning to watch the activity round them, pointing, chattering. From the transport ship they'd just left, slings from derrick arms were lowering nets filled with their kitbags, with boxes and bales of supplies, with odd bundles of miscellaneous military gear. Further aft, a gang of mixed sailors and gunners were swinging out one of the six field-pieces which had come with them and there was a growing pile of material building on the dock, Kaffirs swarming all over it under the tongue-lashing of a red-faced Ordnance sergeant. The wagons were rolling forward slowly, ready to be loaded and move the stuff away, and the band was still playing, behind them now and audible to some extent. Off to one side were several British officers and, from where he stood, Harry looked at them, recognizing some of the badges, some of the elegant uniforms. They were snapped up to attention almost at once, Regimental Sergeant-Major Maitland yelping at them, then stumping to where the C.O. and the officers were grouped. Half a minute later the officers were saluting and moving to their squadrons, and the C.O. was marching stiffly to meet a British staff colonel, their hands coming to their hat-brims as they met.

"Good morning, sir. Morrissey, Second South Australian Yeomanry."

"Morning, Morrissey. Welcome to the war." The colonel looked along the ranks of the Australians and consulted a slip of paper. "Two hundred and eighteen, I believe?"

"Right, sir. All present and correct. No casualties, no sick; and anxious to get going, if I might say so."

"Yes, of course." There was no warmth in the words, only something close to condescension, and he hadn't looked up from the paper to see Morrissey's flush. "Well, we've got some livestock for you round the corner somewhere, I daresay. You'll be in the camp-lines out to the north of the town with the rest of us, naturally." He glanced at the waiting troops again. "Bit—er—shoddy, are they, Morrison? Those their best uniforms?"

"Morrissey, sir. And those are the only uniforms they—*we've* got, apart from stable gear." He tried to mask his anger.

"Ah? I thought it *was* stable gear. Never mind—the quarter-bloke might be able to find you something a little more suitable . . . the officers, anyway."

Out of the corner of his eye, Morrissey could see Fishburn, his adjutant, face scarlet with the repressed desire to hit out, but the colonel spoke again before anything happened, looking up as he tucked the paper into his pocket.

75

"Well, now, I'll send someone along to show you where to pick up your mounts and guide you to your lines. Oh—and the general would like you and your—er—officers to dine with him tonight." His pale eye went up and down Morrissey. "Informally, of course. Eight o'clock in the Mess."

Morrissey's hand was still at the salute when the colonel flicked two fingers at him and walked away.

Fishburn let out a gust of breath. "Jesus Christ allbloody mighty! Sorry, sir, but if that bastard's what all these bastards are like I'm—I'm going to desert and fight on the other bloody side!"

"Hold up, Len, hold up! I don't believe there's another bastard in the world like *that* one! Let's get our blokes moving, shall we?"

Sergeant Owen Fisher looked at his horse with some disbelief. He gave it a gentle punch on the shoulder and shook his head when the mare swung a complacent eye round at him and then slumped again. Fisher walked to where his troop commander stood. "Mr. Cowan, sir, a word with you?"

"Hallo, Owen. What's your problem?"

"Me horse, sir. She's a nice old thing. 'Bout as big as a good-sized dog, she is, an' very quiet. I mean she's asleep, properly speakin'. I'm a bit afraid to get on 'er in case she falls down."

Cowan bit back the smile as he looked up at Fisher's six-foot-three-high poker face. "Perhaps you could carry her, Sergeant." He lifted a hand to stem the outburst. "Look, Owen, if you've kept your eyes open you'll have seen we're all in pretty much the same boat."

Further along, Morrissey and the R.S.M. were in conference.

"Well, Mr. Maitland, they're a job lot, aren't they? I don't think you'd make much out of them if you had *them* up for auction at y'yard, do you?"

"I asked one of those Remount johnnies where they come from, Colonel. D'y'know what he said? Said about half out of a hack stables in the city an' the rest was saved from a glue factory they've got set up here somewhere!" Maitland was a solid, tough man, but he looked like a wounded child, and Morrissey gave a ruefully sympathetic smile. "Nothing we can do about it at the moment, anyway. Maybe I can talk to the general tonight. In the meantime, what's happened to the saddles and equipment?"

Maitland gestured to the long shed behind them and the file of men heading into it. "Being issued now, sir. God knows what *they'll* be like!"

Gloomily, they looked at the scene, the Australian troops struggling with their new and unfamiliar equipment, the air solid with curses. A dozen N.C.O.'s in British cavalry uniforms were desperately trying to show them how to stow everything.

Little Peter Pullen, the smallest man in Harry's troop, stood chin up to a Hussar corporal. "What's this fuckin' saddle made *out* of, mate, cast iron?"

The trim corporal stared down, glowering. "For a start, cocky, don't call me mate, call me Corporal, and stand to attention."

"Get fucked!"

The Hussar gasped three times before he got the words clear. "I'll have you! You miserable little Colonial bleeder, I'll have you on a charge so fast—"

"Aw, git out of it! Can't you jokers make yer own argument stick? Whaddya wanna start talkin' about charges for? Yer breeches is pretty, but yer a lotta gutless wonders!"

The Hussar's fists clenched, but he checked himself and spun round calling, "Sergeant!"

Owen Fisher's quiet voice grated right beside him. "Yair. What's the trouble, son?"

Eyes flicking over Fisher's tunic and chevrons, the Hussar said stiffly, "I was calling for Sergeant Jackson of Ours."

"Well, I'm Sergeant Fisher. Of Somebody Else's mind, but I'm still one of Her Sainted Majesty's Holy Sergeants." The voice was suddenly a whiplash. "Stand to attention, Corporal."

The Hussar stiffened and went rigid under Fisher's gaze as he walked slowly round him, examining him from head to toe.

"Very nice! Very nice indeed!" Several of the Australians were bunched around them now, grinning, and Fisher spoke to them. "Trooper Pullen, you midget misery, you, 'ave a good squint at this man. All of ya, 'ave a look. That's a soldier, that is. That's what British soldiers look like, see? Cavalryman, this one. See 'ow lovely 'is uniform fits, and not a mark on 'im anywhere. Brasses like gold, spurs like silver, face all scrubbed. Beautiful!" The Hussar twitched. "Stand *still*, Corporal! Now then, you crude Colonials, just because this man may not 'ave the brains of a sheep in a snowdrift, just because 'e may not 'ave the manners of a blackfeller with a bottle of gin, 'e *looks* like a soldier, so you treat 'im with proper respect, see? Don't make fun of 'im, nor yet the 'orses he's give us, nor yet the saddles an' stuff."

Ted Hewett and Harry had drifted into the listening crowd, and Ted called out, "Sounds like the Ten Commandments, Owen!"

"Well, 'ere's the Eleventh one then, Corporal Hewett. Get this mob moving and ready to ride out. I'm sure this corporal of cavalry will excuse us simple Colonial volunteers." He gave the Hussar a final malevolent glare. "Go on, son, run away. Dismiss!"

The flushed and furious Hussar stalked away, the whistles and catcalls dying as the R.S.M. moved among them suddenly.

"Sergeant Fisher, what's going on here?"

"Nothin', Sar-Major. Just thankin' that corporal there for giving us the benefit of 'is expert knowledge."

Maitland looked at him steadily, but his eyes were gleaming. "Good for you! Now, less chat and more action. The boss wants us away."

That evening they sat around their gear, bellies full and pipes and rolled cigarettes thickening the air in the tent, dulling the light from the single lamp hung to the centrepole.

"Christ, my arse hasn't been as sore as this since m'father took a belt to it!" Hewett shifted from one hip to the other on the blanket padded under him.

"It's those bloody saddles—made out of teak, they are." Peter Pullen, standing, felt his backside with care and lowered himself with even more care onto his bedroll. "Goes right through t'the bone."

Harry stretched himself luxuriously, flat on his back with his stockinged feet propped on the tentpole. "The trouble with you people is you're not really used to riding. You're all aristocratic folk, y'see, used to putting your bums down on cushions, of course. Undoubtedly—" His voice choked off as Fisher tossed a loose blanket over his head, and when he dragged it off, Greville leaned across and said earnestly, "Hey, Breaker— you're a Pommy—why the hell would they want to make saddles like them?"

"Damned if I know, Bernie. I'm inclined to think we'd be better off bareback than on those things. And don't call me a Pommy."

Fisher, cross-legged on an ammunition-box, blew smoke into the pitch of the tent. " 'T'ain't just the saddles, Harry, it's the whole bloody shebang as far as I can tell. I reckon that poor old mare I was up on 'ad sixty pounds useless weight on 'er."

Hewett leapt at the opening. "Git out, Owen, you weigh more than sixty pounds, mate!"

Harry's voice rose above the roar of laughter. "It's my belief the staff's still fighting in the Crimea . . . wouldn't be surprised if Florence Nightingale turned up any moment now."

"With a few of 'er nurses, eh?"

"Gawd, I c'd use a woman just about now!"

The interrupting voice stopped the banter dead. "Well, you lot sound happy enough."

The man with his head through the tent-flap was a stranger; brick-red face with an enormous black moustache halving it and a dark-blue cap topping it, the field-gun badge glinting in the dull light. He looked around the silent group.

79

"Er, don't let me put a damper on things, mateys. Only came along to see how you was settling in."

Owen Fisher said flatly, "Thanks," and the silence settled again. The man in the doorway coughed and stepped in, a haversack swinging from one hand. The three gold chevrons on his sleeve had a smaller version of the cap badge set over them. "Farringdon. Troop Sergeant, G Battery, Royal Horse Artillery."

"G'day." Fisher had made no move. He let the word drop, watching as Farringdon glanced round at the silent men and cleared his throat again.

"Friendly lot of sods, aren't you? And me with a housewarming present." He swung the haversack against his booted leg and bottles clinked.

Harry's eyes caught Fisher's, saw the gleam of laughter deep in them. The others were beginning to smile as their sergeant stood, stretching out a hand to the stranger. "Ah—Owen Fisher, Second South Australian Yeomanry, all of us. Siddown, mate." He shifted along the ammunition box to make way for Farringdon who unstrapped the haversack and passed out three bottles, dark and unlabelled.

Greville took one, holding it up to the light. "What is it—ox-blood?"

"It's a gift-'orse, Bernie." Ted Hewett was working at a cork with his clasp knife. "Don't look at its teeth, son."

Harry held out a mug for Hewett to pour into and sipped at the dark red liquid. "My God," he choked, his eyes streaming. "Take care, you lot, it's loaded."

"Local brew." Farringdon took a deep draught from the neck of the bottle he'd opened. "Our Mess buys it by the dozen." He looked at them all, considering them. "Do I get the feeling you don't think much of us? Not that I was listening—just you had your voices up a bit."

Harry coughed again and answered. "I'm afraid we've had rather a bellyful of the British Army today, Sergeant Farringdon. Nothing against you, of course—"

"Specially since I brought some booze, eh?" Farringdon had cocked an ear at Harry's voice.

80

Little Peter Pullen took the bottle from his lips long enough to say, "Y'see, it appears your Army's got some bloody funny ideas, mate, that's about the strength of it."

"Not used to ridin' scraggy cattle, Sarge." Greville's rumble rode over the top of Pullen's thin voice. "With a cartload of rubbish tied on front an' bloody back."

"An' saddles as sharp as a dingo's backbone." That was Hewett, again changing hips.

Farringdon nodded solemnly. "Uh, huh—bit soft are you?" He ignored the way the smiles disappeared. "You'll harden, my sons. Believe me, you'll harden."

Harry deliberately let the edge in his voice show through. "There's a difference between hardening and setting solid. Seems to me that's what you chaps have done. Set solid—between the ears."

In the silence, Farringdon pointed a long finger at Harry. "That's my stuff you're drinking there. I don't have a lot of time for a man who'll miscall me while he's drinking out of my bottle."

Feeling the tension, Owen Fisher broke in on them, turning himself to face Farringdon beside him. "That's fair enough. What did you say your first handle was?"

"Arthur." Farringdon hadn't taken his eyes from Harry and he was leaning a little forward towards him.

"Fair enough then, Arthur. We got no quarrel with you, mate. Have we, Morant?" He swung to Harry, barking the last words at him. Harry's grin flashed.

"No, of course not. Sorry old son—it's your lords and masters we're grumbling about."

Farringdon relaxed, his face loosening and he drank again. "My lords and masters, eh? You couldn't grumble any more'n we do, I tell you that!" He suddenly realized what had caught his ear before. "Here, you're not Australian though. You're from Home."

"A long way from Home, Arthur."

The last of the tension went. The bottles circulated and the gunner moved to the ground, leaning back against the ammunition box. "You'll get used to it soon enough. Once you get up against the old Boer you'll be surprised how everything seems to fall into line."

"What's it like? Up there?" Fisher's question drew them all a little closer, all watching Farringdon.

"Like? Another bloody world! Not like any war I was ever in, I tell you that. I never fought a white man before, for a start, not in a battle I mean. Makes a difference."

Ted Hewett, irrepressible, chipped in. "Makes 'em easier to 'it in the dark, don't it?" . . . but Farringdon didn't join in the laughter.

"You have your fun while you can, son. You'll be laughing the other side of your face before long. If you got a face left, that is."

They were silent again, thinking about that, till Fisher spoke. "But they're not soldiers, are they? I mean, they're not even short-timers like us; no training nor nothing from what we've 'eard."

"No, they're buggerall like us, Digger. No uniforms, no supply-columns, no base camps. And no rules. Everyone of them's against us—women, nippers, the lot."

"But we're winning?"

Farringdon looked over at Greville. "I dunno what you call winning. We got a lot of country under our belt and a fair few prisoners, but we can't seem to hold the bastards down. See, you send out a column and there'll be twenty or thirty of the Dutchmen up on a bit of a hill . . . and you never see 'em." His voice was low and they craned in to listen, held by his intensity. "A Boer can tuck himself away in a crease in the countryside you couldn't hide a rabbit in. And he'll wait there all day for you, right there in the sun, no food, no water. Patient sod, he is. And when you turn up, he'll put a bullet in you neat as range practice!" He slapped his knee with a big hand, startling them out of their stillness. "And then he's off and away before you know what's happened, and half-a-dozen good blokes with their heads blown out. More, sometimes." He drank deep again. "Very dodgy bird, the old Boer."

The general said, "But I think we've got the measure of him, gentlemen, we've got his measure," and listened with obvious pleasure to the murmur of agreement.

The Mess tent was beautifully disguised. The canvas walls were hidden under dark blue drapes made, Morrissey suspected, from Army issue blankets. There was a framed portrait of the Queen at the far end, behind the General's chair, and it was flanked by cased colours. Two long side tables held a display of silver trophies, and the dining table itself was a-glitter with silverware. There were lamps burning brightly from a number of the support poles and two candelabra of tall candles gave a warm glow to the forty or so officers now slumping comfortably as the port circulated on a miniature gun-limber and the cigars stung the air.

With the exception of the Australians, all the others were in Mess kit or regimentals. Morrissey's 2 i/c, Major Young, who'd brought the rear party into camp late in the afternoon, had hissed in Morrissey's ear when they arrived, "I thought you said it was informal, Bill!" and Morrissey had whispered back, *They* said it was. Maybe this isn't full dress for them." Alan Young had taken another long look and muttered, "What do they wear when they're going flat out— golden armour?"

The General had made them welcome, greeting them in a haze of sherry, but the overall reception had been cool enough to keep the Australians, especially the junior officers, fairly tightly bunched before dinner. At the table, scattered among the other diners, they listened with some puzzlement to drawled conversations about parties in Cape Town, the possibility of organizing a pack of hounds for a drag, a cricket match played the previous Saturday between regiments, and a wide variety of minor scandals and major slanders. It wasn't till the port arrived that the talk turned to the campaign.

Major Young, thrusting and aggressive, listened to the general rumbling about having taken the Boer's measure, leaned forward and said, "I understand from what we heard today, sir, that you've been taking some quite heavy casualties."

The British officers looked at Young, a concentrated gaze filled with something close to pity, although the surgeon sitting well down the table, a sombre patch of unadorned dark blue, nodded his head. The general was unperturbed. "Always casualties in battle, m'dear fellow."

The surgeon's voice was a bitter intrusion. "I don't get many Boers to treat, sir."

" 'Course you don't! Bloody Boer takes 'em off with him, doesn't he, eh?" A languid Lancer major drawled down the length of the table, "I don't really believe you can get a true picture of battle tactics, Doctor, from a vantage point in your—er—butcher's shop.".

In the spurt of laughter at the surgeon's expense, Young caught Morrissey's eye in some disgust. Morrissey shook his head and frowned for his second-in-command to keep quiet. He waited till the laughter had died before speaking up to the head of the table.

"It does seem from what we've been told that the Boer's fighting a rather unorthodox war, sir. How do we tackle him . . . in the orthodox way?"

"The Boer's not fighting a war at all, Morrissey." For the first time the general seemed to be angry. "He's a rebel, fighting a rebellious action. No different from any other native rising, eh, gentlemen?" The murmur rose again, the Lancer major rapping the table with his fingers and sliding out a distorted "Hear, hear!"

The general sipped at his port. "A rising, Morrissey —and it'll be put down by punitive action, just as we've always put the natives down when they've got above themselves."

Young couldn't stop himself. "With respect, sir, mightn't we be better off fighting them with their own tactics? I mean if—"

The staring silence was so profound that his words seemed to sink away in it.

The staff colonel who'd met Morrissey when they disembarked sent his voice slashing along the table at Young. "My dear, good chap! What an appalling suggestion! You couldn't seriously expect the British Army to throw away everything it stands for and go into the field like—like some collection of backwoods farmers?"

Young flushed angrily under the insolent lash, but it

was Ian Burgess, who'd been simmering right at the end of the table, who bit back dryly.

"Maybe it's because most of us *are* backwoods farmers, sir!"

"Now, now, now, gentlemen!" The general was affable again. "Morley here meant no disrespect. But what he said is quite correct, of course. We're not just an army—we're the British Army, all of us. And we have certain standards to maintain."

The surgeon muttered, loud enough for almost everyone to hear, "No matter how many men get killed."

The general didn't hear and plunged on. "We have certain tried and tested methods to use. We've always been successful because of our discipline and our methods, and we shall be successful again, naturally. Just you get your chaps into line with ours, learn to understand the way we do things and you'll do jolly well, jolly well indeed."

Morrissey inclined his head. "As you say, sir."

The general rose and the rest shoved back their camp chairs and stood waiting. "Well then, gentlemen, time we were in bed, I think. No horseplay for you younger chaps tonight, I'm afraid—early start in the morning, eh?"

The Australians clustered together behind Morrissey as the general moved from his place and the rest of the diners began to head down to the door. The general placed a friendly hand on Morrissey's arm. "Colonel Morrissey, gentlemen, a pleasure to have had you as our guests. From tomorrow we shall be comrades-in-arms, what? Just you watch the way we do things, my boys, and I'm sure we shall be proud of you all!"

From behind Morrissey, the surgeon said, his voice sad, "That's right, Colonel, just you watch the way we do things."

The country was waiting for rain. There was a stillness in the hot air which was almost a throb, not a silence and yet not quite sound. Somewhere in it was the muted rustle of a fitful ground-breeze in paper-dry trees and the flutter of the little dikkop birds. All waiting for rain. Especially the Boers, Harry thought.

The little column straggled easily along half a mile of shade where a low ridge humped to its right, the flankers up there silhouetted occasionally against the afternoon sky as they moved. The flankers out to the left and the scouts ahead were invisible in the haze and across the long undulations of the land, but knowing they were there meant that A Squadron could relax to some extent and Harry was letting his horse walk with the others while he half-dozed.

What was it that Scottie sergeant had said the other day—that the Boer commandos were back there in the hills somewhere waiting for the rain? That was it— they wouldn't come out in any kind of strength till the grass was up and green so their horses had fodder wherever they went. Made sense.

He shifted in the saddle, easing himself, the insides of his breeches wet with sweat. The horse they'd given him back there at the Cape hadn't lasted the train journey north and he supposed himself lucky to get anything at all to ride, but the placid beast he was on now was as broad-backed as a plough-horse and uncomfortable to sit for long even at this pace. Dubbin and boiling rags and pounding with a boot-heel had at least reduced the saddle to something like a seat, but the two-and-a-half-foot picket pegs with their ironshod tips were still crossed behind him, lashed to the cantle regulation style and ripping at the thighs on mounting or dismounting. Under command of the Lancers as they had been, they'd found the regulations hard to get away from and they were getting tired of these pointless patrols. The one chance for action back there at the Modder River had been thwarted when they were held in reserve and sat about all day listening to the rumours rattling as sharp as the rifle-fire.

They moved out of the shade of the ridge, and the flare of sunlight pulled his head up to look up the column: Tregaskis at the head with Owen Fisher, then Burgess' troop, then young Cowan leading theirs. Beyond the head of the column a patch of flat country with another, higher ridge to the left a little.

When Tregaskis' hand went up, Harry glanced at the sun, estimating the time at about three. The column halted while the captain and Fisher checked a map, then moved forward again, wheeling left-handed on the start of its return leg; and Peter Pullen, riding to Harry's right, blinked his dusty eyes and said, "We goin' back, are we?"

"Looks like it, Peter. Be nearly dark by the time we get there, too."

Peter was nodding dozily when the man in front of him jerked backwards off his horse, and he reined in, startled, before any of them heard the crack of the Mauser. Harry heard a sharp hiss in the air by his head before anything else, but then it seemed as though the air was full of the hissing sounds and the echoes of rifle-fire from the ridge, now on their left. He yanked his horse's head, fighting to pull the sluggish beast towards the dead ground below the hump of the rise as Pullen went past him shouting, "Come on, Harry—don't just bloody sit there!"

For thirty seconds there was total confusion, Tregaskis shouting unheard orders at the head of the column, Owen Fisher racing past at a hand-gallop roaring at them to dismount, two men down, one rocking in the saddle and screaming, the blood pouring down his chest from a torn throat. And then there was Cowan with Ted Hewett knee-to-knee with him, turning back along his own troop and waving and calling: "My troop—come with me, my troop!"

By the time a dozen men had heard him and followed, Cowan and Ted were in the lee of the ridge, dismounted and staring upwards cautiously. Harry slid down alongside them, the others clumping against the rock. Cowan had his Webley in his hand and looked half grim, half boyishly excited.

"Right, lads. There's a gully there, looks like cover all the way round and up to that little pimple; see it? Up we go, then."

Ted Hewett, not smiling, said, "Bayonets, sir?"

"Yes. Hurry now."

Harry doubted they'd get close enough for that, but there was a feeling of muscle somehow in locking that fourteen inches of steel onto the muzzle of the Lee-Metford. Everyone had said it—the Boer doesn't like the blade.

From the other ridge, the two scouts could see back across the open patch from where they lay on their stomachs, pulled flat by the sound of the first shot. Below the ridge they could see the bulk of the column deployed along the base of the ridge, some of them beginning to inch upwards. Two little forms lay still in the dust and a riderless horse was running aimlessly loose.

"Christ, that was quick! Can you see 'em?"

The second scout squinted down and back. "No, not a bloody sign. You can't spot that smokeless powder they use. Hey up—yair—see in that patch of rocks there? I just caught a snatch of a move."

"Miserable bastards! They let us go right through—"

"You thank yer lucky stars they did, Mick, else you'd be down there with a hole in ya like them others."

Staring, they saw the other movement.

"Who is it? Cowan?"

"Looks like it. Cowan an' Fisher, I think. Harry Morant. The little one must be Pete Pullen."

"Gonna work up that gully an' get behind 'em by the look of it."

"Y'reckon? Good luck to 'em."

He turned onto his back and began to roll a smoke.

High up the gully, Cowan stopped, head cocked, shoulder pressed into the rock. Beyond him there was only sky over the ridge. He turned, mouthing silent orders and gesturing the men behind him into position. Fisher took four of them across to the other side of the narrow cleft and Harry closed up on Cowan, hearing the young lieutenant's shallow rasp of breath, seeing his back tense and his legs set to spring. When Cowan moved, they all went with him, bursting over the lip of the ridge. The Boers were a little below them, eight, ten of them spread along a hundred feet of false crest and the shots from their rear smacking into and round them sent them scattering at once, one of them pitching headlong, one staggering. Cowan suddenly spun about at Harry's side, gasping, his hand going to the reddening patch on his thigh. Below him, Fisher was bounding down the rocks, the others behind him, the long blades gleaming, their shouts echoing off the rocks. Harry heard the clash of a bullet on the rock above Cowan's head and felt the chips sting his face as he ducked, pulling the wounded man lower. A quick look from low behind cover showed the Boers streaming for their horses—there, in a hollow on the reverse slope—and above the horses, a youngster with a rifle. Cowan rolled over, grunting with pain, and peered over Harry's shoulder as he saw the Lee-Metford go up and steady. They both watched as the lad slammed backwards and disappeared. The Boers were away now, two of them on one horse, the rest hurtling down the rough slope to the plain below, the Australians sending a few shots after them. Cowan's voice was thin with pain.

"Good shooting, Harry. Well done. First blood, eh?"

"Only a colt, sir. Pity it hadn't been a stallion."

He slung his rifle and stooped to pull Cowan across his back.

Cowan wasn't badly hurt, the bullet, at close range, having gone clean through the meat of his thigh without touching bone. He'd heal quickly enough and in the meantime, Owen Fisher was being chiacked about his temporary command of the troop and Ted Hewett was suddenly very serious as an acting troop-sergeant. They'd lost two dead and five wounded, one badly, in return for only one dead Boer. They'd stood around looking down at him, an elderly man with a solid grey beard, his long coat dusty and bloodstained over a work shirt and whipcord trousers. Bernie Greville had growled, "Buggered if he looks like a soldier. Looks like old Mullins used to keep the shop at Five Corners 'n' preach Baptist on Sundays."

Harry, belly full of stew, mind on the afternoon's

deaths, walked to the edge of their camp where the medical cart stood, the rifle on his shoulder. There were two men in the cart, one moaning in his sleep, one still. Under a rough shelter of strung blankets lay the Boer boy Harry had shot, eyes wide on the doctor who'd been attached to them, an elderly Englishman from Cape Town. He was stooping over a man from Burgess' troop, tying off a bandage around the man's head, and he turned when he heard Harry's footsteps, lowering the man's head gently and rising. Harry stopped, looking down on the young Boer, a dark-haired boy, perhaps fifteen, face white and shining with sweat, the bandages across his chest and shoulder stained with dried blood.

The doctor watched for a second, then moved closer. "Taking a look at your handiwork, Morant? The boy's shoulder's gone—you smashed the bone to pieces."

Harry, unspeaking, stared down at the boy, meeting the sullen glare.

The doctor's voice was angry. "I thought you came out here to fight men, not to cripple children."

Harry turned on him slowly, slipping the rifle from his shoulder, and the doctor flinched. "He was carrying this. Loaded. He shot young Cowan with it." Harry held it out to the doctor. "Look at it. It's British, a Metford. It must have belonged to one of our own people. I wonder how this—child—got hold of it? Or how many men he's shot with it?"

He swung suddenly to face the boy lying at his feet, the rifle muzzle dropping, his fingers snapping the bolt back and forward, loading and cocking. The doctor started forward convulsively, hand outstretched in appeal and the boy under the blankets froze, his mouth open in fear. Harry held the muzzle steady on the boy's head for a long, long second, then worked the bolt back again, ejecting the round in the breech and reversed the rifle, grasping the barrel, raising it and smashing the stock down on the ground, striking downwards again and again till the weapon broke. He threw down the pieces and walked away, the doctor, white and shaken, staring after him, the boy crying now in great, tearing sobs.

Farrier-Sergeant Pollock was a beefy man, suety, pink and white like pork, fingers like sausages and a head, as Pullen once remarked, "Same size, same shape, same 'ardness as a chopping-block." He spotted the man he wanted, sitting in the shade of a supply cart, and plodded across, the bulk of his shadow attracting the man's attention.

"G'day, Morant. I wanna talk to you about a little bit of a job I got in mind."

"Haven't you heard, Sarge—we've got three days' rest. And that's just what I'm doing." Harry stretched elaborately and relaxed again. Pollock hunkered down beside him, flopping a very big hand on his shoulder.

"Look, Morant, I've butchered steers bigger'n you. I wouldn't want to think you was being awkward or anything."

Harry opened his eyes and looked into the steady gaze of the farrier, realizing he was serious. "Righto. I can't beat you. I'd better join you." He sat up and took a cigarette from a flat tin, offering one to Pollock and lighting them both. Pollock looked at him, head on one side.

"I wanna get one thing straight first. I know it's said, but I wanna be sure. You *are* the right Morant? The one they call The Breaker?" Harry nodded, wondering. "Goodoh. Then I got a job that's just your mark. I want you to pinch some horses."

Harry stared at him. "Hold on, now, you're not serious! I'm not a bloody horse-duffer, Pollock."

"Simmer down, simmer down. The way I see it is if you pinch something from the Army—specially the British Army—it's not really stealing at all. D'y'agree with me?"

"Well, yes, I suppose so. But horses?"

"Right. See, the boss bailed me up just now and he says we're mounted like a lot of drunk clowns—as though we didn't know it—and he wants something done about it. He says we got three days to pull the horses into shape and I tells him it can't be done because they're no good from the off—"

"That's true enough."

"Right. So he tells me to do something about it, and when I asks him what I'm supposed to do he says he don't much care. Just so long as I do *something.*"

"Well, that seems straightforward enough. So you're going to steal some, is that it?"

"No, son. You are." The big hand went up, stopping Harry's reply.

"Now wait on. I can't do it—I'm too damn big and slow for this kind of a job. But *you* can. You've got a way with horses—everyone knows that. And all you'll have to do is snaffle 'em. I've done all the organizing."

"That's very civil of you! What's it supposed to mean?"

"It means that if you take a bit of a stroll round the back edge of this place, you'll see there's a sort of a house over in the corner of the lines. It's Headquarters, and the Brass lives there and has their scoff there and there's a lot of nice clean tents roundabout where the base wallahs live. Know where I mean?"

"I think so."

"And behind that house there's some horse lines. Very nicely laid out, they are, and there's dry standing for the beasts and two nice English sentries plodding up and down all night."

"God in Heaven, you're not seriously talking about swiping the staff horses? You'll get me shot!"

"Never! Not if you use a bit of common. See now. We're supposed to hoof off out of here before dawn on Thursday. That gives you tonight and tomorrow night to have a good squiz at the place, then you go in and pinch the stock say about three o'clock Thursday and we're off and away."

"Oh, bloody wonderful! You're mad, Pollock, you're a lunatic."

"I'm also the farrier-*sergeant,* Corporal Morant, so watch your tongue."

"But there wouldn't be anything like enough horses there—"

"Enough for the colonel and the officers, most likely. And you can take your pick of what's left. How about that?"

"Very generous." Harry was hard put to it not to laugh at the impudence of the scheme. "Look, I couldn't do it on my own. I'd have to have some fellows with me."

"Up to you, son. Just so long as you get it done."

From inside the supply cart against which Harry was leaning, Owen Fisher's voice echoed, mordant and muffled. "Harry, you make a move without me an' I'll 'ave yer tripes for picket-ropes!"

Morrissey had watched Pollock go and had called Fishburn, his adjutant.

"I'm not going to see the brigadier on my own Len. I need some help . . . and I want someone else there if he turns me down."

Headquarters, in the sprawling house Pollock had told Harry about, was an elegant and smoothly organized bustle. The general, immaculate in a scarlet tunic, greeted the two Australians cordially and spread a map across the table between them, anchoring it with —as Fishburn later told the Mess with delight—a velvet case filled with medals and decorations, a silver mug of brandy, a lady's shoe half full of Havana cigars and a fox mask mounted on a small wooden plaque. As Fishburn said, "You could see the old josser's whole life laid out there on the corners of the map."

Jabbing his finger down like a drill, the general rapidly ran through a summary of his own dispositions of troops and his assumptions of where the enemy was and in what strength, then sat down, apparently exhausted by the explanation. There were no chairs on the other side of the desk and Morrissey looked down on the general when he spoke.

"That's very clear, sir, but are we sure about the Boer? That he *is* holed up across there?"

" 'Course we're sure! I've had vedettes from the South African Horse out that way for a week now and the Jocks have made two patrols in some force and

93

received fire. Logical place for the Boer to be anyway, you see—all that high ground there."

"Of course, sir, it's just that it seems a little too logical if you see what I mean."

"No, dammit, I don't!"

"Well, if I was in their shoes, I should have a fairly strong position up here too—" Morrissey's finger sketched a line high on a rise of land almost at right-angles to the slopes the general had indicated. "I don't believe I'd miss the chance to enfilade people attacking frontally across there."

"Ah, yes, I see what you mean, Colonel. Quite. But I think you're giving the old Boer a little more credit than he deserves, don't you? He's not a soldier, you know."

"Yes, sir."

"Good. Well then, m'dear fellow, if you're quite clear—"

Fishburn muttered, "Er, there was one other thing, sir—"

The general cocked a surprised eye at him. "Not about the plan of attack, surely, Captain?"

Morrissey took over. "No, not that, sir. But I was wondering—sir, may I be frank?"

"By all means, Morrissey! Don't hold back if there's something on your mind."

"Well then, sir, you've got us brigaded with the Lancers here, on the left of the centre-line. My fellows aren't cavalry, you see, not in the way your fellows understand it—"

"Oh, come now, that's too modest by half! Why, your Australian horsemen have reputations second to none. Whole Army knows that!"

"Horsemen, yes sir. But they've had no training as light cavalrymen, only as Yeomanry. We're Mounted Rifles, sir."

"Ah now, you're quibbling, Colonel. The Lancers will be delighted to have you along, delighted! And—this is between ourselves of course—Henry Gore, their colonel, well, he's rather a fussy fellow. Won't ride

94

with just anyone. And he told me personally that he'd be *most pleased* to take you along with him. There!"

The general beamed happily, missing the look of distaste on Morrissey's face at the thought of being "taken along."

"I'm sure we shall manage it, sir."

The general was standing and an orderly appeared from nowhere at once with his hat, gloves and crop.

"There is just one other thing, sir."

The general checked, the smile slipping easily from his instantly cold face. He made no response, just stood waiting, and Morrissey heard himself speaking rather too quickly.

"We have something of a problem with our horses. They're poor quality and the remounts we're getting are even worse—"

"I'm afraid we're all in the same boat, Morrissey. Not a decent nag to be had just now. I have written to Whitehall—"

He made a small, final gesture and began to pull on his gloves.

"Is there no chance—?"

"None whatever, Colonel. As I've just said, we're stretched to the limit." The general let the smile slide back as he grasped Morrissey's arm, urging him towards the door, Fishburn trailing behind them with the orderly. "Now then, what about a whisky-soda before Mess? I can't dine you tonight I'm afraid; my old regiment's putting on a dinner for me. No? Ah, then I shall see you at a later stage."

The salute was a graceful wave of the crop and he was gone.

"Congratulations, sir." Fishburn's voice was dry.

"Thanks. Now you see why I wanted you along. None of our blokes would believe it otherwise."

There were four of them—Harry, Owen, Ted and little Peter—paler shadows in the deep shadows. Bernie Greville, like Pollock, had felt he was too big and awkward to come with them, but he was waiting back where the trees ran along the rear of the row of tents.

There was no moon and the sky had darkened early, building rain-clouds moving in and hanging now in a thick pall that shut out the stars. Harry lowered himself quietly to the ground, pillowing his head on his folded forearms and letting his breathing slow. He felt a hand on his stockinged foot and then the others were close beside him as he slid his head around the back corner of the house, smelling the horses thirty or so feet away. Looking round he could just see the others —Peter was on his left, Owen and Ted on his right, and Harry tapped Owen's shoulder and gestured for him to move. Owen's fingers touched Harry's shirt-sleeve, rubbed across the two chevrons there, then took Harry's hand to his own three chevrons, the gleam of his teeth a little bar of lightness. Without knowing whether the "up you" signal could be seen, Harry made it into Owen's face and moved out, smiling.

Neither of the sentries heard them, shifting in their socks across the night-damp ground, up out of the blackness behind them at either end of the horse lines. A hand across the mouth pulling the head back, a knee in the small of the back and a twist to put the man down and the soft blapping noise of a flour sack with a pound of sand in it.

Ted and Peter came up, tugging their unconscious sentry with them, Ted swinging the man's rifle. Owen was already working on their man and he hissed up, "Get his boots off. Take 'em an' the rifles an' the coats and any ammo. They'll think the Boer's been in."

Harry had gone at once to the horses, hearing them jinking a little at the new noises, hearing a hoof pawing at the earth, a quiet snort of breath. Owen joined him as Harry's knife cut the running-line near a picket-peg and he slid the headropes off the cut end, murmuring to the sleepy horses as he did it, stroking their necks, chirruping gently to them. He worked along the lines, cutting the ropes, his face damp from the muzzles which came out to him, passing the headropes back to Owen then to Peter and Ted, just hearing them as they walked the horses quietly away into the night. Harry took the last three himself, adding in his mind till he reached thirty-four, finding it hard to suppress the laughter building in him.

As he joined the others with Bernie and the horses it began to rain and the soft hiss covered the little noises they made back to their tents where lamps were already flickering as the squadrons made ready to leave.

The colonel's galloper streaked back alongside the column, shouting for officers and troop-sergeants, his call floating behind him with the dust. Harry and Ted wheeled away from the troop, cantering ahead of them with the others towards the colonel. Morrissey looked unhappy, a paper in his hand and his mouth tight. He returned their salutes and looked round at them.

"Orders, gentlemen. We're to move on up. H.Q. Troop, remounts and sick over in that gully there. The rest of us up on the left. We're to come under command of the Lancers."

There was a groan from the group and a curse or two. Morrissey stared them down, waiting for silence.

"I said it was an order! We don't have to like it, but we obey it, understand? Right, column of squadrons, me leading. Go on." He watched, waiting till the rearmost riders had reached their troop, then swung his horse about, Fishburn and Maitland behind him, at the head of the column. His raised arm moved them forward and they walked along the track, round the knoll on their left and onto the flat land sloping gently downwards towards the hills that cupped it. Glancing up as they rode into the open, Harry could see a cluster of men high on the forward slopes of the knoll, a scarlet coat, a blue coat and off to one side the sunwink of a heliograph. Bernie Greville had followed his look and growled, "Bloody staff. Well outa harm's way, as usual."

They'd heard firing earlier in the morning as they'd moved up, but the valley ahead of them was silent now as they halted and Morrissey cantered forward to where the Lancers were deployed in line, the sun dancing along the rows of steel points high above the horses' heads.

Harry looked past the Lancers, lips puckering. "They've been working at it, Bernie. Look there." He pointed with his chin.

The ground ahead of them wasn't truly a valley. It was perhaps a mile and a half long, running down to a ridge of grey-red rock which burst up out of the plain to a height of about four hundred feet, extending more than two miles across the gradual slope. At the left, the same ridge swung almost at right-angles, dipping a little at the join, then coming back towards them for close to half a mile. The knoll on which the staff stood looked as though it had broken away from this main mass in some volcanic upthrust. Away on their right was a belt of old and massy trees running along the twisted line of a watercourse.

Between them and the frontal face of the ridge, well towards the rocks themselves, they could see the pattern of the morning's work in the scattered figures lying still in the dusty grass, one or two moving a little from time to time. Beyond them and in the rubble at the base of the slope, the khaki dolls were more numerous, grouped closer. In one place there was a neat line of them.

Peter Pullen, on the other side of Bernie, had edged his horse in a little closer and spoke across the big man.

"Nasty sorta setup, Harry."

"Usual Boer setup, Peter. Aren't you used to it yet?"

"Oh, *I'm* used to it all right, mate! Don't look as though them bastards is, though." His scornful thumb jerked upwards towards the top of the knoll.

To the right of the Australian column and several hundred yards forward of them, the infantry were grouped, the men standing easy or sitting slumped on the ground while parties moved among them distributing ammunition and food. Behind them the medical wagons were busy and behind them again a couple of field-kitchens were sending up black smoke signals and the smell of stew carried back towards the Australians, mingling with the smell of spent cordite in the still air. On the ridge and its flanking ridge, there was no movement.

Morrissey rode to meet the Lancer colonel, a bulky, red-faced man with a large smile.

"Ah, Morrissey, we meet again!"

Morrissey reined in, eyes on the ground ahead of them. Without looking at Gore he said, "I understand we're to go in with you."

"You're to come under my command, yes." Gore's voice was a little edged. He waved at the ridge. "There's the Boer, along that lump of rock there. The general has put the K.O.Y.L.I.'s and the Jocks at them a couple of times, as you can see, without doing much good. So he's come to his senses and asked us to go along and winkle them out for him with the footsloggers to follow us up."

Morrissey looked at the Lancer silently, then back at the lie of the land. Behind him, Fishburn and Maitland tried to avoid one another's eyes.

"I should be glad if you'd extend my left, Morrissey. We'll advance squadrons in line and your chaps can wheel in a bit just before the charge."

Morrissey was still looking past Gore, but now he swung his eyes directly to him. "I think not."

For a moment the Lancer missed the Australian's meaning, missed the blunt denial in his tone. Then he scowled. "What d'you mean—you think not?"

"I mean, No. I'll not be a party to anything so damn stupid."

Fishburn heard Maitland suck in his breath and then start to whistle low and tunelessly between his teeth. Gore's scowl turned to open amazement. "Do I understand you to be refusing my order, Colonel Morrissey?"

"You do. You're clearly out of your head even to suggest that sort of attack. We'll be cut to pieces—"

"You, of course, have a superior plan!"

"Yes. Ride hard round the ridge there. Dismount. Hit the Boer from the rear, just the way he'd do it to us."

"I see. You realize you'll have to face court-martial charges for your behaviour?"

Morrissey stayed silent, and Gore turned in the saddle, waving for one of his officers to ride forward.

The Lancer major rode up, saluting, and Gore said, "This is Major Carteret, my adjutant. Carteret, I want you here as a witness. Now then, Morrissey, for your information, *we* are a regiment of cavalry, not of mounted infantry. *We* are used to obeying orders and fighting like gentlemen, not Boer rebels. Or backwoodsmen. I shall offer you one final chance to save yourself. Join my left please, Colonel Morrissey."

"I will not have my men butchered needlessly."

"Then you will have to be dealt with. After my regiment has taught the Boer a lesson."

He wheeled furiously away, Carteret shrugging his shoulders and galloping after him. Morrissey spun his horse and rejoined the Australian column without speaking to Fishburn and Maitland.

High on the knoll, the general sat in a canvas chair finishing a chicken leg. Below him the scene lay stretched like a sand-table battle map and he watched as a column of horse began to edge out onto the clear ground. A staff major standing a little forward with a glass to his eye lowered it and turned to the general.

"Lancers moving out now, sir. The Australians don't seem to be with them."

The general tossed the chicken bone to the ground and stepped forward, looking down, the rest of his staff clustering round him. A gunner major edged in and caught his eye.

"May I move my guns down now, sir? I could give the cavalry quite heavy support."

"No, no, no, Major!" The general snapped the words impatiently without even looking at the gunner. "I don't want those guns committed. Once you get out there the Boer will send out snipers and we shall lose you. Couldn't have that."

"But, sir, a screen of infantry with us—"

"No, I won't have it. You'll stay where you are. The cavalry can handle this little affair."

Furious, the gunner stalked back to his waiting battery. The staff major said, "Still no sign of the Australians, sir."

"Can't rely on Colonials." The Guards captain drawled it out, face expressionless. "Especially part-timers."

"Ah well, gentlemen, the Lancers will have to manage on their own. Shouldn't have much trouble anyway."

The Australians had moved fast but they heard the rataplan of Mauser fire while they were still halfway up the rear slopes of the flanking ridge. Somehow they all knew by then what had happened between Morrissey and Gore, knew it with a mixture of derision and disgust on the one hand and a swell of goodwill towards Morrissey on the other. They'd followed him at a full gallop when he wheeled them about and raced for the end of the ridge, riding under the knoll so that the staff major above them hadn't spotted them, then swinging right to dismount and begin the scramble upwards.

Cowan's troop had been sent by Morrissey to walk their horses up the less steep slopes at the very end of the ridge as a mobile follow-up force and now, as Harry's horse crested just behind Cowan and with Ted Hewett a little to his right, they saw their own men topping the rocks further round and saw the spurts of flame as the Australians began to drop fire onto the Boer positions from above and behind. By that time, though, the Lancers had come far forward in their ludicrous advance, urging their mounts up over the loose scree at the base of the ridge. From concealed positions on the forward slopes, the Boers had already poured a slashing fire into the advancing and slowing horsemen and there were two neat windrows of them lying in the rubble, men still, men twisting and yelling, horses bleeding and running and trampling.

With the shots from behind, the Boers began to drop in their turn, began to break and scatter to where their horses were, but the Australians were already there and now Cowan, yelling incoherently, waved his troop on and down. Harry kneed his horse at the downward slope. She was a big roan, a hunter, his part of the loot from the Headquarters raid, and she was used to rough going. He let the reins hang slackly looped over his left arm, bringing his rifle down and firing into a group of Boers as they cut into them, feeling the jar as the roan's shoulder knocked one of the running men flat, feeling her change pace to avoid the body, seeing a bearded face disappear in a blast of blood.

Then his magazine was empty and he reversed the rifle, swinging it like a mace across a running man's neck, hearing the clean crack, and then he was through them and the roan was running across still Lancer forms and swerving to avoid crawling Lancers. Harry slid the rifle back into the scabbard on the saddle, feeling the stock greasy with blood, and slowed the horse, seeing suddenly the lurching figure ahead of him go to its knees and struggle up again, crouching, weeping.

He yanked the horse to a stop, looking down at the man, seeing the colonel's insignia on the Lancer uniform, wet with blood at the side of the stomach. The face above was contorted, blood seeping from the hatless head over the right cheek and caking quickly. The mouth was wide open making uncouth noises and tears were mixing with the blood. Harry walked his horse alongside, ignoring the flick of bullets from Boers still hidden on the frontal ridge, looking down with disgust. Leaning over he grabbed the mouthing, weeping man contemptuously, slinging him across the saddle in front of himself, face down like a sack of rubbish. He pulled his horse away at an angle, trotting back to the end of the ridge, rock splinters and pieces of metal whining about him as he rode, and he looked down on the bloody and heaving back and spoke with hatred.

"Never mind, pretty man. They'll find you some more toy soldiers to break, I expect."

Henry Gore went into hospital and then back to England, broken and mad. Carteret, his adjutant, had been killed outright in the first few minutes of the Lancers' abortive attack and there was no one to press charges against Morrissey. On the way back to camp —they'd learned by then to call it "laager"—the Yeomanry had discussed the whole bad business and determined that if anything happened to their colonel, they'd go after the Lancers themselves and show them what was what! Morrissey got to hear about that, of course, and he growled, "By God, I believe the mad bastards would, too!" He was smiling when he said it but there was dampness in his eyes.

They'd learnt a lot by then. Harry looked at his troop as they moved easily across the country on patrol. They looked different from the other troops with whom they came into contact, different from the men they were when they arrived. Now that they were operating under their own command, more or less, they'd discarded virtually everything they considered either useless or an encumbrance. They wore no tunics or braces, riding in breeches and shirts, the sleeves up and bandoliers slung across their chests. Their slouch hats were now unclipped, the wide brims comfortably bent to shade their eyes and necks, and every man had somehow or other contrived to get hold of a British greatcoat for wear during the chill, sometimes the frost, of the open nights. Largely thanks to Harry's group of thieves, they were well mounted and had a string of remounts which they guarded with a terrible ferocity, so that other marauders gave them a wide berth. They'd also managed to "find" half a dozen light carts and a number of mules to pull them, and so the men rode unencumbered by the mass of paraphernalia considered essential by the British horsemen. What they did carry was what they felt was vital to them and their operations—an extra water canteen each, spare bandoliers, a bag of feed, hard rations and some warm clothes. They were mobile, fast, self-contained and at home on the face of the country they fought in.

Owen Fisher had strolled across to where Harry was sitting, a pad on his knee, scribbling a hasty note to Paddy, and his long shadow had darkened the paper before Harry heard the footsteps on the rocky ground. "Righto, Harry, you've got fifteen minutes."

"Splendid! That's exactly what I need! Fifteen minutes to get this letter finished."

"Yer can write yer memores later. You've now got

fourteen and a half minutes to get yerself straightened up. Get a tunic on and fix yer 'at."

Harry put down the pad and pencil and looked up. "Are you taking me to a dance or something, Owen? Won't the others be jealous?"

"Fourteen minutes."

Getting to his feet, Harry tucked the pad and pencil in his saddlebag and turned to Fisher again. "I'm sure you'll want to tell me what it's about sooner or later, Owen. I mean, even a squadron sergeant-major isn't supposed to keep secrets from his men."

Fisher lifted the corner of a lip in a mordant grin. "You've been elevated, Sergeant Morant. Yer joinin' the staff."

"I'm *what?*"

"Fact. The Old Gent with the medals sent a message to all mounted formations—" he let his voice drift into a ludicrous imitation "—Ai would be pleased if you would be so good as to be so kind as to supply to me one orficer below field rank and one sergeant to act as starf gallopers durin' the forthcomin' ection."

It had drizzled fitfully during the night and now, in the first true morning light, the sky was overcast. Harry glanced up at the clouds.

"No heliograph, of course. Why me?"

"Ah, well, y'see, the colonel says to me, ' 'Oo's the best sergeant for this kinda rort, Owen?' an' I tells 'im you are, of course. I says yer educated an' pretty an' can just manage to sit on yer 'orse if yer sober, see? Perfect man for the job."

"Very civil of you. What the hell am I supposed to do?"

"Mr. Burton out of B Squadron's the officer an' you're supposed to meet him up there where the colonel is in—" he checked his watch—"ten minutes flat. Clean, bright and slightly oiled, Harry. Come on, I'll give you a hand."

Three-quarters of an hour later Harry stood by his horse on the slope of a long spur of land rising out of the plain a little over two miles from the river.

There were four sergeants altogether, a Lancer who kept a fair distance from Harry and two men from the South African Horse, known to one another and deep in conversation. Harry had walked a little away from them, hearing again what the staff captain had said when they rode in.

"Right, you chaps. Just stand by here, will you? The general will relay messages by officer-galloper. You people will act as supports to them, carrying duplicates of the messages by an alternative route. Do you all understand that?" He waited for their response. "Good. Then you may stand easy. Somebody will arrange some rations for you in a while, I daresay. Don't unbutton your tunics. The general wouldn't like that."

The general was about twenty yards away at a field-table set up under a stretched tarpaulin, the centre of a busyness of officers and orderlies, a bluff and square-faced man, his white hair and drooping cavalry moustache stark against the redness of his skin. Harry watched him, wondering how it felt to command twenty thousand men and be preparing for a major battle.

When the Yeomanry had moved into their assigned position late the previous evening they found themselves part of the largest force they'd yet seen. Highlanders, Irish regiments, gunners, half a dozen other infantry regiments and the Colonials were spread in laager over a couple of miles of country behind the spur on which the staff was now established and their fires reflected pinkly off the low and weeping clouds. Ted Hewett had strolled around with Harry and muttered, his voice unusually sombre, "I tell you what, mate, there's a big old stoush brewin' up here."

"Been on the cards for some time, hasn't it, Ted? We've been chivvying them back and back for weeks now. They'd have to stand somewhere, surely."

"Yair, well if I know the old Boer, they'll have picked their spot all right. It'll be bullets for breakfast, Harry, you mark my words."

\*    \*    \*

Looking down now, Harry wondered how right Ted had been. There was no sign of an enemy anywhere between himself and the horizon. Directly across from where he stood the land rose quite steeply in a series of rough folds, the top ridge perhaps six hundred feet above the plain. Two miles away on the left, a small village huddled, the white buildings grey in the lack of sunlight, the massed trees in and near them showing the presence of water. The river ran through a cleft in the hills beyond the village, the single road across the veldt entering the village by the same cleft and leaving as a track leading down to the river bank where a plank bridge crossed the water, perhaps thirty feet wide at that point. The river swung away just past the bridge and made a long loop, turning back again across the plain and forming a salient of land inside the loop which looked to be about a quarter of a mile on each side. There was the thin scar of a track cutting into the side of the loop nearer Harry and it ran into the water at what seemed to be a ford. Down there nothing moved on either side of the river.

Harry's horse suddenly jibbed and danced as the guns opened up and he saw the plumes of greeny-black smoke rise in and around the village. There was a battery of the Royal Horse Artillery just forward of the base of the spur and he could see the gunners serving their guns, the new lyddite shells coming out of the limbers as fast as they could be handled. Past the guns and under the arching flight of the shells, a mass of men was advancing in near-perfect order— Highlanders, Harry realized, as he caught the flash of bare knees under the khaki aprons over the kilts. Out to their left he could see a squadron of South African Horse cantering forward in a wheeling movement which would bring them in on the far side of the village. The other sergeants had moved to join him, the Lancer still staying a little apart.

One of the South Africans said, "Well, there go our boys. Don't you wish you were with them, Dick?"

The other spat tobacco juice in a brown blob. "I

wish I was at home. And if I can't be at home, I'd just as soon be up here, my friend."

Harry heard his name called and turned to where Lieutenant Burton, the officer he'd ridden in with, was sitting his horse.

"I'm going back down to the colonel, Morant. Thought you'd like to know our lot's being held in reserve."

"The colonel will be pleased about that, sir, I'd think. Looks like a big affair building up down there."

Burton looked down to the village, the troops now drawing close, the buildings almost obscured in the rising smoke. Behind the infantry there were already numbers of dead and wounded, but the formation moved forward steadily, seemingly untouched, the dull wink of the bayonets among the khaki.

"Mmmm . . . from what I've just heard over there, it seems those blokes are to clear and take the village and the main force is to cross the river. The Boer seems to have left that clear."

Harry swung his eyes across the bridge and the loop of water and the ford, then lifted them to the slopes above.

"No sign of anything there, is there, sir? But we've seen that sort of thing before."

"Too true. Still, the Old Man seems to know what's what. Well, I'm away."

"Do I come with you?"

"Not this time. I'll be back in twenty minutes."

He wheeled and put his horse into a gallop down the track and Harry walked back to the others, noticing that they were now looking down and away from the village.

Below them, the main body of the army was moving on the river. Coming out of the re-entrant below and behind the spur, a huge rectangle of men was edging forward, a khaki, multi-legged insect inching out onto the plain, more of them and more again till they covered a mile of country and spread across a half-mile front. Behind and around this main body, Harry could see the others, the Hussars and Dragoons wide on a flank, two batteries of field-guns jouncing and rattling behind their teams on the opposite flank and then, towards the rear and halting now as the infantry advanced, a troop of 4.7s—12-pounder guns from the Naval Brigade, easily picked out by the uniforms and straw hats of the gunners.

There was a sudden stir over by the general's table and the raising of voices. An imperious arm waved and the Lancer captain serving as galloper moved into the group, running out a moment later and starting his horse into a walk, hopping one foot on the ground till he swung into the saddle.

The Lancer sergeant mounted, waiting for his officer, who was calling now as he rode close, "Sergeant, take the near flank and ride for Colonel Hart of the Irish. Tell him a spotter has observed the enemy on the ridges there—some guns too. Ride, man!" The two of them were gone in a swirl of dust and Harry and the two South Africans looked at one another and then across at the slopes beyond the river.

The naval guns below them opened up and the slopes they were staring at began to fade behind a mass of the distinctively green-black smoke, but a freshening breeze which began to open the clouds above them also shifted the smoke so that the flashing blows of the shells could be seen. But that was all—there was still no sign, no movement, no response.

On the plain, halfway to the river, the gunners had now raced their guns and limbers past the head of the infantry column and perhaps two hundred yards wide of the marching men. Harry could see the two Lancers flogging and spurring their horses up the flanks towards the head of the column and stayed watching, fascinated, as a South African Horse lieutenant took one of the sergeants with a message for the gunner commander to halt and engage at no closer range. The thought ran through his mind that at the rate the guns were being driven, they'd be across the ford before the gallopers reached them.

He saw the sudden darting wink of a signal from the column below and turned, seeing the heliograph in operation from close to the general's post, realizing that he was standing now in bright sunlight and that the need for his services was probably gone. Burton went trotting past him, waving a casual hand as he returned from their own regiment.

The shells were still beating into the ridges and there was still no answer, no slightest sign of an enemy. The two field batteries were now less than a quarter of a mile from the ford and Harry saw the commander's hand go up and the teams check and wheel, swinging the guns and limbers so that the muzzles faced across the water. Before the drivers had the chance to unhitch, or the crews to go into action, Harry saw men and horses begin to fall.

The South African sergeant beside him gripped his arm with crushing fingers. "Oh, Christ, the Boer's got them in rifle range! Look at it!"

"Where *are* they? Where's the fire coming from?"

With the question, they both saw the bobbing heads and the little straight lines of rifle barrels, saw the long line of men in trenches on this side of the river, trenches dug into a natural fold above the banks and invisible to the men on the plain, almost invisible from up here. The heliograph was blinking and staring now but there was no answering light from below and the tiny points of fire from the concealed riflemen stabbed into the guns, dropping men and horses in little clumps around the unfired weapons.

Four gunners fought to control the rearmost team as they kicked and plunged in panic, fought to wheel them and move away from the scythe of fire. Then they went down together, men and horses, and Harry thought he could hear the human and the animal screams, though he knew it was only his horrified imagination. Within two minutes there were only dead and wounded men and beasts there and the guns stood, whole and unserved, limbers full, muzzles forward, only four hundred yards from the Boers.

The infantry column moved stolidly on, although a body of men, about a half-company Harry thought, swung out towards the guns, closing on them with the obvious purpose of pulling them clear, rescuing them. Some of them got close, but all of them went down without reaching the marooned batteries. Harry realized the South African was still gripping his arm, and he prised the fingers loose, seeing the man's white and shocked face, mouth open, and wondering whether he himself looked as ill.

The fire from the trench was now dropping onto the flank of the infantry and there were men dropping, being stepped over, left to lie, but the column was well advanced into the river's loop and Harry could see that another couple of hundred yards would take them to the ford on one side and the bridge on the other and would mean they'd flanked the hidden rifles. The Hussars and Dragoons were pulling in to close on the infantry front, making for the bridge to head them across.

And then the slaughter began, the same lines of heads, the same spears of light from the same kind of unseen entrenchments all around the loop.

More than half the column was now inside the loop and the cavalry was well towards the bridge and they were enfiladed from three sides, a wicked, a killing fire that struck inwards at them and was joined by the deep bark of field-pieces from the slopes across the river, shells dropping in to the centre and rear of the column, boxing them in completely.

It was like harvesting, like running a line of reapers round a long field of wheat, the blades cutting inwards towards a shrinking centre, the fallen stalks lying in an increasingly wide band. From the first line of fire, figures were racing out now to the abandoned guns, swinging them, loading and firing them into the flanks of the decimated infantry at close range, killing them with their own weapons, their own shells. Alongside him the South African sergeant was crying, great dry, choking sobs, hands on his knees, head low; and Harry glanced at him, then back to the butchery below him, seeing the Irish and the Scots and the Yorkshiremen break and try to turn back through their own pressing ranks, seeing the Dragoons and their horses piled like a wall near the entrance to the bridge, the Hussars dropping behind them as they tried to wheel between the marching, dying men and the sharp points of fire.

Burton's voice in his ear was loud and strained. "Come on, Morant! Get down there, for God's sake! Make sure you reach whoever's left and tell them to get out, get to Hell out of that death-trap. Tell them to try for the guns, not the river. Understand—not the river!"

Burton was gone and Harry mounted and kicked his horse away after him, knowing it was too late. As he rode he could still see the flash he'd had of the general's face, grey now and the white hair and moustache seeming grey and his big frame slumped in his camp-chair as he dry-washed his hands together. The clouds were in again and the 4.7s were still coughing and the shells were still hitting the slopes across the river. There was stillness from the village and it seemed clear the attack there had been successful, but in the flat Harry rode only among the bleeding and the screaming and the dead. The volume of fire ahead of him was slackening and he realized he was riding now through men coming towards him, retreating from the slaughterhouse, and he knew he could do nothing with his useless message. His horse whinnied with unease, standing among wounded and dead men, wounded and dead horses, and Harry held him still with some difficulty, watching the ghastly parade that came past him, unseeing. A sergeant in kilts marched by, eyes straight ahead, head up, leading twenty or so Highlanders, their rifles at the high port, bayonets slanting up over their left shoulders and Harry saw the sergeant's hands clamped tight across his stomach where the blood had gushed down the front of his apron and the green and yellow and mauve of his guts were sliding out of his grip. He saw a tall Dragoon, dismounted, staggering back with one hand holding the side of his face together and a light infantryman, a King's Own Yorkshireman, one leg gone at the knee, arm looped about another man's bleeding shoulders, a long and wavering line of blood seeping into the ground behind them. Just ahead of him a disembowelled horse lay kicking feebly,

111

half a man wound into its pouring intestines; and Harry's horse checked, pawing and head tossing. Harry looked down, seeing the half-body, wondering where the legs and balls and stomach were, recognizing the smeared face as Burton's. He leaned over his horse's neck, vomiting and retching and remembering the cheerful rubbish he'd written to Paddy, back there in the other world of a couple of hours ago.

The night had that special blackness which the dark of the moon brought to a deep gully, and Harry's patrol wound slowly in file, the men barely able to see, guided only by the noise of the men ahead. Harry, in the lead, listened to the clicking rattle of the hooves over the loose stony surface and cursed under his breath, realizing how far the sound carried in the night stillness, calming himself with the knowledge that they'd been through here only two hours before on the way out without a sign of Boers anywhere. Not that that meant a bloody thing, of course.

The shots came from both sides, stabbing sudden jerks of flame into the darkness, and the patrol broke. Harry shouted over his shoulder, "Spurs—ride for the open!" and kneed his horse ahead, trusting to her to find her own footing while he snatched the carbine from the saddle bucket. Behind him he could hear the wild clatter as the rest of them burst into what speed they could make, a thin scream rising above the gunfire and bouncing off the rock walls of the gully.

At least, he thought, the bastards can see no more than we can, and then he was clear, not so much seeing as feeling the closing walls falling away from him and picking up a little breeze on his right cheek as he rode. Again he shouted. "Break clear, fellows. Don't try to fight 'em! Break clear and scatter!" He pulled the horse's head hard to the right, feeling and hearing the noise change as the track went away from them and they were on looser soil and grass, hearing the noise sink as the patrol—how many left?—cleared the gully. He wanted to call to them to head east, but daren't take the chance of pinpointing his own position or letting the Boer know which way they were heading; but he knew his men were all right, knew they'd find themselves and the camp.

He'd made perhaps half a mile, sweeping in a long curve south, then east, the ground rising underfoot, when the horse checked and faltered. He was out of the saddle at once, the carbine cocked, and the thought ran through his mind that this was a bitch of a place to be alone in the dark with a foundered horse. Thank the Lord they'd had their old Lee-Metfords replaced with these magazine Lee-Enfields—no time for single-shot loading if he was caught out here. The exploring hand ran down the near foreleg and the horse winced, lifting the hoof up and inwards, the pulled muscle jerking with pain.

Harry took a deep breath, absently running his hand down the horse's neck, considering. What he needed was a place with some cover . . . no damn use trying to head across the flat like this, walking, and with the Boer out for game. If he could hole up for the night, strap the hurt leg, wait for dawn and the first of the army patrols, he'd be likely to have a chance. He looped the reins into the back of his belt, leaving both hands free, slid the bayonet out of its scabbard and locked it quietly onto his rifle muzzle, and felt for the uphill tilt of the ground, moving forward and up slowly and as quietly as he could.

Three things stopped him. The barely perceptible loom of a mass of rock ahead of him, confirmed by his probing hand, was the first. Then the realization that the edge of the rock was very faintly outlined in a thin pinkish glow. Then the muted whinny of a horse. His hand flashed back at once to his own horse's muzzle, closing on it to prevent an answering sound, and he edged forward in fractional moves, the cocked rifle steady ahead of him.

The glow came from a small shielded fire set to one side of a cupped hollow in a ring of rising roughness. A horse was stretched on its side near the fire, legs loosely hobbled, neck stretched, and another gentle whinny jerking its head up a little as Harry watched.

The man hunched over the horse had his back turned, head down, and Harry's fingers went to the back of his belt, loosing the reins. He stepped out, clear of the rocks, moving his feet with great care so that the spurs wouldn't catch or clink. Ten feet from the crouching back, the bayonet and muzzle tilted down, he spoke, his voice level and crisp.

"Keep quite still. There's a rifle at your back."

The man's hands, working at the horse's shoulder, stopped for an instant and Harry saw the blood on them in the firelight. Then they went on with their task. Harry moved to one side of the fire, placing himself so that he and the other man could see one another clearly.

"Get up! Unless you want to be shot."

The man glanced up, a flash of eye-bright in the glow of the flames, then down again at his hands. His voice was as quiet as Harry's and showed no passion.

"Look, redneck, if you're going to shoot, then do it and be damned! If you're not, then sit down and wait. I've got a sick horse here." Intrigued, hearing the reasonableness in what the man said, Harry lowered his rifle and moved closer, looking down. His finger was still on the trigger, the muzzle a yard from the man's neck. The horse's shoulder was bleeding fairly freely and the crouching Boer moved a hand to its head, holding it steady while the point of the knife in his other hand edged gently into the centre of the patch of blood. Without thinking about it, Harry uncocked his rifle and put it down, kneeling on the other side of the horse, his hands going to the twisting head, the little soothing chirrups coming from his lips. The other man looked steadily at him across the horse.

"Good for you, redneck."

Harry ran a gentle hand across the wound and around it, feeling the sticky hair.

"Bullet?"

"Ricochet, I think. Not big, but pretty deep."

"Can you reach it?"

The knife-point went deeper, moving in tiny touches
114

from side to side. "Just touching now. Damn, it's right into the muscle!"

Harry's fingers spread, a hand on either side of the knife-point, the wound opening under the gentle pressure. He forced the flesh down as evenly as he could, his hands and the Boer's hands touching, the blood sliding between them. The Boer sucked in his breath and the knife moved quickly, in and along and up, half an inch of rough metal coming with it, the horse jerking wildly and whinnying with the pain, Harry's horse in the darkness answering it. Harry patted the sweating neck, his other hand deep in his pocket, dragging out the flask. He pulled the stopper with his teeth and tipped a little of the spirit into the wound, feeling the horse start and try to leap up as the Boer mopped at the shoulder. Then they let the horse rise, his head swinging round as he tried to nuzzle at the wound, the Boer wiping blood away from it, ripping away a piece of rag and packing it into the jagged little hole. He looked up at Harry and they grinned at one another, two men with a task successfully done. In a spurt of flame as a small log shifted in the fire, Harry saw the square face under the flap-brimmed hat, the wide mouth over the fringe of beard, the light eyes. He thought, God, without the beard he could be old Paddy! He passed the flask across the horse's back and the Boer took a deep draught, shaking his head and coughing at the sting of the spirit.

"Ach, that's good brandy!" He took another drink. "Looted?"

"Looted. From a British cavalry Mess!" They grinned again and Harry walked around to look at the wound. "He's going to be stiff for a while. You won't be riding tonight."

"He'll be well enough by dawn. He's a tough old horse, that one."

Harry glanced around. His own horse had edged in and stood now, muzzling at the Boer's.

"Mine's lame. He'll need a strapping before it swells too much."

The Boer nodded judiciously.

"Have you food?"

"Some corned beef. Some beans."

"I have bread and biltong and coffee." He looked very straight at Harry, lips pursed before he spoke again. "Truce, redneck?"

Harry's smile was a white flash and he put out his hand. "Truce, Boer."

An hour later they sat leaning back against the rock, the fire between their stretched feet. The two horses were nearby, hobbled, Harry's with the paleness of a wet puttee strapped around its foreleg. The men had barely spoken, tending to Harry's horse, draining and repacking the other horse's wound, feeling for more wood for the fire, eating and drinking the shared rations. Now they sat, smoking quietly in the lee of the rock, hearing the night wind picking up to a whistle above them, knowing it was strong enough to carry the smoke and coffee smells away.

The Boer edged a coal into the fire with the toe of his boot. "You have done this before, redneck; slept by a fire in the open."

"How can you know that? Except that all soldiers do it sooner or later?"

"No, not as a soldier. As a life." He gave Harry that level look again. "Oh, it can be seen if a man looks for it. See—a man who is used to a roof over his head doesn't sit quiet like that in the open. Neither does he check where the breeze is and sit away from the smoke. Neither does he scrape his plate into the fire as soon as he has eaten. No. This you have done before."

Harry nodded. "Many times."

"But not in England. In England I think they do not learn such things."

"No. Australia."

"So? That is why you think first for the horses. You from Australia have given us some trouble, you are not like the English ones. You are more like us."

"Well, a lot of us are bushmen. Stockmen, cattlemen, farmers."

The Boer's face lightened. "That was me also—a farmer. Good farm. Cattle, goats, pigs, chickens, mealie

116

corn, a little fruit." He sighed. "Good farm. *Was* a good farm." The half-smile on his face had gone.

Harry let the silence hang a moment, but he had to ask the question. "Was? Did our people——?"

"No." The Boer shook his head, smiling again, grimly now. "No, your people didn't get the chance, redneck. The Kaffirs raided; took what they could and put the torch to the rest. Killed my bywoner." He saw the puzzled look and let the smile loose. "My foreman."

"And your family?"

The smile broadened, a touch of pride in the voice. "Ah, Mamma took the big shotgun to them and the girls had each a pistol. But not in time to save Jannie. He was a good foreman. Now the women are with my sister safe, but the farm is——" His hands turned palm up, spread, tossing to the wind.

"Have you no sons to care for your women while you're away?"

The Boer barked a short laugh, eyes squinting in enjoyment.

"Oh, I have sons, my friend! Paul and Klaus and Pieter—big men, those kerls! They ride with Christiaan de Wet's commando. All with red hair." He laughed again. "You mind yourself if you meet three big men with red hair, soldier-boy!"

Harry said, seriously, "I'll remember."

They sat silent again for a minute or two, each of them staring into the fire, seeing different things. Harry broke the silence, voice sounding tired. "It's a rotten war, this. Burning farms and homes, killing men who speak the same language."

"The same language?" The Boer's voice was tighter, a barb in it. "So you speak the Taal then . . . Afrikaans?" Harry stared at him, caught by the sudden near-vehemence. "No, redneck, of course you don't! You're not a Boer, you're a Uitlander, a foreigner." He shook his head, holding down the anger deliberately. "See, my friend, the colour of the skin, even the sound of the tongue are not the matters that count. It's the way to live that counts . . . the freeness. From Australia you should know what that means, as I know, as all of

117

us here know. But those in London—how can they know? So long they have lived with their laws and their commands and their little minds in their big Empire—" the scorn was open "—they cannot know how a man can be free and happy without them."

"You sound like some of the men I know in Australia. They talk about the English like that."

"A strange people, the English. They make laws for themselves and their dirty little patch of an island and then they try to keep the same laws for other people in other places. That way they lost America. That way they will lose us. One day they will lose you Australians and the Canadians and all the others, even the black men in India. Either they will lose in blood or they will just give up. They cannot win."

Harry listened to the words echoing—They cannot win—and fought down the sudden shiver.

"They're winning now. This war."

"So, you believe that? Because they have taken so much land and so many towns and so many miles of the railway line? *Us* they haven't taken, and this is what matters. *Us* they cannot take, because they are stupid and try to fight us as they fought with Bonaparte and then the Russians. *We* are alive and we fight, and so the Englishmen cannot win."

There was the ring of total certainty in his words, Biblical pronouncements, a prophet in a high place, and he was saying in a different way what Harry had heard so many soldiers say, what he'd said himself.

Yet somehow he had to make a defence. "You know Kitchener's taken over? That might make all the difference."

"Perhaps. You change your generals as a woman changes her hats. A new hat does not make a new woman." He tapped out his pipe and changed his tone, smiling. "But there will always be a place under the sky for a little fire and a pipe and a talk . . . with a friend."

Harry thought again as the Boer smiled, how much like Paddy he was, and he watched as the other man lifted his face to the sky, sniffing the now still air.

118

"Four hours till dawn, and then I will guide you to your people. Now we must sleep." He began to pull a blanket over his shoulder.

"Both of us? No guard?"

"What need, my friend? If my people or your people come, one of us will speak for the other, no? Sleep." He shrugged himself down into the blanket and Harry pulled his up to his chin. Under the blanket he felt for his belt, lying near his shoulder, and slipped his revolver from it, placing it within easy reach. He saw the movement across from him, the Boer placing his pistol also near at hand, and they smiled openly at one another and settled quietly.

The half-light of pickaninny dawn held them in a grey world, chill and damp and Harry shivered, pulling his British greatcoat closer round him. His horse was moving well enough and the Boer had cleaned his own horse's wound again half an hour ago so that it walked only a little stiffly. The Boer's hand was out suddenly, stretched wide, palm back towards Harry halting him, and both men leaned over their horses' muzzles. From somewhere in the dimensionless greyness came the guttural rattle of talk, the thick Afrikaans echoing flatly round them. The Boer listened, head cocked, and they heard the voices stop and the thin sharpness of hooves on rock, dying away soon into nothing. They rode on, still quiet, still cautious, and then the greyness opened out and became blackness below them, a blackness punctured by the small red and yellow holes of scores of fires on the plain. The Boer pointed.

"Your people, redneck."

Harry's lip twisted. "They don't exactly hide themselves, do they?"

"It would be easy to attack them from here."

The Boer sounded almost wistful and Harry wondered whether they had the strength in these hills to mount an attack anyway. He followed the signposts of the fires, working out where the lines were, where the creek ran, and he smiled without real humour.

"You might have some trouble if you did attack.

That dark patch on this side is where *we're* laagered. You wouldn't get past us."

"Perhaps, perhaps not. Now you must go before the true dawn. This is where *we* patrol while it's dark. You can have it in the daytime, when we can see you properly through the sights." The smile took the sting from the words.

Harry reached out the flask again, nearly empty now, and raised it. "Thank you. And good luck." He drank and passed it, watching as the Boer also raised it in a toast and drained it.

"Good luck to you, redneck. Watch out for my three big sons . . . and ride safely. Tot siens."

"Ride safely, friend."

They didn't shake hands, just wheeled away in opposite directions as the first tint of pink slid into the dawn greyness.

It was a cage, a large square of wired-off dust, guarded and patrolled and surrounding nothing but half a dozen cooplike huts at one side and perhaps three hundred inmates.

It had stood empty when the Yeomanry rode into the town but the Boers had been driven in the previous day, a long, uneven line of them, dirty and ragged, walking, not marching, between files of armed soldiers. Harry had been struck by the fact that they didn't look like prisoners then, nor now, inside the wire. There was a look and a feel about them which may have been compounded of sullenness and hate and revulsion, but which added up to pride, to self-containment. He thought of the Boer with whom he'd spent the night in camp, and could see men like him in there, behind the wire.

Most of them were bearded men, not all old but bearded in the Boer way, the face hair allowed to grow as soon as a boy turned sixteen, as soon as he was recognized as a man, a fighter, capable of taking on the British Army in all its solidity and strength.

Harry eased his way through the crowd of soldiers clustered at the wire near a corner, watching the prisoners, occasionally jeering at them. A stooped old man, bare-headed and grey-square-bearded was the centre of a swelling group of Boers, his voice rising over them as though he was preaching a sermon, his hands steadying a ragged newspaper against the fitful wind.

Near Harry a soldier called, "Oi, Grandpa! What's all the garglin' abaht?" but the old man's voice droned on in Afrikaans above the catcalls from the watchers. Another soldier shoved his face against the wire, shouting, "Ya got the results of the Grand National, old man?" and the laughter rose again.

The old Boer lowered the paper and stared at the men outside the cage, then moved across, standing close, the mob of prisoners following him. The two nearest sentries looked at one another anxiously and came closer, nervously fingering the bolts of their rifles. When the Boer spoke, his voice was thick, gutturally accented.

"Do you truly wish to know what I read, you rednecks?"

The man he addressed turned a mock-surprised face to his companions. "Gawd, it walks an' talks just like a man, don't it?"

The laughter this time was just a little uneasy now that the old Boer was close, could be seen to be tired and pale. But strong.

"I read to my comrades how the world hates you British." He flourished the paper, seeming to wave down the growl that rose from the troops. "I read how in Germany the Kaiser gives us his blessing and how in America people collect money for our cause—"

Behind him many of the other prisoners were clenching their fists and one of them spat through the wire. The troops surged inwards and two strands of wire began to bend. One of the sentries cocked his rifle and waved at the other, an urgent wave which sent him running towards a nearby building. Beside Harry, Ted Hewett raised his voice.

" 'At's all very well, you old fool, but we're not English. Some of us is Australians."

"Then that is worse, *because* you are not English!

121

Why do you fight for them against us?" His voice rose in contempt. "Jackals! You Australians are very bad people—"

He was close now, close to Harry, only a foot separating their faces across the wire, and Harry looked hard at the contorted face.

"Why, old man? Because we fight as you do? Because we don't march about and wait for you to shoot us down as the British wait?"

The shouts of abuse were building from both sides now, the noise dragging more men to the outside of the cage. From somewhere to Harry's left a voice called, "You're finished with fighting, you lot! It's near enough over. You've lost, mate. Why don't you admit it?"

The prisoners were still suddenly, still and silent, and the silence spread across the wire. The old Boer gripped a strand with both hands, the knuckles whitening, his beard pushing through.

"Finished? You think we have lost because we are in this cage, because you have taken back some towns? I will tell you when we will have lost, rednecks. When we are all dead, that is when! Only when you have killed us all, every one. And if you do not kill all of us, then you cannot win! See—" he pulled aside his long coat and ripped at his shirt, exposing the naked chest, grey-haired and the ribs showing through the skin. "Shoot me now! Or one day I will shoot you."

There was a roar from the men behind him and they all tore open their clothes, baring their chests, grinning with triumph as they saw the looks of the soldiers.

Sick, the bile in his throat, Harry shoved backwards out of the press and walked fast across the dusty square away from the cage.

"Harry! Harry Morant!"

The voice jerked him to a stop, eyebrows down in thought. Then he spun about, eyes going wide as the calling man ran to him. His hand was crushed in the other man's grip, and then they were pummelling one another and laughing, a pair of British privates watching them in disbelief. Harry leaned back, holding the other man at arm's length.

"By God and the bloody devil. Lenehan! *Captain* Lenehan!"

"And *Sergeant* Morant! Show a little respect, man!"

Their faces wide with grins they stepped apart a pace or two. Harry snapped to attention and whipped up a formal salute, answered with total gravity by Lenehan. And then they burst into hilarious laughter again, staggering away with their arms linked. The two British privates watched them go, one of them muttering, "Fuckin' Australians. They're madder than the Boers!"

Harry pushed stockinged feet towards the woodstove and stretched his arms rackingly above him, then slumped again.

"This is without doubt the most luxurious room I've been in in Africa! My Heavens, but you're living soft, Lenehan!"

"Only lately, m'friend, believe me! We got down here last week." He busied himself with opening a fresh bottle. "We've had quite a busy time lately, as a matter of fact. You know, they finally decided if they wanted to get the job done properly, they'd better send for the old New South Wales Lancers."

"We heard you'd been quite badly cut about. Was it sticky?"

"Oh, sticky enough." He flicked Harry's tunic where it hung over the back of a chair, looking at the clasp on the breast. "You've been seeing a bit of action too. Was this for picking up that Lancer lunatic?"

Harry nodded. "Quite some time ago. I've a new job now."

"Oh? Safe?"

"Safe as the Bank of England. Staff galloper. None of your common-as-muck soldier-men for me nowadays. I only mix with the Brass Hats." His voice went low and bitter. "And a dull bloody lot they are too."

"Dull? Wouldn't have thought that was the word. From the little we've seen of 'em I'd have said they were very pretty."

"I'll give you that—they're lovely to look at! Trouble is they're all corpses above the collars."

"Not Kitchener, from what I hear. He'll soon put a short fuse under 'em."

"I believe you could put a cartload of gunpowder under 'em and they wouldn't even hear the bang!"

"Ah, now, let's not spoil a reunion by talking about that lot. Where's that old rascal of an Irishman you used to ride with? Out here?"

"Not Paddy! No. He's at home near Adelaide." He reached for his tunic and took a picture from his pocket. "He sent me this a little while ago. That's Harlequin with him."

Lenehan looked at the stiff pose, Paddy in a much-creased suit, the black and golden head of the horse near his shoulder. "Fine looking horse that."

"The finest. Never been ridden by anyone except me. Never will be." He gulped at his drink, then said brusquely, "I had to shoot Cavalier. Sorry, Lenehan."

"Yes. Well, it comes to all of us, doesn't it?" He looked embarrassed. "Er—did you know Julia married? She has three boys."

Harry's smile was reminiscent, gentling his face. "Julia. I'd almost forgotten Julia."

"Well, she didn't forget you. Her oldest lad is called Harry. She didn't think you'd mind."

Harry looked up, seeing Lenehan's dry smile, and dragged the cushion from behind his head, shying it across the room at the other man. It flew across the opening door, almost catching the newcomer in the face, a lean and smilingly quizzical face behind a bar of black moustache.

The man shut the door and leaned against it, looking at them. "I know Australians are supposed to be uncouth, but it can be carried too far, old son!"

He stared inquiringly at Harry, and Lenehan moved forward.

"Burleigh, come in, come in, do! You two should meet. Harry, this is Bennet Burleigh of the London *Daily Telegraph* and this is Harry Morant, an old friend from Australia. Also known as The Breaker."

Harry shook hands, liking the other man on sight. "I've read some of your dispatches. You seem to have a very clear understanding of the war, sir."

"Do I? I only see it from the sidelines. You chaps are *in* it. And don't for God's sake call me 'sir'—makes me sound like your grandfather! Why do they call you The Breaker?"

Lenehan broke in. "Wait till you see him on a wild horse . . . you'll know."

Burleigh had found a glass and poured a large drink, sucking it down with obvious relish. "How on earth am I supposed to see a wild horse out here? I've never seen a worse collection of hacks in my life. They don't even taste good! They won't let me write about it, of course. My editor says it might cause despondency at home!"

Harry waved a generous hand. "You'd better come and see our horse lines. We manage rather well."

"I wish I knew how!"

Lenehan laid a hand on Harry's shoulder. "Ah, well, it's a mixture of skill, cunning—"

"And outright theft!" Harry hardly looked repentant, and they settled down laughing. Lenehan put fresh wood into the stove.

"What are you doing this far from the action, Burleigh? Not like you."

"Oh, every now and then I like to come back to where the comforts are and spend a day or two watching the antics of the Gilded Staff. I'm waiting for that crucial moment when they cross over into the nineteenth century to join the rest of us. No sign of it yet, I'm afraid."

Harry watched him while he spoke, the face solemn, but the eyes dancing.

"The sign will never come, Burleigh; not unless old Kitchener sets to and boots the lot of 'em out."

"I saw Kitchener in London—great tall chap with the coldest eyes I've ever seen and a voice like God." He drank, recalling the man. "They say he's got a plan. . . ."

Harry interrupted. "Plan be buggered! They've all

125

got plans, most of them a century out of date! Can't they see the way to fight these people is on their own terms? Irregular units. Fast riding. No baggage, no spit-and-polish, no manoeuvres in review order. Hit 'em hard and move away—*that's* all the plan they need. We've got more men by thousands. We could break 'em in no time like that!"

He leaned forward and stabbed the poker fiercely into the grate of the stove, while Lenehan and Burleigh looked at one another across his back. Burleigh said, "Pity you're a sergeant, Morant. You should be a general." There was no malice in what he said, and Harry smiled up at him, clanging the poker down.

"I shan't be a sergeant much longer. I'm to be commissioned."

"Congratulations."

"Well done, Harry! In your own regiment?"

"No. They're off home in a few weeks—enlistment's up. Quite a few staying on one way or another. I put in for the Cape Police."

Burleigh had been studying him quietly. "Then it shouldn't be hard to get you detached for a bit, should it?"

"Detached? What the devil for?"

"Oh, I don't know. Come riding round with me for a bit. Have a looksee at things. Give me the benefit of your fiery opinions—that sort of thing. Would you like to?"

"Can you get whisky?"

"My dear chap. I can get anything . . . except information out of the staff!"

"Then I'm your man!"

Staring into the grey-blue wisps of smoke rising under the pannikin, Harry wondered how many fires he'd lit, how many meals he'd cooked like this, out in the open. All the way up the coast and inland in New South Wales, he thought, and on up north and west into Queensland and down again across Victoria and into South Australia . . . and the eye of his mind blurred them all into one picture, spinning right up to now, the last of many impressions of a hundred fires in a hundred parts of South Africa. Like this one, a neat little fire, set in a rough ring of flattish stones on which the pannikin and a billy could rest, dry grass for kindling, little gum branches for flame, some knotty thorn-tree branches for solidity and a banking of dried horse-turds to hold the heat in and raise the slightly acrid smoke that helped keep the flies away. His mind had walked carefully through all these details while his hand stirred the meat stew in the pannikin and his chin sank lower . . . and it was Burleigh's voice which jerked him upright, a hand grabbing instinctively for the rifle near his foot, then relaxing.

"God, that smells good! What is it?"

Burleigh was stretching and twisting himself upright, the two hours' sleep under the thorn tree's shade leaving him now wide-awake and hungry.

Harry shook his head, dispelling the daydreams of the afternoon heat, noticing how much longer the shadows had grown. "Don't be inquisitive. It might spoil your appetite." He spooned thick meat into their dishes and Burleigh sniffed deeply.

"Well, it still smells good. As long as it's no one we know."

They ate in silence, watching the blue fingers of shadow creep along the plain and down the tilt of land behind them where it rose into the foothills of the great range further back, listening to the calls of the first of the night birds. Burleigh leaned forward to toss a handful of tea into the billy.

"You should have shaken me earlier, Harry. I've some work to do, you know."

"About what? The war?" He inflated his voice. " 'A dispatch from the back of the front by our sleeping partner and holiday correspondent, Bennet Burleigh.' I don't believe either one of us has the slightest idea what's happening to the war, Ben."

Burleigh sat up, smirking a little. "Ah, that's the trouble with you ordinary chaps—the brutal and licentious soldiery. No mastery of Grand Strategy, let alone tactics. *We*, the correspondents, *we* know everything about the war, even if we're nowhere near it." He dragged a large notecase from his pack and flourished it. "Here you have the garnered wisdom of the past year, my Military Morant, the gleanings of a supreme intelligence, saved for just such a moment! Before we go back, I shall have transmuted this into pluperfect prose about which my editor will rhapsodize, the staff will enthuse, Her Majesty will doubtless confer on me a significant Order and the public will rush shouting into the streets!"

"With nooses tied and cabbages to throw!"

The past five days had brought these two men close, Burleigh watching with admiration Harry's self-possession as they moved across the land, seeing his skills at bushcraft and adaptation, at providing food, at settling them in some degree of comfort each afternoon. He liked his quietness. Harry had enjoyed the conversation, the irreverence of the correspondent's comments on senior soldiers and statesmen, his scorn for the timidity of his editor, his clear liking for the soldiers, the men who were working the rough end of the war. Each of them had the same dry humour and the liking was mutual and deepening. Harry waited now till Burleigh had eaten and had poured the black tea, adding lime from a flask and rum from a bottle, then he took the pad of papers by his side and said, "I've saved you a job, Ben. Here—" and tossed the pad across, moving a couple of branches so that the fire spurted high. They were many miles from any likely Boer activity, only twenty miles from camp and on the British side of the sprawl of troops across the countryside. Burleigh leaned in towards the firelight at the heading on the first page: "Kitchener's New Proposal for the Conduct of the War," looked up, startled, then down again and became absorbed, while Harry considered their position. Even where they were in a short fold in the plain and with a screen of trees to one side of them, even this far from the last reported Boer parties, he knew they needed to take some care and he checked his rifle and both revolvers, planning to bank the fire low as soon as the light had gone. About an hour, he thought.

Burleigh rested the pad on his knee, eyes blank, then suddenly focusing brightly on Harry.

"Did you write this? Good God!" He studied Harry's look of mock modesty. "Damn my eyes! It's good, it's bloody good!"

"Then you'd better put your name to the bottom of it. Wouldn't do for me to be known as the author."

"Oh, but look here, Harry, I can't do that! This is splendid stuff, quite masterly, really. Right in my style too, you bugger!"

"So much the better—no one will know, will they? Take it in payment for getting me away from Base for this past week. I've enjoyed it. And you *did* bring the whisky . . . which you might now be good enough to pass!"

He woke in the silent darkness, the taste of the whisky still in his mouth, and knowing something was wrong. Habit kept him still, eyes only slitted open, ears wide for sounds . . . Burleigh snoring quietly to his right and a hiss of breeze in the dry grasses. Nothing else—except he knew there was something. His hand slid very gently up under the blanket to the revolver by his shoulder and he winced as a boot crushed down on his wrist. The voice above him was deep and matter-of-fact.

"Stand up rednecks! Up, quickly!"

A boot kicked into the fire and in the little flare Harry could see there were four of them, one standing over Burleigh, another by the fire with a rifle levelled across the scene, the last bringing their horses to stand, all headroped together with the Boer ponies. Harry looked at the man who'd roused him, judging him to be the leader, seeing the solid features, the hard eyes, red with the fireglow, the tight mouth.

"My friend is no soldier. Let him go. He's only a civilian writer."

The Boer looked briefly at Burleigh. "A writer for the newspapers of London?" He accepted Burleigh's nod. "As bad as a soldier then. I have seen the lies that his sort has written about us." He saw Burleigh's

129

dispatch-case and, in a swift move hooked it to him with his boot-heel and kicked it into the fire. Burleigh's involuntary move forward brought two rifle muzzles close to his chest and the Boer leader laughed without humour.

"If you don't like the treatment, scribbler, you should have stayed safe in England."

Harry had taken half a step forward, mouth open to object, but the leader's butt moved through a short, vicious arc into his ribs, doubling him over with the pain. Burleigh saw the mad flare of light in Harry's eyes. The Boer leader stood over the crouched man.

"You keep your English mouth shut, hear? We will eat and sleep a little before I decide what to do with you. And don't worry about being rescued, rednecks; your nearest friends are seven miles away and my brother's patrol will have them by now. Turn around."

The two men were manhandled together, rifle-muzzles forcing them to move, and their hands were tied behind them. A rawhide rope was lashed two or three times round their chests as they stood back-to-back, and then the leader's hands on their shoulders crammed them down to the ground, sitting awkwardly, knees high, away from the fire. Two of the Boers were systematically going through their saddlebags, pulling out the little food they had left, taking the clothes, tossing other things aside. The prisoners watched as the Boers began to prepare food. Burleigh, his head craning back and half-turned, whispered, "What d'you suppose they'll do, Harry?" He tried to keep his voice calm, but Harry heard the slight tremble in it and thought, No point in not telling him the truth.

"Knife us, I should think, Ben. Makes no noise . . . and saves bullets."

Burleigh's back tensed against his, then relaxed. "That bloody Boer was right, wasn't he? I should have stayed at home!"

Harry's grin was dry. He moved his head with care, looking around the patch of near-dark ground beyond his stretched legs. His bedroll was about six feet from him and he could see what he was looking for, just clear of the blanket. When the Boer boot had held his wrist down, no one had picked up the revolver he'd been reaching for and now he strained his foot towards it, realizing at once that it was too far away. He twisted his head, holding his voice to a bare murmur.

"Ben, listen! My gun's over there on the ground. I can't reach it. We have to get closer somehow. When I give you the word, start a scrap. Start arguing with me and be prepared for me to pull you about a bit, d'you hear?"

"Yes, all right. But your hands are tied—"

"Shut up and stop worrying! Now, go!"

Over by the fire, the four Boers heard the sudden outburst, Burleigh shouting, "You stupid bastard! If it hadn't been for you we wouldn't—" He was jerking at his bonds, seeming to want to turn and hit at Harry, who pulled back, also shouting.

"Keep your dirty mouth shut, you bloody moaning civilian. I'd sooner have old Dutchie here than you!"

Their struggles had toppled them sideways, heads away from the fire and three feet nearer the blankets when the leader stood over them again, sneering.

"No wonder you can't fight us, English! You are too busy fighting each other. Now be quiet!" He turned away, then turned back and kicked Harry savagely just below the ribs. "And don't call me Dutchie!"

Harry was gasping from the pain of the kick and he took a moment to gather himself before muttering again, "No good, Ben. I've got to get about two feet further this way." He felt the slight shrug in Burleigh's shoulders as the journalist whispered back, "Oh, well, here we go again."

This time they began struggling silently, writhing and kicking at one another, and all four Boers moved quickly to look down at them. The leader was holding his reversed rifle, the butt menacingly over their heads, his voice angry.

"Mad English, stop it! You stop it now or I'll bang you on the head!"

The wriggling men lay still as the Boers went growling

back to the fire. Burleigh spat dust from the side of his mouth and whispered, "Well?"

"Got it! I kicked it about four or five feet to the left there. Now it's just a matter of waiting."

The first grey light saw the Boers stirring, one of them mending the fire and the smell of coffee reaching the prisoners, their mouths watering as they listened to their captors drinking and chewing on the last of Harry's rations. Then the leader and one of the others had jerked them upright, laughing as their stiff limbs wobbled under them. The sun was beginning to edge up, sliding colours into the greyness as the leader poked them in the ribs with his rifle-muzzle.

"All right, my little English, strip! Take off your clothes. Everything off, and quickly."

The man with him slackened their chest ropes and cut through the ties around their wrists and they stood chafing the skin, dragging the circulation back again. Harry could see the four Boers were all ragged enough . . . the leader and the man with him watching them closely, the third man stamping down the fire and the last of them tightening the girths on the horses and swinging the bags onto their backs. The leader prodded at them again. "Come on, no wasting time. We can use those clothes to fool more stupid soldiers. Get them off."

They began to strip, Harry hopping first on one foot, then on the other as he tugged at his socks, each hop taking him six inches nearer the clump of scrub where he could just see the dew-pearls on the pistol. Urged by the rifle-muzzle, Burleigh was standing in his drawers, stooping now for his socks. Harry had socks and trousers off and unbuttoned his shirt, watching as the other man near the leader answered a companion's call to help him with the horses. Harry's hands went to the bottom of his shirt and he tugged it up over his head, feeling the morning's coolness on his skin. He was perhaps two feet from the Boer leader when he pulled the shirt free, arms taking it upright above him, and then instantly sweeping it down across the rifle-muzzle as he threw himself sideways and backwards towards the hidden gun. He rolled, feeling the pebbles and the sharp grass-edges cutting into his thighs and buttocks, but the gun was in his hand, cocked and the barrel up in a shining line as the Boer, raging, swept the flannel shirt away from his hands and his rifle. The two fired almost together and Harry felt the sting of the bullet as it struck a small rock near his shoulder . . . and saw the Boer's throat go away on one side in a spurt of red. His second snap shot caught the man at the fire in the thigh and there was Burleigh beside him, the Boer leader's dropped rifle steady in his hands, and the other two Boers letting the horses go, grabbing for a second for guns, then raising their hands while they looked down, shocked, at the bubbling throat of their leader. Harry stood up and looked at the man by his feet. "He'll be dead in five minutes. Forget him. Ben, get dressed while I hold these beauties. Then we'll take them along, I think."

The little room at the end of the railway platform was stifling, the one window giving only onto a shed a few feet away from it, the air motionless and thick. Behind the desk, behind the massed piles of papers, the colonel was red and sweating, his tunic patched across the chest and shoulders and under the arms with black stains and his balding head and thick face running with sweat. He glared at the captain who followed his knock at the door with a rushed entrance, envying his slimness and youth, wondering why the young shit wasn't fighting instead of working here at the railhead like an old man. The captain seemed agitated.

"Sir—excuse me, sir, there's a war correspondent to see you. And a sergeant. Australian."

The colonel wondered what the hell the young fool was grinning at. "I've got no time to talk to correspondents and Colonial sergeants, Maxwell. Chuck 'em out!"

"Yes, sir. But they asked me to tell you—sir, they say they've got a present for you. To be given personally, sir."

The colonel threw his pen into the desk-top like a dart, running wet hands down his wet face.

"What the bloody Hades are you talking about, man? Oh, for God's sake let's have them in, then."

The captain swung the door and Harry and Burleigh walked in, Harry saluting smartly, Burleigh nodding, a finger to his hat-brim. Before the colonel could speak, the two men moved a little apart and led in three Boers, watching the colonel's eyes widen, hearing the smothered laughter from the outer office, seeing the captain's great crack of a smile. The Boers were stark naked except for their hats and boots, and the rough bandage around the thigh on one of them. Their bodies were red-scorched with the sun through which they'd walked and their faces mixed fury with desperation. The colonel closed his mouth, slapped the desk with both hands, sending papers flying everywhere and exploded in a huge guffaw, choking and gasping till he could speak.

"By the living God, Sergeant . . . what's your name, man?"

"Morant, sir. Second South Australian Yeomanry, detached."

"Detached for what . . . collecting naked Boers?" He roared with laughter again.

"No, sir, pending commissioned transfer into the Cape Police. This is Mr. Bennet Burleigh of the London *Daily Telegraph*."

"Well, Sergeant Morant Detached, if I could do it I'd make you a major in the field, I would! A bloody general! I'd hang a medal on you, by Jesus and the Apostles!" He turned, scarlet, to Burleigh. "You too, sir, if you weren't a stinki—sorry—if you weren't a civilian."

Burleigh was quite unperturbed. "That's perfectly all right, Colonel. I've got my best story in years, thanks to Morant here."

"Quite, quite. Very proper attitude! Maxwell, get these—these—children of nature out of here and find 'em some clothes." He looked at the red-raw backsides of the prisoners as they were led out by the grinning captain and roared again with laughter.

"God, that's done me a power of good! Now then,

Morant, where d'you belong, eh? I'll get a signal to your C.O. You too, Burleigh?"

"Thank you, sir. My commanding officer's Colonel Morrissey, but he's in the field. I'm due for leave, sir."

Burleigh said, "I'll travel with Morant, if I may, Colonel. I want a bath and a telegraph."

Answering the colonel's shout, the smiling captain returned.

"Those laddies are locked in that empty stores hut, sir. They're all standing. . . ."

Harry and Burleigh kept straight faces, but the colonel went into another jerk of laughter, fighting his way out of it at last.

"Leave, eh, Morant? By the Lord Harry you deserve it. You'll both lunch with me first, though—bugger the protocol, Maxwell! I want to hear all about it. Then we'll get you on a train for Base. Maxwell—a compartment, mind, not just a couple of seats. Back to Australia for you, my lad!"

Harry smiled quietly down at the Colonel. "Not Australia, sir. I'm going home."

# ENGLAND

It rained lightly as the train pulled away from Exeter, a thin mist of rain that swallowed the cathedral in a gulp and took the city with it before thinning further to let the sun begin to show through. The greens were all dark and fresh and the cart-roads to the farms and the ploughed or fallow fields were red, the soft bronze-red of West Country clay. Harry, alone in the compartment, tugged at the leather strap that held the window closed and leaned out, sucking his lungs full of the smells, grinning at the lushness of it all, the neatness of the line curving away ahead into a toy greystone tunnel.

There were oaks and beeches growing thickly up there where the road and the rail ran across the Torridge, high with the last of the spring rains and the salmon weirs splashing with the leaping fish. The last time he'd made this journey he'd been a lad, with a pocketful of warnings from people to whom he owed money and a confrontation with his father looming. By God! he thought, I was scared that day! A Post Captain in a rage was no welcome for a one-ship lieutenant. . . .

He settled back, considering that he was still a lieutenant, and the captain was now a retired admiral, but what a whole whirling world of difference there was between them. He'd chosen to change into uniform that morning, wanting to make it plain that he was coming back in Service, as he'd been when he left, and he straightened the blue tunic now, glancing down at the campaign medals and the clasps, at the fine cut of the pale khaki whipcords and the chestnut of the boots.

He was damned if he sneaked home in mufti, not after the last year, certainly. The carriage porter slid back the compartment door, grinning in, a massive watch in his hand. "Rackon us'll be pullin' in to Bideford 'bowt seven minutes now, sir. I s'll get thee bags down, s'll I?" The broad burr brought a smile to Harry's face and he stood, stretching, as the man pulled down his cases and slid the tin trunk to one side, dropping a half-sovereign into his hand and gravely returning the one-finger salute. In the little oval mirror above his seat he stared at himself, realizing he was nervous, smoothing back his hair, feeling the light damp of sweat on his hands and forehead. The khaki slouch hat with the big silver badge, chinstrap just under the bottom lip, made him look less anxious, and he scowled, then laughed. Out there, in the pale sunlight now, the land rose towards Appledore and Westward Ho and below his feet he could feel the first juddering as the brakes began to lock the wheels. Bideford. Home.

Head out of the window, holding his hat against the wind, the brim curling away from his face, Harry could see only steam, sweeping back with the smoke from the stack and blotting out the station platform in a cloud of grey and white. There were noises and voices up there, the squeal of the braking wheels and a bell ringing and a voice calling "Bideford—Bideford Station!" and then the red gravel end of the platform cut through the smoke and the stone side of a building and a large-lettered sign and the steam and the smoke were in his eyes and he could feel them stinging with the moisture, the dampness on his cheeks and he ran the back of his hand across his face and swung the door wide and stepped out, standing stock-still, crying without shame.

The three of them there. Father, shoulders stooped a little now, whiskers white, a solid figure in Donegal tweeds, his hard hat square on his head. Father staring at him, gripping the old black cane like a sword. Mother was tiny still, a bird of a woman, her small gloved hands strangling the life out of her purse, her face as wet with tears as his own. And Helen, topping mother by a head, a slim and stately young woman where he'd left a little girl. And they stood there, ten feet apart while the world moved, and then there was no distance between them at all and mother's arms were about his neck and he could feel the crepe-paper fineness of her face against his and her lips covering his and hear the little murmuring wordless noises and Helen, an arm around each of them and weeping and laughing and saying in a crackly sort of voice, "Oh, Harry, welcome home, welcome home!"

And then they loosened, the arms and the lips, and there was father and Harry realized that he'd pulled off his hat when he left the train and he put it back on and pulled himself upright and stared at the old man levelly and saluted him, holding the hand there at the brim of his hat for a long, long moment. And father very stiffly, face unmoved, raised his own hand and took off his hat to his son and then threw the hat to the ground and ran the three steps between them and they met chest to chest there on the platform while the people around them stared and Damn the people to Hell and the white whiskers rasped against Harry's cheek and he felt his father tremble and shake but the grip of the arms was strong on him. Harry leaned back.

"Father . . . ? May I come home, sir?"

The light eyes were brimming, but the voice was a growl. "Don't be bloody silly, boy! You *are* home! Helen, pick up my hat!"

The house had never been big, not when it was built somewhere in the mid-1700s, not when it had been added to nearly a century later by Harry's grandfather, the plain, neatly-columned front with a low wing on either side. The poplars along the drive were taller and the laurels had grown and thickened and the ancient and twisted oak among whose branches the boy Harry had climbed was gone, the hole of its passing filled now with roses in a formal bed. More than anything yet, Harry realized how the loss of that old oak marked the loss of the years.

Leitch the coachman had managed to edge alongside

Harry as he left the carriage, managed to mutter, "Raight glad to see you 'ome agen, Muster 'Arry," and the roll of the voice out of the corner of the almost still lips suddenly reminded Harry of the man . . . no, the lad, who'd worked about the stables once, staring up at the young master with wide round eyes. And then there was Parker, old Parker, his back as stiffly upright as ever, his pink face purpling with the effort not to grin, allowing himself only a smile with his bow and a quiet, "The staff wishes me to welcome you back, sir. It's very good to see you. *Very* good, sir, old times come again." Harry shook hands but could only nod, standing there at the foot of the eight wide, shallow steps, looking up at the house, at the servants waiting there, his throat swollen with an insane desire to shout and to cry and to laugh.

Helen had wanted to come upstairs too, but his mother had said firmly, "No, dear, you just go and freshen yourself and make sure luncheon is ready. I'll take Harry to his room," and they'd walked up the curve of the staircase, her hand trembling a little on his arm, the thin sunlight striking as it always did late in the morning along the upper hall with the two side-tables and the pictures of grandfather Morant and grandfather Chetwynd and the very bad painting of father's first command, a sloop, *Virginia*. The first door on the left was father's room and the second was mother's and the door opposite those two had always been known as the sewing-room, though mother was much more likely to be writing letters, drinking endless cups of tea or chattering.

Then there was Helen's room on the right and beyond mother's bedroom, Miss Tunstall's, the Nanny, the door wide now so that Harry could see it was obviously a room used by Helen . . . a white-and-gold piano, an easel and some racked canvases. Then the end door on the right, the corner room that looked out over the wing at that end, its window offering easy access to that lower roof and to the roof of the greenhouse behind it and the forbidden nightworld, poaching-world beyond that.

"It's still your room, Harry, my dear. It always has been." His mother's gentle hands on his face pulled him down as she kissed him. "We'll wait luncheon for you . . . but not too long. We've a long time to make up for. But you're home now, my son." She kissed him again and was gone, hurrying down the hall, through the sunbars.

Now he lay on his back in the bed that had always had a little lump on the left side of the mattress no matter how often it was turned, and he knew where everything was. Everything as he had left it.

He'd let his mother turn down the stairs and then pushed open the door, eyes closed for a second and feeling the sun on the lids. He didn't open them till he was inside.

A big, square room on the corner of the old house, the bed with the same dark blue counterpane with the light blue pattern on it over in the far corner. The desk, once his grandfather's, in the opposite corner in the angle between the windows. The enormous old wardrobe filling all the wall up to the doorway. The cabinet of shelves and the campaign chest which had been his mother's brother's. The white and gold striped wallpaper a little more faded. Everything clean, everything neat . . . fresh flowers in two bowls, roses in a big one on the chest and a little jar of periwinkles on the round table by the bed. Books tidily on the shelves and papers straight on the desk; and the smell of the lavender his mother always wore everywhere in the room. He stood there, knowing she had been here not just today, not just to make sure it was right, but many times.

The windows were beginning to assume shapes, less-than-black rectangles against the more-than-black of the room and Harry shook himself lower in the bed, pressing and curving his body not just into the sheets and under the blankets but into the house itself, into the country, into the life. He remembered quite clearly the last time he was in this room, the room in which he'd grown up. He'd taken the coach from Dartmouth up to Exeter and then another rattling and bumping its

143

way across to Barnstaple. Hiring a horse there had used all but a few shillings of the little money he had left, but it meant he could time his ride down to Bideford, skirting the town and coming onto his father's land from the seaward side. The spinney at the top of Seven Crosses Hill had given him a clear view of the house and gardens spread a mile below and he'd spent six chilly, hungry hours there, the smoke from the kitchen chimneys blowing up towards him, carrying, so he imagined, the smells of lunch with it. It was well after two that afternoon that he'd seen the light carriage wheel round to the steps and the boxes and cases being lashed on behind. That was better than he'd thought—it meant his parents were off, probably for the weekend, and there'd be no real need for hurry. Not that he'd wanted to prolong things.

Parker had seen him ride down the hill and through the little pear orchard and was waiting on the steps when he dismounted, his uniform crumpled and damp from the night's travel and the long morning in the trees.

"Oh, Mister Harry, the captain's left sir, and Lady Dorothy—to the Amorys, sir, for the shooting."

"It's all right Parker. I'm not on leave," he had said. "Just overnight. Get someone to rub this beast down and feed him, will you?"

He'd run up the steps, not wanting to talk, not wanting to face the puzzled look, and had heard Parker calling for a groom. Harry had his tunic off by the time Parker came tapping at the door carrying the leather valise with the H.H.M. stamped on it.

"Your bag, sir. I'll have a bath drawn directly; and you'll be wanting some dinner?"

"See what you can find me now for a start—anything. Some cold meat and some bread and cheese. Up here on a tray. And some cider, please."

By the time the butler had brought the tray the room was a shambles. Harry had sold the rest of his clothes two days before, sneaking into the dingy pawnbroker's at Dartmouth and out again with three guineas jingling thinly in his pocket. Almost everything he'd left at home was too small for him now, but he'd piled some socks and drawers and shirts on the bed, leaving the rest strewn around.

Parker put the tray down on the chest, looking around with a worried frown. "Is there something wrong, Mister Harry? Something I can do?"

Parker had been a footman when Harry began to walk, as much a part of the family as any relative. Harry had tried a smile, knowing that it wasn't working, knowing too that if Parker sent a groom riding to the Amorys on a fresh horse, his father would very likely be back here by nightfall.

"No, nothing wrong, Parker—not really. Look, I've changed my mind. I shan't stay over, so don't get cook started on one of her Fattening Young Harry feasts. I'll eat here while I sort myself out and then be off. I'd like Rajah saddled, please."

"But sir—"

"No buts, man! Just do as I say!" He saw the wounded look and cursed his abruptness. "Look, Parker, I *am* in a touch of bother but I shall only need a day or two to sort it out, believe me. Just get along and see to Rajah for me, eh?"

He bustled the man out and locked the door, sick at the lying, and tore at the sliced beef on the tray while he went on cramming things into his valise. A rapid search through all his pockets and the various drawers in the room yielded a little over eight pounds and he sat on the disordered bed finishing the cider and looking round, wondering about a note. Below the window he'd heard voices and looked out seeing Rajah, his own hunter, being held there, Parker and the groom talking together. Damn, he'd have to ride away in uniform, otherwise they'd suspect even more. He'd crammed on his hat, snatched at the valise and then, not able to go otherwise, crossed to the desk and scrawled on a piece of paper, "Dearest Mother and Father, I'm truly sorry. Goodbye. All my deepest love. Harry."

Then he'd slammed the door and run downstairs and ridden away. . . .

Now he was back.

He slid out of bed, feeling the morning chill and shrugging into the dressing-gown of his father's which had been on his bed last night. With the curtains pulled back the first of the day looked clear, a dew-frost on the lawns just beginning to sparkle, and he leaned against the side of the window looking out, forcing himself to believe, remembering the words he'd once said to Paddy in a smelly hut high on a winter hill across the world. . . . Nothing will take me home again, will it? So it doesn't matter, does it? But it did, it mattered, and he felt the quick start of tears again, smiling to think how old Paddy would love to see that!

There was enough light for him to see his unshaven face in the mirror. His mother had left all the old invitations, stuck in the frame . . . "request the pleasure of the company of . . . ," ". . . Hunt Ball . . . ," a pink and deckle-edged one ". . . the birthday of their daughter Felicia . . ." and the scrawl across the corner of it—*"Please* come! F."

He pulled the bell-cord and bundled the invitations together into a drawer till the tap at the door came. It was a new face, smiling and saying, "Ayliffe, sir. Footman these three years. 'Morning, sir."

"Oh, yes. Good morning, Ayliffe. See if you can find me some hot coffee, will you? Nothing to eat. I'll come down to breakfast later."

"Very good sir. Draw your bath?"

"After the coffee, please."

"Yessir." The smile was back, wider. "Big day today, sir."

Not that Harry saw much of the events in the house during that day. The thought of suddenly being thrown back into the wild waters of the county's social swim made him nervous, his mind refusing to let him forget how long he'd been gone and under what terms he'd left. The one dominant thought was the hurt to his mother if people should choose not to accept invitations, or come in order to bite on some tasty old meat of scandal. But by the time he'd bathed and breakfasted alone, it was clear from the neat double-stack

146

of acceptances on the table in the hall that the place would be packed that evening. The whole ground floor was a whirling scuttle of servants and Harry got out as fast as he could, a startled lad in the stables saddling a steady-looking mare for him and the gravel of the drive spurting as he cantered away.

By the time he got back the poplars were sliding long pencils of shadow across the lawns. The great double-doors were standing wide to the warm air and the hall was a banked mass of flowers, the eight man-high brass candlesticks that his father had brought back years ago from Hong Kong spaced about, candles as thick as Harry's wrist waiting to be lit. Parker was there looking as though he had just come fresh from a special fitting at a superb tailor's, and a constant stream of maids and footmen moved to and from him for the quiet and unruffled answers to their questions. He waved two of them away as he saw Harry and came forward, taking his hat and gloves and passing them behind him to a youngster who seemed to move with him like the Dog Star with the moon.

"Mister Harry, Lady Dorothy asked me to let you know she thought you were very sensible to get away into the fresh air and out of the—er—turmoil, sir. She and Miss Helen are dressing."

"Been a bit of a madhouse, has it, Parker?"

"Busy, sir, busy enough. But we've managed very well." Just a tiny touch of pride there, Harry thought, Parker the Centre of the Universe. Probably right, too.

"The admiral suggested you might like to take a sandwich and a glass of sherry with him, sir. In his dressing-room." The raised eyebrow was question and answer all in one. Will he do it . . . and if not what will I tell the old gentleman? I'll think of something.

Harry clapped him affectionately on the arm. "I'll be there in five minutes. Just a quick wash first, right?"

Harry dawdled over his wash. He hadn't been alone with his father since he got home and he felt rather like a schoolboy on holidays after a poor term report. He straightened his shoulders, crossed the upper hall and tapped at his father's door, not waiting for an answer before going in. There was a quiet fire in the grate and Harry remembered how his father had always felt the chill, the legacy of years spent away from England under blood-thinning suns. The admiral was propped comfortably in an armchair to one side of the fire, feet up on a stool, a tattered old gown round him and a tray of chicken sandwiches on a low table alongside, with a decanter and glasses.

"Father, may I come in?"

"In or out, boy, but shut that damn door! Draught's like a sword." He poured some of the very pale sherry and waved at the other armchair. "Sit down, Harry, and have something."

It was awkward for them both as they sat sipping and chewing at the sandwiches, staring into the fire, each wanting to start, neither knowing how. It was Harry who broke the silence, leaning forward to refill the glasses, eyes down as he spoke.

"It's very good to be home, Father."

The admiral coughed, and again. "Good to have you here, boy. Dammit, I don't suppose I should be calling you 'boy', should I? Not any more. You've grown well, Harry."

"In a number of ways, Father. I've—I've not always done things you'd approve of."

The old man smiled for the first time, the heavy face softening at once. "You never did, you bloody young rogue! Always went your own way." With the smile they both relaxed.

"I was pretty much of a fool, Father. You do know how sorry I am for . . . all that business, don't you? I—must have hurt you badly."

"You did, boy. Hurt your mother worse. I'm stronger stuff, of course. You should have told me about it, not run off like—" He stopped, not wanting to say words that would sting, then went on, his voice quiet. "Harry, it's all past and done. No point in dragging it all up again—it's over. We've missed you here, all of us, and your mother looks twenty years younger now you're home again. And you've done good things, boy. I'm proud of you."

He blinked, staring back again into the fire, and Harry was astonished at the fierce stab of affection he felt for the old man opposite, saying gentle things. The silence this time was longer, but there was a comfortable softness in it and when the admiral said, "Well then—what was it all like? Australia and the war and all that?" Harry began to talk, the fire lowering, the room darkening, their heads closer together, the old man often breaking into a barking laugh. At one stage he said, "By the God, that feller Magee sounds like a sensible chap! I think I should like him," and Harry suddenly realized that his father and Paddy would probably get on like lifelong friends. And for a moment, he missed Paddy deeply.

Then the tapping at the door and Parker saying, "Excuse me, Sir George—Lady Dorothy asked me to let you know it *is* getting a little late," and Harry stood and his father stood by him, a little shorter with his stoop. Parker's eyes were alight as he saw the old man's arm across Harry's shoulders, pushing him affectionately out of the door. "Go on with you, you smooth-tongued young devil! Get your fancy duds on! There are people coming to stare at you. And watch the old women, boy! They'll be wanting to grab you off for their daughters!"

The long morning room was to the right of the hall and, to the left, the dining room and then the library. The tall panelled doors between all these rooms had been leafed back so that the whole wide front of the house splayed light and music and noise out into the gardens and along the arc of the drive. Sheltered behind a bank of shrubs, an eight-piece orchestra was lilting its way through a polka and the two long buffet tables were surrounded by a constant shift of people, the three men and two maids behind the food slicing and serving with barely a pause. The punchbowls were on the oak table by the library wall with Parker standing nearby, a careful eye cocked on the man attending to the bar. There were several tubs of ice, the gilt caps of the wine bottles glinting out of the blue-whiteness, and a silver tray for the cluster of whisky and brandy bottles.

Parker had listened, sometimes with amusement, sometimes with anger, to the splinters of conversation piercing the overall fabric of the noise. A bonelessly elegant young man had slid past him, balancing three glasses of champagne and drawling to the girl giggling with him, "I'm told he actually worked as some kind of farm labourer. I mean, as *a workman!*" The girl had glanced at Harry, tall by his mother's side, and said, her eyes running up and down him, "Well, it doesn't seem to have hurt him, Arthur." Another girl was asking her escort, "What *is* that funny uniform Harry's wearing?" The young man in infantry scarlet with the green facings and the three Devonshire castles of the 11th of Foot, said, "His sister tells me it's the Cape Police, of all things. Not properly military at all, of course. 'Pears he's been commissioned into them."

One of the older women swam out of the stream and anchored herself by Harry, a thin hand on his arm. "Shall you be home for long, Lieutenant Morant?"

"Six months, Lady Wemyss. I have that much leave."

"How very nice for your dear mother." Her fan tapped his shoulder. "You must call on me soon. I've a niece I want you to look over."

Harry caught her look and they laughed together. "I knew a man in New South Wales, Lady Wemyss, who used to talk to me about horses in just that way."

"Ah, well, you might find the similarity doesn't end there, young man. I'm afraid my niece isn't exactly a great beauty."

"But you'd like me to—er, look her over?"

"Oh, indeed yes! Teeth and stance and so on. You might even run a hand over her fetlocks!" She gave a great guffaw of laugher and Harry's mother turned inquiringly, meeting Harry's smile as Lady Wemyss moved away.

"Is old Elizabeth being coarse again, Harry dear?"

"Not really, mother. Just inviting me to make a bid for a niece of hers. With a touch-trial first."

"Harry! How awful!"

"Yes, I gathered she was."

His mother giggled and he kissed her, edging into the crush. Over by the bar-table, Parker heard a beefy Grenadier say, rather too loudly, to one of the admiral's young cousins, "Don't see what the fuss is about really. Out of some strange Colonial Yeomanry into the African police and everyone treats him like bloody Wellington! Quite extraordinary!"

The cousin, a quiet man in the blue and gold of a commander's full-dress rig, looked with care at the Guardsman. "Ah, well, he *has* seen some action, y'see. Bit different from Palace duties, I imagine." Parker thought, Good for the Navy, and leaned back a little to the tight group of chattering girls behind him.

"Helen told me he's written a lot of poetry . . . some of it quite . . . well, you know—"

"Really! Oh, I'd love to persuade him to read me some of it!"

A third voice said, drily, "From what I've heard of Harry Morant, you wouldn't have any trouble persuading him to do anything . . . not with your bosom cut that low, dear!"

"Good—then I shall have to do something about it, shan't I?"

Parker watched her pass him, a plump girl, pouting her chest so that her very full breasts almost leapt out of the blue silk, thrusting them ahead of her to where Harry was moving towards the door at the end of the library, the door to his father's study. He smiled with quiet enjoyment as Harry passed through the door, leaving the girl tight-lipped and scowling.

Harry pushed the door almost shut behind him, muting the sound of the violins and the conversations out there. The study was immediately below his bedroom, another big square corner room, rich now with the cigar-smoke overlaying the old leather smells from the two walls of shelves and the headiness of port and brandy fumes. His father was leaning against the mantelpiece, his frock-coat unbuttoned, listening with the rest of the seven or eight elderly men there to one of his near neighbours. General Sawyer's face was almost

151

exactly the same scarlet as his tunic and his eyes were sending pale-blue flashes of fire around the group.

"I'm not saying the Boer *can't* fight, dammit! What I'm saying is that he *don't* fight! He shoots a bit and hides a bit and bloody well runs away!"

The lean old man across the group was in the regimentals of the Duke of Cornwall's Light Infantry, his throat and chest glittering with the cheerful ribbons and shining metal of a dozen past campaigns. He opened his tight lips just enough to rasp out, "Well, if that ain't fighting, John, you'd better have another look at the casualty lists. Half the Army's been shot to pieces —and that's *since* Botha surrendered!"

"Gentlemen," the admiral broke in, "all I can say is things must be in damn bad shape for the Army to have to call in a Naval Brigade to help them out! Bluejacket gunners, by the God! fighting on land!"

The tubby man at the other end of the mantelpiece leaned forward, bald head gleaming. "Ah, that was just to let your sailor-boys see a bit of real action, Morant—"

"Real action my arse!" General Sawyer was spraying tiny drops of port as he sputtered. "There ain't any real action any more! It's all this—this commando stuff the Boer's started. No discipline, no uniforms, elect their own officers, all over the place like a pack of mangy dogs!"

The admiral chipped in, forestalling any of the others. "Well, Kitchener'll soon put a stop to it all. D'you see today's report in the *Telegraph?* That chap Burleigh says K's ordered a line of blockhouses right across the fighting front."

"What the blazes is the good of blockhouses? Only hampers the troops—you can't form line in a bloody blockhouse!"

"Well, I don't know, John. Burleigh says they're going to clear the whole damn countryside and toss all the civilians into camps of some kind so the old Boer can't sneak about and get supplies and so on."

"Supplies, is it? He'll have no trouble about that, not with the bloody Kaiser shipping him guns through the Portuguese at Delagoa Bay. Mark my words, gentlemen, the Kaiser's going to have to answer for the way he's supporting those damn rebels!"

The tubby man leaned forward again. "I just hope Kitchener gives our cavalry a chance to get at 'em. From what I hear from my old regiment, there hasn't been a single decent cavalry action yet. Just not using 'em!"

Harry had been listening quietly, his face twisted cynically at the edge of the group, when the quiet voice came from the far side, away from the light of the two desk-lamps and the fire.

"What a load of manure!"

General Sawyer started and glared. "What's that? Speak up, young feller!"

The voice said, a little louder, "Sorry, sir. I said I'm not so sure."

Harry grinned and shifted to see who had spoken, but his father had pulled the other man forward by the arm and Harry saw a tall and slender man, hair the colour of tow, face thin and sunburnt. His Hussar blues clung to him and the furred pelisse across his left shoulder partly concealed the light silk sling holding his wrist. The admiral said, "I don't believe you know young Hunt, John. General Sawyer, gentlemen— Captain Geoffrey Hunt. On leave, like Harry." He turned to the general. "Hunt's been out there, you know . . . the Cape."

The general hadn't taken his eyes from the young Hussar, only nodding at the introduction, Hunt's last words still clear in his mind. Now he shoved his red face forward.

"What do you mean—you're not sure?"

Harry was struck by the quality of repose in Hunt, standing, elegant and relaxed in the circle of older and more senior officers. It wasn't insolence, he thought, but it wasn't a long way from it. Hunt looked back at General Sawyer.

"I was considering the remark about the cavalry not being used, sir." He half turned and made the slightest of bows to the tubby man. "I can assure you, all of

153

you, from personal experience that we are indeed being used. And used very badly."

The tubby man's voice rose above the murmur, shrill with indignation. "Damn your impertinence! What d'you mean—used badly?"

Harry edged a little closer, seeing that Hunt's face was entirely calm and that he faced the obvious hostility around him almost with enjoyment, looking down on the bald head of the tubby man and answering him directly.

"Sir, with respect, we've been used in regimental and brigade advances just as though the Boer didn't have expert marksmen with the best Mauser magazine rifles. *And* Maxim guns in concealed positions. We've been ridden at the centre of strongpoints where we couldn't see the enemy at all—never did see him. We've been used as though nobody's learned a thing since Balaclava."

The silence was thick with anger and embarrassment. Hunt alone seemed unmoved and it was Harry who spoke, deliberately.

"How would *you* suggest using the cavalry?"

"Send 'em home." The immediate response brought a growl from the others, with Sawyer stepping close to Hunt, snarling at him.

"Send 'em home? I find it difficult to believe that an officer—"

Harry pitched his voice just high enough to top the other man's. "And replace them with what, Hunt?"

"Mounted infantry, of course. *We're* no damn use against the Boer. You can't charge uphill into rocks and get a point into an invisible man who's shooting at you." He swung to look round them. "As a piece of first-hand information, gentlemen, let me advise you that the Boer can find his mark in good light at a comfortable thousand yards. He aims generally for the thigh or the leg, so that his round passes through the man and gets the horse too. Disgusting, isn't it?" The mockery in his voice was open now. "No, the answer's mounted infantry. Horses to get 'em in there, dismount 'em and tackle the Boer with well-trained riflemen —magazine rifles would be nice—and machine-guns."

The tubby man was almost dancing with rage. "I'm —I *was*—a Dragoon, sir. I'm damn glad I wasn't a Hussar, if you're an example of the Light nowadays. You should be—"

Again Harry interrupted. "I beg your pardon, sir, but I have to say that Captain Hunt is voicing the opinion of almost everyone who's actually fought against the Boer, especially the younger officers. The situation's a little different when you're actually there, of course." He'd said it as coldly as he could and just had time to catch Hunt's wink before the admiral moved forward, determined to relieve the tension.

"Er—Harry, why don't you and young Hunt go and —er—enjoy the dancing?"

Taking the cue, Harry nodded around the group. "Of course, Father. Gentlemen, I'm sure you'll excuse us. You must have many memories to recapture."

His father walked him to the study door, Hunt following them. The admiral's whisper was loud enough for only Harry to hear. "You young snot-nose! Now I shall have to settle 'em down. But you were right, boy! Stand up to 'em."

Harry gripped his father's shoulder hard for a second, knowing suddenly how much alike they were, and slipped out of the study, heading straight for the bar. He gestured at an opened bottle and the man poured champagne into two glasses, a blue-and-gold arm reaching past Harry for the second one. Hunt said, "I say, you must be Morant, the long-lost-son-of-the-house fellow."

Harry kept his face straight. "You're not really a British cavalry officer, are you?"

Hunt drank down the champagne and passed the glass back to be refilled, using his empty hand to make a sweeping gesture at himself. "I must be. All this glory could never grace a footslogger!"

Harry shook his head in apparent disbelief. "I'd never have believed the day would come when I'd hear a cavalry-man talking sense! You astound me—and I'm bloody glad to meet you!"

They gripped hands hard, neither of them noticing the girl who'd moved close to them, her hair as light as

Hunt's, her eyes as blue and the old-gold gown hugging her to the hips before flaring out in a golden swirl. She spoke across Hunt to Harry.

"Then I hope you'll be just as bloody glad to meet the rest of the family."

Both men wheeled, startled, and Hunt's voice was sharp. "Margaret! Behave yourself!" He turned to Harry. "My apologies—my sister doesn't stand much on ceremony."

The girl blew him a little kiss. "Don't be mealy-mouthed, Geoffrey. Introduce the nice gentleman properly, please."

Harry didn't wait for the introduction. He made a leg, the deep bow almost a caricature. "Morant, Miss Hunt. Harry Morant. And I'm delighted to meet the rest of the family, I promise you. I don't believe I've ever heard a lady say 'bloody' before."

"Then you've led a rather sheltered life, Harry Morant—which I find it difficult to believe. Besides, I'm not much of a lady."

Hunt sounded outraged. "Now look here, Margaret! Morant—"

He realized they were ignoring him completely, Harry staring down at the girl, only an inch or two shorter than himself, deliberately letting his look dwell on her breasts. She stood, hands by her sides, aware of his inspection and accepting it calmly, chin up to study his face. Hunt whistled tunelessly between his teeth, turned to the bar and held up three fingers to the man there. He turned back, a glass of champagne in his hand, to find them gone, moving easily together in the waltz the violins were sighing over. He stared after them for a moment then downed the champagne, then the second, then picked up the third. Parker watched him, smiling, and the smile widened as he looked past the young Hussar to Harry and Margaret Hunt.

Harry couldn't describe it, even to himself. The sense of well-being, of satisfaction, of something like completion, was so much around him that he could only accept it, wrapping himself in the almost tangible blanket of enjoyment. Sometimes it seemed to him that he was dead and in the Heaven he'd been told about as a little boy, a place where the sun always shone, the birds always sang and no one was ever unhappy.

Within a week of getting home he'd snatched up the thousand loose threads of his old life, plaiting them into strong ropes, binding himself once more to the things and the people he'd never expected to see again, and he found the long years behind him were sliding away fast, sliding backwards into a piece of his mind that belonged to someone else, like a book he'd read or a play he'd seen. The real present was being home again. And Geoffrey. And Margaret, most of all Margaret.

When they swung away from her brother in that first waltz, they moved into a separate world. Harry looked down into her face, looking up into his, and began a smile. Margaret quite deliberately turned him into an angle of the crowded room, a corner where the lights reached less well, and moved herself against him, laying the full length of herself onto his body, still moving in the rhythm of the dance, so that he could feel the swell of her breasts and the roll of her thighs. He tightened his grip on her, staring down at the eyes that hadn't shifted from his own.

"Do you know what you're doing?"

Then she had smiled, widely and with a happy triumph.

"Oh, yes, Harry Morant, I know exactly what I'm doing. Don't you?"

And she'd pressed herself to him again, then twirled him back into the crush.

It had gone on for weeks, the days spinning away in a reel of pleasure, Harry and Margaret constantly together, Geoffrey almost always with them, the county ladies buzzing and winking over their teacups, the Hunts and the Morants delighted, the engagement ring a sharp fire of diamonds and the women lost in a wild fantasy of fashions for the proposed wedding.

And it went sour.

157

July brought early rain and cold winds and the two men rode back to the house with their cloaks dripping. The train had hissed wetly away into the mist with their families, hellbent for a frenzy of London shopping, and the house seemed strangely quiet. In Harry's room the fire cracked and glowed and they kicked off their boots and let the warmth wrap them. Geoffrey slumped into one of the two big chairs with a relaxed sigh, propping his stockinged feet on the fender. Harry had walked to the window and stood staring out at the trees tossing in the wind which was throwing handfuls of rain at the windows. He didn't turn when Parker came in with a tray of coffee, the paper and a small bundle of letters. He glanced at Harry's stiff back and coughed gently.

"Er, coffee, Mr. Harry?"

"Thanks, Parker. Just leave it, will you?" His back was still to the room. "Oh—and put some brandy out, will you please?"

"Yes, sir." Harry could hear the clink of the decanter and glasses. "The morning post is here, sir. One for Captain Hunt, sent on for you, sir."

Harry looked around and nodded as Parker passed the letter to Geoffrey, then swung back to stare emptily out of the wet window again. Hunt waited till Parker had closed the door behind him before speaking, the unopened letter balanced in his fingers.

"Harry. Something wrong?"

"No. Just this damned rain, I think."

Geoffrey poured coffee, clattering the cups.

"Well, then, sit down for God's sake. Have some coffee."

Harry swung round and slumped in the other chair, reaching for the decanter and pouring two stiff shots of brandy. He ignored the little pile of mail till Hunt asked, "Aren't you going to open your letters?" then riffled through them and dropped them on the floor by his chair.

"Oh, just the usual ration of bills and invitations."

He drank his brandy and poured another at once, not touching his coffee, and the silence stretched. Hunt leaned forward to poke down a log. "I suppose by the time Margaret gets back she'll have bought half the fashion houses in Town."

Harry grunted.

"She's used to spending pretty freely, Harry. Won't be cheap keeping her."

"I suppose not. We'll manage."

"Er—perhaps I shouldn't ask, but as the prospective best man—how long an engagement d'you two have in mind?"

"Engagement? Oh, Hell, I don't know! Haven't really pinned things down to a date yet."

"Oh, I see." Hunt shifted uncomfortably. "You don't mean—er—you're not . . . ?"

"No, of course not, Geoffrey, don't be bloody daft! We're engaged and we're going to be married. I'm just not sure when, that's all." He gulped down the brandy and refilled once more.

Hunt started to speak, thought better of it and followed Harry's example, watching the other man cross back to the window and stare out again at the driving rain.

He called across the room. "I suppose it's as hot as Hell in Pretoria."

Harry spun about, almost smiling. "That's funny. I was just thinking the same thing. I think I've got what the troops call itchy feet."

He slumped into his armchair again, unfolding the newspaper across his knees while Hunt stared at him, one eyebrow raised, a grin twisting one side of his mouth. "Itchy feet, is it, Harry? I think I've got what *I* call guilty conscience."

"What the devil have you got to be guilty about?"

"Oh, all this. All part of what's been fretting me for some time. Sitting on my bum doing nothing. Enjoying myself—or pretending to. My arm's in fine shape now . . . I ought to be back at work."

"Back in action, d'you mean?"

"I suppose I do."

"That's a damn silly thought! You've still got weeks of leave. Me too."

159

"Christ! You sound thoroughly miserable about it! I believe you feel just the same way I do."

"Don't be ridiculous!" Harry rattled the newspaper up in front of his face, holding it there for a minute or two before dropping it again. "You're right of course, Geoff. I don't think I can take another week of this . . . dinners and parties and soirées and all the rest of it!"

"Exactly! We're not meant to lie about, Harry. We're meant to be doing something. We should be back in harness."

"Listen to this—*The Times*. 'Now that the first of the enclosed areas has been completed the strength of the Commander-in-Chief's plan is evident. The Boer forces under De La Rey have been forced to move back from the cleared and protected country and have been thrown upon very meagre resources. Nonetheless, they continue to fight a hard and savage guerilla action.' " He crumpled the newspaper and tossed it across the floor. "I keep thinking of our chaps out there and wondering what the bastard hell I'm doing here!"

"I know." Hunt's voice was quiet. "I know just what you mean."

Harry made no answer and Hunt, tightening his lips as he looked across at his friend's grim face, ripped the flap of the letter Parker had given him, noticing that it came from the Cape. His yell jerked Harry's head up.

"Oy, Harry, listen to this—it's from MacEvoy, one of our people at Kitchener's H.Q.! He says, 'and there's a great deal of conversation about a new formation to be raised called the Bush Veldt Carbineers. They say it's already recruiting both officers and men and that it's to be a highly irregular affair working well away from Base. You can imagine the effect it's having on some of the old diehards.' Harry? Did you hear that?"

Harry was leaning forward. "Highly irregular, did he say?"

"That he did! 'Highly irregular' and . . . where is it . . . 'well away from Base'."

Harry's hand slapped onto his knees and he jerked

to his feet, a look of amazement on his face. "My God, someone's woken up at last!" Hunt's groan pulled him around.

"All very well . . . but we're not there, dammit! If only—"

"If only be *damned!* We can soon *be* there, can't we?"

"How? You mean—cancel our leave? Can we?"

Harry stalked forward grinning, and his hand took Hunt's shoulder hard. "Of course we can! Shall we?"

They stared at one another, eyes brightening, the grins spreading. Then Harry was at the door shouting. "Parker! Parker—find me a shipping list, quickly! And get my trunk out! Oh—and Parker—get someone to bring Captain Hunt's horse round at once." He slammed the door in Parker's bewildered face and laughed at the gaping Hunt. "You'd best get home and pack, my son!"

Hunt was tugging on his damp boots, laughing. "We're really going to do it? God, how marvellous!"

Harry pulled him up and began jigging him around the room in a wild polka, the two of them chanting "Highly irregular" till the entire house seemed to shake and they fell gasping against the door and Harry opened it and began shoving Hunt out, urging him to hurry.

Hunt gasped, "Harry, what about Margaret?"

Harry stood stock still, face suddenly sober. "Margaret? Margaret will understand, Geoff."

Below them in the stables, the horses were shifting quietly in their stalls, and there was the hissing crunch of teeth in a feedbox. Up here, in the loft, the cracks and chinks in the roof let in slim shafts of pale sunlight across which dust and wispy ends of hay floated. Margaret's fist pounded at his shoulder.

"No, I *don't* understand! I don't understand it at all, Harry!"

"Darling . . ."

"Keep away!" She wrenched herself around, her back half turned to him. "How can grown men be such fools! Such—such children!" Turning back to him she

161

shook her head in puzzlement. "Harry, you're supposed to love me. We're engaged to be married . . ."

"I *do* love you and you know it!" He held her fast, his fingers gripping her shoulders. "And we *will* be married—"

Struggling against his grip, she panted at him. "And in the meantime you just run off back to your damn war! It's not sense—not fair!"

He managed to reach her cheek with a kiss. "Margaret, please . . . surely you understand it's the chance of a lifetime?"

With a sudden violent move she pulled free, staring at him. "Chance of a lifetime! Oh, you—you schoolboy, you!"

Angered by the scorn in her voice he leaned away from her, letting his voice chill. "You seem to forget I'm still a serving soldier. And there *is* a war going on."

"And you're on leave from it—"

"A leave which I feel it necessary to cancel. As does your brother."

"Then you're both fools!"

"We're both quite old enough to make logical decisions."

"Logical! And I can go to Hell, I suppose?"

"And you can—" Abruptly he leaned towards her again, softening. "You can surely wait for me?" With her silence his anger returned. "Look, I'm not a tame hack that you can hobble to ride just when you feel like it!"

As she swung her head a shaft of light struck fire from her eyes. "Oh, tell the truth, Harry. You're escaping! You're running away—again! You're quite happy to bed me but you're scared to wed me, that's the truth of it, isn't it?"

She stopped on a gasp, suddenly frightened of what she'd said, frightened of his reaction. But his voice was sad and not much above a whisper. "That's not so, Margaret. You know it isn't so."

And she was in his arms and the tears were shaking her as his hand stroked her hair.

"Harry . . . Harry, why do you have to go?"

# SOUTH AFRICA

After the sunlight, the Bush Veldt Carbineers head-quarters was almost dark, a sergeant looming suddenly from behind a table on their right and a dim figure at the end of the room. Harry's hand was halfway to the salute when the figure leapt up and almost ran towards them.

"Hallo, Harry! Welcome to the Bad Boys' Club!"

Lenehan looked older, thinner, greyer, but the smile was as wide and as welcoming and the handshake hard. Harry stared, open-mouthed, finally managing, "Well, I'm damned! Are you the boss?"

"Indeed I am—you're all mine. I've been waiting for you." He half turned. "You must be Hunt?"

"Yes, sir, Geoffrey Hunt. Am I classed as a Bad Boy now?"

"Oh, the old fuddy-duddies seem to think we're all either bad or mad in this show. Come in, come in, find a chair."

Harry slumped, tunic unbuttoned and looked at Lenehan. "Major now, I see. I thought you'd taken your discharge and gone home long since."

"Thought about it. Then they offered me this and I couldn't resist it."

Geoffrey leaned forward. "Caught us the same way, sir. Are we the last?"

"Just about." Lenehan waved at the sergeant. "Potter, go and ask the other officers to step in, will you? And the sar-major, please." He turned back as the sergeant went. "Still a few odds and sods to come, but you're the last of the officers. Actually, the whole blasted show's made up of odds and sods. I think you'll know one or two of them, Harry. Some of 'em are a bit rough . . . but you'll find out for yourselves soon enough." The mutter of voices and clink of spurs could be heard outside and Lenehan forestalled the knock by calling, "Come straight in, you chaps."

Harry was to learn these men intimately in the weeks that followed, but he never forgot his first sight of them, the impression at this first meeting that someone had gone out of his way to collect a job lot of junior officers for a nasty task. . . . George Witton, slight and slim and foxy-faced, with a fuzz of gingery hair and artillery badges; Tom Fletcher, all angles and brown-leather skin, managing to look like a gypsy, even in his N.S.W. Lancer's uniform; the great blacksmith's bulk of Peter Handcock swelling through his Bushman's tunic, tough ropes of hands jutting from the sleeves which still carried the outlines of a farrier-sergeant's chevrons and insignia; Alec Picton, plump and gentle-looking, like a schoolmaster, round-eyed as though astonished to find himself at war; Ivor Summers, a slender reed of a lad, thin fair hair flopping across a red-burnt face above an elegantly-cut Lancer tunic. They clumped into the little, airless room, raising the temperature perceptibly, and draped themselves across the desk and against the walls and cupboards. Geoffrey caught Harry's eye in a look that said, unmistakably, Jesus! What *have* we got into?

The touch on Harry's elbow was light but firm and he turned, feeling a sudden gush of emotion in the throat as Owen Fisher smiled at him—an apparently unchanged Owen, one side of the thin mouth crooked up in a grin, one black eyebrow up above it.

"Owen—by God, Owen! What the hell are you doing here?"

Fisher saluted, but Harry grabbed his hand down and wrung it, unable to stop smiling. Fisher gestured slightly with his head to take in the others, watching with interest and some amusement.

166

"As you see, Harry—sorry, sir. Came along for the fun. Good to see you again."

Harry, with Geoffrey on one side of him and Owen on the other, felt that things couldn't be bad.

Lenehan's briefing was concise and pungent, his finger sweeping across the sketch map pinned to the wall as he showed them their area of operations. Kitchener's plan was well advanced, great sections of countryside cleared of all Boers, crops and farms, even small villages burnt, and the inhabitants moved back into huge camp areas. The commandos had been forced out of this growing belt of devastation, pushed away from the settlements and farms which had sheltered and fed them, which had been their depots and command-posts. And while the massive juggernaut of the armies pounded forward slowly and irresistibly, the Boer troops were moving back and around and away, into the rough country, the higher country, where they were difficult to reach. And, despite reduced numbers and almost non-existent supplies, they were still darting down in fast raids, wreaking havoc on the lines of communication, cutting into the flanks of the main forces, living off British food, firing British ammunition.

The Bush Veldt Carbineers were to fight them at their own game. In quick stabs, Lenehan's finger marked their battleground on the map . . . a waste of dust and rock and scrap vegetation, a tangle of single-beast tracks, a sweep of hills arcing round at both ends to a half-dry river. One far boundary was a spur railway-line, and the main track south cut into it at an angle forming another bound. It looked like tough and hard-working campaigning, and the group of men sucked in their breath and whistled gently as the scope of their area became clear. Lenehan looked sombrely at them.

"Yes, I know, it's bloody enormous, isn't it?"

Tom Fletcher, slumped in a corner like an old brown saddlebag, broke the considering silence. "How many of us will there be, Major?"

"When we're full up, a hundred odd, including us."

Fletcher's voice was dry. "Ah, then they'll give us a week or two to win the war for 'em, I s'pose."

Lenehan overrode the ripple of laughter. "It's not as bad as it sounds. The last intelligence puts the Boer round here mainly," his hand flickered across the sweep of rocky hills, "about four hundred they reckon, but in small groups, scattered. We've got to stop 'em getting together. If we don't—well, we shall be in the shit!"

"What about my guns, sir? When do we get them?" It was George Witton, ginger head bobbing up across the room, and Lenehan hung onto a pause before answering.

"I'm sorry, George—we don't, I'm afraid." He forestalled Witton's objection. "I know you and your fellows came as gunners, but that's not the sort of fight we're likely to get into. Of course, you're free to go back to your regiment as soon as you wish—"

"Good God, no!"

There was a roar of laughter at Witton's indignant squeak and he sank back out of sight, his face scarlet. Harry called across the room, "What about the men, sir?"

"Mixed bag—just like us. They're/going to need a bit of shaping up." He listened to the murmur that rose. "I think we all are, gentlemen." The others stilled at the more formal address, and Lenehan let his voice become a little crisper, pulling them back into the feeling of command. "I intend to work in troop patrols when we get going, but I'm allowing two weeks for us to shake down and get to know one another. Hunt, you're next senior rank, so you're now second-in-command for your sins. We'll manage without an adjutant. The rest of you will be allocated as soon as I can sort it out. Questions?"

Peter Handcock's voice was a heavy rumble. "Horses, sir. What are they like?"

"I don't know, Peter. We haven't got more than a dozen yet. Tell you what—I'll leave The Breaker to find some for us, eh, Harry? Think you can do that?"

Harry kept his face straight. "Shouldn't be surprised, sir."

Owen's lopsided smile was back and Geoffrey noticed the slanted look of appraisal that came up from Fletcher, although he said nothing. It was Handcock, shouldering through the rest who said, "Hey, are you *that* Morant? Well, it's a pleasure to serve with you!" and who wrapped Harry's hand in one of his own enormous ones, shaking it till Harry had to ask him to stop. Under the cover of the general murmur of chatter, Geoffrey whispered to Harry, "Didn't realize you were famous, old boy. I shall have to mind my manners." Harry hissed back at him, "You'd better mind your flapping tongue, *Captain* Hunt, sir, or I'll clip it for you. As soon as my hand heals . . ." and he looked down ruefully at his fingers, reddening again as the blood came back into them.

Lenehan had been right. The men did need shaping up and the ten days that followed that first meeting were a continual grind. Fisher, squadron sergeant-major, never seemed to raise his voice, but its flat rasp was there all day, barbed and prodding, as he put the troops through basic drills time and time again, shaking them back into routines they thought happily forgotten, pushing them to the point of exhaustion, stripping what little fat there was away from them and drawing fast responses and unhesitating movements. They split the duties, each of the officers taking a spell at the drilling, as much for their own needs as for the men, but each of them also spending time on their special skills. So Peter Handcock took over the horses as they came in, setting up a little smithy and ending his days black and reeking, his huge body browning to an oak colour and his hair bleaching paler and paler. George Witton, deprived of his guns, scrounged a couple of discarded limbers and a collection of broken and rusted parts and, with a couple of his gunners, more or less invented a Maxim and a Hotchkiss. Alec Picton made their maps, riding hundreds of miles with a couple of men who'd run chains for Government surveys, borrowing instruments, stealing paper and spending long evenings turning out probably the only detailed maps of that part of the world. The wispy Ivor

Summers asked for and got permission from Lenehan to use the six Lancers he'd brought with him as a reconnaissance troop, disappearing with them for three and four days at a time and coming back with his men exhausted and himself seemingly dustproof, heatproof and immune from thirst and hunger, to give Lenehan information about Boer detachments in the sort of detail which meant he must have been within touching distance of them. Harry, with Tom Fletcher, rode out every morning and came back every evening with horses. Neither man would say where they came from, although Fletcher usually muttered, "Ah, we found 'em strayin' out in the bush," and grinned . . . but Handcock and his assistants spent a fair part of their time running out new brands.

Geoffrey Hunt got to know the track from the B.V.C. area to Field H.Q. intimately. Once the morning routine was over, he'd jam a saddlebag with that day's pile of requests, indents and reports and ride out, spending his days chasing equipment, ammunition, weapons, rations, and vainly trying to speed the movement of their action orders. After ten days he threw himself down on his camp-bed one night, his normally good-natured face screwed up in disgust. Harry, propped on an elbow in the other bed and reading a month-old newspaper, grinned across at him.

"You look like a sulky kid who's been kept in after school."

"Oh, shut up, for Christ's sake!"

Harry's eyebrows shot up and he pretended to cower. "Oh, please, Captain Hunt, sir, please don't hit me! I'm sorry if I offended your Hussarship!"

For a long moment it looked as though Geoffrey was going to hit him, then the scowl gave way to a rueful laugh. "Sorry, Harry. It's just that I really didn't come back to act as a dogsbody messenger-boy, you know. God, I think I'd sooner be at one of old Mrs. Darby's dinner parties. At least there'd be some decent food!"

"Ah-hah!" Harry swung himself upright. "Now we have the truth of it! Gallant Hussar misses action!

170

Under pressure, Captain Hunt admits he'd rather be feeling knees under dinner-table than carrying out necessary wartime tasks!" The pillow caught him full across the face before he could duck.

Later, lying half-asleep in the dark, Harry spoke quietly. "Geoff, you're not sorry, are you? About coming back?"

"No. Wouldn't be anywhere else for quids. You?"

"No. Except for Margaret."

The name hung in the still dark and Harry felt the quiver in his body as he thought of her, thought of her willingness and warmth, and rolled savagely onto his side, trying to force himself into sleep.

By the end of the second week, the Volunteers looked a much more workmanlike body of men. Differences in uniform had been simply overcome—everyone, officers and men alike, wore plain khaki tunics and breeches, and rank badges were the simplest cloth ones. No one wore shiny brass or pipeclay and the only distinguishing feature about them as a unit was the strip of green cloth each man wore as a puggaree around his bush hat. Rifles and pistols were standard issue and most of the men carried either bayonets or long knives as well, while George Witton's two little guns travelled lashed to either side of a home-made limber which could, if necessary, be handled over rough ground by two or three men. Watching them ride out just after dawn one morning on a field exercise, Lenehan noticed how quiet they were, how well they sat the fair horses they rode, how few orders were given beyond simple hand movements, and he was satisfied. He turned to Hunt. "Geoffrey, I'm coming with you today. We will, by God, beard the general in his unsavoury lair and bloody well force him to give us some work to do. Come on!"

Riding easily at the head of Geoffrey's troop, Harry saw Lenehan and Hunt move out along the track to Field H.Q. and silently wished them luck. He knew the men were sick to death of drills and exercises, just as he knew they needed some action as a unit to pull

171

them really tight. He wondered how his own men would work together, wondered about the trouble-makers, wondered whether he'd done the right thing.

Earlier that week he'd sat half-slumped in the saddle watching Owen Fisher put the troop through their paces. The two files of fifteen men had halted their horses and were sitting at attention, but from where he sat, Harry could see that three of the troopers in the rear file were muttering to one another, their horses jibbing a little out of line. The end man had already been before Harry twice during days of duty as orderly officer—Booth, a dark-faced and surly man from London with a record as a trouble-maker. When Harry had once asked him why he'd re-enlisted, Booth smiled unpleasantly and answered, "Chance to make some money, sir." The tone had made it plain he had loot in mind. Now, as Harry started to edge his horse forward, Fisher's voice snapped out.

"Booth! When I want two of us talking at once I'll let you know!"

Harry, closer than Fisher, heard the low-voiced snarl in reply. "Bloody nice of you, mate!"

Fisher wheeled his horse as Harry rode up, and saluted. "Troop present and correct, sir."

"Thank you, Sar-Major." He dropped his voice as he answered the salute.

"I wouldn't say Booth's all that correct, Owen, would you?"

"Bloody nuisance, that man, Harry. Needs a bit of action to work it out of his system."

"Well, we all need that."

"True enough. Just the same, I'd be happier with Booth somewhere else, I think. Trouble-maker, he is."

"Good soldier, though? In a scrap, I mean?"

Fisher considered. "Yair. I reckon he could look after himself."

"Well, we might be able to make use of him then, mightn't we?"

Harry reined his horse back a little and swung to face the troop, pitching his voice up a little. "All right, you blokes, sit easy. Well, it looks as though we might

172

get off this damned square before long and start tackling the Boer again." He sensed the stir and gave it a moment to settle. "You can take it that this is probably close to the end of training. You can start thinking about some real work."

There were a few grins among the listening men. "I'm going to assume that we'll be on the track tomorrow, so we'll stand down now and take it slack for the rest of the day." The grins widened and there was a mutter of appreciation. "All right, properly at ease now. Fall them out, Sar-Major."

As soon as Owen had dismissed the men, Harry muttered to him, "Tell Booth I want to see him now; behind the supply shed."

Fisher's face was immobile, but his eyes were smiling as he nodded.

Harry heard the man coming and set himself. As Booth rounded the corner of the shed on the edge of their area, Harry's hands shot out, locking hard into the front of Booth's tunic, forcing his chin up and back, and Harry pivoted, slamming him flatbacked against the shed wall so that the breath burst out of him in a great gasp. He held the man there, almost on tiptoe, face purpling and hands plucking uselessly at Harry's wrists, while he spoke to him, quietly and conversationally.

"Trooper Thomas Booth, slum-boy and troublemaker, right? Right?" He slammed him against the shed again till Booth nodded tightly. "Well, Trooper Thomas Booth, you're making a nuisance of yourself, you and your nasty friends. You're not behaving yourself, lad, not the way I want you to behave, and I'm going to have to teach you a lesson, eh?" He threw Booth contemptuously from him and watched as the man controlled his breathing and straightened his tunic, his stare at Harry malevolent.

Still panting a little, Booth spat out, "That's contrary to the Articles, that is, *Mister* Morant! You struck me—you could be locked up for that!"

"Indeed I could—if you could prove it, Booth. But there aren't any witnesses, you see—just you and me.

173

Now then, you're a strong lad and you've got all sorts of ideas of your own. Here's your chance to try them out. Come on, let's see just how good you are."

For a moment Booth tensed, fists clenching, setting himself for a spring. Then he relaxed. "Oh no, oh no, you don't! You'll not get Tommy Booth on striking a superior officer! Not on your life, cully!"

Harry smiled coldly. "Good! Bears out what I thought—you've got a brain in your head. Now let's see if you can start using it. You've got a year's service, Booth. You ride well and apart from your disgusting bad manners, you make quite a respectable soldier. But you've got to learn who's the boss, Booth. Understand?" Booth stared back at him, trying to hold his gaze, then nodded. Harry bore straight in.

"The answer is 'Yes, sir.' "

"Yes. Sir."

"Ah, now we're getting along famously. We shall be friends yet, you and I. And just to show you how friendly I can be, I'm going to make you up to corporal." He watched the wash of amazement on the man's face and smiled grimly. "I'm going to give you some responsibility. Make you give a few orders. You'll like that, won't you, Corporal Booth?"

The other man was silent, mouth open, eyes blinking. "Lost your tongue, man? Never mind. I don't want to be thanked. Just you take care, though, and behave yourself. You've got something to lose now, you see." His voice suddenly snapped. "Straighten yourself up!"

Booth pulled himself together, composing his face but unable to hide the suspicion in his eyes. Harry held down a grin. "Good. Now, just to show there's no ill-feeling, let's shake hands on it, shall we?"

He stretched his hand and Booth instinctively met it. Harry slid his grip along, moving into the hollow where Booth's thumb ended and across the little joints at the back of the hand, locking his own fingers in and down, hard and steadily, seeing Booth's eyes go wide, then fill with tears of pain, his face twisting. Harry was expressionless and he kept his voice low and friendly.

"I'm sure you'll remember who's in charge here, won't you, Corporal?"

Dropping his hand, he turned on his heel and was gone.

Now, glancing back, he could see Booth with Dawes and Rattray, his two cronies, riding together. There'd been no further overt trouble from any of them but Harry sensed the hatred in Booth whenever they were near and again he wondered whether he wouldn't have done better to get rid of him. Shrugging the thought away, he wheeled off the track, gesturing the troop to follow him.

Dinner had been over an hour ago and the little Mess hut was thick with tobacco-smoke, hanging in blue swirls in the still heat of the night. Harry was resting on his shoulder-blades in the wreck of an easy chair someone had salvaged, idly watching Peter Handcock hunched over a letter, the pen almost invisible in his massive fingers. Witton and Summers were bickering quietly across a chessboard and the others were trying to find something new to read in the pile of ancient newspapers and journals. All heads raised and swung as they heard the horses canter in. When Lenehan and Hunt came through the door, everyone was up and surrounding them at once, Witton gesturing to the orderly for two whisky-sodas. The latecomers were dusty and obviously tired and Lenehan shoved his officers aside impatiently, slumping into Harry's chair and taking the drink from the orderly.

"For God's sake, chaps, let's get our breath! Thanks George—cheers everyone!" He gulped the drink down. "All around, please, orderly."

Harry caught Geoffrey's eye and felt a surge of relief at the beaming smile and the wink that went with it. He leaned in towards Lenehan.

"Well, sir, what's the word?"

Lenehan let the others fall silent while he sipped at his second drink. Then, "We're off!"

There was an immediate hubbub, Handcock capering round with little Alec Picton till the room shook.

The orderly darted out to spread the word and ran back in a moment later with two fresh bottles. Lenehan rose and crossed to a table, hitching himself onto it and yelling at them to calm down. In the comparative quiet he said, "Look, this isn't a bloody picnic outing we're going on, you know—"

Summers' boyish voice crossed his. "Well, we—we have rather been waiting, sir."

"Well, the waiting's over. We've been cleared by H.Q. and Geoffrey has the orders here . . ." he stretched out his hand for the bundle of papers and rustled through them to find what he wanted . . . "orders to 'engage in actions against the enemy by means of vigorous and offensive patrolling'."

It was half a minute before Geoffrey, balancing on a rickety chair, could lift his voice above the noise. "We did try to find out what that meant exactly, but there wasn't a manjack there prepared to commit himself!"

Witton called out, "Good enough. Leaves us a pretty free hand, don't it?"

"Sir! Sir, did you see K himself?" Ivor Summers sounded more than ever like an excited schoolboy.

Geoffrey answered, "Kitchener? Oh, we *saw* him all right—at a very considerable distance. He's got a flock of aides and secretaries ten deep to keep common soldiers like us away from him!"

"But he did sign the orders?"

Lenehan took up Harry's question. "He did. Or to be strictly accurate, somebody signed them for him. And as George suggests, we've got a pretty free hand, the way I see it. So, we start tomorrow. Two patrols." There was an immediate silence as he looked round. "One's mine with George as 2 i/c and Geoffrey will take the other out with Harry." He frowned down the swell of complaints from the others. "You'll all get your turns, never fear. We shall all be out inside a week." Not letting anyone interrupt, he went straight on, "There's one other thing. No prisoners." The silence was intense and he spoke quietly into it. "That's

176

what we were told at H.Q.—no prisoners will be taken."

Again it was Summers who spoke. "They can't be serious! That's unheard of!"

Tom Fletcher, businesslike as always, asked, "Did they put that in the orders, sir?"

"Not in the written orders, no. But we were told, Geoffrey and I, that Kitchener wants it made plain. Anyone under arms or sheltering an armed man is to be shot at once."

"To Hell with that!" Harry's voice was tight with rage. "Sorry, sir, but—"

"That's all right, Harry, I quite agree. If they shoot, then we shoot them. Otherwise, we take prisoners—on my authority. We might be irregular but that doesn't make us bloody barbarians." There was a slackening of tension. "Now then, what about a stirrup-cup?"

In the first light of the next morning, Geoffrey, leading his patrol, turned to Harry and said, "There's something to be said for it you know—this no prisoners thing."

"You're never serious! You mean just shoot 'em?"

"Yes. Why not?"

Hunt's voice was quite flat and Harry stared at him in surprise.

"Is this the Gentle Geoffrey, Meek and Mild? Ravening round the countryside like a murdering Mongol?"

Hunt stared back at him levelly. "I'm serious, Harry. Remember how often we've talked about fighting them on their own terms? I think that's just about what I meant. They don't hesitate to shoot our wounded. By God, you've seen it happen! Why should we hold back?"

"You couldn't do it, Geoff. None of us could."

"Depend on the circumstances, wouldn't it?" He half smiled. "Perhaps that's the difference between us professionals and you toy soldiers."

"Hmm. I'll remember that the next time I see you handing over your bullybeef to some hairy old Boer brigand."

The soft thump of hooves came from wide on the flank and they reined in, waiting for the scout to reach them. He swung alongside in a cloud of dust, the grey beginning to turn gold in the light of the new sun. "Farm just across that little rise, sir. Small place—don't look much."

Geoffrey checked his map and nodded. "Right, thank you. Back you go." As the scout cantered away, Hunt turned. "Harry, take your half and circle round to the south there, will you? I'll give you a couple of minutes to position then I'll come in on this track. We should be there just about nicely together."

Harry saluted solemnly and, just as solemnly, asked, "Do we take prisoners, sir?"

Hunt smiled widely. "Only the young and pretty ones."

Harry, wheeling his half-troop away, was smiling too . . . but the thought was there that old Geoffrey was a harder customer than he looked. Harry wondered whether he himself was as hard as he thought.

Harry led his half-troop through a thin screen of scrubby trees to one side of the farmhouse as Geoffrey's half swung through the gate on the track. An old Boer came out onto the stoep, watching silently as the troops moved in. Owen Fisher, riding with Geoffrey that day, fanned his hand outwards and four men took post wide beyond the fence corners. The rest of them dismounted and led their horses into a patch of shade, then spread out quickly. Geoffrey, Harry and Fisher sat their horses, waiting till the quick inspection was over, then swung down. Fisher beckoned two troopers to follow them as they moved towards the stoep. The old man there snatched off his hat, jerking his head in a kind of bow.

"Good day, mynheeren. Will you come inside?"

He gestured at the open door, bobbing his head. Geoffrey and Harry, hands on pistol-butts, stopped outside the door and Fisher led the two troopers inside, rifles ready. Geoffrey and Harry followed them in.

It was cool and dim in there, a wide square kitchen with a low fire muttering in the stove, the huge chimney sucking the heat away. An old woman stood grimly to one side, a younger woman by her and two children half-hidden behind them. It was silent except for the heavy ticking of an old clock on the overmantel. The troopers slid to either side of the door, covering the room. Geoffrey sketched a perfunctory salute to the women and the old man stepped towards him.

"There is nothing here for soldiers, mynheer."

Ignoring him, Geoffrey nodded to Fisher who pushed through the door across the room and began a rough search. The old man started after him, then swung back. "Why do you search my house like this? For what do you search?"

Geoffrey's smile was cold. "You don't' know, of course."

"I am a farmer." He spread his hands and hunched his shoulders. "How should I know the ways of soldiers?"

"Well, Mynheer Boer, the ways of soldiers are these —to search for guns, for ammunition, for hidden fighters, for supplies. But you know of none of those things, of course."

"I have said I am a farmer only. I know nothing of these other things."

"Then I may just shoot you for *not* knowing." The old man stepped back hastily and the women gasped. Harry looked in astonishment at his friend. He had spoken flatly and without a trace of emotion and Harry felt he meant what he had said. He pursed his lips in a noiseless whistle. This was the "professional soldier" with a vengeance.

Owen Fisher came back into the room, slipping his pistol into its holster and shaking his head minutely. Geoffrey strolled about the dim room, lifting and dropping the lid of a storage bin, flicking open a cupboard door, the children's eyes, enormous, following him as he went. He stopped at the overmantel, tapping his pistol muzzle against the bobbled fringe, staring at the family photograph there, the people in the room posed in a formal group with three young men. He lifted the picture down and looked at it, speaking with his back to the room.

"There are no young men on your farm. Have you no sons?"

The old man barely hid his smile. "Oh, ja, I have three fine sons, mynheer. See, there in the picture."

Geoffrey turned, also smiling faintly and handed the picture to Harry who put it back on the mantel. Geoffrey walked close to the old man.

"Where are they, these three fine sons?"

"Oh, Petrus, the oldest—the father of these little ones here—Petrus is in Pietersburg. He sells two oxen and buys a horse. In the place of those your soldiers have taken from us."

"And the others?"

"Josef and Nicolas are working for a friend of mine on the other side of the valley. Just for a few weeks."

Hunt nodded in apparent understanding. "Of course." He strolled to a corner where a gun-rack stood empty. "No sons here. No horses. And no guns?" And he turned again to the old man.

"These also the soldiers have taken."

"Which soldiers, old man—ours or yours?"

The old man made no answer and Hunt flicked an eyebrow at Harry and Owen as he moved to the doorway. "I shall want water for my men."

"Of course, mynheer, of course. There is a barrel of fresh water just outside here."

He darted forward, obviously glad to get them out of his house and Geoffrey followed him. Harry, seeing Owen Fisher move back into the room, paused to watch. Fisher walked to the younger woman and gently shifted her to one side so that he could see the children . . . a girl of perhaps five and a boy a year or two older. Digging into a tunic pocket, Fisher brought out a slab of thick toffee and held it out to them, seeing the eyes grow big and round, staring first at the toffee then up at their mother. The mother's hands went around the children's shoulders, pulling them close and Fisher straightened, shrugging. He put the toffee on the table by the children and made for the door. Harry saw the little girl's hand sneaking out, but the mother's hand was there first and she snatched up the sticky sweetmeat, tossing it into the stove. She spat after Fisher and Harry, face wrinkling in disgust, turned away outside.

The old man was at a big water-butt by the end of the stoep, its lid partly aside, baling water out into a couple of tin jugs. Two of the troopers were filling canteens from the jugs as Harry mounted, and he unlooped his canteen and passed it down, walking his horse alongside Geoffrey's as they waited. He leaned closer.

"Geoff, I believe you *would* have shot that old bloke."

Hunt didn't turn his head and his voice was calm. "Yes. If he'd given me the slightest reason, I think I would."

Wondering about it, Harry watched the watering, and a sudden sharp look on the Boer's face caught his attention. It was almost a smile, just for a second, almost a smile of . . . what? Triumph? He watched closely, accepting his own dripping canteen back without shifting his gaze. He uncapped the canteen and lifted it to his mouth, seeing the sudden dart of the old man's eyes, then he kneed his horse gently forward and leaned down, holding out the canteen.

"Here, drink some, old man."

The Boer looked up, not moving, and spoke politely. "Thank you mynheer. I am not thirsty."

"Not for thirst. For a toast—to your three fine sons."

Geoffrey had stepped his horse closer and the men had stopped to watch, sensing something happening. The Boer still made no move and Harry straightened, calling.

"Sergeant-Major Fisher!" Owen shouldered through the men. "Give this old man a drink." He handed the canteen to Fisher and drew his pistol, cocking it deliberately. Fisher held the canteen to the old Boer's face.

"Here y'are, Grandad, take a swig of this."

The Boer jerked his head away, staring up at Harry. "Mynheer, I do not wish to drink, believe me!"

Harry said, "Old man, I believe you. Drink!" And he lowered the pistol's muzzle till it was centred on the

Boer's forehead. The man snatched at the canteen and made some pretence at drinking, his eyes locked on the pistol. Then he threw it aside and tried to run, a dozen hands on him at once. Harry looked down at him.

"Give him a drink. A good stiff one."

Harry grinned a little at Geoffrey's inquiring glance above the struggling men but said nothing, watching as they held the Boer still and forced the neck of the canteen between his lips, pinching his nostrils closed so that he had to open his mouth. He swallowed, and again, then gagged and retched and, as the men let him go, dropped to his knees vomiting.

Harry holstered his pistol. "Tip that water-barrel over, some of you men."

A couple of the troopers got their shoulders to the butt and rocked it till it swung off its blocks onto its side, the staves and hoops cracking apart and the water dashing out to disappear almost at once in the dust. A deep growl came from the watching men as they saw the mass of filth in the wrecked barrel . . . a well-decomposed bird of some kind, and what was obviously the contents of the farm's sanitary bucket. On the stoep, the man's family had watched the scene and now the old woman ran forward to her husband, clutching at him protectively. Geoffrey's face was white with revulsion. Harry said, "I imagine the well will be clean, Geoff," and was answered only by a nod. Then Geoffrey looked round.

"Right. Corporal, take four men, empty every canteen and refill them at the well. Sergeant-Major, we'll have that ox butchered right away please. Send someone into the house for some cloth to wrap the beef in. And I want the poultry collected."

As Fisher saluted and the men began to move, Harry caught Geoffrey's sleeve. Geoffrey turned to him, unsmiling.

"Don't worry Harry, I'm not going to shoot them, though God knows I should! But I *am* going to teach them a lesson." He called, "Corporal Booth, I want all the rest of the livestock, no matter what—get everything over by that well. When the canteens are full, kill the stock."

Booth grinned. "Yes, sir. Kill the stock it is, sir."

"Oh, and Booth—the dogs too."

"Kill 'em? The dogs, sir?"

"Everything. And cut the guts open. Then throw the bodies into the well."

He jerked his horse around and rode to the gate, his back turned to the farm.

Booth muttered to Dawes and Rattray, "Fancy shooting the dogs, eh? I'll lay you that was Bloody Breaker Morant's lousy idea."

Now that they were close the sound had lost its ghostliness. From back there, back in the flat dark out of which they'd ridden, the sound had come catlike, a thin and inhuman skirl in the blackness, snapped into unequal lengths by the skittishness of the night wind. They hadn't seen the light till they moved through the trees, and right to that moment there wasn't a man among them could have said from which spike of the compass the sound was coming. The dim and yellow light tied it down for them and Harry urged his horse forward a little faster, glad that he knew where he was heading.

Moving cautiously down the loose scree slope into the shallow valley, Harry knew he and his men were very tired, just as he knew that they were never careless any more. There were fewer of them now, the flame-stabs in past nights had thinned them a little, but they were sinew-taut. They rode without talking, falling easily into the night-patrol formation, wide of one another, no two men in file, no man completely out of sight, no points or flanks to be picked off by a silent knife or a thin rope.

Plump little Alec Picton had gone that way, relieving one of his men out on a flank and stumbled over half an hour later, stripped to the drawers, his head grotesquely sideways on his pudgy neck and the rawhide buried in the cut flesh. Patterson, a quiet trooper from Auckland had gone unquietly, bubbling a pink froth into the night, his voice full of aerated lung-blood as he gasped how a Boer had been riding alongside him. Whatever their past experience had been, they'd all learned something these past hard weeks, they'd all seen things that held them quiet. In the sudden and un-expected fight at Van Maal's Post, when the place erupted nearly fifty Boers, Ivor Summers had been dismounted, had lost his carbine, had emptied his pistol and with his back against a corner-post in the angle of a fence, had fought five men with a rake, whipping his slender body about like a demented swordsman, his shoulder bleeding from a bullet graze. And when Harry had cantered up and burst into the Boers, blowing one man's head apart, Ivor had cursed him for getting brains and blood all over a good tunic. Peter Handcock had gone silently berserk in that fight, picking up a Boer and using him like a flail, walking in among the thick of them and swinging the broken corpse as though he was beating a carpet, his face deathly still and a frown of concentration pulling his brows down. When it was over he remembered none of it and cried when they told him. Tom Fletcher, leathery and sardonic, had taken to riding with a stockwhip looped over his shoulder, and Harry had seen him ride into the direct fire of a group of Boers, the metal tips of the lash cutting wickedly till the Boers broke and ran, yelping and demoralized. And Harry had seen Geoffrey in action, unruffled, deliberate and unhesitating, as often as not with an unlit cheroot jutting from the corner of his lips and a cold mercilessness keeping him firing at the enemy as long as there was a movement to fire at.

As the half-troop crossed the narrow floor of the al-most-flat valley, the light ahead of them brightened and the building stood out a fraction darker against the dark sky. The singing had stopped a couple of minutes earlier but now started again, the solid cadence of the hymn ringing out, nothing ghostly about it now. "A Sure Stronghold is My God," they sang . . . forty or so of them, Harry thought, as he peered through the window of the simple wooden church; praising their God and not a fit man among the lot of them.

Harry's sergeant, Parker, had moved the men around fast and silently in an arc twenty feet wide of the church and was waiting for Harry at the door. Grinning without humour, Harry waited till the "Amen" was fading, then slammed the door back and stepped inside, the shuffle of feet and a wild squeak from the harmonium the only sounds for the moment. It was a narrow-shouldered building, unadorned and shabby, the uncomfortable rough-hewn pews leading down to a small platform—a lectern, a plain table with a massive old Bible on it, and the harmonium. Behind the lectern, the Predikant stared at them for a long breath, then ignored them, coughing out the harsh gutturals of the Taal as he began his sermon. The congregation at once turned to him. The soldiers might just as well not have existed. Harry gestured, and Parker and a couple of troopers moved down the sides of the church, one of the men snatching his hat off with an embarrassed look at Harry, standing still in the doorway, pistol in his hand, his eyes on the dyed hessian curtain behind the Predikant.

On the other side of the curtain, the children had frozen at the first alien sounds. The hessian covered the door leading to the small room at the end of the church, a storeroom of sorts, with a couple of broken pews in it and some empty boxes. There were five children. Two boys, perhaps twelve, were in the pit in the ground, the wooden flap held up by an older girl. Another girl stood near the door and the third boy, not more than ten, was motionless just outside the door, hand clamped hard over the muzzle of the donkey there, harnessed into the shafts of a flat cart. He was the only one who could see outside, the only one who could see the mounted soldier walking his horse along the fence, head turning, carbine ready. The second soldier swung dimly into sight and the boy heard him call, not knowing he was hearing Corporal Booth.

"Well, you goin'ta be all bloody night, Mick?"

The first rider turned back. "Nothing here, Corp. They're all in there."

"Aagh, we oughta put a match to the place. Get rid

185

of a double lot of trouble in one go—bleedin' Boers and Bible-bashers all in one. Come on!"

The boy waited till they went, then hissed into the storeroom. At once the other children began to move, the boys in the pit passing up the rifles and the bandoliers, the girls passing them out, the other boy sliding them soundlessly into the bed of the cart and pulling old sacks over them. Beyond the door and the curtain they could hear the rumble of the Predikant's voice.

The voice didn't falter as Harry walked down the narrow aisle, but the passionate hands became knuckled fists. Skirting the lectern, Harry stepped up onto the platform behind the preacher and flicked the hessian aside, seeing the door there, nailed up, trying it and finding it fast. He waved to Parker, signing him to get outside and check the other side.

The children heard the rattling of the door and hurriedly passed out the last two rifles, dropping the lid on the pit and edging a box over it. Four of them slipped noiselessly away along the fence-side of the church, and the fifth one, the boy, hand again over the donkey's muzzle, began to lead the animal away, the cart's wheels nearly silent in their axle-beds of grease.

As Harry reached the door of the church again, the sermon ended and the harmonium gasped and sucked in air and belched a sour chord. The first notes of the hymn came with the shots and the singing stopped abruptly. Glaring back at the Predikant, Harry saw him gesturing fiercely and the music rose round him again as he ran outside.

Two shots, then another, and some shouting and the pounding of hooves and the mad bray of a donkey. Harry stood still by his horse, waiting, and they brought the wagon to him, Booth leading the donkey, two other men carrying Parker. In the yellow flare from the window Harry could see Parker's chest dark with the gush of blood and knew he'd lost a good sergeant. Booth gestured with a thumb.

"In the wagon, Mr. Morant. It's only a bloody kid. He shot the sarge."

Harry stepped close and looked down. "Oh, Christ!"

The boy was slim and weighed very little as Harry cradled him, the torn throat still pumping blood which he could feel seeping through to his skin. He walked back to the church, the gape-mouthed head lolling against his shoulder and walked again down the aisle. The singing didn't falter and the Predikant's eyes were fixed on a point above Harry as he sang. Down the aisle and to the front and turn and hold the little body out to the people. The singing went on, seeming to rise louder, and though there were tears on the faces, the mouths kept opening and closing and the singing went on as Harry dropped the boy's body on the table and ran from that terrible church.

As they rode away, Parker's body in the cart on the Boer rifles, the singing was still there, swelling into the night.

It was the morning after the next before he had a chance to write to Parker's wife, sitting on an ammunition box outside the tent he shared with Geoffrey. Beyond them the men of their troop were relaxing, knowing there was something planned for that night. Geoffrey, back propped against a saddle, watched Harry seal the letter and put it to one side with a small canvas bag of Parker's personal belongings. He tossed away the end of the cheroot.

"That's a job I hate more every time."

"Writing to the next-of-kin? Yes, I know how you feel . . . never really know what to say to them."

"Who was that—Parker?"

"Mmm. Only been married six months, I believe."

"Dear Widow Parker, I regret to inform you your husband was shot by a Boer boy aged eleven who was killed in our counter-attack. God!" He turned his head away and they sat unspeaking till they heard the sounds of horses coming into the bivouac and stood up, stretching and slapping dust. Hunt said, "That'll be Peter with Owen Fisher and the rest of the men for tonight. We might as well let them all know about it now, I suppose."

Looking across the sprawling ring of men, Owen

Fisher thought again what a well-matched pair Hunt and Morant were for this kind of work. Between them they showed everything that was needed—Harry's dash and fire, Hunt's cold calculation and the undoubted boldness of them both. The night was likely to be a hard one and he was glad enough to have these two men to lead them. They were crouched together now on the far side of the ring, comparing their maps, Harry looking chunkier than he was against the slim height of Hunt, elegant as always, as plainly dressed as the rest of them but in khaki cut specially for him, the breeches neatly patched in many places but worn in preference to Army issue. Now Hunt stepped forward.

"Right, pay attention. We're going after the Dutchman in some style tonight. The word is that there's a clutch of them concentrating at De Koven's. We don't know how many but we'll assume a fair crowd. And there's another lot meeting at Klinger's, across the ridge from De Koven's. I think you all know the ground there well enough, but Mr. Morant has maps for you to look at later. You'll notice that the major has sent Mr. Handcock along with an extra half-troop and the sergeant-major and we're going to go for both places at once." He let the murmur rise while he lit a cheroot, then quieted them and went on, scratching a diagram in the dust with a stick. "Now then, the farms are about a mile and a half apart, but there's the ridge and a dry gully between them. I shall take my troop and Mr. Fisher's people to De Koven's and the rest of you will hit Klinger's with Mr. Morant. Questions?"

One of the men called, "What about Mr. Witton's lot, sir? They coming with the pompom?"

"No; we thought about it but I think they'd be more trouble than enough on that ridge. And if we get close enough in they'd be a danger to us anyway."

"Hot meal before we go, sir?"

"Yes; and eat up well, lads. It'll probably be a long night." He caught Owen's eye. "Yes, Mr. Fisher?"

"I brought up some—er—medical supplies sir. The major's compliments."

Geoffrey grinned. "If that means what I think it means, there'll be a rum issue when we stand-to. No rum in the canteens, please, you N.C.O.'s."

The lounging men stood as Geoffrey and Harry moved away to where Peter was checking the horses.

The last red sunlight was smeared across the edge of the sky when the rum went round to the men standing by their horses' heads along the track. Corporal Booth, sucking the thick liquor through his teeth, scowled at the two men in his file. "Stupid bastards! Why can't they leave well enough alone? Another night chasing the fucking Dutchy!"

Rattray pushed his nose down into the tin mug, inhaling the rum fumes. "If we left 'em alone they'd be down on us before we knew what was what."

"Get out of it. Them Boers are buggered, mate! We been runnin' 'em ragged. They couldn't damage a girls' school!"

Dawes, his ferret-face twitching, broke in. "I could —by God, I could!"

Booth sneered at him. "Oh, you're always crutch-hungry, you are, Sid! Anyway, that's something else we won't get tonight."

Rattray finally gulped down his rum and licked his lips. "Ah, there's always a flopsie around the Boers, Tom, y'know that. They do the cookin', among other things."

Dawes snapped out a thin laugh. "Gawd, y'not fussy, are ya? Them old crows, they're all made of leather."

The corporal spat into the dust by his boot. "Aside from which, Mr. Captain Bloody Hunt and Mr. Lieutenant Bloody Morant wouldn't like it!" He spat again. "I tell you, this coulda been a very handsome few months, this could, if it hadn't been for them toffee-noses." He screwed up his face and affected a drawl. "No lootin', chaps, an' hands off the gentlewomen! Christ!"

The word came down the line to mount, and they

swung up into their saddles. Rattray settled himself and leaned closer to Booth. "Well, one thing, Tom—you'll not catch me chasin' after a bullet tonight. Me for a nice thick rock."

"Yeah, well leave room for me, mate. And Sid."

At the head of the column, Harry and Geoffrey were comparing their watches.

"All clear then, Harry? One hour to get into position. No noise, no action till you hear my three signal shots."

"Right you are. Just don't keep us hanging around all night. Ready, Peter?"

Handcock nodded and Hunt raised his hand. Quietly the file of horsemen moved out of the bivouac area, separating almost at once into their two columns.

The moon was still low and only in its first half, but it was a clear night and there was starshine and the shadows were black enough for the ground ahead of them to be visible in relief: a slope, dropping about thirty feet in the hundred down to the fence. Beyond that Klinger's farm humped black and solid. No lights, no movement, but the slim breeze lifting towards them from down there carried the smell of woodsmoke to where Harry lay with Peter Handcock. Harry held his watch close to his face, then leaned sideways to whisper in Handcock's ear.

"Ten minutes yet, Peter, but you'd best get along to your blokes now and start working down. I'm going to move down now with my people. I want to get in the lee of that barn before the party starts. Give it another couple of minutes and then bring your lot down to the fence-line."

He felt, rather than saw, Peter's nod as he elbowed himself back to where his half-troop was waiting, and he checked them quickly before beginning to work transversely down the slope, heading for a clump of trees which would screen their passage to the barn.

They were still twenty yards from the trees when the single shot came.

\* \* \*

Across the ridge and the gully, Geoffrey Hunt had positioned his men quickly for the closing move on De Koven's farm. It was a more awkward attack approach than Harry's, since the farm buildings were placed in a rough square with a yard in the centre, and the gully took a sharp swing alongside the main building, running away behind it and giving excellent cover for anyone needing to get out fast. Owen Fisher had held his watch up to show Geoffrey there was a little more than ten minutes left and Geoffrey nodded, deliberately relaxing.

Ten yards back and to the left, Booth, Rattray and Dawes had found their rock, a solid shoulder jutting out of the slope, and they were stretched behind it, Booth and Rattray still and silent, Dawes fidgeting and jumpy.

"How long d'you reckon, Tom?"

Booth pulled away. Dawes' mouth was close to his face and his breath was rancid. "I don't know. Too bloody soon I expect. Shut up and keep still."

Dawes wriggled away a foot or two, edging his head around the base of the rock and trying to see ahead. His fingers played nervously with the safety of his cocked rifle and, as he half knelt for a view, the rifle slipped from his sweaty hand and toppled a yard down the rock slope. The safety was off and the shot sounded as loud as the last trump.

Geoffrey whipped round, squinting into the dark, aware of the noise in the farmhouse ahead and below, aware of a dart of light as a door opened and shut, of shouting. He heard Owen call, "What bloody fool did that?" and he shouted himself, "All right Sergeant-Major, let 'em rip!" He aimed his pistol into the sky and fired three rapid shots as his men began to slip and rattle past him, the stabs of their fire cutting through the darkness.

Harry had frozen at the sound of the first shot, trying to determine where it had come from, hearing nothing for a long breath, then the three shots together.

"Christ, they're early!" He stood up, calling, "Move in, Peter—move in now. Open fire!"

The fight at Klinger's was half over almost as soon as it began. Within seconds of Harry's call, the two men sent down into the farmyard had put a match to the pile of hay alongside the barn, and the dry stuff went up like a giant torch lighting the whole area. The dozen or so men tumbling out of the house were easy targets. Three of them went down at once, another staggered and was grabbed by two of his friends. Only one got away into the night and the rest bolted back inside. A moment later they began returning fire from the farmhouse windows, but it was clear they wouldn't be able to hold out long. Harry hadn't fired a shot by the time he found Peter again, settled on the far side of the barn from the hay fire. Peter grinned.

"No trouble, Harry. Have 'em out of there in five minutes."

"Yes, it looks good enough. Peter, I think there's something wrong over on Geoffrey's side—that early shot. I think—"

Peter's great hand suddenly closed on his arm and his head cocked. In a lull in the firing Harry caught the sound, the unmistakable heavy stammer echoing off the rocks.

"Oh, God, they've got a Maxim there! They'll cut the guts out of Geoff's lads!"

Peter's face was tight.

"I'll take whoever's clear, Harry—"

"Take 'em all, Peter, all except these blokes here!" He gestured at the half-dozen men nearby. "Go on, *move!* I'll be there as fast as I can."

He didn't wait to see them go, hearing the shouts and the scatter of hooves as he moved among the men left, still firing into the farm. He grabbed Mulholland, a stocky and competent corporal.

"Listen, Mulholland, Captain Hunt's in trouble and I'm leaving you in charge here. You're a sergeant now."

"Goodoh, sir. She'll be right."

"Get it cleared up fast and get your men over to De

Koven's. If you've got prisoners and they won't move, break their bloody legs and leave 'em."

"We'll sort 'em out, sir. Be there in no time."

Harry ran for his horse, hearing Mulholland ordering three of his men to speed up the rate of fire and cover his advance to the farm.

The firing at De Koven's had stopped by the time Harry's horse, blowing hard, had reached the top of the ridge. There was a tongue of flame licking out of a window at the end of the house and he could see figures moving together in the yard. He plunged down the slope, jerking the horse back onto its haunches as he came on a group of men standing and lying by a clump of rocks.

He grabbed a trooper's shoulder as he hit the ground. "Where's Mr. Hunt?"

"Don't know, sir. Down there was the last time I seen him." He gestured down towards the farm, now beginning to burn fiercely.

"Where are the N.C.O.'s?"

Booth moved in before the man could answer. "I think I'm the only one left, sir. Since the sar-major got hit."

"Where's Captain Hunt, Booth?"

"Must be with the others, sir. They had a Maxim."

Harry began to run down towards the burning farm. Just inside the gate a man was kneeling by three still figures and he looked up, recognizing Harry and beckoning him urgently. In the flame-light as he knelt, Harry could see Owen Fisher, face wrenched with pain. Owen plucked at him with a weak hand and Harry took it, feeling the chill wetness of it.

"Owen, quiet now, man. We'll get you back in a bit."

Fisher's mouth gasped for words. "Hu—Hunt—"

Harry bent lower. "Where? Where is he, Owen?"

The mouth shut, clenching against the pain and Harry looked down, feeling sick as he saw the bloody and tangled mess of Fisher's belly. The sweaty fingers tightened in his and the gasping voice came.

"We—we went against the farm, Harry—the Maxim. Hit us with the Maxim." Anger lent him strength and his voice became louder. "They wouldn't back us up, the bastards—"

Harry could hear the shuffle of boots as men gathered round, and the sharp sound of hooves drawing close. "Who, Owen? Who wouldn't?"

Fisher tried to lift himself and Harry slid an arm behind his shoulders, propping him. He stared round, his head wobbling, his eyes fierce in their need to see clearly, and he jerked his chin at Booth.

"Him. And his mates . . . wouldn't support us. Mr. Hunt was hit—"

He fainted then and Harry laid him back gently, wiping his hands on his breeches as he stood. He remembered the sound of horses and called over his shoulder.

"Sergeant Mulholland, are you there?"

"Sir!"

"Bring Corporal Booth here, please."

Harry looked round the yard. They'd taken a number of casualties and there was a growing line of still or moaning figures by the fence. Several of the troopers were scouting nearer the buildings. Mulholland coughed quietly alongside Harry and he took a deep breath and swung to face Booth, standing at attention. Mulholland was holding two rifles and Booth's empty fingers were clenching and unclenching. He spoke as soon as Harry looked at him.

"Sir, we was advancing and that Maxim opened up and a lot of the men was hit. I didn't know Mr. Hunt was hit, sir. I saw Fisher go down and I—I pulled the others back, sir. To—to regroup and attack again."

Harry looked past him, speaking to the others. "Is that what happened?"

There was a moment's uneasy silence in which Dawes and Rattray glanced at one another and shifted a little away from Booth. One of the troopers spoke out of the ruck.

"Not properly, sir. Mr. Fisher was yelling for us to
194

come again—we heard him. He shouted he was hit and for us to rush the flank—get Mr. Hunt."

Booth burst in. "I had to make a decision, sir. It would have been murder to go into that bloody Maxim—"

It wasn't till Peter Handcock loomed up by him that Harry realized he hadn't seen him there till then. The big man's head was down and when he looked up, Harry saw his face was wet with tears and wrinkled like a baby's.

"Harry, we found Geoffrey. Over there behind the farm. They must have dragged him in and then left him when they shot through."

They walked together round to the back of the building and Peter pointed, standing there weeping as Harry went the extra couple of yards alone. Geoffrey was lying a few feet away from the back door and Harry felt the bile come into his throat and pain grip his stomach. He bent over, gagging, then straightened, sucking in air and fighting for control. His voice was quite steady when he called.

"Bring Booth here."

He groped in his pockets, finding his message-pad and a stub of pencil and waited till Booth was standing there, his lips trembling. Harry jerked a finger downwards.

"Kneel down." Booth hesitated and Harry's rage overcame him, so that he shouted into the man's white face. *"Kneel down, you shit!"* and his hand on Booth's shoulder forced the man to his knees alongside Hunt's body. Harry thrust the pad and pencil at him.

"Now write this, Booth." There was no sound from the watching men as Harry dictated, speaking coldly and steadily, his eyes fixed on Hunt in torment.

"Captain Hunt's body was struck by a bullet at close range. It passed through his right shoulder. This was a simple wound and did not cause his death. When found the body was stripped naked. The sinews at the backs of both knees and ankles had been severed. The forehead was bruised and the right cheekbone crushed. Captain Hunt had been castrated."

He choked and spun away, vomiting onto the ground. Peter Handcock, wet eyed, gestured to the men and two of them came forward, kneeling by the kneeling Booth to roll Hunt's body in a blanket and carry it away. Peter watched as Harry walked to his horse, mounting as though he was exhausted and walking it away up the slope. He turned to Mulholland.

"I gather you're a sergeant now, Les." The other man nodded silently. "Right—send someone you can rely on to stay with Mr. Morant and get a galloper away for a couple of carts for the wounded. Then let's get this mess cleared up."

It was almost dawn when they were finished and the flames from the burning buildings were beginning to pale as the sky lightened. The men stood by their horses, not talking, faces drawn and tired in the dawn chill. There were eight graves in a row beside the track and another a little further away under a scrubby tree. Harry stood bare-headed and slump-shouldered looking down at it, at the rifle jammed muzzle-down into the pile of rocks. Peter Handcock stepped forward, touching his arm gently and Harry straightened painfully, then shook himself and took a deep breath. He walked to his horse and pulled himself up into the saddle, waiting till the men had mounted before speaking. Then he looked along them, face set.

"Don't bring me any more prisoners."

He turned his horse's head along the track.

"Y'ave 'ardly touched a thing, Mr. Morant, sir." Craddock's crinkled nut of a face showed his concern as he shuffled the tin plates about on the folding table. "That was a nice bitta corned beef 'ash, that was."

Harry neither answered nor moved, sitting slouched in a canvas chair, glass in one hand, bottle in the other, and Craddock thought he looked like an old man. He clattered the plates together and let a note of reproof creep into his words.

"Y'got to eat somethink, sir. Y'can't go without eatin'. Y'll get sick."

He waited for some response from Harry but there was none. Craddock sighed, twisting his lips in thought. "Will I make some fresh tea, sir, eh? Nice strong cuppa—"

The bottle slammed down on the table, shaking it and slopping gravy off the edge of a plate, and Harry stared at the little man with dull anger. "Oh, for the love of God, stop jabbering! You sound like an old woman." He saw the wounded look and shut his eyes, calming himself before speaking again. "All right, all right, I'm sorry, Craddock. Just clear that stuff out of here."

He got up and stalked to the side of the little hut, looking down on his bed, littered with loose gear and clothing. The open trunk alongside it was half-packed with Geoffrey's things and Harry turned away from it, sick of the business of making Geoffrey finally gone.

"Craddock, go and ask Mr. Handcock to come in."

"Yessir. Er, fresh tea, Mr. Morant?"

The murderous look sent him scuttering from the hut and Harry poured himself another drink, carrying the glass as he walked idly about, picking up papers and clothes and putting them down again in other places. Handcock's voice took him by surprise and the thought shot through his mind not for the first time that for all his bulk, the man moved like a cat.

"Did you want me, Harry?" The rumbling voice was tentative, and Handcock stood only halfway through the door. In the days since they'd got back from De Koven's, Harry had been almost unapproachable, although they all knew Lenehan had spent an hour with him late that afternoon.

Harry waved the glass. "Yes. Come in." He watched Handcock walk to the table and stand awkwardly, shifting his massive weight from foot to foot. "Don't stand there like a bloody tree, man! You give me the jumps."

Not speaking, Handcock sat, chewing at his lower lip and Harry felt a swell of self-hatred, knowing how easily the man was hurt. "I'm sorry, Peter. I'm—I'm a bit off tonight."

197

"That's all right." He glanced at the mess. "D'you want some help?"

"No, thanks. I'm nearly finished. There's some other stuff at H.Q., but they'll look after that, I suppose." He swept the loose items off the bed into the trunk and kicked the lid down. "Not much to show, is there?" Abruptly, he moved back to the table and slumped down in the other chair. "I'm to take over Geoffrey's troop."

"Yes, we expected that. I'm glad."

"Are you? You may not be. You're to be my second-in-command."

"I'm still glad."

Harry looked up, meeting the big man's level stare, then looked away, unwilling to accept or share emotion. He poured whisky into a second glass and pushed it across the table.

"I'd like you to move in here, Peter. Sorry—I mean, would you like to move in here?"

"Well, look, I don't want to push in, Harry."

"No question of that—it makes sense. We're going to be working pretty closely together, Peter."

"Yes, well, of course. I'll be happy to." He gulped down his drink and stood, towering and seeming to fill the room. "I'll go and get my gear shifted. Won't be long."

He paused, seeing Harry wanted to speak, seeing the difficulty he was having. "Peter, thanks. I don't think being on my own would do me much good just now."

Handcock's grin was understanding. "That's all right. But don't push yourself too hard."

"Me? Don't worry about that." His face went stony. "It's the bloody Boer who's going to get pushed hard."

Handcock remembered those words as he watched Harry make them live, driving the troop unmercifully in his chase. The easy-going humour he'd always shown, the readiness for a prank, the thought for his men and their mounts, were all gone; he was drinking heavily again and eating only when somebody put food in front of him and he looked gaunt and grey, twitching with a nervous energy that kept him from sleep and comfort. He seemed in any kind of ease only when they were on the track, only when they found Boers, and then he became an icy demon.

He left the troop with Peter for two days while he caught the train to the hospital in the town seventy miles south, where Owen Fisher was being kept. When he came back he sat slumped on his bed, elbows on his knees, hands slack and head hanging, and his voice was dull.

"Owen and I came out here together, you know, Peter . . . he was a good friend. Now he's lying in that bed there, half a man, while they try to keep him alive. His guts are in pieces and they keep pumping stuff into him to deaden the pain, but it doesn't. His hair's nearly all fallen out and you can see his skull showing through his face and he's mad and he stinks." Harry looked up and Peter was shocked at the naked torture on his face. "And he was crying, Peter—Owen Fisher crying."

He never spoke of Geoffrey, except late one afternoon when they had searched a house on the edge of a little dorp and found an old Snider rifle tucked behind a cupboard. The woman of the house said she hadn't known it was there. Perhaps her dead husband had left it, but Harry had turned her out with her two half-grown boys yoked to a cartful of their belongings and a little girl crying in her arms, and had then broken a lamp against a wooden wall and watched the burning oil spread. Standing outside as her home burnt and the troops walked their horses back and across the little vegetable garden, the woman, dry-eyed, had stared up at Harry and cried out, "You are a pagan, a heathen! You make war on women and children! You destroy food!" She spat and made horns with her fingers at her forehead. "You are a son of the Devil!"

Harry spoke down to her coldly. "Not my choice, Madam. It's an arrangement made between some of your people and my friend, Captain Hunt."

He saluted and turned away, and Handcock felt chill as he watched him.

*　　*　　*

Gradually, though, he seemed to pull himself back, and the news that Owen Fisher was progressing left him almost cheerful. A rider had come into their over-night camp late the previous night carrying the news about Owen among his messages and now, in the clear softness of a Sunday morning, Harry decided they'd rest for the day, and the men lay sprawled comfortably around in the shade of some trees by a small creek, spelling the three lookouts every couple of hours.

Harry was dozing when he heard a flurry of voices and sat up, knuckling the sleep from his eyes. Mul-holland was leading a small group of men across, a Boer in the middle of them and Harry stirred Peter into wakefulness as they approached. Mulholland hunk-ered down by them.

"Got a Dutchman, sir. Dawes spotted him and bailed him up."

Dawes was standing with a self-satisfied grin. Since Booth had gone, his posting away quickly arranged by Lenehan, Dawes had been at pains to keep himself well out of the way, not even having much to do with the very subdued Rattray. Now, though, he'd brought in a prisoner and hoped that might help him. Harry ignored him completely, studying the Boer, a filthy, slew-eyed young man in an overlong greatcoat which fell loosely to his ankles. Standing up, Harry pulled the crushed cabbage-tree hat off the man's head, look-ing at the loose lips and the trickle of slobber on the stubbled chin. Beside him, he heard Peter's snort of disgust.

"Oh, God, he's a lunatic!"

Harry turned to Dawes, whose grin was fading.

"Where did you find this? And why drag it back here?"

Dawes stuttered. "He—he was carrying a rifle sir, and ammunition. I thought—"

"All right, don't go on about it." Harry pulled up a box, sitting and studying the Boer, who grinned stupidly at him.

"What's your name?"

The man's voice was thin and jerky. "Oh, I am Hennie Visser, mynheer. I am a soldier like you."

Harry's face twitched with disgust. "Hardly. Whose commando are you with, Visser?"

"My uncle Piet's commando, mynheer. I am a scout and a very good shot——"

"God help your Uncle Piet, then!"

The man giggled and Harry looked away.

"Mulholland! Take this softhead away. Give him something to eat . . . we'll take him back to the cage with us."

Peter sighed with quiet relief, thinking how, a week or two ago, Harry would have had the man shot for carrying a weapon and Harry, as though knowing what was in his mind, said, "Wouldn't be worth the waste of a bullet, Peter. Christ, the Boer must be getting pretty hard up!"

It had been decided that they'd ride back to Base in the cool of the evening and they ate well at lunch, planning on a couple of hours' sleep while the sun was high. Harry and Peter leaned back against a tree, smoking, relaxed, across the little glade from the men. The prisoner, Visser, sat at the edge of the troops' circle, a tin plate of food under his chin, his lips slobbering. Mulholland walked across.

"All fed except the scouts, sir. I'll relieve them in ten minutes or so. What time for stand-to?"

"Oh, four, I think. That'll get us back into camp around nine in comfort."

"One or two of the horses are looking a bit knocked up, sir."

Peter broke in. "I'll come and have a look at them in a minute, Les."

Harry yawned and stretched. "We won't push them, anyway. I'd like to——to——"

His voice slowed and stopped and the other two followed his stare. Across the glade, Visser had finished eating and was standing, hat off and greatcoat rolled into a bundle to be used as a pillow. Under the coat he was wearing a khaki tunic and breeches, unlaced and hanging loose above bare legs and an old pair of

201

ammunition boots. Harry's move to him was deadly fast and Peter scrambled after him, seeing him spin Visser around. Peter's breath caught in his throat as he realized what had snatched at Harry. The tunic and breeches were military, finely-cut khaki, filthy and sweat-stained, but unmistakable. The patches on the breeches were neat under the grime and the sleeves and collar of the cavalry tunic showed darker markings where badges and brevets had been cut away. Visser, not knowing what was happening, shrank away from the menace in Harry's stare, sinking down onto his bundled coat, but Harry's whisper froze him.

"Stand up, Visser!" Harry reached down with both hands, seizing the Boer's upper arms and jerking him to his feet, his face wincing in pain. The hands tore open the front of the tunic and Peter could see past Harry's arm, the faded but clear label inside: "Gieves, London. G. G. R. Hunt."

Harry threw the man down onto his back, treading him down and holding the tunic open with his foot so that everyone could see the label. His voice was hoarse.

"For pity's sake, get Geoffrey's clothes off that thing!"

Peter tugged at his shoulder, feeling the muscles tense and locked.

"Harry, calm down—he could have—"

Harry ignored him, watching as two of the men tugged the uniform away from Visser's squirming body, leaving him in a torn pair of foul drawers.

"Put him over there!" Harry pointed to a slim tree about ten feet away.

No one moved and he drew and cocked his pistol, his voice low and shaking.

"I said, put him over there."

Visser, blank face distorted and wet, was dragged kicking to the tree, where he stood half-crouched.

Harry walked to one of the saddles nearby and dragged the rifle from its scabbard. He moved back and tossed it into Visser's chest, the halfwit cradling it instinctively against him.

"You, Visser! Shoot!"

The man blinked and wept and held the rifle out to return it.

"Shoot, God damn you to hell!"

Clumsily Visser fumbled with the bolt and Harry stepped a pace closer and fired into his face, blasting the head into a splash of red and white which fanned backwards against the tree, the body arcing back incredibly under the blow and falling clumsily. Harry stepped closer again and methodically emptied the other five chambers into the chest and belly, and no one moved in those few seconds.

He looked round at them.

"Bury it."

No one moved still, as he walked away, reloading his pistol. By his own saddle he turned and called back to them.

"Mr. Handcock, I want that carrion covered up. And we'll ride as soon as it's done."

Half a mile away, the two Boers tucked into a cleft in the rocks across the creek, stared at one another. The younger one, his bearded face black with rage, slid his rifle forward and jerked up the backsight, but his companion pressed the barrel down, shaking his head. For a moment they struggled silently, then the younger man yielded and rested his head on his arm, cursing fiercely. The older man patted his shoulder and jerked his head back to where their horses were tethered, and they wormed their way back, the picture of what had happened clear in their minds.

Lenehan folded the bundle of maps into the scuffed leather case and buckled it down.

"Right then, Harry, that's it. I'll be gone about six days I should think—maybe a day or two longer. You can't rush those idiots at H.Q. Any problems?"

"No John. It's all in hand. Give Owen my regards, won't you?"

"I'll do that, never fear. And Harry, watch yourself. That story about the man Visser. Well, you know what I mean."

"Yes, I know." Lenehan looked at him, seeing the

flint hardness there, and choked back any further comments.

They were at a junction of two tracks, the first time in weeks that the entire B.V.C. had been together. The eighty-odd men were standing easy by their horses, the officers grouped by George Witton's limber nearby. Lenehan was to go to Field H.Q. with half a dozen troopers as escort and Harry would command in his absence. Lenehan handed him the case.

"Well, the maps are all marked and up to date." The rattle of wheels and hooves pulled their heads around to the cart that was being trotted down the line of troops, a corporal leading the two skinny horses in the shafts. "Hallo, what's all this?"

The corporal saluted.

"Stopped this old cove just behind the ridge, sir. Says he's a Bible-basher."

"All right, thanks. You can leave him here."

The corporal trotted away and the rest of the officers drew closer as Lenehan and Harry stepped forward, looking up at the man on the box of the cart.

"Who are you?"

The man, his long black coat and black wide-brimmed hat dusty, looked down at Lenehan, a hand stroking through the grey beard. "I am Jacob Hesse, sir. A pastor and missionary of the Lutheran Church, travelling in the name of God."

"You're not a Boer, sir. Are you from Holland?"

"No, I am from Berlin. I wish to pass through."

His English was heavily accented but quite clear and he spoke with determination; almost, Harry thought, arrogance.

Lenehan nodded. "I see. Excuse me for a moment. Er—won't you get down and have a cup of coffee?"

"Thank you, no. Please to let me pass."

"Shortly."

He moved aside, the others closing on him.

"What d'you think?"

Ivor Summers spoke quietly.

"He looks a little like my old history tutor, sir. Shouldn't he have some papers on him?"

"He'd better have. Harry?"

"Why don't you leave him to me? It's my pidgin now and there's no reason for you to hang about."

Lenehan looked at him consideringly. "Yes, all right. But be careful, Harry." He stepped back and said, "Your command, Mr. Morant," returning the salutes and mounting. "Right, Sergeant, let's have our detachment, please." Looking down, he smiled. "Enjoy yourselves; and take no chances, Harry."

Harry watched the little group of horsemen trot away, then turned back to where the old man sat grimly on the cart.

"My name is Morant, Lieutenant Morant. I'm in command here now. Will you come down, please?"

The old man shook his head. "I do not wish to come down, Herr Leutnant. I wish only to go about God's work."

"And I don't wish to have you lifted down Herr . . . Hesse? I wish only to go about *my* work."

Hesse tried to stare Harry out, but his gaze dropped and his head with it. Tight-mouthed he clambered down, one of the troopers helping him. After a hesitation he took off his hat and gave a jerky little bow. Harry punctiliously saluted.

"You have some papers of identity, sir?"

"Ja." He fumbled inside his long coat, handing over an oilskin packet. "They will tell you only what I have already said."

Harry skimmed rapidly through the papers: a German passport, a travel visa signed by someone at General Headquarters, an impressive piece of parchment with the Prussian crest on it. He handed them back and waved to Mulholland.

"Sergeant, you might take a look in that cart, please."

Hesse watched the sergeant and two troopers rummaging through his gear, his face flushed with annoyance.

"I have only supplies there, Herr Leutnant—personal things, Bibles—"

"No guns? No ammunition?"

"I am a man of God, mein Herr. I do not deal with

guns. They are of the Devil. It is such men as you who deal with them."

Witton broke in. "All very well, pastor, but your people in Germany are doing a bit of devil-dealing too, you know."

The old man looked around them. "I do not speak of war or politics. There are now people in this land who have not homes and have not families and who need the help of the good God. This I go to give them."

Mulholland spoke from the cart. "Nothing there, sir, only what he said."

Hesse pulled on his hat and drew himself up. "So. I may go forward now?"

Harry cocked an eye at the others. Peter rumbled at the missionary, "It's thick with Boers out there, you know. Not safe."

"They are Christians, young man, children of my Church."

"They're also touchy on the trigger," broke in Harry. "Once you pass here, people don't wait to ask questions. If they don't recognize you at once, they shoot. They even shoot Christians."

One of the troopers snorted, and Hesse flushed again. "I tell you Herr Leutnant, I am not concerned with shooting."

"I can't give you an escort."

"Thank you, I have my Escort. You will permit me . . . ?"

The man had a simple dignity now, and Harry shrugged and stepped aside, watching him clambering up again and accepting the reins from a trooper.

He made a last attempt. "You do understand, pastor . . . it's at your own risk. I won't have a patrol along that track for several days."

"I will pray for God's forgiveness for you all."

They watched the cart go, bumping away along the narrow track with a cloud of dust rising to hide it.

"I have a feeling I shouldn't have let him go."

George Witton ran his hand through his gingery fuzz and spat dust away from his lips. "Couldn't really stop him, could we? Sanctimonious old sod!"

"Let's hope his God's riding with him." Fletcher sounded solemn for a change, and Harry looked at him, grinning wryly.

"Well, He's unlikely to be riding with us, Tom." He raised his voice. "Mount 'em up, Sergeant Mulholland —work to do!"

An hour later, a single shot out of the sun took Tom Fletcher just ahead of his right ear. Harry looked down at the shallow grave and said, "I wish that padre was here. He might like to thank his God for His children's work."

The scout was calling as he galloped in.

"Road block, sir. 'Bout quarter of a mile up the track. Round that way."

Captain Gregory's hand shot up and the column halted. He signalled the scout to go back on his tracks and waited while his lieutenant and troop-sergeant joined him. Behind him the mounted infantrymen sat alert, carbines cocked.

Gregory sniffed at the dry air, trying, as he always did, to get the feel of the place. Nothing.

"Right—usual drill. I'll go up the middle this time. Eyes open for signals, please."

Nodding, and without fuss, the two others wheeled away, pulling the column off into three sections, the sergeant leading out wide to the left to cut across the curve and behind a slope, the lieutenant taking his men up the hill on the right. Gregory gave them a few moments to get well under way and waved his own men forward along the track.

Up on the hill, edging just his head above the crest-line, the lieutenant looked down on the block. A cart, tipped on one side and slewed across the track, its contents spilled and scattered. Traces cut, and no horses. The sergeant's party just working into sight below and to the right.

The sergeant saw the toppled cart almost as quickly. From his angle he could also see the humped black body in its lee and the grotesque black birds trenching obscenely into it. He halted his men and looked up, waving to the lieutenant and waiting.

Captain Gregory led his party slowly round the curve, looking up to the hilltop for the all clear, then out to the left for the second reassurance. He moved forward and the three groups converged on the cart, the vultures rising with an ugly clatter ahead of them. By the time Gregory had dismounted the sergeant was kneeling by the body, face disgusted, hands busy. Gregory forced himself to look down, a handkerchief at his nose.

"Anything, Sergeant Matthews?"

"Bible in the pocket, sir . . . foreign. And papers." He passed up the book and an oilskin packet. "Been shot, sir. One in the back, high up—here." He half rolled the body so that Gregory could see the hole in the black coat, just below the shoulder. Lower than that, almost central, much of the man's back was gone in a gaping shambles. "That lot's from the other shot, in the chest, sir. Close range by the look of it."

Gregory nodded, looking round to see that the lieutenant had men spread well on lookout and searching the nearby ground. He opened the packet of papers, then stared up, startled.

"Good Lord, it's a padre! German." He wheeled on the watching men. "All right—get this cart off the track, some of you. Matthews, see if there's anything in his boxes and things. And get a blanket round him. Quickly."

The lieutenant strolled across, face grave, tossing something in one hand.

"I say, Greg, there was this. Lying just over there."

Gregory looked at the bent and smelly can, shreds of bully beef inside it with a few ants crawling stickily about. He looked at the label.

"Our issue. Oh, damnation!"

"There's a fair amount of that stuff leaks away to the Boer, you know. Doesn't necessarily mean . . ."

"I know, I know. Still and all . . . where'd you find it, exactly?"

They walked to where two or three men were still peering in amongst the scrub and small rocks. One of them bent suddenly, picked up something small and passed it silently to Gregory. It was a twisted strip of dark green puggaree cloth, sweat-stained and ravelled from old knots.

The lieutenant looked at it, sombre.

"Hardly likely any of our chaps would shoot a padre, surely?"

"After these past few months, I believe some of 'em would shoot the Archbishop of Canterbury." He turned away, calling again to the sergeant.

"Matthews, I shall want you to take that body back to Headquarters. You'd better put a couple of the horses to that cart and take half a dozen men. Let the colonel know what's happened, please, as soon as you get in. I'll give you a note to him and another for the provost-marshal."

Harry was in his tent scribbling a report when Handcock stuck his head through the flap.

"Column riding in, Harry."

Outside, squinting into the afternoon sun, they studied the approaching horsemen. Handcock grunted.

"Bloody Pommies! Two days late! Suppose they kept stopping for tea and sandwiches on the way."

"Stop picking, Peter. They may have run into trouble." He shaded his eyes against the glare. "Seem to be more than we expected."

The column moved into the camp area, a long double-file of mounted infantry, a young captain at their head with a grim-faced major alongside him. As they led under a couple of tall old trees, Harry could see the major was wearing a provost brassard. Behind him was a section of men in the white crossbelts of the field police. Wondering, he slipped on his hat and stepped forward saluting and smiling as the two officers dismounted, the police following them.

"Hallo, there . . . we've been waiting to hand over to you! I'm Morant."

The others returned his salute and the captain made to take Harry's outstretched hand, but in his fractional hesitation the major spoke.

"Lieutenant Morant, I'm Malleson, assistant provost-marshal."

"Good afternoon, sir. Trouble?"

"Very possibly. Is all your command here?"

"Yes, sir. We've been waiting for—"

The major broke in, tugging a paper from his belt-pouch.

"I should like to see all the officers, please. Immediately."

Puzzled at the man's formality, Harry gestured the others forward. "Of course, sir. Gentlemen—"

Malleson looked at them as they stepped forward. "Lieutenant Morant, would you report your officers to me formally, please?"

Harry looked a query at the young captain who licked his lips and looked past him. Shrugging, he drew himself to attention. "Sir—Lieutenants Handcock, Witton, Summers and Morant reporting as requested."

The four saluted as one, Malleson carefully answering. "Thank you. Gentlemen, I must notify you that I am now placing you all under open arrest." His hand moved a little from his side and his policemen moved closer. "Will you hand over your side-arms, please?"

For a second the silence was complete, Malleson staring into their shocked faces. Then Harry exploded. "What the bloody hell are you talking about? I'm sorry sir, but what in God's name is going on?"

"Your side-arms, please, gentlemen. I'd be most reluctant to place you under close arrest, but I'm prepared to if you make it necessary."

Harry stared at him and around, noticing how the policemen were now in an arc, three wide on either side of the major. He looked at the others, shaking his head. Ivor Summers stepped half a pace forward.

"Look here, sir, what are the charges?"

Malleson was suddenly embarrassed. "You will be advised of the charges at Field Headquarters—"

Now George Witton stepped in, ginger eyebrows lowering. "But that's quite contrary to Queen's Rules and Regulations—"

"Please! I'm acting under direct orders from the Field Commander. Now, side-arms, if you will."

The M.I. captain spoke from behind Malleson's shoulder. "Look Morant, I'd advise you to go along. It's just something—"

Malleson's voice was abrupt. "If you don't mind, Gregory." Then, to the four men facing him, more softly, he said, "I don't like this any more than you do, but I'm afraid I don't have any latitude in the matter. Orders." He held up the paper.

Harry tried again. "Major, my C.O. is at Field Headquarters and I feel sure—"

"Major Lenehan is being detained under inquiry."

There was another silence, the British troops motionless on their horses, the men of the B.V.C. clustering close. Harry saw Mulholland, face worried, and Dawes, an unpleasant grin twitching his mouth. He shrugged and pulled out his pistol, slipping the lanyard over his head and handing it across, butt foremost. The other three followed his lead.

Harry tried to keep his voice light. "I've no idea what this is about, but I suppose this is the quickest way to get it sorted out."

Malleson was obviously relieved. He passed the pistols back to one of his men and sagged a little. "Thank you, gentlemen. I'm sure I have your word you'll cause no trouble and attempt no escape." He waited for their nods. "Now, if you'll get your necessary things together, we'll move as soon as we've had a meal."

"What about my men?"

Gregory came to him, a sheet of buff paper in his hand. "Er—I've been given temporary command of your chaps, Morant. I'll bring them into Field H.Q. in a few days. I've one patrol to make first."

"I see. Well, look after them, won't you?"

"They'll be all right."

Peter, watching Harry, saw the effort at control, saw the little patches of white around his lips, prayed he would hold himself in . . . then sighed in relief as Harry smiled, pitching his voice so everyone could hear, making it cheerful.

211

"Well, the last time I was arrested it was for being drunk and disorderly in South Australia! This time I'm as sober as a judge and as dry as a bone! Would I be permitted to offer you gentlemen a drink?"

The sentry to one side of the metal-strapped door slapped his rifle-butt under the lamplight as Lenehan and the orderly officer approached. The orderly officer, his crimson sash the only warm splash of colour, produced a pass and the sentry banged a flat hand on the door behind him. There was the metal jangle of keys and the grating sound of a bar sliding before the door swung and a corporal of Field Police checked the pass, then saluted them through.

They were halted again on the far side of the room where a sergeant took the pass and they signed the Duty Book, then moved on behind the corporal through the rest room, empty at that moment and to the other door. The corporal's knock brought a face to the barred grille with a nod and a hand sliding a long steel key through the bars.

The corporal unlocked the door, slamming and locking it again behind them. "This way, sir."

Lenehan didn't move, looking down the corridor to where another armed man sat with his back against the far door. He suddenly shouted, his voice ringing and bouncing off the stone and metal.

"B.V.C.! Are you there, my chaps?"

The echoes were alone for a second, then there was a sudden clash and shout, Harry Morant's voice above it all.

"John! John Lenehan, welcome to Liberty Hall!"

Lenehan rounded on the orderly officer.

"Open these bloody doors, man! Come on, smartly now!"

Watched with care by the guards at either end of the corridor, the cell doors were unlocked and the men allowed into the one big cell at the far end on the right, pounding at Lenehan's back, wringing his hands, questions falling over one another in a jumble until he managed to shout them into a grinning silence. He looked at the orderly officer. "I say, there's really no need for you to hang about, is there?"

" 'Course not, sir. I shall have to lock you in, I'm afraid."

Lenehan nodded and the door clanged as the young officer left, turning the key on them. There was a little awkward silence as Lenehan stared round at the four of them.

"Well, are you all right?"

Ivor Summers smiled lazily. "It makes a nice change from chasing Brother Boer, sir. We don't even have to sleep on the ground."

"But we *would* like to know what's happening." George Witton needed a haircut and he brushed the ginger fringe out of his eyes, Handcock nodding alongside him. Harry hadn't spoken and Lenehan cocked an eye at him, meeting that wide flash of a grin. Harry gripped his arm.

"What about you? Are you in the clear?"

"Yes, I am now. I feel badly about not being with you fellows . . . but then I can probably be more use out of here. They tell me I shall be called as a witness anyway."

Peter Handcock's rumble sounded even deeper in that closed room.

"Witness to what, sir? What are we supposed to have done?"

"You mean they haven't—" The rattle of the key in the lock interrupted him and they all turned as the orderly officer led another man in, neat, compact, seeming almost dainty in his spotless uniform.

Lenehan let out a gust of relief. "Well, thank Heavens for that!" He shook the newcomer's hand firmly and faced the others. "Gentlemen, this is Ian Thomas of the New South Wales Lancers. Major Thomas, may I introduce—"

He was stopped again as Thomas stepped forward, his hand upraised.

"All right John, let's leave the amenities for a moment." The voice bore no relationship to the man's size and apparent delicacy. It was strong and vibrant

213

and he used it as an actor does, pitching it with care for the most effect. "We'll all get to know one another soon enough, gentlemen. I'm a lawyer. I'm a very good lawyer and I'm going to defend you." He watched the reactions on their faces for a second, then whipped round suddenly on the orderly officer. "Look here, Captain I-Don't-Know-Your-Name . . . go and see the commandant and tell him I want some chairs and tables in here. And some lamps . . . writing materials. By God! these gentlemen aren't criminals. You're supposed to be guarding them, not burying them!"

The orderly officer's mouth opened and closed but no sound came from it.

Thomas snapped at him, "Go on, man, gallop about a bit!"

Aware of the prisoners' surprised grins, the captain flushed and made for the door.

Half an hour later the big cell looked more like a Mess anteroom, with half a dozen chairs around a trestle-table, a green cloth covering the boards. There were two layback chairs on either side of a small side-table, and some other oddments of furniture, hastily collected, were piled in the corridor waiting for this first meeting to end. Lenehan and Thomas had both brought cigarettes and tobacco and the prisoners were luxuriating in a thick haze of blue smoke as they leaned around the table, looking to Thomas at its head. He finished scrawling a note on the scratch-pad in front of him and slammed the flap of his dispatch case closed on it, leaning back and looking quickly around them.

"Right! So much for the pettifogging details. Let's have your questions first, shall we?"

"When do we get out of this place?"

"What the hell are we doing in here anyway?"

Harry and George had spoken together and Thomas checked them. "I don't know how long you'll be held here. I do know why. You're being held under field arrest on charges arising from a Court of Inquiry into a number of deaths of Boer civilians. I've already told you that."

"But it's a lot of balls!" Peter's voice was indignant.

"Very probably. Nonetheless, the Court has ordered you further held pending continuation of inquiries."

Harry let an edge of irritation creep into his voice. "Come on now, Major, you can swallow all the formal flapdoodle. What's the situation in plain language?"

The others murmured agreement and Thomas grinned at them without real mirth.

"Simple language, eh? Well then—someone's stewing something up."

George snorted. "And what's that supposed to mean?"

"It means that rigmarole at the Court of Inquiry where they gibbered at John Lenehan there, all of that was a lot of claptrap. Didn't mean a damn thing as far as I'm concerned. There's something else hatching, and they're hanging onto you people while they sort themselves out."

Lenehan leaned forward, face anxious. "Can they do that?"

"Properly speaking, no. But there's a war on you know, and the bloody-minded men in the Judge Advocate-General's office *are* doing it! I'm having the devil's own job—"

He bit the words off short as the guard corporal knocked and entered, a flat package in his hand, a long envelope on top of it.

"Letter for you, sir, and a package for Major Lenehan."

Lenehan ripped open the envelope, smiling as he handed letters across the table. He'd not told them about his arrangement to collect their mail in case something went wrong, but now there was something for each of them and they chattered and laughed over their letters like schoolboys at the end of term. Harry looked at his two envelopes . . . one from Margaret and one from Paddy. Smiling quietly he tucked them away to read later and leaned close to Lenehan.

"What have you really heard, John?"

Lenehan hesitated, then spoke quietly. "I wasn't

215

going to mention it, but the word is out that there's going to be a court-martial."

"But that's absurd!" Lenehan frowned a caution to Harry to keep his voice down, and he controlled himself with an effort. "It's absurd," he repeated. "I mean there was only an inquiry because everyone knows old Kitchener's a stickler for military form!"

"Harry, it's only what they're saying in the H.Q. Mess. That there's to be a court-martial and . . ."

His voice died away as he realized the others had stopped their chatter and had heard him. Ivor Summers was pale. He was the only professional soldier among them, a British officer at that, and the sound of a court-martial had a peculiarly horrifying ring about it to him. "But good God, we only did what we were told!"

Handcock's voice was loud with rage. "You know that, sir—the orders were clear enough!"

Lenehan tried to answer but George Witton cut in. "Not as though we were the only ones, even if there *was* any truth in it all. And every damn civilian over the age of six was out to get *us!*"

Harry's head had swung to the others and he now spoke to them all. "The point is, can they make any charges stick against us, anyway? Surely they'll never do it!"

"They're going to have a bloody good try."

Thomas had been silent since he opened his letter, but the others hadn't noticed in their elation at receiving mail, then in their fury. Now his voice was flat and dry and it silenced them at once. Thomas was staring down at the papers, his hands flat on either side of them, and when he looked up his face was grave.

"Gentlemen, I have now received information from the office of the Judge Advocate-General. I am advised that you are severally and together to be arraigned before a Field General Court-Martial on a date to be set."

George, as usual unable to contain himself, burst out, "What the fuck's a Field General Court-Martial?"

Thomas looked at each of them in turn before answering, keeping his voice deliberate and uninflected.

"It's a court comprised of three officers. It has the power to impose a sentence of death." He went on looking at them in complete silence, reading the shock and puzzlement in their stares.

"Why?" It was Harry, asking for them all. "What for?"

Thomas pretended to consult the pages in front of him before he answered. He found it difficult to hold down his own sense of outrage. "The material brought forward at the Court of Inquiry will be taken into account and there will be three separate charges to which you must answer. These concern the deaths of certain Boer civilians on two occasions." He paused again, again looking round at them. "The principal charge concerns one Jacob Hesse, a German national—"

Peter interrupted. "Hesse? Harry, that's that crazy old missionary—"

Thomas overrode the interruption. "—who was found shot to death in suspicious circumstances within the area of operations of the Bush Veldt Carbineers under temporary command of Lieutenant H. H. Morant. You are being charged with his murder."

It was rather like being locked inside a stone, Harry thought, like being a fly in ambergris. The floor beneath his feet was stone in slabs and the walls were stone blocks. The ceiling was of heavy wooden planks, but they were grey-painted and had the look and closeness of stone around him, like the door, strapped wood and metal bars. The single window was high and narrow and close-barred and he had to stand on the end of the hard bunk to look out of it, seeing nothing then but the flat waste of beaten earth on that side of the prison, and a few lights from the town in the hollow beyond. Each of the cells had an oil-lamp on a hook by the door and the yellowness fell at a sharp angle through the bars, striping one corner with poor light.

Harry propped himself there to look through the letters again, trying to feel from Margaret's words something of home, something of her warm flesh and the

217

comfort of her body and her love. This letter had taken seven weeks to reach him here, in a stone box, and the last of her scent had gone from it somewhere on the way. She hadn't known then about Geoffrey's death and he could only feel an emptiness when he re-read her messages to the man under the tree, out of the world, inside the past.

And yet Paddy's carefully-formed writing, the letters large and rounded and a little aslant across the pages, Paddy's letter brought him all the smells of the bush somehow. Even there, even barred and blocked, the simple letter seemed to carry with it something of freedom.

*Harlequin is doing well and I sometime find it hard to keep my promise which you placed on me not to saddle him up and go for a good old run. Im sure he would like that Harry old friend and you migt care to give it some of your thinking. Last Thurs. old Mac Taylor from out by Downs River was thro this way and stayd here with me for three days. We had a fine time talking on the old days and he sents you his Very Best Respects. I showd him all the newspaper pices I been keeping in a box about your Exploits and those of the Gallant Boys which left from here. He was glad to hear you are now an Officer which I said was No Surprise to me and he agreed. Where are you now Harry and what are you doing? I have it reckoned out that you will be halfway to being up with your Enlistment and look to see you Home again with your Lovely Lady. Harlequin and me will be pleased for that day to come. Write soon and remember Your Old Freind, P. Magee (Paddy). P.S. Are you writeing any Poems still?*

He found the light was poorer than he thought as he folded the letter, unwilling to admit to himself that his eyes were wet. When the guard walked along the boot-banging corridor a few minutes later turning off all the lamps except those at the ends, Harry lay on his bunk fully dressed, and stared at the far wall, seeing the barred lines of the window creep out of the first blackness and listening to Thomas' voice in his head telling him he would be charged with murder.

By now the big cell had come to be called the Common Room and the three weeks which had gone by had given it a lived-in look, almost one of comfort. The four men were allowed to move freely between their own cells and the big one until ten at night, and they took their meals together there, Thomas having arranged for the Commandant's Mess to provide for them. Hasleton, the Commandant, had become a friend —an elderly colonel, pining for the active days when he'd commanded his own infantry regiment and considerably out of sympathy with what he called "Arse-faced Authority locking up good young fighting officers."

At Christmas, he'd gone out of his way to bring them something of the traditional cheer, providing them with a pudding and a fine turkey, cold ham, glazed sweets, several bottles of wine and some excellent brandy. Thomas had brought a stunted tree in a box, its lack of relationship to a fir tree considerably disguised by the small decorations he'd managed to fasten to it and the gaily-wrapped packages below it, cigars and books. John Lenehan had arrived with a bundle of letters for them and parcels from Ivor's family, and on Christmas morning, the guard sergeant, his face scarlet with shyness, had carted in a box of gifts from the several Officers' Messes in and near the town. The four prisoners felt, for the first time, that they weren't alone, that there was a great swell of friendly feeling around them—and not simply because of the time of the year.

But it was a short interlude and by Boxing Day the prison feeling was back with them, stronger for the previous day's gaiety. On Christmas night, Harry, Peter and George had lain silently in their cells listening to Ivor sobbing quietly.

They'd settled into a routine of sorts. Lenehan would

call on them every day with newspapers and letters and gossip, often staying for a meal. Thomas, too, made at least one visit each day, even when there was no real need for it, and they'd come to appreciate the toughness of this dapper little man and his no-nonsense methods. The food was good and they were able to supplement it occasionally when one or other of them was able to arrange for some funds. What they all missed most was the company of other people, the chance to talk outside their own confined circle, the chance to walk somewhere other than on the baked earth beyond the prison wall for a half-hour a day and under guard. Chess and bridge, reading and writing letters, reminiscing—everything grew stale quickly and they found in the third week that they were spending less time together. They were all scared of abrading one another, of becoming quarrelsome. But they met for dinner each evening, scrupulously cleaning up and dressing as well as they could, making of the unelaborate meals a ritual of normality, trying to lose sight of the bars and the drab stonework as they sat around the table in the Common Room, a couple of plain candlesticks from the Commandant's quarters softening the circumstances a little. And they tried to keep the conversation general, away from the war and their immediate problems, each of them able to contribute an aspect of talk, of life, which was new to the others. Inevitably, though, it seldom lasted a whole evening. Always they'd drift back to the fighting.

Thomas had brought them a box of cigars this evening and now, with the dinner things cleared away, they sat puffing into a lapse in the talk.

Handcock, bulking over the table on his elbows, admired the length of his ash and spoke casually to Thomas. "What's this rumour about Kitchener halting operations, Ian?"

"Not a rumour." The others cocked their ears. "Not a halt either, really."

George had never tanned easily and the past three weeks' confinement had left his fair skin almost white. He grinned crookedly out of that pale face. "Well, that

220

makes almost as much sense as the average High Command statement."

Thomas smiled back, nodding his head in rueful agreement. "No, it's just that he's got everyone sitting more or less still, that's all. The blockhouse line's finished, the country's cleared, the camps are full and the place has got a garrison of sorts every twenty feet or so it seems."

"And the old Boer's doing nothing, is that it?"

Thomas snorted at Harry's question. "Hardly. He's just moved back into your stamping-ground and he runs out every now and then and chews us up and runs back again."

"Splendid!" Harry let the sarcasm knife out. "They keep us stabled here and our men sitting on their backsides waiting for their enlistments to run out and the bigwigs chaffer over the politics of it all. And the Dutchman goes on doing what he was doing last year!"

There were silent nods from the others, even Ivor Summers. They'd noticed how much quieter he'd become, his lazy humour seeming to have gone completely these days.

The mood lifted when Lenehan walked in a moment later, a bundle of journals under his arm. "Here, you blokes, papers are in." He sat down, accepting the cup of coffee Thomas poured him and riffling among the newspapers to find the one he was looking for. "There's some rather odd news from Burleigh in the *Telegraph*." He folded the paper flat and pulled a candle closer to read. " '. . . and it is believed that the Kaiser has made the strongest personal representations to His Majesty to follow the German Government's recommendations to Downing Street in the matter of the death of the missionary, Hesse. Informed sources in Berlin report that the essence of these communications is of reparations rather than of justice. . . .' " He stopped and looked up at them.

Peter rumbled, "Pity we hadn't stopped that bloody Bible-bird that day, Harry."

Harry was savage in reply. "Pity we hadn't *shot*

221

the bastard! And put him underground and forgotten about him! We'd have saved all this bother."

Thomas frowned across at him. "Hardly a sensible attitude, Harry—and it won't help if anyone outside here hears you."

"Oh, for God's sake!" Harry shoved his chair back, toppling it, and went to his own cell, slamming the door hollowly behind him.

He could hear them still as he stood perched on the end of his bunk, looking through the window-bars without seeing anything. He could hear the thick silence which followed his walk-out and then the gradual growl of conversation for a while, even a laugh or two. But the "Goodnights" came quickly and the rattle of footsteps and the locking of the end door, and then near silence as the others drifted back to their cells. It was only when he realized that there was slightly more light in his cell that Harry looked round, seeing the loom of Peter standing in the doorway.

"Harry? All right?"

He stepped off the bunk, sitting on it and leaning back against the cool stone wall, his knees pulled up.

"Hardly, Peter. I'm in prison . . . hadn't you noticed?" The bitterness rang in that hard room and he rose again to stare out into the night, speaking back across his shoulder. "Sorry. I'm afraid I get a bit edgy when I'm cooped up for too long."

Peter settled on the other end of the bunk and lit a pipe, his silence companionable, undemanding. Harry's voice softened as he half turned from the bars.

"It's a bit like the country the other side of Adelaide, over the hills."

"Mmm, a lot of South Africa's like home, hadn't you noticed? Makes me quite homesick sometimes." Peter chewed his words round the stem of the pipe. "You wouldn't be homesick for Australia though, would you, Harry?"

"Oh, it's not the places I miss so much. It's things I miss and the way I like to do them. People, too."

"Know what you mean. All this must be unpleasant for your fiancée. . . ."

222

"Margaret?" He looked down at the big man in the dim light. "You know Geoffrey Hunt was her brother?"

"That must have been a hard blow on its own. How's she taking all this?" The pipe-stem took in the cell, the prison, their lives.

"Taking it? As you'd expect, of course. But it's finished. I've written to her and told her it's finished. I wouldn't want to bring her more trouble."

"That's a bit down, isn't it, Harry? The court can't do anything to us. They've nothing at all to go on."

"Oh? Go and have another look at that piece of Burleigh's." He turned to the window again, chin on his folded arms on the ledge, face close to the bars and the night breeze. "Wonder how Harlequin is? Be a grand night for a gallop."

Thomas was back immediately after breakfast the next morning to tell them the Court would begin to sit the next day and to take them again through the procedures and the material he'd collected. In the previous weeks he'd talked to each of them separately several times, covering page after page of paper with his dashing script, checking and cross-checking everything. It wasn't until he'd collated everything they'd told him that he met with all of them together and with Lenehan present. He looked pleased on that day, slapping the neatly ribboned pages together on the table.

"Well, you're all square as far as I'm concerned. Not that I didn't expect it, but it's reassuring to know one's clients are cutting from the whole cloth. I just wanted you all to know I'm completely confident of your stories and I don't doubt the Court will be too. Splendid!"

On this day he spent most of the daylight hours with them, picking at lunch, answering every question patiently, turning up references for them, trying to impress them with the impartial justice of the law, working to build their confidence, to lift them out of the worry and depression of the weeks gone by. It was particularly hard with Summers and Thomas followed him into his cell, closing the door behind them.

"Mind if I spend a minute with you, Ivor?"

"Take your time, Ian. I'm not going anywhere."

There was no humour there, only a resigned listlessness.

"Well, actually you are, my lad. You're going in front of that Court and then home. Before too long, I shouldn't wonder."

"Perhaps."

"Oh, come now, Ivor, you mustn't mope like this! Good God, if you answer the Court that way they'll—they'll smack your bottom and send you to bed!"

A thin smile rewarded him and he pressed on. "I realize it looks unpleasant for you, but you wouldn't be the first officer to have made a damn good career after being cleared by a court."

"You're sure we're going to be cleared?"

"Aren't you? Don't you believe they've no case against you?"

"I know I've—we've—done nothing wrong."

"Well, then!"

Ivor's face came alive for a moment.

"You're a good chap, Ian. I'm sure you won't let any of us down in any way. It's just that I don't believe there's anything left for me in the Army after all this. There'll always be—you know—hints, stories."

"Be damned to them! Fight back!"

"I think my fighting days are over. Whatever happens."

Thomas was appalled when he realized Ivor Summers was crying.

Breakfast was a strange meal next morning, the four of them alternately chattering as though they were going on a trip, then lapsing into deep silences. In a way, Harry supposed, they were taking a trip. The Court was to sit in the building beside the prison, a meeting-hall of some kind, and this would be the first time they'd been outside the walls for more than the daily half-hour's exercise, the first time they would have seen people other than Lenehan, Thomas and the prison staff.

Hasleton came to see them as they were finishing breakfast, pouring himself tea and injecting a mood of belligerent cheer, eyes beaming in the scrubbed pink face, fingers plucking at the tobacco stains on his white moustache.

"Well now, laddies, off you go, eh? Up against Arse-faced Authority! Almost wish I was with you, begod! I'd tell those blinders a thing or two, spending their time chivvying good young fighting officers about instead of letting them get on with their work! Not good enough! I tell you what, now, I know the fella who's sitting over this Court—'bout as much use as a eunuch's cock!" He suddenly realized that that was hardly a comforting statement and made haste to recover. "Mark you, he's fair! Got to be truthful—he's a wank and an arsehole, but not an unfair man!"

His confusion, far from depressing them, brought them to laughter and they were still laughing when Lenehan arrived. He listened to them for a second, hearing the thin, faint edge of hysteria.

Then Hasleton caught the eye of the sergeant at the door and abruptly pulled himself upright, tugging down the flaps of his tunic and putting on his cap. He walked to the door and turned to face them, coughing loudly till he had their attention.

"Gentlemen, I must inform you that I am about to parade you for handing over to your escort. Perhaps you'd be good enough to collect your requirements and stand by your cell doors?" He was flushed with embarrassment as they filed past him.

The guards led them out of the corridor and through the rest room into the hall. The outer doors were closed and the day guard was drawn up along one wall, armed and at attention. Facing them, the Commandant and the orderly officer stood together with a young captain in Rifle green who stepped crisply forward as the prisoners halted.

"Good morning, gentlemen. I'm Crookes of the Six-tieth, Escort Commander. I should very much like to be able to stand down my men—if I may have your word . . . ?" He let the question hang and Harry glanced around at the others, seeing their immediate agreement.

"That's kind of you. Of course you have our word."

"Splendid. Then we'll stroll across as soon as I've signed you out." He turned to the guard sergeant and scribbled his name where the man's finger was poised on the great ledger, then turned back to the Commandant, his salute seeming to make the air crackle. "Thank you, sir. The Prisoners' Escort is ready."

Hasleton winked approvingly as he casually flopped a salute in return. "Well done, young Crookes. Off you go."

The doors swung and Crookes led them out, a Rifles sergeant bringing the men there to a crashing attention. Crookes waved an airy hand at him and said, "All right, Sergeant. Dismiss," and led them along the wall at a saunter, rather like a prefect taking a group of junior boys along to see the headmaster, Lenehan thought as he followed behind.

Crookes smiled easily around him. "We'll be doing this every day till the Court rises, you fellows. Do please let me know if there's anything I can do to—er—ease things along, won't you? Can't discuss proceedings, of course, or smuggle hacksaws or anything of that kind. Anything else though, within reason." Waving aside their thanks, he looked at Ivor inquiringly. "I know you, don't I? You're Summers, you were at school with my ass of a little brother—Simon."

Ivor's face flushed with pleasure. "Good Lord, yes! I'd no idea—how is he? We were really quite good friends, you know."

"So I gathered from his letter. Knew I was in these parts and asked me to look you up and tell you not to fret and so on. He'll be bucked up no end when he knows I've seen you."

"Is he out here? On service?"

"Yeees . . . doing rather depressingly well for a tiddler. Gunner, you know."

Watching Ivor's animation, Harry blessed the chance that had brought Crookes to them. As they walked between the guards outside the Court, they all, strangely,

226

felt an ease that had been noticeably absent for some time.

Malleson, the assistant provost-marshal who'd arrested them, was standing just inside the doorway and accepted Crookes' salute as he came forward.

" 'Morning. You've been tolerably well looked after, I hope?"

"For prisoners, yes, sir." George was unable to keep the sharpness from his tongue and Malleson gave him a dry smile.

"Witton, isn't it? Yes, well, I'm afraid we have to accept the fact that you *are* prisoners, gentlemen, until the Court decides otherwise, of course. The provost-marshal has appointed me to be here throughout proceedings. You understand that your—er—quarters and Colonel Hasleton come under his jurisdiction, and the rules require the presence of an officer from his staff." They nodded in understanding as both Lenehan and Thomas joined them, listening silently as Malleson continued.

"I can see by the fact that you arrived under this officer's escort only that you've paroled yourselves to him. I'm directed by the convening officer to let you all know that no one desires these proceedings to be any more onerous than is absolutely necessary. Proper military forms will be observed, naturally, but otherwise I think we'd all prefer that things moved along as comfortably as possible."

Harry, biting back the temptation to say they'd be more comfortable with the positions reversed, restrained himself to nothing more than an uninflected, "Thanks."

Malleson accepted it with a quick nod. "You are, nominally, in the charge of the provost-marshal—which means in my charge as things stand. Captain Crookes is your escort and I don't propose to interfere in any way with the arrangements he makes with you for your movements between these two buildings, as long as there is no trouble of any kind." He let the last words hang for long enough to let it be plain they were a warning, then smiled suddenly and disarmingly, and relaxed the stiffness of his stance. "It's always a bloody business, this. I'm afraid I have to be a bit pompous about it at the start, but I'm sure you'll understand the need. I'd really prefer you to think of yourselves as being in my care, rather than in my charge. Good luck to you."

He was gone quickly, a solid and erect man marching through the door across the hall. Crookes muttered, "Good chap, that. Mustn't be put off by all the provost-marshal stuff. Malleson's quite human for a bobby."

Thomas paused by them long enough to say, "Feeling better now? Good. Lots of people on our side, you know." Then he followed Malleson.

A moment later Crookes led them off into a side room, the one window firmly closed and locked and the only furniture a bare table and a number of hard chairs. Crookes perched himself on a corner of the table and passed cigarettes around.

"Be a little while, I should think." He nodded to the second door in the room. "Court's in there. They'll be ploughing through all the paperwork for a bit before they send for us." He sent a long streamer of smoke up to the ceiling and smiled round at them. "One thing about a Field Court like this—none of that fol-lol with swords and gloves and so on. Much more comfortable this way."

It was plain that he was trying to keep the feeling light, not to let them think about the day, but they were silent, George and Ivor sitting side by side, gazing vacantly ahead, Peter patrolling in his strangely silent way and Harry drawn irresistibly to the window.

Beyond them, inside the court-room, there was the shuffling of feet and a low rattle of talk. The knock at the door was startling when it came and they were all on their feet at once, staring at the sergeant there, holding the door wide and saying to Crookes, "President would like the accused paraded now, sir, please."

Crookes stood, tall and suddenly sombre, stubbing his cigarette into an empty tin on the table.

"Right, sergeant, thank you." He turned to the four. "Well, then, gentlemen, time we went in."

Through the open door they could hear a sharp voice calling, "The Court is open," and an increase in the noise as a number of people moved in from the hall. Crookes gave them an encouraging little smile.

"Straight line, please. I'm going to march you in."

A moment later, Harry leading with Crookes on his right, they stepped smartly into the Court, marching a dozen steps, halting on the quiet command and turning right, standing at attention facing the long table. From somewhere off to one side, just out of Harry's range of vision, three men moved to stand behind the table, its length covered in green baize, a number of heavy books and several pads of paper and some pencils scattered along its length. The three turned, facing the four accused men—a Buffs major, elderly and solid; a Gunner captain, thin-faced, fair-headed; another captain, thickset and freckled under his tan, his tunic bearing the double-headed eagle of the King's Dragoon Guards.

They spaced themselves out behind three of the four chairs there, and another man moved in to stand by the empty chair to the major's right. His tunic was plain, the General Staff badges and lack of medal ribbons giving no indication of his status, only the major's crowns showing his rank. The Buffs major glanced at the others, sat and gestured to them to sit and Crookes' gentle touch on his elbow turned Harry and the other three to a row of chairs behind them. In the few seconds of turning and sitting, Harry could see that there were several rows of chairs in the body of the courtroom and he caught a glimpse of the dozen or so faces there, none of them known to him. Thomas was at a small table to the right, a younger officer bent over the papers there with him. To the left, a similar table was empty, but a moment later two men walked quickly to it, their arms full of files and books and sat down. Crookes leaned close and whispered, "Prosecuting officer; name of Llewellyn."

The Buffs major's voice was brisk and clear as he glanced around the room, his fingers pulling a sheet of paper from the open file in front of him.

229

"I should like silence, please. I shall now read the order for the convening of this Court." He cleared his throat in the hush that followed, then read, quickly and almost without inflection:

" 'On Active Service, this nineteenth day of January, 1902. Whereas it appears to me, the undersigned, an officer in command of His Majesty's Forces in South Africa, on active service, that the persons named in the annexed schedule, being subject to Military Law, have committed the offences in the said schedule mentioned; and whereas I am of opinion that it is not practicable that such offences should be tried by an ordinary General Court-Martial; I hereby convene a Field General Court-Martial to try the said persons, and to consist of the officers hereunder named. President, Major James Courtney Bainbridge, the Royal West Kent Regiment; members, Captain Leonard Edward Briggs-Cope, the 205th Field Battery, the Royal Artillery, and Captain the Honourable Michael Stuart Patrick Holding, the King's Dragoon Guards.' This Convening Order is signed 'Kitchener, General Officer Commanding and Convening Officer'." He placed the paper neatly at the bottom of the file and looked directly at the four men. Crookes leaned forward a little to glance at Thomas who stood, gesturing to the four to stand also.

The major, now known to them as Bainbridge, and the president of the Court, checked a new sheet of paper before him. "Lieutenant Harry Harbord Morant, Bush Veldt Carbineers, you now have the opportunity to challenge all or any member of this Court now convened. Do you wish to make any such challenge?"

Thomas had briefed them on this point and it was clear in their minds. One after the other they answered "No" to the president's question, Ivor Summers stuttering and flushing scarlet.

Then they sat while the room grew warmer round them, watching and listening as the president introduced the lean, grey-haired major by his side as the appointed Judge Advocate, and as he, in turn, swore in the president and the two members of the Court.

To Harry the whole thing had the feel of unreality about it, the swimmy feeling of half-waking from sleep after a heavy night of drinking. The people around them appeared less than tangible somehow, mouthing echoing words and making unusual motions. The court orderly, the sergeant who'd called them from the side room, was standing rigidly in the at-ease position off to one side and Harry watched him fascinated, seeing the fly crawling across his face and seeing too the man's fight not to move to brush it away, the corner of his lips twitching as he puffed at the insect without dislodging it. Harry wanted to dash across and brush the fly off and the desire grew and grew in him till he had to grip the edges of his chair to keep himself still. When the low talk and the shuffling of papers at the long table stopped, he dragged a long breath of relief into his lungs at the thought that now something was going to happen.

"The accused will stand."

They rose, unconsciously stiffening themselves to meet the president's level stare along the four of them.

"Number 918, Lieutenant Harry Harbord Morant, the Bush Veldt Carbineers, you are charged on three counts. Charge Number One is of the unlawful destruction of civil property during the months of October and November 1901 within the area of military operations designated as Area 6 in Field Operational Order 132; Charge Number Two is of being instrumental in causing the unlawful deaths of certain civilian persons, namely one Christiaan De Beer, aged eleven, and one Hendrik Visser, aged twenty-six, within the same designated Area; Charge Number Three is of the unlawful murder by shooting of a German civil person, namely Jacob Hesse, aged sixty-one, within the same designated Area. How do you plead to the first charge?"

"Not guilty."

"How do you plead to the second charge?"

"Not guilty."

"How do you plead to the third charge?"

"Not guilty."

Bainbridge entered each plea meticulously on the

paper in front of him and looked up again. "Do you wish to apply for an adjournment on the ground that any of the rules relating to procedure before trial have not been complied with, and that you have been prejudiced thereby, or on the ground that you have not had sufficient opportunity for preparing your defence?"

In one wild second Harry recalled the arguments they'd had with Thomas about the way they'd been arrested without knowing on what grounds, how they'd been held for six days without information and without being allowed to talk with one another or receive visitors, and he remembered Thomas saying, "Drag all that up and we'll alienate the Court at once. They'll know about it, because I'll make it my business to *make* them know about it. Keep mum and they'll think the better of you for it." Now he breathed deeply again and shook his head.

"No, thank you, sir."

The routine dragged on, each of the others being charged in precisely the same way and being asked exactly the same questions, each of them answering as Harry had done. A light mutter of talk had risen behind them during this and when the president had signed to the four of them to sit down again, he frowned over their heads and raised his voice.

"This is a military Court. The persons entitled to speak here are those directly concerned with the charges and proceedings, and no one else. At all. If conversation continues among the visitors—who are here by courtesy, I would remind you—I shall have the Court cleared."

He waited to be sure there was absolute silence, his mouth grim under his moustache, then spoke directly to the four. "I'm sure your defending officer has been at pains to explain the procedure of this Court, but I will go through it quickly so that the members and I may be sure you know what is happening. The prosecuting officer, Major Llewellyn, will first of all conduct his examination, the examination-in-chief. The defending officer may cross-examine each witness and the prosecuting officer may then re-examine if he wishes. Evidence for the defence will then be brought and the same procedure will apply. Witnesses will be brought into the Court as required. At the end of all evidence, the two counselling officers will sum up their cases, after which I may or may not present my own summation. I shall keep a record of proceedings and I shall consult with the Judge Advocate here," he nodded to his right, "should the Court require information on specific points of law. The Judge Advocate will take no other part in these proceedings." He paused and studied them with care. "I consider this to be a court of military law—and of justice. No reasonable legal or military request will be denied to the accused, but I expect proper behaviour within the Court at all times. Is all of this clearly understood?" He accepted their nods with no change of expression and Harry remembered Hasleton's opinion of the man—"a wank and an arsehole, but not unfair." Bainbridge spoke again. "Major Thomas—Major Llewellyn—you have established, I understand, that none of the accused has been tried before now with any of the offences listed in the schedule?" Thomas and Llewellyn glanced at one another for a second, then said, "Yes sir" simultaneously.

"Good. Then I think we may proceed, gentlemen. Major Llewellyn—"

For more than an hour and a half, Llewellyn spoke fluently and in a surprisingly gentle voice, the Welsh cadences becoming more marked when he made emotional points in his background story. Harry found himself leaning back, relaxing, listening with fascination to that singing voice telling a story which, after the first few minutes, seemed to be just that—a well-told tale, an entertainment. Llewellyn took the Court through the raising of the B.V.C., dwelling lyrically on the type of war they had fought and in what fierce terrain and under what physical hardships. He painted an engrossing picture of their operations against the larger backdrop of the conduct of the campaign as a whole, and stressed the success of their actions in meeting the

233

Boer on his own terms. Once the president interrupted as Llewellyn paused for a sip of water.

"Major Llewellyn, I wasn't aware that we needed this detailed statement about circumstantial affairs. Do you propose to continue for long before calling evidence to the charges?"

Llewellyn dropped his chin on his chest and considered before replying.

"Mr. President, I am perhaps going to considerable lengths to establish the—er—circumstantial affairs, because I feel it is essential for the Court to understand clearly some of the things which caused these charges to be brought against the four accused officers. I have no wish to prolong proceedings, sir, but I am sure that this explanation in advance will enable the Court to see points made later in a much clearer light."

Bainbridge grunted and waved to him to continue, and Llewellyn did, at the same pace and in the same almost eulogizing way. Harry, puzzled, glanced at the others to see that they were in the same case. George Witton caught his look and raised his gingery eyebrows high, shrugging his shoulders a little. Beyond him, Harry was surprised to see Ian Thomas slumped in his chair, his face twisted in a fierce scowl.

At lunch in the side room, Thomas cleared the point for them. "Clever little bastard, that Llewellyn. He's silk, you know—King's Counsel. What he's done is steal a good deal of our thunder, d'ye see that? He's put you people in a bloody good light—you and the B.V.C.—and I can't get at him for that. I can't even capitalize on it much. Now he'll start calling witnesses and begin to pull you to pieces and he'll try to give the Court the impression that he's doing it unwillingly— that he's conforming to the letter of the law and being forced, in all honesty, to argue your guilt *even though* you're a band of gallant heroes!"

The court-room seemed strangely familiar when they were taken back into it after their lunch, as though it was a place in which they'd spent much of their lives. Within seconds of the president's nod, Llewellyn called his first witness and the sergeant, acting as court orderly, called through the main door of the room, "Captain Viljoen, please." Viljoen, a flat-backed little man in the khaki of the South African Horse, took the oath and stood steadily, impassively answering Llewellyn's opening questions in monosyllables as the prosecuting officer took him briefly through his background as a Transvaal-born soldier against the Boers.

"And are you presently in command of an irregular unit of horse in the Northern Transvaal?"

"I am."

"This unit is known as Viljoen's Horse, and is established on lines very similar to those of the Bush Veldt Carbineers?"

"The name is right. As to the rest I don't know."

"I see. Well, perhaps you will tell us briefly of your establishment, Captain Viljoen."

"Yes. I have one hundred and ten all ranks. We work as four troops and engage in offensive patrol activity in our area—"

"That's the one designated as Area Seven in the Field Operational Orders?"

"Yes. Area Seven. We are under orders to engage the enemy as we do."

"These are written orders?"

"Yes."

"Do they include any order which states that you shall not take prisoners?"

"No."

"*Do* you take prisoners?"

"Often." There was the flicker of a smile on the still face.

"Have you ever, within your command, shot, or ordered the shooting of prisoners, civil or military?"

"No."

"Thank you." Llewellyn's wave to Thomas was both graceful and condescending.

Thomas stood directly in front of Viljoen and looked at him hard. "You are locally-born, Captain Viljoen, yet you fight on the British side. May I ask why?"

Llewellyn was on his feet at once, but the president gestured him to sit down again before he could protest.

235

Viljoen's lips tightened a little. "It is a matter of belief, of conscience."

"I see. You do not believe the Boer cause—the cause of your own people—is the right one to follow?"

"No."

"And you have engaged in military activity for British arms since the outbreak of hostilities?"

"Not since the outbreak, no."

"No. Since the formation of the first of the irregular units, such as your own and the Bush Veldt Carbineers, is that right?"

"Yes."

"A late decision." Thomas' tone was dry and Harry caught the glances among the members of the Court. "How many prisoners has your unit brought in, Captain?"

"How many? I don't know . . . a number. It has been several months—"

"More than a hundred?"

"Possibly."

Thomas held his hand behind him and his junior passed a paper to him. Without looking at it he pressed on. "If I suggested one hundred and nineteen, would that sound right to you?"

"It could well be." Viljoen's eyes were on the paper and Thomas now looked down at it.

"One hundred and one women and children. Eighteen men, all over the age of sixty-five with the exception of one man who was crippled in both legs." He stared at Viljoen whose face was now reddening. "These are the official returns, Captain. Do you agree with them?"

"I—I must. They are official."

Thomas passed the paper to the president.

"In how many actions has your command engaged?"

"I could not say, not without the records."

Again, Thomas' hand went back and received a clipped bunch of papers. He passed them to Viljoen.

"These *are* the records, Captain. Please correct me if I'm wrong. In the past five months, your command has engaged in a total of sixty-one patrols of which thirty-eight have resulted in actions of a minor or major kind. Is that correct?"

Viljoen waved the sheaf of papers. "If that is what the record says, yes."

"It is. And in that time, during those actions, no prisoners under arms were taken by your command?"

"The Boer fights hard. He fights to kill and we do the same."

"Thank you, Captain Viljoen. I take that to mean that you agree that during that time, in thirty-eight actions, *no prisoners under arms were taken by your command.*"

He sat down at once, and Llewellyn rose to re-examine. "Captain Viljoen, have any charges of any kind relating to the treatment of prisoners, civil or military, ever been brought against you or any person under your command?"

"No, sir. None." With obvious relief, Viljoen spoke loudly, assertively, and Llewellyn, smiling a little, sat down. Viljoen, excused, was a little less flat-backed when he left the Court.

During the rest of that afternoon, Llewellyn called officers from four other irregular commands, establishing with each of them the pattern of their operations as being similar to those of the B.V.C. In none of these cases was Thomas able to move as he had against Viljoen. All of the men were British and all had fought against the Boer from the outset. The records of their actions showed that many prisoners had been taken, and the best Thomas could do was compare their figures with those prepared by Lenehan to show that, on balance, they were much the same.

When the Court adjourned that evening, all that Harry could feel was that the work they'd done in the field had been made to look shabby, and he was beginning to hate the softly singing voice of Llewellyn.

It took Llewellyn five days to work his way through his witnesses, five days with a weekend interrupting them, and the four men sat through the hours in the court-room bewildered at the parade of people brought in to testify to their crimes. During the weekend, Ivor Summers said in a suddenly petulant voice, "Well, I don't care! After what those people have said this week, I just don't care a stuff any more about any of it! If the world wants to think I'm that kind of black-guard, the world can go to hell!"

Harry looked across their common room at Thomas. "That chap Llewellyn *has* been dredging, hasn't he?"

"A good lawyer does, Harry—part of his trade. I've done a bit myself."

"All very well, but fancy dragging in those women! Of course we routed them out . . . we had to. God damn it, Kitchener did the same thing on a bloody sight grander scale than we ever did—turned people out, burned their houses, burned their crops, took their stock. Isn't that what we were there for?"

George broke in. "Ah, yes, but you see, Harry, it's not the Brass that's in there on trial. It's us." His voice had grown waspish in the past few days. "Unless Ian proposes to call Kitchener in evidence. Ian?"

"Hardly. But I think you're losing sight of the fact that Llewellyn hasn't really been able to establish a single valid point. So far, anyway. We've been able to counter all along, and always with the same business of precedent, of accepted fact throughout the Army. He hasn't hurt us yet, you know."

George reddened with anger. "Hurt *us?* You make it sound as though you're being tried too! He has hurt *us,* you know. Not you—*us!*" And he half ran back to his own cell, leaving a dull silence behind him. Thomas pursed his lips and looked at the others.

"I'm sorry. I hope you understand what I mean?"

Harry nodded and Ivor sat as though he'd heard nothing. Peter stood and stretched his great frame till the bones cracked.

"Don't worry, Ian. We know you're doing everything you can. It's just that it sounds so—you know, dirtify-ing. All that stuff . . . it makes us sound like a lot of shits."

\*   \*   \*

On the morning of the fifth sitting day, Llewellyn rose at the outset and said, "Mr. President, I shall conclude my evidence today. I have three final witnesses. May we have Colonel Burnham Harrison called, please?"

Harrison was tall and stooped, an ageing man who looked like a mild-mannered schoolmaster and who attested that he was on the headquarters secretariat and that his responsibility was the drafting of orders and the supervision of their dispatch.

"And you held this same position at the time of the formation of the unit designated the Bush Veldt Carbineers, and drew up their operational orders?"

"Yes, that is so. I handed the orders myself to Major Lenehan, the Officer Commanding that formation."

"Mr. President, I have here copies of those orders from Colonel Harrison's files, their veracity agreed to by my learned friend." He passed the papers to Bainbridge. "These orders, Colonel, have only one thing to say about the treatment of captured persons. Would you be so good as to read the relevant section from my copy?"

Harrison took the orders, pulled a pair of thin spectacles onto his nose and peered down, his finger searching.

"Ah, yes. Number Seven, which states—and I remember this quite clearly—'Persons captured under arms against British forces in the field shall be treated as laid down in the Manual of Military Law. Persons found to be sheltering or otherwise aiding such persons under arms shall be arrested and placed within the jurisdiction of the nearest Provost Marshal or Garrison Commandant.'" He stared up over the glasses and Llewellyn took over at once.

"Did Major Lenehan question any part of these orders when you handed them to him?"

"Quite the contrary. He seemed delighted to receive them. He had been badgering us for them for some days and was anxious to get into the field. Captain Hunt—"

"Did he read the orders in your presence?"

239

"No, he handed them to Captain Hunt and went immediately to talk with the quartermaster, I believe."

"Thank you, Colonel. No further questions."

Thomas made his point at once. "Colonel Harrison, you tried to say something about Captain Hunt when my learned friend interrupted you. Would you tell us now what it was you wished to say?"

The president's voice was sudden and curt. "One moment, Major Thomas, please. I'm not sure you can follow that line of questioning. . . . It's—er—second-hand or something, isn't it?" He directed the last part of the query at the Judge Advocate beside him and they heard his voice for the first time, precise and with a slight hissing of sibilants.

"Colonel Harrison has mentioned Captain Hunt's name as being present at the time the orders were handed to Major Lenehan and has said further that the orders were passed to the captain. It would seem then that the captain's presence and actions were introduced into the evidence drawn by the prosecuting officer and that the defending officer may follow that line as long as it has direct application." He leaned back and became immobile again, seeming almost to disappear. The president coughed and signalled to Thomas to go on.

"Well, Colonel. About Captain Hunt?"

"Yes, well, I simply wanted to say that Hunt did read through the orders in my presence, and he too seemed delighted with them."

"He asked no questions about them?"

"Not to my recollection, no."

"And you vouchsafed no additional information?"

"None whatever. It was all there." Harrison sounded offended, as though the comprehensiveness of his work had been questioned, and Thomas let a silence build before his next question.

"Now then, Colonel, I ask you to consider carefully before answering my next question. Did you yourself tell Captain Hunt, or did you hear anyone else in a position of responsibility tell him that no prisoners were to be taken?"

"Certainly not! That's a most reprehensible suggestion!"

"Is it within your knowledge that it was Headquarters policy to advise that prisoners taken under arms should not be brought in?"

"No, it is not!"

"Thank you, Colonel. Mr. President, may it be noted please that I may wish to recall this witness at a later stage?"

Trooper Dawes came into the court-room uneasily, his peaked face pale and twitching. He'd found clean khakis from somewhere and they were a size too large for him, adding to his general air of awkwardness. It was clear he was frightened and Llewellyn took some care to calm him by making the first few questions simple and innocuous. Dawes relaxed visibly and Llewellyn moved in.

"Were you present, Dawes, at the church at Duival's Kloof on the night on which the boy Christiaan De Beer was killed?"

"I dunno what the kid's—the boy's name was, sir, but I was at the church all right."

"There was a service in progress?"

"Yes sir. Hymns and prayers, all in Dutch."

"In Afrikaans, yes. Can you tell us how the boy was killed?"

"Didn't see it meself, sir, not the shooting proper. I was round the front. Mr. Morant and Sergeant Parker and a coupla the men went inside the church and then after a bit, the sergeant come out and went up the side and round the back. Then there was this firing and yellin' and the next thing, they was carryin' Parker back all bleedin' and the boy layin' in his own cart. He was dead, sir, first time I seen 'im."

"And what happened then?"

"Well, Mr. Morant he grabs the corp and he drags it inside the church and some of us followed 'im to see what was gointa 'appen. He walks in there while they was singin' a hymn and he throws the corp on the altar sort of thing."

Harry started up, his face white, but Crookes' firm hand pulled him back into his seat, and the rifleman's face, serious now, warned him to be still and silent.

Llewellyn moved back to his chair, an eyebrow cocked at Thomas. The president's face was grim as Thomas stood in front of Dawes.

"Trooper Dawes, I just want to clear up one or two minor points, if you'll help me?"

"Yes sir, a course." Dawes' smile was cockily friendly.

"Thank you. I think you said you didn't see the actual shooting?"

" 'At's right, sir. It 'appened round the back."

"How many shots?"

"About three, I think."

"All from your own troops?"

"No, sir, there was a Mauser first. Couldn't mistake it."

"This was, presumably, the shot which killed Sergeant Parker?"

"Musta been, I s'pose, sir, yes."

"So it seems logical to assume that someone—possibly the boy himself—fired first, killing the sergeant, and that he himself was killed by the return fire?"

The Judge Advocate and the president had been leaning together as Thomas spoke and now the president interrupted. "Don't answer that question, Dawes. Mr. Thomas, I'm advised that the question is entirely out of order since any answer by Trooper Dawes would have to be pure conjecture. You may continue."

Harry could see Llewellyn's half-smile as Thomas went on. "You've said, Dawes, that Lieutenant Morant *threw* the boy's body onto an altar."

" 'At's right, sir."

"Mr. President, the paper numbered A6 in your file is a deposition by Lieutenant George Cann, Royal Engineers, together with several perspective drawings and plans made by him at the church in question. You will see there is no altar within the church, simply a table upon a platform." The president nodded, passing the papers along the table as Thomas turned back to Dawes.

"Properly speaking then, the body was placed upon this *table?*"

"Well, yessir. I only thought—"

"Placed, Dawes? Or thrown?"

"Well, sir, depends what you mean. Dropped, I s'pose."

"Yes, of course. The boy's body was *not* 'thrown on the altar', but dropped on the table?"

"Yessir." Dawes was quieter, his eyes watchful.

"The—er—cart in which the body was brought from the back of the church. Was there anything in it other than the body?"

"Yessir. 'Bout twenty rifles, some of 'em our issue, an' a lot of bandoliers."

"Thank you, Dawes. You've been most helpful."

Llewellyn wasn't going to leave it at that. "Just before you're excused, Trooper Dawes, let's be quite clear. You were on patrol under Lieutenant Morant's command, some of you entered a church while a service was in progress and as a result of this an eleven-year-old boy was shot to death?"

"Right, sir."

"I have no more questions, sir, but I may wish to recall Trooper Dawes later."

It was eleven o'clock when Llewellyn called Booth, and the hot room seemed to Harry to become stifling suddenly. Booth looked well, spotlessly clean, his hair and moustache neatly-trimmed, the chevrons on his sleeves pipeclayed, his medal ribbons gay on his chest. Llewellyn took him quickly through the preliminaries, then through the actions at the church, apparently seeking to do no more than confirm the impression he'd striven for with Dawes' evidence. Thomas looked puzzled, but approached Booth with confidence.

"Corporal, you joined the B.V.C. as a trooper, isn't that so?"

"Yes, sir. Transferred at my own request sir—chance to see a bit more action."

Harry, watching the members, saw Holding, the Dragoon, give a pleased little smile. Thomas went straight on.

"You were in Lieutenant Morant's troop?"

"Yes, sir, I was. Best troop in the unit."

"Please restrict yourself to answering my questions, Corporal. You were promoted corporal within that troop . . . by whom?"

"Mr. Morant, sir. It was his half-troop then, of course. Captain Hunt was in com—"

Bainbridge cut across the flow. "The defending officer has asked you to restrict yourself to answering the questions asked, Booth. I'm telling you to do so."

"Sir!"

Thomas looked happier. "Lieutenant Morant promoted you to the rank of corporal?"

"Yes, sir."

"On the night of the combined action of De Koven's Farm and Klinger's Farm, the night on which Captain Hunt was killed, did Lieutenant Morant carry out any unusual punishment upon you?"

"No, sir."

"Did he require you—indeed, order you—to kneel down by Captain Hunt's body and write a description of it at his dictation?"

"Yes, sir."

"And you didn't consider that unusual?"

"Well, sir—Mr. Hunt and him was friends. He was upset."

Even Holding looked sceptical at the falsity of the tone.

"So that you made no effort to report Lieutenant Morant's actions or to seek redress for them?"

"No, sir. No reason to."

"No reason to." He paused. "Am I to take it then that you agreed with Lieutenant Morant's actions, that you respected him as your immediate commander?"

"Yes, sir. Always. He got me my stripes, after all."

Thomas waved a resigned hand and sat down, still

puzzled. Llewellyn's re-examination wiped away the puzzlement and replaced it with anger. Llewellyn rocked on his heels in front of Booth, smiling at him.

"At the end of the action referred to by Major Thomas, Booth, the action in which Captain Hunt was killed, and *following* Lieutenant Morant's subjecting you to an indignity under stress of emotion—"

Thomas was on his feet at once and the Judge Advocate, with a nod from Bainbridge, raised a finger to him, addressing Llewellyn.

"That is not permissible, Major Llewellyn, as I'm sure you know. The Court has a right to an apology and should caution you about procedure."

Llewellyn was unruffled. "Of course, sir. My apologies, Mr. President, and I accept your caution. Now, Corporal Booth, what were the final events that night at De Koven's, please?"

"Well, we got the wounded tidied up and into a couple of carts, we rounded up all the livestock and we buried the dead. Nine altogether, sir."

"Including Captain Hunt?"

"Yes, sir. Buried 'em all on a bit of a hill there."

"And Lieutenant Morant was present throughout this?"

"Well, not properly speakin', sir. He sort of went off by himself after—after we found Mr. Hunt. Then he come back when the buryin' was done."

"And did what? Said a prayer, perhaps?"

"No, sir. Not a prayer. He spoke to us though—the men."

"Can you tell us what he said?"

"Yes, sir. He said, 'Don't bring me any more prisoners'."

There was a buzz, quietened at once by Bainbridge's scowl.

"Those were his exact words? 'Don't bring me any more prisoners'?"

"Yes, sir."

Harry could hear himself saying it, looking down on Geoffrey's grave, the farmhouse burning below them.

Dawes, recalled by Llewellyn, was voluble about the incident with Visser.

"Well, sir, he was like a wild animal, Mr. Morant was—"

Thomas was on his feet immediately, hand in the air in protest and the Judge Advocate nodded, hissing something to Bainbridge. The president spoke directly to Dawes. "Trooper Dawes, you are not permitted to make remarks like that about the accused. You'll confine yourself to describing the events without giving us personal comments about people. Go on."

"Yes, sir—sorry, sir. Anyway, this loony, Visser, 'e was just standin' there when Mr. Morant run over an' grabbed at 'im an' tore 'is jacket open. An' then he sorta glared at 'im an' 'e tole us to get the clothes off 'im—Visser's clothes, that is."

Llewellyn was quiet, gentle. "And did you remove Visser's clothes?"

"Not me, no, sir. Some of the others—Sergeant Mulholland was one—they pulled 'em off and the poor geezer was stood there in 'is drores an' 'e was cryin'."

Llewellyn let it sink in, nodding several times before speaking. "Was Visser armed?"

"Not then 'e wasn't, no, sir. But Mr. Morant 'e slung a rifle at 'im an' then 'e just up an' shot 'im. Right in the phiz—the face, sir. An' then 'e went on shootin' 'im till 'is gun was empty."

Llewellyn made him go through it again, stressing points with him till everyone in the court had the gruesome picture clearly in mind. Then he waved him to Thomas.

"Trooper Dawes, these clothes Visser was wearing— did you recognize them?"

"No, sir. Khaki, they was, an' old . . . coulda been any sorta clothes."

"British Army uniform?"

"Coulda been, I suppose sir. I wouldn't be sure."

"Did you see any identifying mark on them or in them—a label perhaps?"

"No, sir. Some of the lads reckoned they see Mr. 'Unt's name in 'em, but I never."

"And what happened to the clothes afterwards?"

Dawes smiled.

"Oh, Sergeant Mulholland took 'em an' burned 'em, sir."

Llewellyn sat back satisfied and declined to re-examine.

They sat silent through lunch, Crookes attempting to raise a smile with his inconsequential chatter and failing miserably. Ian Thomas didn't join them at all and they filed back into the court-room after the recess, still silently. For the first time Harry felt a sense of deep depression.

Llewellyn had advised the Court of the closure of his parade of witnesses immediately before the lunch break and now Thomas walked easily to a central spot, seeming to anchor his small feet firmly, not speaking till he was set.

"Mr. President, I do not propose to speak at length about the background to the charges brought against the accused. My learned friend has already done that admirably." Llewellyn's smile was broad. "Neither do I propose to speak of the military virtues of these men, for their uniforms and decorations attest to these. At the outset I want to state simply that they have entered pleas of Not Guilty to all the charges brought against them. *They* do not believe themselves to be guilty of crimes or offences. *I* do not believe it—and it is my conviction that the Court will not believe it by the end of these proceedings. Now, with the Court's approval, and that of my learned friend, I wish to change the stated order of call of my witnesses."

Bainbridge glanced at the Judge Advocate who muttered to him. Thomas and Llewellyn were waved forward and for a moment or two there was a low consultation, then Llewellyn, clearly angry, stamped back to his chair. Thomas, face impassive, turned to the court orderly, listening as he raised his voice through the doorway.

"Call Corporal Thomas Booth."

Harry spun around, staring, then back to look at

the others, all of them showing their astonishment. Booth marched back in, concern on his face. Bainbridge checked Thomas and spoke across him to Booth.

"Corporal Booth, the defending officer has asked for your recall and for you to appear and to testify as a witness for the defence. I am advised that this cannot be so unless you agree to do so. In the interest of the truth and of justice, I can see no reason for you *not* to agree, but, of course, the decision rests with you."

The implication was plain and Booth's discomfort was just as plain, his eyes flickering between Bainbridge and Llewellyn, who pointedly looked away. Bainbridge snapped, "Well, Corporal?"

Booth swallowed. "Sir, I—I don't think I should."

"Major Thomas?"

"Mr. President, members of the Court, I have no desire to press the point. I would, however, request that Corporal Booth remain within the body of the Court subject to the president's discretion as to his recall."

Again the whispered consultation along the table, the Judge Advocate's hissing sibilants the only distinguishable sounds, then Bainbridge nodded. "Very well. Corporal, you may be excused, but you will remain within this room." He waited till Booth had found a seat in an otherwise empty row. "Now, Major Thomas."

"Thank you, sir. My first witness is Sergeant Gordon Connelly."

The court orderly startled everybody by marching briskly forward to the witness chair instead of calling the name, and Thomas left it to the last moment before explaining.

"This is Sergeant Connelly, sir. The court orderly."

The Judge Advocate leaned almost entirely across the table. "Now, now, Major Thomas. The sergeant has been present throughout the testimony given. It would be entirely improper—"

"With respect, sir. Sergeant Connelly approached me in some distress during the luncheon recess with information which I feel it is vital for the Court to hear, otherwise I would not have taken this most unusual step."

"I am in some doubt, Major, whether his testimony would be admissible, even so."

"With your permission, sir, I have here copies of the sergeant's sworn statement to me, before witnesses. If I may pass them to you, and one to my learned friend, to assist your deliberations?" Without waiting for an answer, he stepped forward, placing papers on the table, then turned and carried one sheet to Llewellyn. For a full minute no one moved or spoke. Then the Judge Advocate looked up and said something quietly to Bainbridge, who nodded his head. The two captains behind the table made the same indication and Bainbridge spoke.

"Major Llewellyn, we would value your opinion in this."

Llewellyn, his face dark with anger, stalked a little forward from his table. "Mr. President, I see no need for Sergeant Connelly to testify. I should like to assure the Court and my learned friend that, had I known of this earlier, I should not have called Corporal Booth as a witness. With the Court's permission, I would suggest that the defending officer read the sergeant's sworn statement and that it be accepted into the record of proceedings." He nodded curtly to Thomas and sat down.

Bainbridge looked approving. "The Court agrees. You may be excused, Sergeant. Major Thomas, please read the statement."

That vibrant voice of Thomas' rang in the otherwise fully silent room. " 'This statement was made voluntarily by Number 25986, Sergeant Gordon Connelly, the Wiltshire Regiment, in the presence of Major Ian Thomas, New South Wales Lancers, Captain Jeremy Andrews, the Scots Guards and Regimental Sergeant-Major Angus Charles Fergusson, the Scots Guards, at Pietersburg on Tuesday, 24th January 1902. I, Gordon Connelly, solemnly swear and testify that on this day while on duty as court orderly at Pietersburg, I was in the presence of Corporal Thomas Booth, a witness for the prosecution at the Field General Court-Martial there being held. During the lunch recess on this day, Corporal Thomas Booth did say, in my presence and hearing, the following words: "That'll do for them, I reckon. I tell you, I'd walk from Spelonken to Pretoria to see Morant in front of a firing-squad." Corporal Booth then spat and walked away.' "

Thomas looked up and there was a shuffle in the Court as everyone, it seemed, turned to where Booth sat, deathly pale.

Bainbridge spoke directly to him. "Corporal Booth, this will become a matter for a separate Court of Inquiry. Is the assistant provost-marshal present?" Malleson stood up at the back of the room. "You will place Corporal Booth under open arrest pending that Court. Sergeant Connelly, you are relieved of duty as court orderly, and I shall write a note of commendation on your conduct to your commanding officer. Thank you. I think, gentlemen, the Court should adjourn now until nine tomorrow morning."

In the common room that evening, even Ivor seemed happy, and Thomas was gleeful.

"It's just what we needed. Pure luck, of course, but just what we needed. It's got everyone with you now, lads, all the sympathy in the world!"

Hasleton, beaming, slapped Thomas' shoulder. "I told you—I told you what he was like, didn't I? Said he was a prick—but fair!"

Dinner that evening was the gayest for some time and when Lenehan arrived he was greeted with shouts of joy and they talked above one another in a swell of sound trying to explain what had happened. Peter noticed Lenehan's apparently listless reaction, and rumbled across the table at him.

"Come on now, John, it's good news!"

"Yes. I'm glad. But I'm afraid I've some bad news, too." He swung sideways to face Harry.

"It's Owen Fisher. He died this afternoon."

\* \* \*

Sleep wasn't easy that night. Owen's face kept swimming out of the darkness . . . lean and brown and with the lopsided grin . . . and then the naked weeping face he'd seen weeks before in the hospital. The messages since then had said he'd been improving but Lenehan had told them that Owen would never have been whole, or wholly sane, again, that his lucid times were less and less frequent and that he had no feeling for life. He'd just screamed one last time and died. When Harry did fall asleep, he dreamed of screaming faces.

The scream was a high yell, nearby, and overlaid with the sharp crackle of rifle-fire. Harry scraped the gum of sleep from the corners of his eyes as he leaned against the wall, peering from the barred window, seeing nothing but the usual barren night-time scene there, then leaped for the door. In the corridor the night-guards were running to where someone was hammering for the main door to be unlocked and Harry shook the bars shouting, "What the devil's going on?" The others joined his shouts and the echoes rang and jolted back along the stones. Then there was more light and voices and keys in the locks and the four of them were in the corridor, Peter gigantically naked, the others in their drawers and the duty sergeant was standing aside to let the orderly officer through, mouth grim and eyes startled.

"Right—let's have quietness, please."

In the moment's silence, the gunfire beyond the walls could be heard louder and closer and there was a bugle ringing somewhere and, faintly, the jumbled thump of hooves.

"We're under attack. The Boers are coming in past us; probably on the other side of the valley, too. The commandant would like you all to get dressed quickly, please."

"How many of them?"

Harry's voice was crisp and it halted the others, already turning back to their cells.

"No idea. A hell of a lot, by the sound of it. Hurry, please. I'll be back immediately."

In the cell, on the outside of the building, the fighting

251

noises were certainly louder and from the edge of the window Harry saw a dark clump of horsemen stretched at a full gallop across the flat and heading down towards where the lights were coming up fast in the town. There was continuous firing in the dip and out of his sight, but the night sky was glowing a little down there with the start of a fire. Harry jerked on his trousers, shirt and boots and ran back into the corridor, finding the others already there and the orderly officer just coming back through the door from the guards' rest room. He was breathing fast.

"Gentlemen, it looks as though—" There was the singing scream of metal on stone as a bullet tore through a cell window and threw itself against the wall of the corridor, bouncing away with a diminishing yelp. They all ducked and the orderly officer took up where he'd stopped, his mouth tilting in a tight grin. "—as though we're under attack ourselves. Colonel Hasleton has asked me if you'll accept weapons under parole and assist in the defence of this place."

Peter growled, "Give me something to shoot with, for Christ's sake, and let's get on with it."

Within seconds, rifles and bandoliers had been passed through to them and they stood for a second, smiling at one another at the feel of it, then automatically turned to Harry. He looked at the orderly officer and nodded.

"Right—you'll have work to do. I'll take over here if you like. Can we get onto the roof?"

"You might—from the back, anyway. Sergeant, get that end door open."

They ran down the corridor to the far end, the sergeant struggling with the stiff lock, then they were outside, the night cool and loud around them. Harry looked up and nodded again.

"We can manage. Off you go." Without waiting to see the other two race away, he tossed his rifle to Peter and stood back a couple of feet. Peter and George, their own rifles on the ground, held Harry's like a bar between them. He took a short step, jumped onto the horizontal rifle with one foot and the other two hoisted.

His hands went up to the stone coping set well above the doorway and he could feel the shove against his feet as the others hoisted the rifle, pushing him up till he grasped the roof parapet and jerked a leg over, dragging himself across and immediately turning and hanging head down to take the rifles as they were passed. Peter lifted George effortlessly and Harry grabbed his wrists, pulling him up and over. Ivor came up like a feather and Harry called down at Peter's upturned face.

"See if you can find us a Maxim, and a couple of boxes for you to stand on. You're too bloody big for us to drag you up."

The grin from below seemed to light the night.

"Yair, I'm big and beautiful all right, Harry. Back in a minute."

Harry rolled back to look around him.

The parapet was no more than two feet high and the pitch of the iron roof ran down into it all the way round, the skylights which lit their corridor by day set into it on either side of the ridge. Between the bottom edge of the iron and the inside of the parapet there was perhaps two feet of flat space which acted as a gutter, the downpiping holes puncturing it at intervals. His urgent wave took the other two after him as he scuttled along that space, moving above their cells to the front corner of the building. The noise was louder now and, risking a quick look over the edge, Harry could see that there was fire coming from the small clump of trees on the far side of the road and from the house, partly wrecked, a little further along. A sudden spurt of flame showed him that there were some Boers in the gully alongside the road. Below them, in the room above the entrance, there was the muffled sound of the return fire and away across the flat where they'd taken their daily exercise, the sound was building into what seemed like a heavy fight. Harry sat in the gutter considering for a moment.

"They're across the road there and in that old house. George, you stay in this corner; and Ivor, you slide along about halfway and you should be able to lob into them easily. They'll spot you as soon as you start firing, so watch yourselves. I'm going back to see if Peter's done any good."

He could hear the two rifles open up behind him as he slithered back.

Below, outside the back door, Peter was staring up, two men with him and the bulk of a Maxim between them.

"Harry? I've got the bugger. If we get the wheels and the shield off we might be able to get it up there."

"Fine. Go ahead and try."

He watched as the axle-pins were banged out, the trail uncoupled and the steel protector plate pulled off. One of the men lashed a rope round the muzzle and breech and threw the end up to Harry. A moment later Peter was alongside him, pushed up on the shoulders of the men he'd brought along and he took the rope and called down, "Right—let's give it a burl." Lifted from below and with Peter's huge muscles heaving steadily from above, the bulky body of the gun came up fast and they wrestled it across the parapet.

"I'll take this, Harry; you bring the belts."

Peter stood, the Maxim cradled in his arms, his shoulder muscles forcing his shirt tight and his face gleaming with sweat; and Harry, struggling with a box of ammunition belts behind him, shook his head in admiration at the great man's strength and surefootedness in that narrow gutter-way.

Bullets began to hiss and sing past them, ripping into and bouncing from the iron roof with tearing clangs, but they were at the front corner within a couple of minutes, George wriggling aside to let Peter lower the Maxim onto the parapet, then taking the box from Harry and quickly feeding a belt end into the breech. Peter, grinning like a mischievous schoolboy, pulled back the cocking handle and squinted along the barrel, depressing it towards the gully and the trees and snapping a short test burst.

Harry banged him hard on the shoulder.

"Good man, Peter. Go to it. George, you stay and load. I'm going up with Ivor."

Boer bullets were smacking into the stonework just

below them and still ripping above their heads into the iron roof, but the heavy stammer of the Maxim took effect very quickly. From the other end of the roof where he and Ivor kept up an accurate fire, speeding up the rate whenever the Maxim stopped for reloading, Harry could see there were now several small fires burning in the town. But he could tell also that the fighting was moving back towards them, that the Boer attack had been held and was being beaten back. A moment or two later, a large group of horsemen came up out of the dip, scattering as they rode fast across the flat towards the road, scattering wider and many of them falling as Peter's fire went in among them. One horse checked and staggered, then veered wildly towards the prison before going down, the rider leaping free and running, head down and arms pumping. Harry squinted, locking his sights onto the speeding figure and squeezed the trigger gently, feeling the butt come back into his shoulder, seeing the little manikin fall, the legs kicking and jerking. He lowered the rifle and muttered, "Go on, scream, you bastard. That's for Owen."

There was a ladder propped against the roof for them to come down by and half a dozen men went up it then to recover the Maxim and the ammunition belts. Outside the back door, Hasleton, tunic unbuttoned over his nightshirt, stood smiling, the orderly officer and several soldiers and field police with him. They were all dishevelled and sweaty.

George jumped off the ladder and flicked a friendly finger at the Commandant. "I tell you what, Colonel— I didn't think I liked this place well enough to fight for it!"

Ivor, his face happier than it had been for weeks, chipped in. "Like it or not, it's the only place we've got, George!"

Hasleton cleared his throat. "Gentlemen, most gallant, most gallant. I'm deeply indebted to you. We all are." He insisted on shaking their hands.

Peter, smoke-blackened, growled, "That's all right,

sir—made quite a change," and Harry added, "It's what we're supposed to be doing after all, sir."

Hasleton looked suddenly embarrassed as he stepped back a pace. "Yes, of course . . . that's quite so. Er— I wonder, gentlemen—" His eyes went to the weapons in their hands and they realized what he meant, realized that the men behind Hasleton were all armed and close. He went on, stumbling, "Little though I like it, lads—er—I'm afraid I must ask you—" he let it die away, his hand sketching a gesture towards their rifles. Harry, his face stony, held his rifle across his body, muzzle down. His fingers went to the bolt, working it fast, sending a stream of shining cartridges in an arc. Then he simply opened his hands and let the weapon drop and turned, walking into the dark corridor, into his cell and slamming the door behind him.

The sitting of the Court the following morning showed things in a new light, perhaps because everyone in the room had been awake for a good part of the night, many of them actively engaged in the fight with the Boers, now known to have been a strong force under Beyers, beaten back with quite heavy losses but leaving considerable damage behind them and a number of British wounded and dead.

Thomas addressed the Court as soon as it was in session.

"Mr. President, gentlemen, I want to depart, if I may, from the business of presentation of evidence in defence of the accused in order to speak briefly about their conduct last night. Everyone here knows of the events which took place; some will not know that these men, accused and imprisoned on charges which the prosecution has not been able to substantiate, willingly gave their parole and accepted weapons in the defence of the very prison in which they are being held. In the defence, Mr. President, of this town and its inhabitants and its military installations. If it is desired, I can call the prison commandant, Colonel Hasleton, and the men under his command, to testify to the gallantry of the accused and to the importance of their contribution to the defeat of the enemy last night. I do not think that will be necessary—it is already common knowledge. Sir, I quote to the Court the words of England's greatest soldier, Arthur Wellesley, the Duke of Wellington. The Iron Duke himself said, and recorded for posterity, 'The performance of a duty of honour and trust after knowledge of a military offence ought to convey a pardon.'" He paused, looking at them, Bainbridge and the Judge Advocate watching him expressionlessly, Holding, the Dragoon, nodding seriously, Briggs-Cope, the youngest member of the Court, looking down as he doodled on a pad. *"Ought to convey a pardon,* sir. Wellington's own words and his own feelings. Since it is undoubted that these men performed a duty of honour and trust after knowledge of a military offence *which has not been proven,* I ask whether this Court is not prepared, is not, in fact, willing, to follow the Duke's dictum. I ask that the accused be granted an immediate pardon."

He sat down in a weighted silence and no one moved until Bainbridge seemed to shake himself into speech.

"The Court is sensible of the conduct of the accused last night. I am going to adjourn to seek the advice of the Judge Advocate and his staff. The accused and all Court officers will remain close to this room for recall, please."

They waited for two hours in the side room, Crookes assuring them that the longer the delay, the more likely the Court would be to accept Thomas' request. Thomas himself spent only a few minutes with them, but seemed quite lighthearted and when they filed back into the court-room, the four men themselves felt a wash of hope. It didn't last. Bainbridge leaned forward on the table and directed his words to Thomas.

"The Court has gone thoroughly into this matter and wishes to commend the accused on their actions during last night. There is, however, no question of a pardon and the proceedings will continue." Harry heard Ivor's low cry above the mutter from the people in the courtroom behind him and Thomas strode forward scowling.

That evening at dinner in their common room, George said, "Remember what Ian told us right at the start . . . something's stewing up, he said. He was bloody right. They're stewing *us* up!" Hasleton looked in long enough to thank them again and to denounce the Court in blistering terms, but none of them felt like talking and they went early to their cells.

Harry thought about that day, about the way the Court had seemed to change its attitude. Throughout Llewellyn's period, virtually no questions had come from the long table, but today, Bainbridge and occasionally Holding had intervened a number of times to question witnesses themselves. The atmosphere had been one almost of hostility. Lenehan had been called early and had been eloquent in praise of his officers' work. Bainbridge had broken into Thomas' line.

"Major Lenehan, no one is disputing their soldierly qualities or their bravery in action. I remind you, however, that the charges against these men are because of actions which were *not* soldierly. We've been told by Colonel Harrison of Headquarters that the orders he drafted for you were explicit and contained no reference to the treatment of prisoners other than those in the Field Orders. We have also been told—at secondhand—that Captain Hunt stated that *he* had been instructed that no prisoners were to be taken. I would like to know whether you were told anything of that kind?"

"No, sir. I had no direct conversation with Colonel Harrison about our orders. But Captain Hunt came to me as soon as he had spoken with the colonel and advised me of the 'no prisoners' information."

"In other words, Hunt was the only one to hear this supposed statement?"

"Yes, sir. But I have no reason to doubt—"

"And Captain Hunt is now, unfortunately, dead?"

"Yes, sir, he is."

\* \* \*

George Witton had, not unexpectedly, lost his temper. Holding had asked leave of the president and questioned George.

"Were you present during the incident at the church at Duival's Kloof?"

"I was not."

"Were you present when the man Visser was shot?"

"No."

"Were you present during the interrogation of the missionary—er—Hesse?"

"I was there when he was brought in and when he left—but there was no interrogation."

"Really? You realize that all three charges laid apply to you, although you say you were not present on two particular occasions?"

"I do—and I'm damned if I see why! None of us should be here—"

Bainbridge's voice was icy. "Lieutenant Witton, I warn you that you must behave yourself. Unless you conduct yourself in a proper military manner and show this Court the respect due to it, the consequences will be serious."

George gaped at him. "Serious! What the hell do you think they are now?"

Thomas leapt up and quietened George, making apologies to the Court and managing to prevent things becoming worse. They were bad enough.

When Bainbridge spoke to Ivor, it was with an ill-concealed contempt.

"You are a British officer, Lieutenant Summers, a regular Army officer, and might be expected to have a clearer understanding of the forms of war. Yet, if the testimony we have is correct, you made no attempt to intervene in the interrogation of Jacob Hesse or the subsequent events. Why is that?"

Ivor was white-faced and clammy with sweat. "Sir, with respect, there was *no* interrogation of Hesse, as Lieutenant Witton has already pointed out. And I don't know what the—the—subsequent events were."

"You say that on oath?"

"I do, sir."

Bainbridge made no reply, but wrote something on his pad with great deliberation.

Peter Handcock seemed taller than the president, even sitting down, and his broad, square face was set grimly when Bainbridge questioned him.

"In the matter of the shooting of the man Hendrik Visser—you were present?"

"Yes, sir."

"What part did you take?"

"None, sir. No active part, that is."

"What part was taken by any person present, other than Lieutenant Morant?"

"None, sir."

"What part was taken by Lieutenant Morant?"

"He shot Visser, sir. And quite rightly."

"I will not accept comment, Lieutenant Handcock. You said, 'He shot Visser' . . . after what kind of trial?"

"Trial, sir? I don't follow."

"Was the court at the trial of Visser constituted like this?" Bainbridge waved his hand about. "Were the appropriate paragraphs of the King's Regulations observed?"

Peter glanced around him and let his look dwell on the officers behind the table.

"Was it like this? No, sir, not half so handsome. We were out fighting Boers, not sitting comfortably behind barbed-wire entanglements. We got 'em and we shot 'em under Rule 303."

There was a titter from the spectators, silenced by Bainbridge's glare, which he then turned on Peter.

"Rule 303, what does that mean?"

"A 303 cartridge, sir. Very effective."

Harry grinned, but there was no answering smile from Thomas.

The succeeding two days brought a string of B.V.C. troopers to the Court, men who testified almost without deviation to the real events at the church, at De

Koven's and with Hesse, reducing Dawes' story to its true dimensions and even further discrediting Booth. Despite persistent questioning from the Court and from Llewellyn, one man after another told the same thing and Mulholland proved an excellent witness, reporting in great detail on the finding of Hunt's body and the effect on Harry, and on the later events with Visser in Hunt's uniform. But while Thomas was able to extract all this with ease and was able to build a solid base of matching testimony, Llewellyn was just as able to reduce much of it by pointing out that the stress of emotion had little to do with the commission of the acts.

When Thomas put Harry up, there was a stir. Everyone realized that this was likely to be the crux of the whole affair, that Morant was the key figure. Thomas, after discussing it with Harry the night before, had determined to use Llewellyn's own tactics and try to cut the ground from under the feet of the opposition by directing his questions as *they* would be likely to do and establish Harry's situation clearly.

"Of those accused here, Lieutenant Morant, is it true to say that you are the only officer who was present during the circumstances leading to the major charges—at the church, De Koven's Farm and the deaths of Visser and Hesse?"

"Perfectly true, yes."

"Is it equally true that there were three men who could very largely substantiate the untruth of the charges against you—Captain Geoffrey Hunt, Squadron Sergeant-Major Owen Fisher and Sergeant Stanley Parker?"

"That is so."

"And that all these valuable witnesses are dead?"

"Yes. They're dead." Harry felt a wave of desolation as he said it.

"So that your testimony, which affects not only yourself but the other accused, stands, in some respects, materially unsupported?"

"It does."

"And you are on oath and realize that this Court is searching only for the truth in these matters?"

261

"Yes."

"Then I ask you, Lieutenant Morant, whether you are guilty of the destruction of civil property by burning or other methods?"

"Yes, I am, if guilty's the word. In the ordinary way of these things, when we discovered a place with arms in it or with Boer troops in it or with evidence to show the enemy had been given aid, we cleared the people and livestock from it and burnt it."

"Was this practice isolated to your area of operations?"

"Not by half! It's quite standard—look at the clearing of the ground ahead of the blockhouse line!"

"Thank you. Now I ask you whether you are guilty of the death of the boy Christiaan De Beers at the church at Duival's Kloof?"

"I am not, and neither was anyone under my command, except that they returned the boy's killing fire."

"And are you guilty of the death of Hendrik Visser?"

"Of *his* death, yes, as an act of war."

"An act of war, you say?"

"Yes, of retributive war. He was armed and wearing the clothing of a British officer who had been mutilated and killed by Boers."

"And are you guilty of the death of Jacob Hesse?"

"No, in no way. We tried to stop him going forward, in fact."

Thomas turned to Bainbridge. "Mr. President, I would like to waive further examination of Lieutenant Morant and request, on his behalf, that he may make a statement to the Court."

Bainbridge frowned, but nodded, and Thomas gave Harry an encouraging wink. Harry straightened and looked at each of them in turn. Briggs-Cope looked away; Bainbridge stared over his head; the Judge Advocate stared back, lips pursed, and Holding smiled faintly.

"Mr. President and gentlemen, I only want to say this, that you can't blame the young'uns—these others here. They just carried out their orders as I did—and they had to do that." His voice went up a little. "We

262

all carried out orders—they obeyed mine and thought they were obeying those of Headquarters. Captain Hunt told all of us we'd been directed not to bring in prisoners, and he and I discussed that—discussed the wrongness of such an order. None of us obeyed that one order, and that's likely to be the only crime of which we're guilty in military law. I did not carry out that order until my best friend was brutally murdered, and then I resolved to do exactly as I had been told. But if anyone is to blame, then it is only me."

No one behind the long table spoke. Bainbridge nodded towards Llewellyn who walked forward almost reluctantly.

"Lieutenant Morant, the vigour and earnestness of your statement convinces me that no words of mine will alter what you say. I shall ask only three questions of you, and then only to corroborate earlier statements made in this Court. Did you shoot to death Hendrik Visser?"

"I did. For good reason."

"Please, answer the questions and no more. Did you shoot to death Hendrik Visser?"

"Yes." Harry's chin was up and his face grim.

"While in temporary command of the Bush Veldt Carbineers, were you actively patrolling in the area designated as Area Six, the area in which Jacob Hesse was shot?"

"Yes."

"Close to the body, two items were found—an empty British bully beef tin and this—" he drew from his pocket the length of ravelled green cloth which Gregory's lieutenant had found, and which had been lying on his table since the first day. He held it before Harry. "Is this a puggaree band similar in every way to those worn by members of the Bush Veldt Carbineers?"

Harry stared at it.

"It's a piece of green cloth."

"Exactly similar to those worn by you and your men?"

"Yes."

"Thank you. That is all I wish to know."

Thomas rose to re-examine and handed Harry a small paper package.

"Lieutenant Morant, would you please unwrap this package and show the Court the contents?"

Harry pulled out a strip of dark green cloth.

"Now would you read the slip of paper enclosed with it, please?"

Harry smiled gently as he read. "Received from Major I. F. Thomas the sum of twopence for one yard of dark green cotton. Signed, L. Braun for Braun's Stores, Pietersburg."

"Thank you. Nothing further, Mr. President."

"Very well. The Court will adjourn until nine o'clock tomorrow morning for summing-up by defence and prosecution. We shall hope, gentlemen, to keep tomorrow's proceedings as brief as is reasonable so that the Court may also sum up. Adjourned."

"Reluctantly, Mr. President, I'm forced to submit that the evidence heard from Colonel Harrison is worthless and irrelevant. A certain conversation said to have taken place between the colonel and the late Captain Hunt, and reported by Hunt immediately to Major Lenehan and later to other officers under his command, was denied by Colonel Harrison. I suggest there has been ample testimony to show that Colonel Harrison was, to be charitable, forgetful of what had actually happened. Attempts have been made throughout these proceedings to link the four accused in responsibilities for a series of so-called 'crimes', and yet there has been no valid evidence to show that crimes were committed, only acts of war—although there *has* been evidence to show that not all the accused were present at these places when the alleged crimes were committed. Attempts have been made to suggest there was no justification for the shooting of Hendrik Visser, although there has been more than enough testimony to the facts of his being an armed enemy when captured in the dress of a *murdered* British officer. No attempt has been made by the Court to consider fairly the conduct of the accused during the Boer attack on this settlement, nor to consider the extreme stress and provocation placed upon one of them, Lieutenant Morant, by the brutal and savage murder of his friend and troop commander."

Thomas had been speaking for little more than a quarter of an hour, his vibrant voice controlled, never raised but reaching every ear in the room. "Further, gentlemen, the charges brought against each of the officers accused implies their complicity in alleged crimes, implies that each of them was, if not directly guilty, guilty as an accessory before or after certain alleged facts . . . not one of which has been proven here! Lieutenant Morant, acting in temporary command of the Bush Veldt Carbineers at the time of the arrest of the four accused, has gallantly stated that he alone is to blame for any fault; but it is my assertion that none of these men is to blame for anything, unless carrying out their duties in the face of hazard and hardship is a matter for blame. And following their arrest—an arrest made in the field, within sight of the Boer rifles, in front of their own men, an arrest made *without explanation,* Mr. President—following that, these brave men were subjected to close confinement and without the benefit of advice or friendship or even information for a period of several days! This hardly seems the way of British military justice. Gentlemen, I submit that the facts are quite clear. The boy Christiaan De Beers was shot during a military engagement in which he himself bore and used arms against our troops, killing one of them. The man Hendrik Visser was shot as an enemy combatant, bearing arms and clearly implicated in the murder of a British officer. The man Jacob Hesse was shot by unknown persons after he had disregarded the warnings given to him by the accused about proceeding further into enemy-held territory. None of the accused did other than obey what he took to be his legal orders. If the Court holds that these men were mistaken in their views about what they were entitled to do, then certainly the accused are open to censure. But not to a charge of murder."

Thomas sat down to a shuffle of feet and a buzz of

muted comment and Llewellyn, responding to Bainbridge's nod, moved slowly forward.

"Mr. President, members of the Court, let me say at once that the matter of the military conduct of the accused, in general, is not and has not been in dispute. Had there been any doubt of their gallantry, their actions during the attack here recently would have dispelled that and, in fairness to them and to my learned friend, I must add my voice to those which have said that Wellington's dictum might well have been taken into stronger account as a result of that night's work."

There was a gasp from the spectators and a quick handclap before Bainbridge slammed his hand down on the table, and again. His face was angry.

"That is quite enough! There *will* be silence in this Court!" He waited until there was no sound, then pointed at Llewellyn who went on undisturbed, the Welsh in his voice more marked now.

"Having said that, sir, I trust it will be clear that I do not in any way feel that the accused have been brought here wrongly charged, nor do I believe they are other than guilty as charged. Emotional attempts to plead stress and hardship and the loss of close friends do not weigh against the Manual of Military Law. Such things are the lot of every soldier on active duty in the field. There is not one grain of evidence to show that the young lad, De Beers, eleven years old, sir, fired the shot that killed Sergeant Parker, or, indeed, fired any shot then or at any other time. Yet he was killed. There is not a shred of evidence to show that there was a connexion between the death of Captain Hunt and the wearing of his clothes by Visser. He could have come by the clothes through purchase, barter, even theft, yet the accused chose to believe he was concerned in Hunt's death and Visser was killed. Summarily. Without trial." He walked slowly to his table and took a drink of water, then walked just as slowly back to the same spot before continuing.

"There is, however, more than a shred of evidence to connect the accused with the dastardly killing of Jacob Hesse, a man of the church engaged on a godly mission. There is a length of cloth. Only one formation of troops in this entire area of operations wears such a distinctive insignia . . . and those troops were under the temporary command of one of the accused while the other three accused were on service with him! In answer to my learned friend, let it be said that, gallantry aside, a boy and two men, one a missionary, were shot to death in the area in which a military formation was operating. Troops from that formation were present on each occasion. The accused are the officers in command of those troops. I think those facts speak for themselves."

Harry could see Ian Thomas straightening his files and books and papers and he leaned to Peter and whispered, "That's it, then, old son. One way or the other." Peter rumbled back, "You make it sound like there's a choice! I hope you're right!"

Bainbridge had consulted with the other members and now leaned forward again. "The Judge Advocate will sum up for the Court."

That sibilant voice from the prim lips was brief.

"There is little to be added from the Court. We have noted the conflict of evidence as between defence and prosecution witnesses, and the Court has already instructed that action be taken in the matter of the testimony of Corporal Thomas Booth and that his evidence not be taken into account in these proceedings. The Court has also noted the remarks made by both defending and prosecuting officers as to the words attributed to the Duke of Wellington, and wishes to point out with clarity that these words are no more than that. *Obiter dicta* cannot replace the law, no matter how high the standing of the speaker. Finally, the Court has clearly in mind that the charges which have been brought against the accused are based soundly upon absolute requirements within the Manual of Military Law . . . and they will be considered in that light and in that light only, whether they be true charges or not."

He leaned back, becoming at once the same greyish figure he had been throughout, muttering a few words to Bainbridge and then rising and leaving, a shade of a man.

Bainbridge shuffled his papers together.

"The Judge Advocate has left the Court in the presence of the accused and separately from the members of the Court, as required. The members of the Court will now retire to consider their verdict and the accused will be returned to the jurisdiction of the provost-marshal. This Court is now closed."

When they were signed back into the prison building by the guard sergeant, there were half-hidden smiles around them. Crookes, who usually left them there with a cheerful "Cheerio, see you in the morning" hung about while they filed through the door, through the rest room and into the cell corridor beyond. For the four of them there was a sense of end-of-term, of annual holiday, of a task completed . . . not a happiness, simply a feeling of something over and done with.

It was Ivor who found the surprise.

Harry, peeling off his tunic, heard Ivor's high voice calling from the common room.

"I say, come here, you people, in the common room!" And then a ring of laughter.

They crowded in, their faces cracking into smiles as they saw the table, a strip of white cloth running along the centre of the green baize over the boards, a bowl of flowers in the centre between Hasleton's candlesticks, two flat plates of savouries and a large silver tray with glasses and three bottles of sherry on it.

Hasleton's voice behind them was a benign boom. "Well, go on, go on! In you go, laddies. It's over and I thought we'd better have a bit of a celebration!" He pushed past them, the cork coming out of a sherry bottle quickly, the pale liquor splashing as he spoke. "I just thought we'd have a bit of a drink to the confusion of Arse-faced Authority, eh?" Crookes was there and John Lenehan and Ian Thomas, balancing on his small feet, a quiet smile on his face and there was suddenly a party and the slap and clatter of crossed conversations and the sweet heaviness of tobacco smoke and laughter, while the afternoon sky became the evening sky and the sherry disappeared and they relaxed for the first time in weeks.

But that wasn't all. Hasleton kept chuckling and grinning and hinting at "better things yet, laddies" until, a little after seven, his own batman and orderly appeared to clear the table and begin setting it and they kept coming and going till Hasleton could contain himself no longer and, face flushed with the wine, shouted, "Right, then, gentlemen. Shall we dine?" and bustled about pushing them into chairs around the candlelit table, thumping himself down at the head and beaming across the smoking roast that his orderly put before him, his hands flashing the carving knife and fork like fencing foils.

It was an astonishing evening. Burleigh arrived while Hasleton was carving and there were roars of applause and shouts for another chair and another setting and applause for the bottle of brandy he'd brought. When the grinning orderly carried in a huge dish of strawberries nested in ice, there was more applause, swelling into a shout of joy when the batman staggered after him, a tub of ice cradled in his arms and the necks of six bottles of champagne jutting from it. Hasleton stared.

"Oi, Carter, what's this, what's this? S'posed to be four bottles of bubbly, ain't there?"

Carter, the batman, lowered the tub with a grunt and dug an envelope from his pocket. "The other two come about an hour ago, sir. Message with 'em."

Hasleton tore the envelope open and pulled a candlestick closer, peering at the note, then suddenly slamming his hand on the table so that the plates and glasses jumped and rattled, roaring with glee.

"Listen to *this,* you terrible people, you! *This* is the news of the minute!" He flourished the paper, then read, " 'For the Gentlemen of the Bush Veldt Carbineers, with our apologies for their inconvenience and our sincere Good Wishes for their Successful Futures'." He smiled widely round at them, his eyes almost disap-

269

pearing behind his flushed cheeks. "And it's signed 'Michael Holding and Leonard Briggs-Cope' . . . not so bloody arse-faced after all, eh?" There was an instant of stunned silence, and then they burst into cheers and laughter, Peter grabbing wispy Ivor, lifting him clear of the floor and waltzing round the table with him, yelling, "There you are, son—the bloody Court sent us champagne! *Now* you can cheer up!"

Later, glutted with food and wine and laughter, they sat quietly in a haze of cigar smoke, sipping at Burleigh's brandy. Crookes looked around at them, the candles burning low now and their faces smoother in the mellow light.

"Well, it's all over bar the shouting, you fellows. What are you going to do when they've apologized and let you out?"

"I know bloody well what I shall do." Peter, huge in the candle shadow, his voice deeper than ever, spoke up at once. "When I get home I'm going to start finding out about motors. Everyone thinks they're just a bit of a fad, see, but I reckon they're the coming thing. There'll be motors all over the place before ten years've gone. Horses are going out. Don't see much point in going back to blacksmithing, myself, so it'll be motors for me. The quicker the better."

George, his hair standing on end and his face redder than his eyebrows, slapped Peter's shoulder. "Right, Peter! I'm going back to farming—I reckon if I can handle soldiers I can handle sheep again—an' when you get your first motor running, you can damned well come and visit me! If the thing works, I'll buy one, by God! Sooner run sheep in a motor than a saddle!"

There was a laugh and Lenehan, in the little pause that followed it, said, "Ivor? You'll go on soldiering, of course."

Summers looked the way he used to look, languid and almost fragile, his eyes lit with laughter. "I should think I'll have to, John. Don't know anything else. I remember Daddy telling me once that I was the thirty-first Summers of one kind or another to live in the

270

Army. Never really thought about _not_ being in the Army, so I shall go on. Wind up as an antique colonel in Brighton, I expect—gout and a liver and half a pension."

"Not so much of the antique colonel, you young sprout!" Hasleton's smile was benevolent. "Harry, you're keepin' pretty mum down there. What about you?"

Harry had been half listening to the others, his head down over a pencil and a sheet of paper. Now he looked up and focused properly on them. "Me, I shall hoof off back to Australia with John, here, collect my old friend Magee and my horse and take 'em back to England and hunt a few foxes. Might write a book. Wait for another war. I think chaps like me only really function properly when there's a war going on." None of them asked him if marriage figured anywhere in his plans, but Lenehan leaned over, looking down at the paper under Harry's hand.

"Started the book already, Harry?"

"This? No, this is just a scribble. I thought it might seem appropriate to the occasion."

Urged by the others, he rose, a little unsteadily, the paper in one hand, a dripping candle in the other.

"Right then—pay attention. I dedicate this rhyme to all my friends present, and anyone with the wit to take its meaning.

> _In prison cell I sadly sit—_
> _A damned crestfallen chappy!_
> _And own to you I feel a bit—_
> _A little bit—unhappy!"_

There were cries of mock-commiseration, and he shouted over them,

> _"It really ain't the place nor time_
> _To reel off rhyming diction—_
> _But yet we'll write a final rhyme_
> _While waiting cru-ci-fixion!"_

George called, "Bring on your hammer and nails!" and Peter gagged him with a spread hand that almost covered his face. Harry read on,

> *"No matter what end they decide—*
> *Quicklime or boiling oil, sir,*
> *We'll do our best when crucified*
> *To finish off in style, sir!"*

"Hear, hear!" from Hasleton at the head of the table.

> *"But we bequeath a parting tip*
> *As sound advice for such men*
> *Who come across in transport ship*
> *To polish off the Dutchmen!*
> *If you encounter any Boers*
> *You really must not loot 'em—*
> *And if you wish to leave these shores*
> *For pity's sake, don't shoot 'em!"*

The great gush of laughter swelled and boomed along the corridor and through the walls to the night-guard, grinning at their posts.

It couldn't be heard in Bainbridge's quarters where he sat at his desk, Holding and Briggs-Cope opposite him. They'd dined together, carefully keeping the conversation away from the trial, and now were sitting sombrely, their papers spread before them. Bainbridge looked up.

"Well, then, Briggs-Cope, junior member first. General feelings, please."

The young gunner hesitated. "Er—they're not really general feelings at all, sir. I think I'm pretty clear in my mind about it."

"You *think* you are? You'll need to be more definite than that, you know."

"Yes, I know. Well, the main thing is—there doesn't really seem to be anything that can be called *proof*, does there? Aside from Visser—and even then I'm inclined to feel we must give Morant the benefit of the doubt, all things considered."

"Do you?" Bainbridge's voice was flat and cold, and he stared at Briggs-Cope till the younger man looked down. "Holding, what about you?"

"I'm forced to agree about the lack of actual proof, you know. The first charge is nonsense, surely . . . we've all done that sort of thing, and K has made it part of the policy. The boy's death was clearly accidental—and his own stupid fault anyway, by the sound of it—and Visser was shot quite deservedly, in my opinion. It's the Hesse business I'm not sure about."

Bainbridge leaned back, balancing a pencil below his chin.

"It looks to me as though neither one of you is very sure about anything. I'm going to help you clear your minds. The Hesse business, as you call it, Holding, is one of crucial importance. For more than just the obvious reasons."

He leaned right forward to them and began to talk quietly and forcefully.


Half a mile away in the prison, Crookes leaned elegantly against the wall alongside the very mellow Hasleton, watching as the others fought and struggled in a game of touch-rugger with a rolled-up tunic as the ball.

"Certainly lettin' off steam, sir, wouldn't you say?"

Hasleton belched comfortably. "They need to, young Crookes. Poor bastards, locked up in this place all this time and then subjected to all that palaver by those cock-faces out there! Let 'em rip. I don't care if they wreck the bloody prison!"

The tunic-ball came flying out of the tangle of bodies towards them and Crookes caught it neatly, his lean face suddenly smiling very youthfully. "Oh, good, sir. Then if you'll excuse me—" He howled like a banshee and dived full tilt into the laughing scrum.

\* \* \*

February had opened in a swirl of heat and a letting-down of emotions. The party to mark the end of the hearing had left them all with sore heads, and the routine of the days in the court-room was no longer there, so that they quickly became bored, a boredom coloured with the sick shades of apprehension, despite Lenehan's assurances.

"Oh, come now, the talk in the Mess is that the delay's because Bainbridge hasn't been well. They say he's got a bit of a cold and has been kept to his bed. Everyone says that they're bound to wipe all the charges out."

Ian Thomas was less sanguine, but far from gloomy. "The way I see it, they'll want to make something stick after all the fuss they've kicked up, so they'll plump for something easy. Probably squash the charges in general and stick Harry with a severe reprimand and that'll be that."

Privately he wasn't so sure. That Bainbridge had been isolated in his quarters was common knowledge, but Ian also knew that the Judge Advocate had been a frequent visitor and that Briggs-Cope and Holding had been there every day. None of them appeared in the Mess.

And then the word came, Thomas and Hasleton arriving on a sultry Tuesday afternoon, with the formal pronouncement that the Court would reconvene the following morning at nine to deliver its findings.

Ivor burst out, "Does that mean we can get out of here tomorrow—you know, if it's all squashed?" He looked pathetically young and eager.

"Well, what happens is that you're paraded in front of the Court and they read off their findings and then you're brought back here until the whole thing's confirmed."

"Oh, Christ—paperwork!" George's waspishness had come back. "How long's that likely to take?"

"Well, the rules say that the convenor of the Court has to confirm the findings—that's Kitchener—but they also say any officer superior in rank to the president can do it if there's a reason."

"Is there?" Harry was apparently relaxed, but Thomas could see the tension.

"A reason? Oh, well, yes—distance and time, you see. It's close enough to two hundred miles along the roads, and it has to be done in person, by signature. Telegraph's no good."

"So somebody local will do it?"

"Yes, the brigadier, I expect. Or a visiting officer if there's one passing through of enough rank . . . takes the onus off the local chap, y'see."

Thomas didn't realize till he was on the way out of the building that his last remark sounded a little ominous.

Crookes was back in the morning, and they went through the familiar routine almost with relief, knowing that something was happening to break the long day's monotony. The court-room, when they were marched in, seemed quite crowded and Harry noticed Bainbridge looked pale and unwell. The chair next to his was empty . . . and then he realized that the two captains flanking Bainbridge had the look of sickness too and he felt his stomach lurch unaccountably. The first formalities quickly over, the four sat, while the men behind the long table leaned their heads together, Bainbridge pointing to a bundle of forms in front of him, then nodding and looking up. When he spoke, his voice was slightly hoarse.

"The accused will stand." He watched them levelly as they rose, instinctively straightening themselves, a short, firm line staring at him.

"Lieutenant Ivor Compton Summers, Twelfth Lancers, detached Bush Veldt Carbineers." They all heard Ivor's breath suck in between his teeth. "The Court finds the charges against you as follows: Charge Number One, Not Guilty; Charge Number Two, Not Guilty; Charge Number Three, Guilty—" he stopped abruptly as Ivor's gasping moan rang through the still room, then bore on. "Guilty, but with mitigating circumstances." He made no pause, no change in inflection as he said, "Lieutenant Gerald George Witton, Colonial

275

Horse Artillery, detached Bush Veldt Carbineers, the Court finds the charges against you as follows: Charge Number One, Not Guilty; Charge Number Two, Not Guilty; Charge Number Three, Guilty, but with mitigating circumstances." Harry could feel Peter's bulk tense alongside his shoulder. "Lieutenant Peter Handcock, Bushmen's Regiment, detached Bush Veldt Carbineers, the Court finds the charges against you as follows: Charge Number One, Not Guilty; Charge Number Two, Not Guilty; Charge Number Three, Guilty as charged."

There was a low grunt, deep in Peter's chest and Harry could only think and think again, My God, they've stuck Peter—they've done for him! He heard the relentless voice rasping his own name and the findings against him, and it sounded like an echo of the previous statement, while his mind spun with vertigo in the knowledge that big, friendly Peter had been smashed. And then he realized it was no echo, that Bainbridge had finished speaking and that the last words had been directed at him—"Guilty as charged."

And then Bainbridge was speaking again, saying, "The Court's findings in these proceedings were unanimous," and he was scratching his signature across the bottom of a form and sliding it to Holding and then to Briggs-Cope for their signatures, while he spoke passionlessly. "The Court directs the prisoners to be returned to their place of confinement within the jurisdiction of the provost-marshal pending confirmation of these findings and handing down of sentences."

Malleson was there suddenly with Crookes, both grim, Crookes' eyes as sad as a spaniel's all at once, and there was an armed guard outside, and Thomas, stock-still at the door, his face covered with a film of sweat and Harry suddenly realized that Bainbridge hadn't referred to the four of them as "the accused." He'd called them "the prisoners."

Hasleton was waiting for them as they were marched into the entrance hall and signed for, Crookes silently shaking hands with each of them in turn. The old colonel's head was shaking and his lips trembled under his moustache as Malleson whispered to him off to one side, then he pulled himself upright, nodding, and walked across to them.

"Gentlemen, under instructions from the provost-marshal, I must inform you that you may no longer be allowed the privilege of the large cell in this establishment as a common meeting room. You will be confined to your own cells except for statutory periods of exercise which you will take individually. This will apply during the remainder of your stay here." He swallowed, then muttered, loud enough for only the four of them to hear, "Oh, the crawling shits! I'm so sorry, laddies." He spun on his heel, signalling to the duty sergeant, and they were marched to their cells.

There was no exercise. It was just after ten by the entrance hall clock when they went in. Harry sat on his bunk, watching the slow sweep of the shadows of the window-bars across the floor, wondering in a mildly puzzled way how people could be so stupid as to find Peter guilty of anything . . . any of them, but Peter, huge and gentle, Peter most of all. He had no idea of the circling of time and when the keys rattled along the corridor and he looked at his watch, he was surprised to find it was close to noon. He heard the steps and saw the heads go past, down to Ivor's cell at the end and then back, a glint of sun on Ivor's very fair, thin hair, and the slamming of the door and then a silence. The whole prison seemed to be still, waiting, and the noise of the return seemed overwhelming. Harry was hard against his cell door, his face pressed to the chill bars and he could see the tears coursing down Ivor's face.

Peter, in the next cell, shouted angrily, "What've they done to you, Ivor? What's happening?"

Summers stopped abruptly, face contorted. "They've cashiered me! They're sending me to Hell!" then stumbled forward again, the guards not looking at him, returning a moment later with George, pale, slit-lipped.

Peter called again to Ivor, but there was only the sound of soft weeping, and he went back to his door,

277

cramming himself against the bars like Harry, both of them waiting, not speaking. George stopped outside his own cell door when they came back and called in a bitter cry, "Mitigating circumstances, fellows—all they're going to do is send me to prison for life. That's all!"

Harry felt sick, felt his guts churn and his throat constrict, the sweat breaking out on his face as he struggled not to vomit. By the time he'd gained control, Peter had gone along the corridor and through the loud door and into the silence beyond it. Ivor was still crying and George shouted at him, "Oh, for Christ's sake, Ivor, I'll change places with you!"

Then there was Peter again, his eyes wrinkled in puzzled concentration, his lips pursed. He passed Harry unspeaking and went straight into his cell, not answering Harry's cry.

Malleson was beyond the door and he led Harry to a side room, knocked and took him through. The sallow-faced colonel at the table looked up and nodded. "My name is Corcoran and I'm the provost-marshal. I have to advise you that the findings of the Field General Court-Martial before which you were arraigned have been confirmed, the confirmation being made by Brigadier Arthur Bernard Doyle, garrison commander. Under the regulations governing this action, it was deemed that there was no reason to delay confirmation owing to the distance between the Court and the present whereabouts of the convenor. Do you understand?"

Harry nodded, and Corcoran glanced down at the form he held. "You have been advised that you have been found guilty as charged of Charge Number Three in the proceedings against you. The verdict of the Court, unanimously reached, is that you, Harry Harbord Morant, being found guilty of the murder of Jacob Hesse, shall be put to death by firing party, the sentence to be carried out at Pietersburg on the next day after this confirmation. March out."

When Thomas turned, Lenehan was shocked by his appearance. All the dapper trimness was gone. His tunic was unbuttoned and it and the shirt beneath it were dark with sweat; his skin was pale and somehow shrunken, so that he looked thinner and unshaven and his hair was tangled at the top and back of his head where he'd been running his hand through it. He stared at Lenehan, gave him an absent nod and turned back to lean again over the corporal at the Morse key and the signaller alongside him with a pencil poised over a pad of message forms. Lenehan pushed through the counter-flap to their bench at the back and stood beside Thomas, looking down.

Thomas spoke without turning his head. "Nothing, John—absolutely bugger all! We've sent three signals in the past two hours and all we're getting back is acknowledgments. Here, look."

He thrust some crumpled papers at Lenehan who flattened them to read the pencilled messages. The first was timed at 1.05, addressed to the Commander-in-Chief, H.Q., Pretoria, and it said, "Urgently request consideration deferment sentence Morant Handcock pending appeal highest authority. Thomas, Defending Officer, Pietersburg." The second was timed at 1.55 and was the same message, preceded by, "Repeat stress urgency earlier message." The third, timed twenty minutes ago, at 2.40 read, "Request urgent permission make direct appeal His Majesty in case of Morant Handcock and your most urgent notification no promulgation execution order pending same." The answer in each case had come within ten minutes of the receipt of the signals at Headquarters—the laconic "Acknowledged."

Lenehan dropped the papers and said, "What else? Shouldn't I ride to Pretoria, or get the train?"

"Two hundred miles? And try getting the gilded bloody staff to rouse K from his virtuous couch?"

"No, I suppose not." His voice was tired. "Ian, it has to be some sort of ghastly mistake. We must be able to do *something!*"

"I'm doing it, damn it!" He straightened, his hand massaging the small of his back. "I'm sorry, John—I feel a bit like Judas, and I expect he got a bit short-

tempered when he heard them carpentering the cross."
He moved through the counter to the door, pulling
Lenehan with him away from the two signallers. "I
don't believe there's been any kind of mistake, my
friend. I believe poor Harry and Peter—and the other
two, come to that—have been put up like sacrificial
bloody lambs on somebody's political altar. I—"

The stutter of the Morse key and the corporal's cry
came together and they ran back to the bench, leaning
across the men's backs as the sharp rattling was trans-
lated into hasty writing on the pad. Thomas reached
down and grabbed the page as the man finished writing.

"Not before time! Here—it's from Kelly, Adjutant-
General's office—'Reference your request deferment of
sentence pending appeal His Majesty. Must advise
cable facilities ex-Pretoria extremely limited. Further
advise unlikelihood appeal successful.'" The key was
rattling again as Thomas read on savagely. "'C. in C.
absent these Headquarters tour of inspection outsta-
tions probably returning Friday. Kelly.' Friday! Oh,
how fucking convenient!"

The corporal glanced up.

"Sir, there's another one . . . it's personal to you
from General Kelly."

Thomas snatched the form from the other man.

"'Personal. No copy retained Headquarters. Deeply
regret situation and aware your feelings. Shared here
by many but orders give no choice. C. in C.'s absence
most unfortunate and no telegraph link his position.
Orders originated beyond this Headquarters and appear impossible appeal. Have done all possible. Kelly.'"
Thomas pushed the form into his pocket in a damp
and crumpled ball. "That's it, then, John. Those daft
words of Harry's the other night were right, weren't
they? Remember? . . . 'while waiting crucifixion'?" He
looked round at the two solemn-faced signallers.
"Thank you both. I'm sure you'll realize the need to
keep close mouths about that last message . . . no
copies, no chat?"

"Not to worry, sir." The corporal's nod was joined
by the signallers'.

"We'll keep mum, and we're very sorry about it, sir."

"Thank you again."

Lenehan noticed that, despite the heat, Ian Thomas was shivering.

Burleigh's normally good-natured face was a black scowl as he loomed over the uncomfortable brigadier in the garrison commandant's office.

"You do realize, I'm sure, what the effects of this sort of thing could be?"

"My dear Burleigh, I realize only too well. Just as you must realize the sort of position in which you're placing me. I'm under orders, man. I may be in local command, but that's the top and the bottom of it. I can't fight Headquarters!"

"Can't or won't? Were you under orders to confirm that damnable sentence?"

The brigadier shifted awkwardly, looking away, and Burleigh stared at him, surprise wiping away the anger suddenly.

"By the Living God, I believe you were!" He felt for a chair and sat silent for nearly a minute while the other man watched him, licking his lips nervously. When Burleigh spoke again his tones were level and polite.

"I am making formal advances now, sir. On behalf of my newspaper, I request your permission to use telegraph facilities to dispatch a story to my editor in London, via Pretoria."

The brigadier stared back at him, tightening his lips.

"I'm sorry, Mr. Burleigh. I repeat, the facilities are not available at this time for other than military traffic."

"Then I request a first priority on those facilities. Will you give me some indication when they *will* be available?"

"I can't do that. Headquarters will make that decision."

"After tomorrow morning, no doubt." He stood, his downward look contemptuous. "I shall let you have a written request within a quarter of an hour. I hope you'll be prepared to let me have your answer in writing—fully—as quickly as possible." He walked to the door and turned. "I'd hate to have to sleep with a military conscience tonight."

The brigadier sat still, listening to the echoes of the door's slam.

At four o'clock, the orderly officer and two guards unlocked Harry's cell and took him out for exercise.

He'd spent most of the time since pecking at his lunch staring out of the window at nothing, trying to get his mind to adjust to not being there any more, not being anywhere. He looked at the young orderly officer vacantly for a second or two, shaking his head, then blinked and came back to the present.

"Exercise? No, thanks. I'd rather not."

"I'm sorry, Morant, the provost-marshal has said it's a regulation. He says you're to have half an hour outside."

"Does he? And suppose I refuse?"

The orderly officer looked momentarily confused, then recovered himself, his shoulders tightening.

"I'm sure you wouldn't want to do that. It would be—awkward. For me."

Harry looked at him, realizing the truth of that, and smiled quietly.

"Yes, of course. I'm sorry, old son. Lead on."

They strolled in a wide circle around the flat pan of baked earth in the late afternoon sun, and he found he was glad he was outside for a while, glad to feel the heat and the first lift of a cool breeze to gentle it, glad to be stretching his legs. The guards walked behind and the orderly officer paced alongside, making no attempt to talk, but offering a cigarette and showing he'd be prepared to chat if Harry wanted to.

Peter was being brought in as Harry was signed into the book. He looked just as tall, but less solid somehow, as though the flesh and muscles were hanging on the great bones rather than being packed hard there.

"Hallo, Harry. Been walking?"

"Yes. You?"

"Yes, out that side. They don't seem to want us to mix now, do they?"

"Doesn't look like it. George and Ivor's turn next, I suppose."

The duty sergeant glanced across at the orderly officer, but no one said anything as they were led back into the corridor and to their cells. Then Harry noticed the two end doors were standing wide open and saw the orderly officer's quick look, and he stopped outside his own cell.

"Have they gone walking already?"

"Er—yes, they have as a matter of fact." He shifted his glance.

"Where? Not where I was—"

Peter, in his own cell doorway, listening, rumbled, "And not on my side."

"Look, will you go back in, please, you fellows? We can't stand about out here."

Harry gripped the door, the bones of his hands jutting through the white skin.

"Have they gone? Have they been taken away?"

A pause. Then, "Yes. Yes, I'm very much afraid they have. While you two were out."

Peter's voice was thick with fury. "You miserable, crawling, Pommy bastards! Wouldn't even show enough stinking guts to let us say goodbye to our mates! Christ, I hate the whole shit-mouthed mess of you!" He shook the heavy door till the hinges grated and the guards stepped close, rifles ready.

"Peter!" Harry barked it out like a command and the big man stopped at once, standing with his arms hanging and his face crumpled.

"That won't do any good, old lad. Although I agree —it was a cur's trick." He rounded on the orderly officer. "I suppose you knew?"

"Yes. I'm ashamed to say I did, but I'd no choice. The provost-marshal decided there was to be no fuss."

Harry could see the pain in the young man's eyes. He was an infantryman and was simply serving a twenty-four-hour duty as one of a string of young officers to take a turn.

"Where've they gone, do you know?"

"Train to Pretoria. On to the Cape then, I imagine. It—they gave Summers some civil clothing to wear. It didn't fit too well." He turned his head.

"Yes, well, it's done, isn't it? Thank you for telling us. Not your fault."

He turned his back and walked into the cell, standing with his back turned and his head in the oblique shaft of afternoon sunlight.

Lenehan watched Harry's hands, firm and steady as they tidied the last of his meagre belongings into neat little piles.

"Did—did Ian come, Harry?"

"Yes, about an hour ago. He was pretty cut up, I'm afraid."

"He feels guilty . . . like Judas, he said."

"He shouldn't be. He did a marvellous job. No one could have done more than he did. He was just up against too much, that's all—we all were. Dear old Hasleton's Arse-faces." He grinned without any humour at all. "You heard about Ivor and George?"

"I saw them. At the train."

"How were they?"

"As you'd expect, Harry. They both asked me to say their goodbyes to you. Poor Ivor asked us all to pray for him . . . it's affected him very badly. They'll be in Pretoria tomorrow morning."

"Yes, well, we won't see much of tomorrow morning, will we?" He opened his writing-pad. "Look, will you take these letters for me, John? And I want you to make sure whatever cash is due to me goes into this one for Paddy." Lenehan nodded, mute. "I've asked him to let Harlequin go. . . ." He turned, his head down, and fussed needlessly with his folded clothes. "The others are to my people . . . and . . . and Margaret." He held one envelope in his fingers. "I'd written one to you too, old man. Didn't think I'd see you again, somehow." He dropped the envelope on the bed. "You won't need it now. I just wanted to ask you to see Paddy and the fellows at the *Bulletin* for me. And to thank you for your friendship."

Lenehan found he couldn't answer, only nod, his eyes blurring, as Harry tore a couple of pages from his writing-case and crumpled them onto the floor near the door. He handed the case to Lenehan and piled some other things onto it . . . his leather box, his wallet and his old gunmetal cigarette case. There was a knock at the cell door and a guard looked in.

"Padre's here, sir."

Harry faced Lenehan.

"Time to go, John. Give my love to Julia." Lenehan's fingers were crushing his own. "And, John, thank you for Cavalier."

Lenehan's foot brushed against the little ball of crumpled paper Harry had tossed down and, as the padre came in, he managed to bend quickly and pick it up without Harry noticing. He walked quickly away down the corridor for the last time.

The padre stood uncertainly for a moment, looking at Harry's back.

"May I talk with you, lad? It's Harry, isn't it?"

Harry turned slowly and sat on the end of the bunk, leaning back against the wall under the window.

"It is, Padre, but you won't do much business with me, I'm afraid."

"You're very close to the Infinite, Harry."

"As close as I've ever been. But then, we always are, aren't we?"

The padre's face was thin and intelligent, and he almost smiled, nodding in recognition of the remark.

"Would you like to pray?"

"For what, Padre? Another crack of the whip?"

"You could pray for God's mercy."

"No, thanks. I'm quite sure if there *is* a God, he knows what he's doing. And if there isn't—what's the point of praying, anyway?"

"Is there nothing I can offer you?"

"A hacksaw mightn't be a bad idea." The padre was startled at the sudden flashing smile. "No—nothing,

285

I'm afraid. But thank you for coming, Padre. Go and have a word with Peter."

"I shall. And I shall pray for you."

"I can't stop you. You might try one for the Court while you're about it. I shouldn't think they'll be sleeping much tonight."

The padre shook his head sadly and rapped on the door. Harry, looking away, heard him go to Peter's door . . . and realized his own door hadn't been closed. The orderly officer was standing there, a bottle of brandy in his hand. He held it out.

"The Commandant sent this down." He gave the bottle to Harry and stood there still. "Look, Morant —we all think—I mean—"

"I know. Thank you. And tell old Hasleton he's a damned decent fellow, will you?"

The door closed and Harry thoughtfully pulled the cork, sniffing appreciatively at the fine cognac. He tipped the neck over his tin mug, emptying half the bottle into it so that the brandy came right to the rim, then took the bottle to the door, calling for the guard sergeant. The man came down, staring at Harry through the bars.

"Sergeant, be a good chap will you. Take this to Mr. Handcock for me . . . after the padre's gone, eh?"

"Yes, sir, glad to." He reached through the bars for the bottle. "Sir?"

"Something wrong?"

"Yessir. The men—they think—we *all* think—well, it's a bloody bad business, sir, that's what!"

"Yes, I suppose it is. But I'm afraid everyone thinks so except the Powers That Be. Thank you . . . and the men."

The sergeant stamped away, passing the padre as he came from Peter's cell. A moment later, Peter's bass roar echoed up the corridor.

"Good on you, Harry. Drink hearty!"

"You too, Peter. Chin up!"

Outside the prison, the sentry saluted Lenehan as the door closed behind him and he walked slowly to one side, standing in the light of a lamp, the bullet-marks on the walls above his head still raw. He shifted the little pile of Harry's things and carefully unfolded the crumpled sheets of paper he'd snatched from the cell floor, tilting them to the light and bending his head to read, not realizing he was reading aloud, the sentry's head turning as Lenehan read.

*When I am tired, and old, and worn,*
*And harassed by regret;*
*When blame, reproach and worldlings' scorn*
*On every side are met;*

*When I have lived long years in vain*
*And found life's garland's rue,*
*May be that I'll come back again*
*At last—at last—to you!*

*When all the joys and all the zest*
*Of youthful years have fled,*
*May be that I shall leave the rest*
*And turn to you instead;*

*For you, dear heart, would never spurn*
*(With condemnation due!)*
*If, at the close of all, I turn*
*Homeward—at last—to you!*

*When other faces turn away*
*And lighter loves have passed,*
*When life is weary, old and grey*
*I may come back—at last!*

*When cares, remorse, regrets are rife—*
*Too late to live anew—*
*In the sad twilight of my life*
*I will come back—to you!*

The writing was neat, unaltered, as though Harry had thought it all in his mind exactly before putting it down. But there was a scrawled line diagonally across the bottom of the page, the writing fierce and angry: "But I won't, Margaret, I won't!"

The sentry heard the anguished, "Oh, Christ!" from Lenehan and saw him bend his head, and called out, "Are you all right, sir?"

Lenehan put the pages in his tunic pocket and lifted his head. "Oh yes, I'm just fine, thank you."

When the sentry told his mates about it later, he said, "I dunno about fine—he sounded as though he'd just been gut-shot!"

There had been muted noises in the night on the flat ground beyond the prison and, with the first of the true light, Harry could see from his perch on the end of the bunk, the two thick posts which had been set into the ground there, a couple of hundred feet away. There was something gleaming near the top of each of them.

He hadn't slept, yet he didn't feel tired. In some way he felt more alert, more aware than he'd ever felt, holding onto, breathing deeply of all the time left to him. Unless something very unexpected should happen. They brought breakfast just after six, a guard carrying the tray in without looking at him, and he'd been surprised to find he was ravenously hungry, clearing the food quickly and calling to ask for more tea. The same guard had brought him hot water in a jug and he'd washed and shaved carefully, changing into the clean breeches and shirt he'd kept out the night before, giving his boots a final buff with the discarded shirt and folding his sleeves back neatly above his elbows. He felt clean and light and vigorous, the thought in his mind that it was such a waste to destroy a firm body with years of action in it yet.

There was little noise in the prison and he made no attempt to call out to Peter, hearing the muted sounds of his movements in the next cell above the thick silence which seemed to envelop the place. He'd kept his watch and he looked at it when the door at the end of the corridor opened and the steps came towards him ... seven-thirty.

The orderly officer was pale, the black smudges under his eyes darker for the pallor, and he swung the door and stood back, not speaking. Harry stepped out, taking one backward look at the cell, at the scuff marks where his boot-toes had dug into the wall the many times he'd stood up there to look out; at his initials, cut into the stone of the window ledge with a nail during an interminable day. By the time he'd turned back, Peter was there beside him, the guards all around them. Peter was pale, too, but smiling, and he boomed, "'Morning, Harry. Fine day for it." Harry grinned back at him, feeling a great affection for this big, calm man, and said, "Good company, too, Peter." Then they were moving down towards the door at the far end, the door through which they'd gone the night of the Boer attack, and Peter looked up and back as they went through, remembering the scramble up there and the muscle-cracking lift of the stripped-down Maxim. Hasleton was there and the sallow-faced provost-marshal, Corcoran, and Malleson, solid and erect and miserable. He was carrying the big ledger from the entrance hall, and the orderly officer signed them out. Finally. Malleson handed the ledger to a guard and Hasleton walked to them.

"Harry—Peter. My dear laddies. I'm ashamed of my uniform for the first time." He coughed loudly, wringing their hands. "God bless you both, boys." Then the guards were about them again, and they were moving around the corner and becoming a part of the ceremony there.

One of the guards stumbled on a loose stone and Peter smiled sideways at him, rumbling, "Pick up the step there, son," but that was all that was said while they marched crisply towards those two posts, the gleam now clearly visible as a steel hook set in the front of each post about a foot from the top. Behind them, Hasleton and Corcoran had moved around along the side wall of the prison, below the windows of the cells, and some distance away to their left there was a file of men halting and turning right into line facing the posts. Harry and Peter looked at them, recognizing the Balmorals and the flash of tartan under the khaki aprons.

They hadn't known Malleson was marching with

them until they were halted by the posts and turned to see him there, a field policeman with him stepping forward and moving behind them. Two of the guards urged them gently back and they felt hands taking their wrists.

Harry cocked an eyebrow at the white-faced orderly officer.

"Mayn't we have a smoke?"

The young man looked at Malleson who nodded and came forward, his case open to them, and they felt the thongs slacken. He lit their cigarettes for them, deliberately standing in front of them to try to obscure their view of the Highlanders, but they could hear the snap of the commands there, each of them preceded by the readying words, "Firing party . . ."

Peter took only two or three drags, deep ones, and dropped the cigarette. Harry puffed once more at his and they smiled their thanks to Malleson, whose face remained unchangingly sad. Peter's hand was dry and big around Harry's as steady as his look. "Goodbye, Harry. It's been a good time. I'm glad we were friends."

Harry looked up at him.

"Goodbye, Peter. If there's anything after this, I hope we can share it."

Then the thongs were round their wrists and the posts were hard and cool against their backs. The field police sergeant moved in front of them and passed a broad leather strap around each chest, someone behind taking the slack of the loop and raising it, not tight but firm, holding them upright, and Harry realized what the hooks were for. Malleson and the orderly officer stepped aside and they were looking across the brown barrenness before them to the firing party.

A sergeant was moving along the line, handing something to each man, and they could see then the single action as each of the men in the line pushed a round into the breech of his rifle. One of them is a blank, Harry thought, and every man there will live the rest of his life not knowing whether he's killed one of us or not. The Highland officer passed down the line inspecting each man briefly, then marched to one side, standing stiffly, his sword a slash of clean silver light. The sergeant positioned himself to the officer's right and a pace behind him.

Harry suddenly realized the padre was there, stepping forward to speak to them. Peter turned his head away and Harry said, "Goodbye, Padre" and looked past him. The man sighed and blessed them both quietly and walked away to the prison wall where Hasleton stood, Malleson, Corcoran and the orderly officer joining them there, a drab little group against the white wall. At the far end, the front corner of the prison, there was a knot of men . . . they could see Lenehan there, and Thomas and Crookes, and Mulholland and half a dozen of the B.V.C. troopers and some others. The road ran past them, a little below their level, but they could see the tops of the trees and the chimney of the wrecked house from which they'd driven the Boers. And they could hear in the still morning air the tattoo of galloping hooves there, too, and everyone's head swung as the rider came in sight, an officer on a lathered horse, a blue-and-white dispatch brassard on his arm and a flat leather case strapped across his back. Harry heard Peter's hiss of indrawn breath and quirked his lips in a mirthless smile, looking straight ahead of him as the rider galloped up to the prison and past it and away, down into the town. The police sergeant was there again, two wide black cloths dangling from his hand, but they both shook their heads and he stowed them into a pocket, taking from another pocket two white discs of thick paper and a couple of long pins. Breathing heavily he stepped close, avoiding their eyes, and pinned a disc to each man's chest, a little to the left of the breastbone, then stepped back and quickly away.

There was a silence and Harry was looking up into the sky, deep and warmly blue. The voice sounded a thousand miles away when it called the firing party to the aim, and he looked down again, surprised to see them so close, the muzzles staring at him. He pitched his voice down to them.

"Shoot straight, you bastards. Don't make a mess of us!"

They saw the flame, but not the smoke which followed it.

## March 1902

*It had rained just a little during the night, but now, in the late morning, the sky was clearing fast and there was sunlight. Paddy walked sluggishly down the foot-worn track from the house to the rail fence, feeling that the brightness was wrong, that there should be black clouds and rain and thunder, something stormy and fearsome. The last newspapers to arrive were spread on the table back there in the house, with the untouched food and the cold mug of tea, and Lenehan's letter and Harry's letter were crushed in his hand as he walked, because he didn't realize his fists were clenched and his shoulders hunched.*

*Across there in the green shadow, there was a flicker of movement and he whistled gently, waiting for the golden shape to come through the shadows. Harlequin danced and sidled out, one big eye fixed on Paddy as he went through his pretence of not wanting to come close, till he realized the man wasn't playing, was just standing there, staring down at the letters in his hand.*

*Paddy lifted his head, letting Harlequin nose against his cheek, and he dredged a big handful of the coarse brown sugar from his pocket, walking with it in his hand to the gate, putting the letters away and slipping the bar to let the gate swing wide. The golden horse stepped delicately through, his turning head and his eyes showing that he was puzzled at this variation. He came close, outside the rails, and put his silky muzzle down into Paddy's cupped hand, while the man gentled him.*

*"Well, there, Harlequin, lad, that's the end of yer*

sugar ration. I made Harry a promise an' I'm going to keep it, so I am. Ye shan't be rode be anyone other than Breaker Morant . . . that was me word, remember?" The horse tossed his head as though agreeing and Paddy looped a hand into the thick black mane and walked him away from the yard, well out to where the land rolled down to the creek on one side and swelled up in a bald, grassy hill on the other. He swung the horse around, facing him up the hill, and patted his neck.

"Go on now, fella. Ye're as free as he is now. Away ye go!"

Harlequin stood there, looking at Paddy, a forefoot pawing gently at the ground. He whinnied a question and swung his head, looking round him.

"Go, Harlequin, go!"

Paddy slapped the firm rump and the horse started away, trotting, stopping, looking back. Then he began to run, a long and easy gallop, across the face of the hill till he stood on the skyline, the sun on the deep golden sheen of his hide. He called once, a high neigh, then he turned and was gone below the crest and there was only the sky.

Paddy walked back to the house alone.

# Now that you've finished . . .

There are one or two things you may be interested in knowing.

Harry Morant and Peter Handcock *were* executed by a firing party from the Cameron Highlanders, at Pietersburg on the morning of 27th February, 1902. They're buried near where they were shot.

The real George Witton went to prison on the Isle of Wight, serving nearly three years of his life sentence, then being released in haste and secrecy after petitions and a great deal of political pressure had been brought to bear.

There *was* a Major Thomas—not Ian, though—and he was disgusted at the whole miserable affair, and wrote of his conviction that the executions were carried out for international policy reasons.

And there was, of course, a Kitchener. During his visit to Australia in 1910 he was asked to unveil a memorial to Boer War dead at Bathurst, in New South Wales. It's recorded that he refused to unveil the memorial to those volunteers unless the name of Lieutenant Peter Handcock was removed from the roll and, to the shame of the men who ordered it done, it was removed. It was replaced afterwards and I've seen it there, centrally placed on a separate strip of bronze.

I've been to all sorts of sources for material for this book. The poems quoted *were* written by Morant and I found them, together with a wealth of other stuff, in the only factual record of any worth about these events, *Breaker Morant—A Horseman Who Made History,* written by F. M. Cutlack, out of print and kindly loaned to me by the publishers, Ure Smith.

Finally, if there seem to be errors in fact of military law and its methods, they're either because I am at fault, or because the way in which it was interpreted in the case of Morant and Handcock seems to have been grievously wrong.

Since their execution, no Australian soldier has been tried on a capital charge by a British Army Court.

Wentworth Falls,
Blue Mountains,
N.S.W.
1972.